For Jud

SPELL OF INTRIGUE

But wait! - there's more...

MAYER ALAN BRENNER

1/19/92

DAW BOOKS, INC.
DONALD A. WOLLHEIM, PUBLISHER

375 Hudson Street, New York, NY 10014

Cover art by Tom Kidd.

DAW Book Collectors No. 834

First Printing, November 1990

1 2 3 4 5 6 7 8 9

PRINTED IN THE U.S.A.

"ALL HANDS ON DECK! PREPARE FOR—WHAT?"

Shaa shrugged. "The unknown."

"Aye," said the captain. Then, shouting again, "Prepare for the unknown!"

People spilled onto the deck. Shaa was only peripherally aware of them as he gazed intently at the hole which had suddenly appeared ahead of them in the water. With a gurgle and a swoosh that were clearly audible to the watchers on the ship, the edges of the hole spread out and the water on the walls inside began to revolve in earnest. Then, suddenly, the whirlpool cone started to fill explosively, to fill and *overflow.* A mound of water, no, a *hill,* built above what had just been a hole, a surging mass of green and brown river water, green and brown except for the streaks of white inside of it. Streaks? No, not streaks, but part of a single rushing shape, and the water was light green, not dark, and not just a mound but a frothing tumbling—

The top of the water erupted. Spray flew to all sides, showering the boat a hundred feet away. Out of the mass of hurtled water burst an iceberg which was fully twice as wide as the beam of their ship. As it fell back onto the water, setting loose another titanic sheet of spray, the iceberg began to move directly toward the ship.

Shaa was bracing himself for the impact, when he heard an electric whine. He turned toward the Great Karlini just in time to see something clear and shiny ripple past. The thing hit the iceberg a bit left of center and immediately slid like oil out across its surface. The note of the whine deepened and fissures appeared on the iceberg's surface. Shaa dove for the deck and covered his head with his arms as the iceberg exploded with incredible force, and life-threatening boulders of ice began pelting down upon everyone on the deck. . . .

Mayer Alan Brenner's
delightful DAW fantasy series—

THE DANCE OF GODS:

CATASTROPHE'S SPELL (#1)

SPELL OF INTRIGUE (#2)

For Sunny and Matt

TABLE OF CONTENTS

1
THE WORLD ALREADY IN PROGRESS

Fradi had recently died, which made it all the more remarkable for him to realize that he was once again awake. That is to say, on the one hand he was rather surprised, but on the other hand he was scarcely surprised at all. He was aware that "recently" was a relative term under the circumstances, but his attendance at his own deathbed, surrounded by those glad to see the last of him, did seem to have taken place not long before. That, in any event, was not the point. By any standard it was a refreshing situation. He was not in pain. He *had* been in no shortage of pain, and had expected (if anything) to awaken into an environment where the continuation of mere physical pain would be the least of his worries. Renewed life after death was an article of faith, but the multiplicity of faiths differed sharply on the nature of that life, and on the correlation of one's circumstances in the next with one's behavior in the last. Out of self-defense Fradi had cleaved to a faith that stressed accomplishment rather than slippery value judgments of good and evil, but he had always harbored some residuum of doubt. He was quite happy, though, to be reassured. One so rarely gets an article of faith confirmed.

Nevertheless, it was surely a miracle. "To the gods," he began ritually, "I offer thanks—"

"You're welcome," said a voice from behind his head.

He opened his eyes. Above his head was a ceiling of cunningly carved stone inset with patterns of dancing light. The vision through the fovea of his left eye was clear, unblurred by the annoying swirl of white whose curdling presence had significantly impaired his accuracy with a bow. In fact, all his senses seemed to leap at him with unparalleled clarity, his deadly hands unhindered by knotted joints, the paths of his thought undimmed, his natural (or, as one brief adversary had maintained, unnatural) vigor fully restored. He was resting on his back in a long coffin-shaped basin whose sides he could see right through, covered with a white togalike garment fringed in gold. The figure of a woman, presumably the one who had spoken, moved into his field of view. She would not actually *be* a woman, of course, since the circumstances were what they were, but to his newly restored eyesight no divergence could easily be found. He suddenly discovered that another anatomical feature to whose activity he had long since bade farewell had also returned abruptly to consideration.

A squared-off scepter whose face glowed in mysterious patterns was in her hand. The figure extended it toward him, examined its patterns searchingly, and then moved it slowly in the Swirl of Sinalla. He raised his own hand and made the Swirl himself, concluding with the extra touch of fingertips above his heart. The figure smiled at him, a benign smile. "Behold," she said, "for your master approaches."

The transparent bier pivoted downward, leaving him perched halfway between the horizontal and the vertical. The carved wall ahead of him seemed to dissolve into mist. Beyond the mist was a vast open place of darkness above an endless silver plane. In the middle distance was a pillar of steam. From the midst of the pillar he felt the force of a Presence.

The pillar spoke. "Fradjikan! You have been called!"

Fradi felt the words rumble through his body with an almost-curdling resonance as the pillar felt silent. Although the cloud exhibited no feature that might be considered an eye, still he felt it examining him with a deep and searching gaze. Then, somewhat to his surprise, he heard a low, virtually subterranean peal of laughter; no, not *laughter* really, but more of a chuckle. A chuckle?

"You have aroused Our mirth," said the pillar, "for reasons that are Ours alone to know. However, *this* you may know. In reward for your virtue, your devotion, and your dedicated development of such a useful set of skills, you have been honored with Our grace."

He found he had to fight an urge to babble. "I am honored beyond all honors, O Preeminent One. I sing your praises. There is no way to properly show my abasement, no way to adequately repay—"

"This is true. However," the voice of the Presence said consideringly, "there is a certain thing you can do. Indeed, We have granted the benison of our favor in anticipation of your accomplishment of a specific task."

Underscoring the benison, the steam pillar smiled a beneficent smile. "The name of this job is Max."

"Not much to look at, is he?"

Two men stood over a third. The one who had spoken had hair that cascaded in curls past his shoulders, and a light brown mustache to match. He wore a cloak of severe, high-collared cut but of expensive weave and fabric. A set of reading glasses slouched low on his nose; a wide-brimmed hat wound with fur trim rested on the table beside him. He was, in short, a merchant, and not a struggling one.

"No, Meester Groot," said his companion. "Companion," of course, would by all accepted standards of the day have been too strong a word, implying a degree of social equality that even enlightened merchants would rarely lower themselves to. The relationship between Haalsen Groot and his employees, though, was scarcely typical, since the esteemed Meester Groot did not restrict his activities—or his colleagues—to those a scrupulously proper merchant might assume without reproach. The third member of the tableau, the recumbent one, provided ample illustration of this point.

Admittedly, Haalsen Groot was no colossus. Nevertheless, for a figure half again as tall as Meester Groot, the mass and bulk of the man on the cot should have been proportionately greater as well. Where one would have expected only the sleek curves of corded muscles, though, the sight of stretched, somewhat mangy skin and the protruding angles of bones, sunken cheeks and hollowed eye sockets betrayed a barbarian swordsman far from home and lost in the strange convolutions of civilization. He had yet to open his eyes. Instead, he was spending his time and energy on the occasional fever chill, uncontrollably chattering his teeth and contorting his body into strange representations of the fetal position, as perhaps illustrated by one of the members of the Nightmare Realism school of modern painters. Following this line of thought, Meester Groot commented, "Life may be life, but aesthetics are certainly aesthetics," to which his clerk replied, as was his habit, "Indeed so, sir." The barbarian interrupted with a deep liquid cough, a fine froth of pink bubbles appearing on his lips.

"You *are* sure you found the right man," Meester Groot said suddenly.

"He was booked under the name of Svin," said the clerk methodically. "The arrest record listed his last job as caravan guard, so the circumstances would seem appropriate. Once fed, cleaned, and healed, he'll most likely match the description as well; he *is* fairly distinctive for this far south. Should I make further inquiries?"

"No, Julio, I take no exception with your effort. I suppose you'd best send for the doctor. Sounding a bit tubercular, our friend here, don't you think?"

"Indeed so. I expect the physic momentarily." Julio gave a cough of his own, but a much more discreet and refined one. "Do you have any idea why Meester Maximillian wanted you to secure this particular specimen, sir?"

Haalsen Groot kept his gaze on the barbarian as he spoke, but, behind their lenses, his eyes appeared to be looking somewhere else entirely. "To Max, adventuring is an improvisational art. He likes to have a varietal selection of raw materials at hand from which to mold." He also has a streak of excess sentimentality, Meester Groot reminded himself, as well as a certain philosophy of the world. Most likely he met this fellow on a caravan and thought he could make a modern man out of him. Whatever the exact details of his interest in Svin, here, Max was rousing himself to more activity than Groot had seen in years. Things promised to get intriguing. They would not be safe, perhaps, and they would be (most likely) ill-advised, but they would certainly not be boring. He reminded himself to order more sandbags.

Bellowing an inchoate battle cry in an impressive display of sheer vocal power, the former Lion of the Oolvaan Plain pushed off his perch on the heavy iron chandelier, dislodging half-a-dozen lit candles in the process, and plunged downward, his massive sword twirling lethally around his body. His opponent, who had been peering inquisitively around the room trying to determine what the Lion might be up to *this* time, brought his own rapier up. As the Lion descended, his mightily thewed legs curling into a crouch beneath him, his adversary's blade caught him in a sharp rap behind the calves, introducing an unexpected element of angular momentum. The Lion began to revolve backward, the floor came up as his opponent stepped smartly out of the way, and with an unwelcome *thud* he found himself flat on his back looking up at the expanding formation of still-flaming candles following him like dying comets toward the boards. The tip of a rapier appeared in his field of vision, blurring into a glint of red highlights as it caught the reflections of guttering fire. Pieces of candles bounced away to all sides.

The sounds of swishing and slicing died. The Lion moistened the thumb and forefinger of one hand against his lips and raised them to his forehead, crossed his eyes, and pinched gingerly in the midst of the glob of wax coagulating above his eyebrows. He was rewarded by a quick sizzle that faded off into a gurgling hiss. "You missed one," the Lion said.

"It's your own damn fault," said his adversary. "Chalk it up as a lesson in humility. Who the hell ever accomplished anything with one of those big grandstanding moves in the first place?"

"I'll have you know I once ambushed a bear."

"By falling off a lighting fixture? And which scar did that one leave you with, hmm?"

The Lion snorted. "Shut up and help me off the floor. My back's killing me. And toss me one of those towels."

A moment's leverage, suitably applied, resulted in the Lion becoming vertical once again. He draped the towel over his naked chest and led the way to the sideboard. "I've got half a mind to join you," he said after a moment, easing the words out around a large chunk of roast beef. "I've missed the last two Knittings, and the one before that must have been, oh, twenty, twenty-five years ago."

"Sure," Max said, "go ahead, come. Forget all that stuff you were telling me last week about how you're the only responsible force holding this city together and getting the warehouses rebuilt on schedule, not to mention the good government seminar you're putting your old friend Kaar through. Let Roosing Oolvaya sink back into the river—who needs it anyway?"

The Lion glared at him, an effect somewhat spoiled by the protruding cud of half-chewed meat in one cheek. "It's my kids," he said, "I should never have had kids in the first place. That was the beginning of the end. They warp your whole sensibility. You should have some."

"You forget," said Max, "I do have some. I have yours. Don't think I don't regret it, either."

The Lion resumed chewing, a look of satisfaction on his face. He might have been the one who'd ended up flat on his back on the floor, but that didn't mean he was the one who'd lost. "So, you think you can teach my son something?"

"He's got two arms and a brain, and at least a full complement of normal senses," Max said cautiously. "I don't see why not. Should be able to put a little maturity on him, at any rate, if he doesn't get carved up first."

A rather feral grin curled the left side of the Lion's mouth. He ran the towel over his forehead, catching the sheen of water draining down past his headband from his long black hair. "You studied with no master you'll lay name to, you fight with a mad hodgepodge without recognizable style, no part of the room is safe from you, either, and on top of that you know the value of life—by damn, I like that in a man! Are you sure *you're* not my son?"

Max raised an eyebrow and glanced at the Lion. True, they were about the same height, and they both had straightish black hair, although Max's ran more toward the wavy and the Lion's was running significantly toward gray, but Max had a lighter, more lithe build than the Lion's heavy-boned, mass-of-the-earth eastern-plains solidity. Max was also fully at home with the company of a highly functioning mind. The Lion, Max had discovered, had a brain with which no one could find fault, but was reticent to the point of pulling teeth about actually using it, rather than the largest convenient sword or the nearest wieldable chair. Beyond temperament, there was also the issue of age to consider. "It would seem unlikely," Max said. "Then again, who can say? If you can provide a reasonable inheritance, though, you're welcome to adopt me."

"How did you pick up that nickname anyway, the 'Vaguely Disreputable'?" The Lion had retrieved his sword and was idly using it to cut a thin slice of corned beef from the other large hunk on the serving platter. Suddenly he whirled, flinging the slice of meat off the end of the blade toward Max's eyes and launching the rest of his body after it. Max immediately fell backward and tucked into a roll. He'd been preparing himself for something of the sort, having found that the Lion enjoyed trying to lull his opponent off guard before flailing out in some unexpected attack. The corned beef flew over Max's body and hit the wall behind him but the Lion's sword, following it, slashed down instead.

Max stopped his back somersault perched on his shoulders and reversed direction with a sharpness that implied he'd had this move in mind from the start, springing forward first to a firm-footed crouch, then to a clinch directly up against the charging Lion's chest, and then, grasping the towel still dangling around the Lion's neck and giving it a twist and a stiff enough yank to bring a flush of sudden purple to the Lion's face, and using his pull on the towel to amplify his vertical momentum, flipped himself head-over-heels over the Lion's shoulder as the Lion catapulted forward toward the floor.

Max landed atop the sideboard, carefully keeping his

feet clear of the food. The clang of the Lion's sword against the floor was followed immediately by the familiar sound of the rest of the Lion joining it. "Acrobats," said the Lion in a muffled voice. "I've always detested acrobats. Rabbits, the bunch of them, always hopping out of your way."

"I keep telling you," said Max, "agility can outmaneuver the mass of a broadsword any day."

The Lion sprang back to his feet with a fair show of agility on his own part and retrieved his slice of corned beef from its perch on a wall sconce. "Tell the world about it," he said. "Acrobatics are fine if you do them just right. If not, you've just set yourself up for the strike of death." As he swung back toward the sideboard, he saw Max standing on it, his arms folded, tapping one foot next to a bowl filled with roasted potatoes. "Oh, all right," the Lion said, "I'm finished for today. Go ahead and make yourself a sandwich."

"Never fit will," said a croaking voice from beneath the table, "this." Something black and leathery moved behind one of the table legs, virtually lost at the back of the cabin in the shadows cast by the single lamp hanging by a chain from the ceiling. A wooden crate grated raspingly along the deck boards under the table and then crunched up against the wall.

"It does seem, if I may be so bold, that we *have* been spending the majority of our effort on merely moving the household from one location to the next," another voice remarked from just outside the door. A large heap of books precariously bound up with a net appeared in the doorway, followed by the speaker, who was attempting to balance the volumes in a pair of unnaturally long and slender arms that appeared to be wrapped so securely around the bundle that they were bending not only at the elbows but also, although that was certainly an illusion, midway down the exaggerated forearms as well. The skin of the exposed forearms was colored a more than incidentally greenish hue.

A muttering black cloak emerged from underneath the table and scuttled off to the side as the taller figure let the books subside with a heavy thump onto its upper surface. The top of the cloak's hood was barely higher than the level of the tabletop, revealing that working under the table was no serious inconvenience to its wearer. "Job did take I not with sole purpose furniture to arrange," said the mutterer.

A third being, this one human, had been sitting at the table in question trying desperately to remain engrossed in deciphering a letter. This being looked up from the heap of netted books which had just entombed the letter to a depth precluding immediate recovery. "What was that, Haddo?" he said, with an air of resigned disorientation.

"The matter on which Master Haddo was commenting," said the green-skinned one, stretching out his kinked arms, "was that of the purely menial activities to which our employment with you has led us of late."

"Plainly can speak for myself I," Haddo croaked. "Intercessor for need nil is." The hood swiveled to peer accusingly upward, revealing a continued expanse of fuliginous black broken only by two glowing orange sparks at around the right position for eyes. "Speaks yet Wroclaw truth."

"Oh, come on now," said the man at the table. "You know the situation. You know I'm not real fond of it myself."

"Yet sit you table at," said Haddo, "while heavy bundles drag we."

"But I'm the boss," the Great Karlini pointed out. "I'm supposed to sit at tables and think. You're supposed to handle things like packing and lifting, that's what I hired you for."

Wroclaw gave a discreet cough. "Not quite true, if I may remind you, sir."

"Said not you, 'For all is one, and for one is all'?" Haddo grumbled indignantly.

"If you don't like the job, Haddo, you're not bound to it," said Karlini. "I don't own you; you're more than welcome to take off and go back to wherever you came from. Where was that, by the way?"

"Hinterlands," said Haddo. "Do not say I, to wish

leave I. It the right of civilized beings is all complain to, admit you."

"Then what do you want, Haddo? You want another raise?"

"Satisfying current contract is. Rightful appreciation wish I, or treatment of equality."

Karlini glanced sidelong at Wroclaw. "Wroclaw?"

"I believe Master Haddo would wish either to see you yourself sharing in the heavier work, or, lacking that, to be properly entreated to continue bearing the burden himself."

"Ahead never get will you," Haddo snapped at Wroclaw, "when coat your words you sugar with. Question one have I: why beg you not I?"

"You want me to *beg* you to keep working?" said the Great Karlini. "Why should I do that?"

"Fringe benefit," Haddo stated. "To contract refer. Also, for you is no skin off."

"Oh, very well," said Karlini. "Please, please, Haddo, won't you stay and continue this demeaning but nevertheless essential work? I beg you. How's that?"

"Bad," said Haddo, "not is."

"What about me?" inquired Wroclaw.

Karlini pushed himself to his feet and glared at Wroclaw. Then he transferred his glare to his stool, growled "Do you want me to beg you, too?" in its direction, abruptly drew back one booted foot and swept it forward, connecting with one rod of the stool's tripod base with a solid thunk, and turned and stalked out of the cabin, limping slightly. Haddo and Wroclaw looked at each other, then stared after Karlini as he made his way onto the deck. "Fancy that," Wroclaw commented.

The deck of the river barge was covered by bales of fabric wrapped in watertight cloth, lengths of neatly cut hardwood, barrels of pickled fish, and whatever else could be sold for more at some other spot on the river away from Roosing Oolvaya than it had originally cost at Roosing Oolvaya. Over it all were the scrambling members of the crew, stowing the goods in the center of the craft away from the sweeps or beneath the benches for the rowers. For all Karlini knew, they'd be covering the benches next; the barge would be traveling downstream, with the current, so you'd figure there wouldn't be much need for rowing, but Karlini was the first to admit he was no sailor. He stepped aside as two wharfmen came up the gangplank from the pier propelling a recalcitrant goat between them and then made his way gingerly across the deck.

A woman was sitting on the port gunwale, her legs dangling over the side, wearing the same breech-and-tunic traveling outfit as Karlini. She had an inkpot balanced on the gunwale to her left, a quill pen perched behind one ear, and an open ledger book in her lap, and was gazing with an abstracted stare out across the harbor, occasionally eyeing the dark-haired young woman seated to her left. Karlini seated himself to her right, keeping a watchful eye on the inkpot, and gave her a quick kiss on the cheek. She turned toward him with a small start.

"Ouch," said Karlini. He rubbed at the long streak of black ink tracking across his right cheek toward his ear.

Roni dropped the offending pen into her book and set both off to the side. "What do you expect if you sneak up on me like that when I'm working?" she said. "Don't do that, you're only smearing it."

Karlini inspected his hand. It was indeed largely covered with ink, that probably was a fairly good indication of what his face now looked like. The young woman on Roni's other side emitted a strangled yelping sound, her mouth screwed shut and her face contorted into an agonized expression of controlled repression. Her hand flew up to cover her mouth as yet another yelp escaped.

"Go ahead, why don't you," Karlini said, a note of what was hopefully only mock exasperation coloring his own voice. The girl's face uncorked, a spasm of chuckles spewed out like the cloud of bubbles from a shaken bottle of carbonated wine, and then she doubled over, clutching her sides, overcome by the wave of giggling. "I must really look wonderful," he announced with resignation.

"Hold still," said Roni, producing a cloth from a side pocket and applying it to Karlini's cheek. "Tildy, why don't you go and try that new problem set, and I'll go over it with you later."

Tildamire, the oldest known child of the former Lion of the Oolvaan Plain, managed a nod, swung off the gunwale, and staggered off across the deck, holding her exercise book to her chest. "She's a good kid," Roni continued, "and I think she's going to turn out to have a real flair for math, so don't get exasperated at her. Promise?"

"Oh, very well," said the Great Karlini. "But do I really look *that* ridiculous?"

"Of course, dear," Roni said serenely. "How's our loading coming?"

"The staff's restless again," Karlini said. "I don't blame them. We'll all feel better when we're on the move."

"I suppose. Did you untangle the letter from Groot?"

"Haddo and Wroclaw are decorating the room over it. Anyway, it's probably only another warning to be careful with his boat."

"I don't know," Roni said. "Something's been making me nervous. There, now you can appear in public. Give me your hand. Do you think we can trust the crew?"

"It's Groot's boat," said Karlini. "It's Groot's crew, too. You might as well ask if we can trust Groot."

"Well, can we?"

A seagull flapped down and perched itself on Karlini's shoulder. He ignored it. "As far as anyone, I guess. Depends on where the profit is. He's always had a soft spot for Max, though."

"Haven't we all," remarked Roni. "That's better. Try to wait at least five minutes before disgracing yourself again, will you please, dear?"

"You knew what you were in for when you married me," Karlini said.

"Right. I told you I didn't want children immediately, and instead I ended up married to one."

"Would you like me to give you back your receipt?"

"Shut up," Roni said, "you idiot."

"Very well, dear," Karlini said, affecting an aggrieved expression. "How's the research coming?"

"It's hard trying to work out of boxes, with the apparatus packed away, but I think the trip won't be a total loss. I do have enough data put by to just sit and think about stuff for awhile."

"You won't, though, if I know you. You still think all this is leading somewhere?"

"Oh, yes," said Roni, "no question about that. The biologically cellular roots of magical power, no less. Whether we can understand it well enough to harness it, of course, still remains to be seen."

"We all have confidence in you," Karlini said.

"Confidence isn't the point. We're dealing with intricate systems, tremendous energies, things we're not even close to comprehending. Traditional magic is dangerous enough as it is, and that's when you already know what you're supposed to be doing, and yet here we are trying to forge new tools out of a whole new field. It's intimidating as hell. If you ask me, I'll take pure research over this any day."

The seagull, which had been nibbling inquisitively at Karlini's earlobe, hopped into the air, beat its wings once for balance, and landed nimbly atop his head. "Why does this thing keep following me around?" he said, craning his eyes upward in an attempt to gain early warning of the gull's next move.

"Maybe it thinks there's something lovable about you. There's no accounting for tastes, I suppose."

A leathery, attention-getting "hurrumph" sounded from behind them. Karlini shifted his position to crane his head around without dislodging the seagull. It was Haddo, the bright sunlight doing no more than the gloom in the cabin to reveal a single detail within his hood. "Bird," announced Haddo, "must fly I."

"Go ahead, Haddo," said Karlini, "and thank you. We'll see you later."

Haddo scuttled away. " 'Thank you'?" said Roni.

"Don't ask." They watched the passing water traffic for a moment. Then Karlini said abruptly, "Don't let Max stampede you into this, dear. He'll survive."

"Yes, but that's just the point, dear, don't you see?" Roni said. "Will he? And will we?"

* * *

I took a last look around my office. I know it's ridiculous to get sentimental about places, especially rental ones, but the office and I had covered a lot of ground with each other, so to speak. At any rate, I couldn't begin to count the number of times I'd covered the floor of the office with my own body, and for all I knew some of the copious amounts of organic fluids I'd spilled in that place were still dripping through knotholes to the floor below. The room was as bare as I'd found it, which really wasn't *that* bare; I'd known that anything personal I brought in was as likely as not to wind up smashed against the wall, if not across my head. The old bashed-in shield still hung over the entrance door. It had come in with the place and would go out with it, too. It was only in the last few weeks of investigation that I'd discovered that the shield had not actually been mine, receiving its dent in some campaign of my youth, but then it had only been a few months or so before, when I'd fallen in with Max and his crew for the first time, that I'd realized I had virtually no memory of my life before I'd arrived in Roosing Oolvaya seven years earlier.

The Curse of Namelessness, as Max had called it, was apparently not something you ran across every day, even if you were a sorcerer specializing in that sort of thing. Max wasn't that type of specialist, or at least I didn't think he was; his strongest talent that I'd been able to identify was an absolute genius for driving people crazy with cryptic references and vague allusions he would consistently refuse to amplify. Well, two could play at that game, I'd thought initially, but it was turning out to be harder than I'd figured, since one of the major items of analysis was my own mind. Don't get me wrong. I wasn't nearly at the end of my patience with Max, as exasperating as he could be. Any aggravation I went through with him was pretty mild compared to knowing I might still have a serious enemy out there, somewhere, who had hit me with this spell in the first place and had not only wiped out my past but even any knowledge of my own name.

Magic. Things always come back to magic, don't they? I hate magic. Of course, more and more my own life was coming to be wound up with the stuff. I knew I was in trouble when I found myself hoping that my memory problems could be traced to merely being hit over the head one too many times, but Shaa, the physician, had assured me that my condition was not, as he put it, "a simple organic amnesia." Realizing I'd rather have physical brain damage than have to keep dealing with magic didn't make me feel more secure about my sanity, but—

There was a knock on the closed door.

Oh, *no*, I thought, not again. The last time there'd been someone at that door who'd managed to approach without triggering a squeak from the staircase I'd adjusted specifically to act as an adjunct doorbell, it had meant trouble, big trouble; the trouble, in fact, that had landed me with Max and his friends in the first place, and had nearly resulted in the destruction of all of Roosing Oolvaya to boot. While I was contemplating escape through the side window and over the roof, the locked door opened and a woman came in.

Unlike the last time, when the visitor had been pale and tweedy and merely radiated an air of deadly purpose, this one had the burnished skin of a person who spent a lot of leisure time sitting on a tropical beach listening to the waves. And watching the sharks at play. The major thing about her that reminded me of Gashanatantra was that aura of "We'll do it my way or we'll pull off a few fingers and then try it again," the kind of attitude that probably passed for conventional light chitchat in her usual circles. I didn't need the warning tingle in the back of my head to know that whatever the mess before had really been about, it was back in motion again.

I was about to say, "How's your pal, Gash?" thus getting in the first word, bolstering my fortitude with a typical display of hard-boiled effrontery, and making it appear that I understood everything that was going on, and then some. But even though it seemed the perfect way of opening a conversational match of wits between us, an uncharacteristic burst of caution froze my jaw. Instead, I merely leaned back against the side wall next to the window, crossed my arms over my chest, and eyed her with as unflinching a gaze as I could muster on such short notice. The door swung shut behind her of its own accord, a cute trick I was sorry I'd never practiced myself while business was slow, and she planted her feet firmly on the floor in front of it, spread at shoulder width, letting her arms hang, the palms open and facing toward me and the air curdling slightly within their grasp. Her eyes were the color of lightning.

The seconds ground slowly past. I felt like something invisible was trying to mash me backward through the wall, but that my body was shrugging off the pressure with the well-mortared firmness of a barricade of bricks. It could have just been my mental state. It could have been, but I knew it wasn't. Unless I missed my guess, the metabolism link Gashanatantra had hooked me with was automatically drawing on his own personal protection field. At the moment, the shunt that linked us appeared to actually be giving me some help; if so, it was just about the first time. Fortunately, the protection effect was totally automatic. My own attempts to draw deliberately on the link had primarily revealed that where magic was concerned I had deep reservoirs of total incompetence whose surfaces I had barely begun to scratch. There was one thing I could do, though, that fell in my own department. Rather than merely glower at the woman by the door, or let my jaw assume its practiced wide-open position on my chest, I forced my face into something approaching a sarcastic grin. I figured the effect was less than completely successful on the sarcasm front, but I was hoping the subtle element of mockery I was aiming for would balance that out.

After a moment whose true length I wouldn't have ventured to guess, the eyes across the room narrowed. Her fingers folded inward as the tortured air in her hands rippled and became clear. The pressure against my body eased. "So," she remarked. Her voice had the tenor of a violin string plucked with a pick of broken glass, smooth and lyrical above a whiplash spike.

I kept my grin from widening with relief; this had probably been only the start. "So," I said also, for good measure.

" 'So'? All you can say is 'So'? I'd have thought better of you, *you*, always so proud of your reputation for having the perfect thing to say at the right time. Or do I still hold that much of a spell over you?" She tilted her head up and to one side and chuckled, but her chuckle held a disturbing hint of some nasty joke in it, barely contained.

"My reputation is occasionally expanded in the telling," I temporized. As far as I knew, I had never seen her before in my life.

"In a way," said the woman, "I suppose this was the perfect refuge for you. I'm almost embarrassed how long it took to track you down." That's what she *said*, but she didn't *look* embarrassed at all.

"Really," I said. "How nice. I'm sorry I put you to so much trouble. To what exactly do I owe the honor of all that effort, as well as the pleasure of your visit?"

"Now that I see you I'd know you anywhere," she said musingly. "Even if you do have a different body, even if you *are* hiding out in a rattrap room in a flea-infested town. Scarcely your style at all, which is, of course, the beauty of it. I can even understand your not giving me a proper greeting. Rest assured, though, my dear, certain things can survive any number of new bodies. Come over here and kiss me."

I tried to keep the gagging feeling in my throat from becoming loud enough to be heard across the room. "Don't you think that should wait?" I said instead, hoping I didn't sound too much like a drowning frog.

She scowled. It was a mean scowl. I was glad it wasn't directed at me, only at whoever she thought I was. I was only sorry that whoever that really was didn't happen to be around at the moment. "Very well," she said finally. "So that's the way you're going to be about it. I would have thought you would let yourself unbend that far, but then again, I do know you, so perhaps not. Nevertheless," and the scowl crawled again toward her equally nasty grin, "I *am* still your wife."

"How are you feeling?" said Jurtan Mont.

"When one considers the alternatives," said Zalzyn Shaa, "not too bad." He plopped down to sit on a convenient rock. "After all, look around us." A sweep of his arm took in the shrub-covered hillside, the neat patches of farmland falling away from them in long cultivated waves, the low gorge of the River Oolvaan and the beginnings of the mountains beyond, and, slightly downstream to their right, the sprawl and bustle of Roosing Oolvaya.

"Yeah," said Mont, following Shaa's gesture, "what?"

"Come now. Surely you have more of an aesthetic sense than that. Or have I been wasting my time on a toad?"

Mont dropped the sack containing the herbs Shaa had been collecting next to the rock and lowered himself to the ground. "Okay, it's a nice view, but what does that have to do with how your heart is?"

"If one is going to push one's limits," Shaa said sagely, "one might as well do it where there's something pleasant to look at. If one's limits obligingly retreat, then the pleasant vista can serve as sufficient instant gratification for attempting the exercise in the first place. Even if the limits remain in force, one can at least console oneself with the thought that one might easily not have anything to look at at all, pleasant or otherwise."

"So you've got more energy?" Shaa had set a fairly brisk pace up the hill. "Your breathing seems pretty good."

"To complain would seem churlish," Shaa agreed. At least, Mont *thought* that's what he was doing; it was always hard to tell with Shaa. "Have you finished packing?"

Mont grimaced. "Yeah, I guess. I don't know. I don't even know what I should be packing anyway."

"Whatever you can carry without unduly aggravating the horse."

"Why do I have to be *going* on a horse? I don't like horses."

"Neither does Max," said Shaa. "However, he is less fond of walking. It's known as a trade-off."

"Well, I don't like Max either. Why can't I be going with you? Why do I have to go to start with?"

Shaa opened the sack, peered within, fingered thoughtfully through his latest collection of weeds, selected one slender stalk of dusty and purple-edged green, mashed its bulbous end between his thumb and forefinger, and inserted the oozing tip in the corner of his mouth. "Did you ask a question?" he said.

"You're like trying to punch smoke, you know that?" Jurtan said. "You know perfectly well I asked a question."

Shaa rolled the weed around with his tongue for a moment before responding. "Maximillian has, rather valiantly I might add, offered to assist in your seasoning. I'm not sure I understand why, but then I'm not certain I understand why I've been spending so much of my own time with you when you persist in being so urchinish. There are some who would pay for the opportunity that is being thrust upon you gratis, but from your lips does a word of thanks fall? Not in my hearing, and I venture not in anyone else's either."

"I never said I wanted to be an adventurer," said Mont, "or whatever you all think you are, and I don't particularly want to try to fight with a sword. I'd rather work on the—well, the other stuff."

"They are not, as you are well aware, mutually exclusive, and the swordwork may not only help to occupy you on the way to the big time, but may help you when we get there."

"The big time? I thought we were going to the City of the Empire."

"Merely a synonym," Shaa said, "as you may come to appreciate if you survive, a state which may have something to do with your not exasperating one of us beyond the bounds of our professional courtesy."

"Well, excuse me for living," Mont said sarcastically. Shaa was pleased to note that his command of the proper tone was improving. Then again, of course, as Shaa didn't mind acknowledging, he did have more than one expert teacher. "But what if this adventuring stuff isn't for me, anyway? I mean, you've got an excuse. You've got your curse."

"I do indeed, and I am heartily sick of it. This time there may actually be a chance of slipping out of it; that is why *I'm* going."

Mont snorted. "You're not sick of it at all. I mean, you may be sick of the curse, but you're not sick of adventuring, I know you're not. You like it."

"I like it more when I have some discretion about the situation. The thought that it is quite likely to bring about my death does not exert a calming influence, either."

"I thought adventuring was supposed to be risky."

"This is true. Yet my risk factors are not merely those of the typical job description," Shaa said, "as you know perfectly well."

"That's a pretty good one, when you think about it," said Mont. "You're cursed to keep running after something that's probably going to kill you."

"Hmm, yes," Shaa commented, "it is rather classic. My brother did know what he was doing."

Mont actually made a small whoofing noise, as though he had been punched unexpectedly beneath the diaphragm. His mouth fell open. "Your—" he said. "Wait a second. I thought you had a sister."

"I do have a sister. I also have a brother."

"But I thought your sister was the one causing you all the trouble."

Shaa swiveled an eye in Mont's direction. "One of the major things you have yet to learn is not to presume that just because you know one fact, you know all, or just because you know facts, you know their proper interpretation."

"But—" said Mont, "but—"

"Why should I tell my life's story to a lout who wants to rot in Roosing Oolvaya for the rest of his days?"

Mont subsided into a sullen pout. "I'll go with Max," he said eventually.

"Don't do me any favors. You still appear reluctant," Shaa observed. "Is there some other hidden frustration you wish to vent?"

"No," said Mont. "Yes. Why do we have to go off and try to get in more trouble, anyway? I mean, Roosing Oolvaya's an out-of-the-way kind of place, nothing much ever happens here, and now that that whole bit with the coup and Oskin Yahlei and so forth's finished with, I'm sure nothing's going to happen again for years and years, if it ever does, so why can't we just stay here and do the same training and—"

"A characteristic example," stated Shaa, "of limited thinking, wishful at its source, narrow in its development. Events have a way of seeking one out, under their own momentum, or—" Shaa lengthened the word, so as to override the objection Mont, backtracking toward literal-mindedness, was about to voice—*"or"* (he repeated for good measure) "the characters behind the events, caught up in the same momentum, are the seekers; the difference is of semantic concern alone. The fact remains that events, once loosed, are as difficult to contain as vapor in a burst balloon. There may in fact be some entropic correlation. We may want to consult Roni, I believe that falls in her area."

Mont, his jaw set, was clinging grimly to his original idea, always a difficult thing when you happened to be waging a conversation with Shaa, but then he *had* been getting a lot of practice, at *that*, anyway. "That's ridiculous. Why couldn't I just stay here and be a clerk or a merchant or something? Things like you're talking about never seek out clerks."

"These events may not, although I could recite a list of counter-examples that might curdle your hair, but what about your father? Would *he* seek you out, hmm? And another point for your consideration, just as a reminder. Yes, I have a curse, but you have a gift. Tell me, my friend—which is the stronger motivator? Perhaps you *could* just stay at home, though, at that," Shaa mused. "Would you want to?"

Mont opened his mouth, then paused, his head tilted slightly to one side, visions of heroism (Shaa suspected) no doubt circulating in his mind. "I guess not," Mont said slowly. "I just want to know my options, that's all. I don't want to be dragged around like a toy with a pull string. I want to be able to make choices for myself."

"What more does any rational person want? A valid goal, if an ambitious one. How, do you suppose, would one go about achieving it?"

One of these days, Mont thought, he might learn to see these coming. "Luck?"

Both of them knew that Mont had merely been tossing out a useless response to buy himself some time to really think about the question, but Shaa was willing to grant him some at the moment; he was feeling expansive. "Far too random for a man planning to rise above the march of fate. You might as well say you hope to hide from the gods, from destiny, from good fortune as well as bad, indeed, from the world at large."

"Uh," said Mont, "as a matter of fact, that thought *had* crossed my mind. Why *not* hide out? Isn't that what Max has been doing, and what about you, yourself?"

"Ah," said Shaa, "indeed. Hiding out can without question be a valuable strategy, if not a totally open-ended one, but that doesn't mean it's at all a matter of sitting back and staying off the streets. How effective do you think it might be for someone whose primary skill is a reliance on luck?"

"All right, all right, I can tell what you're getting at. If you want to try to control your fate, you have to know what you're doing, and if you want to do *that*, you've got to have skills. Experience. Right?"

Shaa raised an eyebrow, the expression on his face affable, and then let the motion of his forehead draw his head back for an appreciation of the clear sky above. A waggling speck moved far overhead, a speck that could perhaps have been a large bird.

"But what's the urgency *now?* Why do we have to leave town all of a sudden now, after sitting around for a month. I mean, nothing's happening *yet*. Is it?"

"One never wants to be the last to know," Shaa said sagely. "One must always expect the worst. There is a certain attitude one must strive to cultivate. One must always think, in the midst of the clearest sky, that something could be happening already."

2
A CRISIS OF IDENTITY

"Since you want to bring *that* up," I said, "you might as well sit down."

The desk was staying with the office, too, not that I'd have had much use for it on the road, and along with it the two chairs. I took the one at the business side of the desk and the woman I'd never seen before took the other. Then we sat there and stared at each other. I couldn't begin to guess what she was thinking, but at the moment that was the least of my worries. My concern centered around the things she had given me to think about already.

I'd never been a particularly promiscuous guy; at least, not as far as I could remember. The "not as far as I could remember" part was the kicker in that sentence, of course. I wasn't sure which was going to be worse: having her realize she'd mistaken me for someone else, or having her recognition of me as her husband actually be correct. I didn't remember having been married, and it didn't seem like the sort of thing I'd be likely to forget, but if you were in an inquisitorial mood you could probably say the same thing about my name. Even if I took the tack that I could have been married to her and totally forgotten it, I didn't think that was the answer. She'd implied that she'd recognized me even though I'd changed my appearance. I had a feeling she hadn't been referring to my hairstyle, either, but to some major total body rework that sounded like pretty heavy magic indeed. I suppose it was possible that whoever had hit me with the curse had put me through such a transformation. As long as I was playing the odds, though, it made a lot more sense to go with the most obvious explanation. The one named Gashanatantra.

I'd been wondering why I hadn't heard anything from him. There was no clear reason he'd want to leave his metabolic link active indefinitely, since it had to be a drain on his resources, yet as far as I could tell it was still perfectly intact. Now I knew. He was still using me as a decoy. The woman hadn't recognized *me*, per se, she'd recognized the trace of Gash that was flavoring my aura through the link. She thought I was really him. She thought the taste of Gash's own aura I was still carrying was really a little bit of his true identity trickling through an otherwise comprehensive disguise. That ring business he'd set me up with before had been pretty tricky, but it was looking like I hadn't seen anything yet. At least the ring bit *was* business; this mess seemed unmistakably personal. What had I ever done to him?

There was another reasonable explanation though, as long as I was running through the range of possibilities. She could have merely been out of her mind. I liked this explanation even less than the others. She had struck me as both a powerful and a nasty customer, and that was assuming her activities had some rational reasoning behind them. If she was delusional or outright insane, well, my best bet was to start finding out if I remembered any good prayers. After falling in with Max and Shaa I'd gone back and made a few back payments to Phlinn Arol, the Adventurer's God, just in case, but I had no idea if that had put me into his favor or not, or if I'd ever even been there in the first place. The gods work in mysterious ways, they say, which I always figured was just as well. Of course, back then I hadn't yet gotten in the habit of staring across my own desk at gods who were working mysteriously on me. "It's been a long time," I said. "When we last spoke . . ."

"I know," she said. "I know you told me you never wanted to see me again. I know you hated me because of that time with Kortese."

She paused. I fixed her with a stern gaze. She swallowed, and said, "Do you think I would tempt your wrath without a very good reason?"

"I don't know," I said, "would you? Here you are, and yet I haven't heard the barest hint of any kind of reason, good or otherwise, wouldn't you admit? As you saw fit to bring up, I suppose we *are* married, or at least someone might try to make that case, but what does it really mean, anyway? And let us not forget your initial greeting. I would say that smacked more of the preemptive first strike than a preamble to polite conversation, hmm?"

Her gaze was perhaps less sardonic, less sure of itself than it had been at the outset. "All right, then, I'll be direct. I want the ring. If I could have taken it off your smoking body, I would have."

"Ah," I said. "Now we appear to be getting somewhere. But where, indeed? There are many rings floating about, and even a few worth blasting one's in-laws over. Which one do you have in mind? And why do you think I might have it?"

"Don't start playing games," she snapped. "You know perfectly—"

"No games?"I said in an aggrieved tone. "Just what did you expect, pray tell? If you know me at all, my dear, you know that convolution is my life's blood, so to speak." I was riding the odds. Shaa had told me something of Gash's reputation as the Mad Plotter, the Devious, master of stratagems and counterplots. "I'm rather disappointed in you, you know. I'd have thought during your association with me something might have rubbed off. Instead, what am I met with? A frontal assault, if an expectedly weak one, followed by a retreat to declarative statements? Oh dear, oh dear." I tsk'd at her once or twice for good measure.

She looked at me, and in her face I read a mixture of emotions. On the surface was a flush of rage, no doubt aimed at me, no doubt well-earned by my belittling remarks. Beneath that was her initial layer of arrogance torn through now by the shreds of doubt. Beneath *that*, though, was something else, rising up like a leviathan from the great depths of the ocean. Like the hidden leviathan, it made only the barest ripple on the surface;

unlike the leviathan, which stays in the deep water because it can't breathe in the air, she was deliberately hiding this particular emotion, which meant, by extension, that she was deliberately letting the other emotions show. What was she up to?

"As long as you're being declarative," I continued, "I'll try to play *your* game, how's that? What did you think you were doing when you walked in here? Why did you bother to attack in the first place? You knew you'd never lay me out with your power alone."

"No," she said. "You're right." Suddenly her original nasty smirk was back. No, more than that. Suddenly the leviathan had emerged from the abyss, hurling its mass clear of the water in a thunderclap of shrapnel spray. "That's why I brought *this.*" She reached into the air, her hand sliding into a spot above the center of the desk and disappearing from sight along a neat dividing line as though she'd stuck her hand behind an invisible wall, giving me a good angle to view the rest of her wrist and then her forearm in a cross-sectional, apparently severed state. The view of chopped-off muscles and pulsing arteries, and the yellow of living bone, made me sorry Shaa wasn't around to fully appreciate it; I prefer my anatomy neatly confined to outer surfaces. I didn't have to watch that particular parlor trick for long, though, since she quickly grasped the thing she sought in the invisible compartment and drew it out into sight.

A mass of writhing worms was my first impression, gray and black and ceaselessly squirming and making a disgusting squelching sound; I hoped it wouldn't start oozing ichor all over the desk. Then I realized that the wormball might not be solid at all, since the worms seemed to be freely passing through each other at will, overlapping and parting like the multiple images from a particularly rotten barrel of fermented oat rotgut scarfed down in the kind of long flashy swig that would probably leave you unconscious at its conclusion, either from lack of fresh air or the unmitigated kick of the brew itself, and if it didn't leave you sprawled insensate on the floor you'd wish it had. The worms were treating her hand with respect, not trying to merge with *her* flesh, only their own, but as I noted that fact I also realized that a sparkling film had appeared over her hand and arm like a painted-on glove. The glove effect was one I hadn't seen before in my limited experience with magic, and since I had no idea how to duplicate it myself I had a feeling that the worms might not treat my flesh with the same level of restraint.

It *did* look impressive, I had to admit. However, the effect was to some degree lost on me, since I unfortunately didn't have the slightest idea of what the wormball actually was, other than more trouble, but that much was only common sense. Gash, I was sure, would have recognized it immediately; he was that kind of guy, and it did sound like the sort of thing that would be up the line of his professional specialization. He still didn't seem to be around, unfortunately, and he sure wasn't sending any helpful messages either. "So," I said, "you've got a new toy. Do you expect me to collapse at your feet, to beseech you in tones of supplication?"

She peered at me, momentarily nonplussed. Her eyes took a quick glance at the worm thing, almost as though she wanted to make sure it was really there, and active; I half expected her to shake it to see if it would rattle. She didn't. Instead she fixed that grin firmly on her face and extended the thing toward me. I felt a sudden flush of heat as though the door to an oven had been opened in front of my face. Unlike an oven, I didn't feel the sensation on the surface of my skin, but down behind my eyes in the center of my skull.

"So what are you trying to tell me here?" I said. "You're willing to go for a divorce?"

"I'd rather be a widow."

"Easier said than done."

"No, I don't think so." Her hand paused. The wormball was close enough to my face that I had to cross my eyes to see it clearly, and the heat was extreme. So far I'd kept myself from shrinking back in the chair, but the next time she started moving I figured I'd better be prepared to do something fast. "You know," she commented, "I'm enjoying this more than I'd expected, and I'd looked forward to enjoying it quite a lot."

"Don't say I never show you a good time," I said. "Just out of curiosity, suppose you actually succeed in frying my cerebellum with that thing. How do you plan to get hold of the ring you mentioned then? The ring you say is the main reason you've come after me in the first place."

"I said I'd take it off your smoking body, and I still will."

"Ah, yes," I responded, "you did say that, and in so many words. What would you do, though, if it didn't happen to be *on* my body, as indeed it does not?"

"That's the oldest bluff there is."

"No doubt. It happens to be most effective, however, when it's true."

"True? You've never said anything true in your life. You wouldn't recognize a true statement if it—"

"You're sure you're ready to take the risk? It's a little hard to go back once I've become a smoldering corpse, you know. What would you do then if you found you'd guessed wrong? More to the point, what would your associates do?"

It was a calculated gamble. True, she hadn't mentioned any partners. She didn't seem nearly as sharp as me, though, or to be more precise, as sharp as the being she thought I really was, and I had a hunch she knew it, too; it may have had a lot to do with the fact that the two of them were distinctly on the outs. That being the case, I didn't think she would have decided to go after me-or-him on her own, ring or no ring as inducement, and if she wasn't in this alone she was in it with somebody else.

Continuing to be conversational wasn't my last-ditch gambit, either, by any means. My walking stick was within reach, propped against the side of the desk, for one, and for another I figured I was capable of more frenzied agility than she was used to expecting from Gash. Physicality was always a useful last resort, or an option to turn to when you couldn't think of anything else and figured you'd might as well do *something*. But I *did* have a brain, or so I'd been told, and I figured it would be a reasonable idea to find out just how good a weapon it could be on its own terms, before I started in on my more usual behavior of trying to throw it at people, using its gross characteristic of mass in an attempt to knock them out before I lost consciousness myself through the impact of cumulative whiplash.

She had the corner of one lip between her teeth and was gnawing it absently in thought as she watched me. Not moving her eyes away, she fumbled around her neck with her free hand, got hold of a round palm-sized crystal disk hung from a silver chain, raised it in front of her face, and then squinted at me through it. "You say you don't have the ring?"

"I don't have the ring."

As I said the words again, a regular pattern of silver motes ran across the surface of the disk like a school of tiny minnows. Her frown deepened. Her pursed lips narrowed to an ominous line. Abruptly, she thrust the wormball out straight into my face.

My head was whipping back out of gut reaction as she moved, but I felt a fiery lash across my forehead and heard the quick sizzle of hot grease. She was the one who yelped, though, as she fell backward into her chair. Her arm was jerking uncontrollably, the forearm twisting spastically back and forth. The worms that had covered the front side of the floating colony, the side that had barely grazed my skin, were crisped, and had melted droopingly all over her palm. An evil-looking brown smoke was rising off their twisted bodies. The rest of the worms had broken entirely out of their ball and were slinking their way out of the vicinity in every direction—off across the tabletop and up along her lashing arm. She stared at me for a second, this time with a clear mixture of shock and fright, and then turned her attention to the worms, cupping her free hand and pointing it down at them. A flattened vortex appeared beneath her palm. The worms leapt or were sucked off the table, some coming free with a reluctant slurping *pop*, and the bunch of them darted in a straight spinning cloud toward the vortex like arrows off a multiple-fire crossbow heading for a competition target. Sparks showered out, and then the last of the worms were gone.

Singed tracks wound up her forearm. I figured my forehead probably looked the same. What I couldn't figure was what had happened, and why. Obviously that wasn't what she'd expected. It sure wasn't what *I'd* expected. What I did while I thought, though, was release my grip on Monoch, the sword disguised as a walking stick, fold my arms, and grin at her.

She didn't grin back. "I *told* him this wouldn't work," she said under her breath, "but I never expected *that.*"

Okay, I thought, *I have the advantage.* I had her off-balance. It was a perfect moment to hit her with a mop-up blow. The major problem was that I still didn't know what to use for a mop.

The ring; I should concentrate on the ring. She wanted the ring, but I didn't have it. Any way you looked at it, that was going to be a problem. I could take one of two approaches: either keep on trying to convince her I really didn't have the ring, or go for letting her believe I *did* have it but just didn't want to turn it over to her. Or that I had it hidden and I'd lead her to it. If I could get her to accept that I didn't have it, the unavoidable question would be where it was. Under the circumstances, I doubted she'd buy the line that I didn't know what she was talking about; I could keep on trying it, but it would be a holding action that wouldn't hold long at all, I could tell. Maybe I could sort of tell her the truth, that I'd been working with others and I'd turned the ring over to them, but I'd have to tell her who the others were and then it would be their lives on the line. Unless I didn't identify the *right* others. . . .

Who did I know who I'd want to sic this harridan and her pals on?

Then it hit me that that wasn't the only way to go about this. "Very well," I said. "Let's discuss this ring. Let's *discuss,* like adults, not chew up each other's flesh like razor-tooth rabbits. Razor-teeth are beneath us, perhaps you'll agree now?"

She was in some pain, it seemed; not much, but enough to make her more receptive. I was in some pain, too, but my edge there was that I'd *expected* it. "It's clear you're interested in getting your hands on this ring," I continued. "I think perhaps you'll believe me now when I tell you I don't have it. I *did* have it, though, if we're talking about the same ring, and I presume we are."

She blinked at me. She'd probably thought I'd just kick her out the door, or through the wall, or into the next dimension, as long as I had the drop on her. I was playing the role of Master Plotter, though, or at least I thought I was, so I was trying to live up to a higher standard. "The plot for the ring was mine, but not mine alone," I said. A small gleam of triumph appeared on her face; she knew she'd scored one, even if it was a point I was letting her win. "Mine was the plot, but not the implementation. With me in this scheme was someone you will recall, whose name I am sure I will not need to mention. Especially under the circumstances, it would be unwise were I to do so. Things between us after we acquired the ring did not go according to my plan. As a result, as I said, I do not now have the ring. Suffice it to say I was outwitted; there, are you happy?"

She was, I could tell. She looked *real* happy. I figured the reluctant self-incrimination and embarrassing abasement of an admission of failure would sit well with her, considering her current attitude toward me, particularly since her alertness might be slightly clouded by the pain of the worm burns. But would she take the bait?

In the midst of her glee, her face assumed a thoughtful air. "Do you mean who I think you mean?" she said.

I wanted to say, "If you think I mean who you think I mean, then I think you catch my meaning," or words to that effect, but somehow I thought it would spoil the tenor of the exchange we were having. Instead I simply raised an eyebrow, tossed her a smile and left it at that for her to chew on.

I watched her mastications for a moment before I decided to give the cauldron another quick stir and toss in an extra pinch of seasoning. "As I'm sure you'll be pleased to have me admit, I felt unable to go and retrieve the ring myself, single-handed, lest I risk annihilation more closely than you will remember I prefer. I had pretty much written the thing off, if you want to know the truth. As I said, brushing against annihilation isn't worth it for a ring. Your coming here today and pressing the issue has made me reconsider, however. With you, your partners and myself united, we may very well be able to succeed where I by myself had given up."

"How would we divide the ring? Why would you want to get involved with another partnership, after you've just admitted the last one fell apart on you?"

"I don't know how much you really know about this ring," I said. "Just let me say that its benefits do not have to be limited to one bearer. Aside from that, though, the issue for me is no longer merely one of the ring itself. There are reputations to think of, and accounts, you will agree, to settle."

"We've never worked a job before," she commented, "not even when we sort of got along. Do you think it's a good idea to be talking about doing that now?"

"No," I said. "Do you?"

She gave me an actual grin, for a change. "I don't either," she told me.

"Good," I said. "Then we're agreed. The situation speaks for itself. I'm willing to admit I haven't been in my peak form, primarily due to lack of motivation. If I'm being sloppy and you can't even get *me* to give up a ring I don't have, you're never going to pry it loose by yourselves from the one who *does* have it. Let's go talk to your partners. They're hanging around somewhere in town, right?"

She gave a crisp nod and headed for the door. I grabbed Monoch and followed her. I picked up the pack I'd leaned next to the door earlier, when I'd come in to look things over before my rendezvous with Max, and closed the door behind my back. I didn't turn around, even though I didn't think I'd ever set foot in that room again. Like I said before, sentimentality about that crummy office was the last thing I thought I could afford right then.

I knew I'd never carry this off over an extended period of time. I didn't know who the players were and I had only the most rudimentary insight into what the game really was. At the moment, though, long-range planning didn't occupy nearly the same priority for me as the short-term question of staying alive and un-crisped through each successive minute. Maybe I'd set something in motion and maybe not, and even if I had let something interesting loose I didn't know if it would wind up in a brief shoving match or an all-out war of the gods, as grandiose as that sounds; all I was hoping for was enough confusion to slip myself off the hook I'd found myself dangling from by the collar of my coat. Whatever it was I might have expected, I had the uneasy suspicion that the true outcome was going to be something else entirely.

I'm not perfect, never claimed to be; all I try to do is learn from my mistakes and not to make the same ones over again. The problem is that like most folks, I'm creative. I've got a totally demoralizing talent for coming up with entirely new mistakes even worse than the old ones. I wondered just which one I was sticking my foot into this time. I'd seized the initiative, true, or at least I thought I had, and so I was heading out toward the next trial in a better position than I'd hoped. I'd known when she'd walked in the door that the only way she'd be walking out alone would be if I was dead; she wasn't just going to stroll peacefully out of my life and let me go back to whatever I'd been doing. So we were leaving together, but we were doing it more as a mutual standoff and less as her dragging me. The end result was the same, but the game of position between us had me with the marginally better hand. It was a circular argument, of course. The spot my "better hand" had put me in was off the ladder and onto the high wire.

We headed west through Roosing Oolvaya, on foot, away from the river and toward the caravan grounds. I'd been hoping we'd pass someone I knew so I could try to slip him a message, but I hadn't really believed that hope would pan out and it didn't. Roosing Oolvaya went through its normal routine of waking up, stretching, and getting about its business around us. Carts with fresh produce, pens of cackling chickens, and once even a tank of live droop-whiskered fish clattered past on their way to the central market; a little late in the morning for them to be arriving, perhaps, but apparently someone thought it made sense. As we drew closer to the west gate that let onto the caravan grounds, though, traffic got tighter and denser until we were virtually clawing our way upstream. At the gate—in fact, right in the middle of the gate—the explanation revealed itself.

Two wagons were mashed up together in a pile of loose wheels and fragments of wood siding, one canted onto its nose with both front wheels gone and the axle shattered. The rest of the traffic, wheeled, mounted, and two-footed, was forced to edge its way around through the narrow space left between the wreckage and the stone arch of the gate wall. A group of people were trying to pull the wagons apart and drag them through the gate out of the way. Unfortunately, they didn't seem to have agreed on which side of the gate they were moving them to, and so seemed to be largely nullifying each other's efforts. As we wedged our own way through the gate, past a tangle of shouting men, including the wagon drivers, a group of city guards, and some frenzied partisans who had probably been normal citizens just passing through a short time before, I noticed a big crumbly gap in the overhead curve of the gate arch. Directly below it, I could now see more clearly, was the wagon with the crushed front axle, the top of a big stone sticking up above its sideboard.

I didn't think that much of it all. You built a gate, or a bridge or a palace, for that matter, and there was no getting around the fact that eventually it would start to fall down. Then you'd fix it up or just tear it down entirely and start over; that's the way things went. All you hoped was that you didn't happen to be standing under it when it started to let go. Sometimes you got real lucky and built something that was still standing around, in reasonable repair and with minimal maintenance, a thousand years later, but that sure wasn't the way to bet.

Like I said, that much was only common wisdom. Maybe it wasn't in the old days, I mean the *really* old days, but since then civil engineering has become something of a lost art. Not by chance, and not because people lost interest in it, of course, but because the gods had decided we'd all be better off if we gave up technology and went back to a purer, grubbier world. Or at least the gods had decided *they'd* be better off. I'd always disliked the gods because of their general high-handed attitude, and their aversion to the world's use of technology was the perfect case in point. Now that I had my own private god out for a stroll, though, perhaps I could voice my objections in person, and maybe even find out from the horse's mouth, so to speak, *why* they'd always acted this way, aside from naturally wanting to run the world and everybody's activities in it. I glanced at the woman. Somewhat to my surprise, I found she was eyeing *me,* as though she was trying to decide whether to ask *me* something on the same order of interest to her as my own question was to me. We stared each other down for a second or so, then turned our heads to the front and resumed plowing on through the traffic jam.

We cut off down a regular strip of open ground kept clear as a road. There weren't any official roads in the caravansary, of course, just a sizable expanse of flat ground mashed into dust and fenced off for the season into rentable plots by local entrepreneurs. The irregular roads tended to converge at the various wells, though, and off ahead of us I could see the tall water-barrel winch poles atop one of them as we approached. Unexpectedly, the traffic, which had begun to thin a bit as we got away from the mess at the gate, started to coagulate once again. I wondered just what was going on around the city today—a contagious case of bad luck? We broke through the crush of people and came face-to-face with yet another woeful situation.

Ahead of us, two guys in travelers' robes were standing nose to nose, waving their arms around and yelling in each other's face. Behind them was another learned-looking fellow with a long beard; he was rubbing his chin with one hand and casting a sage eye over the proceedings with the air of someone who was about to make a pronouncement. An ox stood next to one shouting man, pawing the ground nervously with its right front hoof. There was blood on the ox's left horn. As a sort of centerpiece to the scene, a bloody sheep lay on the ground between the two men who were going at it. The sheep wasn't moving, but if the two men were any good at sympathetic magic, I expected it to leap up and break into a jig any second from the level of emoting going on.

Instead, the man who I figured for the owner of the sheep made a grab for the tether dangling from the neck of the ox. The ox, already spooked by the excitement, danced back out of reach. Unfortunately for the ox, it had neglected to look over its shoulder first, and so it backed into the low crumbling wall around a wide water well. The wall crumbled further under the force of the ox's hurled mass; the ox, its hind legs knocked out from under it, sat down hard on the remains of the wall; and with a crunch and a small rumble a stretch of wall centered on the ox disintegrated entirely, propelling the ox, still in motion, backward into the well. The crowd heard one frenzied ox-bellow, the ox's head and horns disappeared from sight, and then the crowd fell silent. The two guys froze, their arms in mid-wave, their mouths open in identical circles. In the midst of the sudden silence we heard a loud PLOP of displaced water. That cut things loose again. The two original guys were joined by a third, apparently the owner of the well, and then the *crowd* joined in with a general shouting and arm-waggling. The original sage, too, had been supplemented by two others, and the three of them had their heads together in scholarly consultation, trading citations of tractate and verse in their own rapid crossfire.

As we tried to edge around the commotion, one of the people who was trying unsuccessfully to grab hold of the ox's tether or otherwise drag it out of the well clutched at his chest with a look of horror, pulled out an obviously empty drawstring bag suspended by a thong from around his neck, and began hollering, "My jewels! This well has swallowed my jewels!" He swung around to join the owners of the ox, the sheep, and the well in their grievances, elbowing the man next to him in the back. The man thus elbowed, who had been pulling hard on the dangling tether of the ox, overbalanced and went headfirst over the wall into the well. Ox and man bellowed in unison. I turned my head; I'd seen more than enough.

My companion was regarding me with a clear look of admiration. "Which one was you?" she said. "I was watching you the whole time, but I couldn't even pick up a flicker. It was the ox—you caused it to back into the well, yes? Or did you start the entire thing? Was it the sheep?'' She shook her head in amazement. ''Such a stylish example of your philosophy, too—a small nudge here, a small kick there, and then the momentum of the avalanche. I hadn't been certain before, in the other incident with the displaced stone in that gate, even though it seemed to have the touch of your personality, but now there's no doubt about that either, is there?''

I did my best to show her an inscrutable smile. I thought I'd just learned something valuable. Not *reassuring,* necessarily, and probably not useful, either, but it did begin to add some depth to my knowledge of the person I was supposed to be impersonating. ''A bit flamboyant, perhaps, if indeed it was me,'' I said.

She cast me another sidelong glance. ''I think I like you more this way. Your arrogance was always one of your most obnoxious points. I never thought you could change, but perhaps your time spent slumming with these mortals has done you some good after all.''

''Don't take it to the bank,'' I said. Behind us now, the crowd fell silent again for an instant, then resumed with increased vigor. I didn't want to look. She led me around another corner, though, and down past a camel corral on our left and a maze of tents on our right. We went around the back of a medium-sized tent and she pulled aside the door-flap, then indicated the interior with an open hand.

''You told me *I* was slumming?'' I said.

Her mouth pursed as her mood regressed to its earlier state, and one corner of her lip curled down in a small snarl. ''Just go in the tent,'' she told me.

I brushed past her. A few small incense burners were scattered here and there on low tables and next to cushions, and the canvas walls transmitted additional light from the outside, so I had no trouble seeing the figure of a man perched comfortably on a large pillow at the far end of the tent, his legs crossed, a puffing hookah at his side; no, I had no trouble at all. The trouble was with the interpretation of what I saw. I'd never seen *her* before, but I'd sure seen *him.* He was the guy I knew as Gashanatantra.

3
BUT NOT FORGOTTEN

"Why doesn't this surprise me?" Max muttered.

"Rest assured," said Shaa, "something will come of it."

"Something? You mean something good?" said Jurtan Mont.

"Good, bad, the difference is primarily a referential one," Shaa told him. "Events are Max's basic philosophy, stirring them up and then improvisationally molding the flow. To channel a current, one needs motion, not merely a stagnant pool." Shaa indicated the rolling surface of the River Oolvaan visible past the gunwale and the other moored barges, and then smoothly pointed a finger at a passing vessel easing downstream with the swell.

"Are you going on with that philosophy bit again?" said Max. "You've been trying to hook me with that line for the last ten years."

"If the line fits," Shaa said blandly, "one could do worse than hang from it."

Max snorted. His perch atop the aft deck cabin of Haalsen Groot's barge let him see over the top of the usual wharfside clutter of crates and the rising form of the winch-driven crane, its reconstruction lagging typically behind schedule. Many people were visible to his gaze but the Creeping Sword had not yet been one of them unless he'd strolled by in disguise, and why would he want to do that? The Sword was several hours overdue. Even if he didn't know his own name, forcing them all to resort to that cheesy nom de plume when they needed to refer to him, one thing he *had* proven himself to be was relatively punctual. Although Max's own timeliness was often a matter of relativity itself, he was willing to appreciate it in others.

"Are you perhaps considering a visit to his office?" Shaa continued, after a moment for mutual contemplation.

"I'll go through the motions," Max said. "Of course I'll go through the motions, but he won't be there. I only hope that whatever he's gotten himself into is going to help out in the long run. I just wish I knew when he was going to pop up again."

"You think we'll see him again?" asked Jurtan.

"Yeah, we'll see him again, probably right in the middle of some mess like the last time."

'Unless he's dead, of course," Jurtan added, trying to adopt the same natural tone of full-blooded yet abstract appreciation for the world's twists and turns that Shaa and Max seemed to spin naturally around themselves merely by breathing.

"Dead?" said Max. "What's that supposed to have to do with anything?" He cast a glance down at Shaa. "I thought you were supposed to be tutoring this kid."

Shaa shrugged. "Every day, or perhaps every other, something of significance appears to sink in. The younger generation is not what it used to be, if indeed it ever was. I wish you better luck."

"You sure you don't want him?" Max said hopefully.

It didn't bother Jurtan, not any more; at least that's what he kept trying to tell himself. "Do you mean death in general isn't something he has to worry about, or that the Sword's curse means he can't die?"

"Tricky thing is curse," muttered the voice of Haddo from within the cabin. "Relevant death may be, or may not."

"What Haddo says is quite correct," said Max, raising his voice so that he could be heard in turn by the cabin's occupants, "but I was thinking more about the gods."

"Always think you about gods," said Haddo. "Ulcer get will you." A small trapdoor in the roof intended for cabin ventilation suddenly popped open next to Max; a black hood and a glowing-coal eye appeared through it. "Envious perhaps are you, of gods their power, of gods their knowledge?"

"You know me better than that, Haddo," Max said. "I don't envy the gods, I hate them. I'd love to wipe them out, or at least bounce them back down to mortal status."

"Join them you would not?"

Shaa and Max exchanged unreadable looks. "I'd die before I'd join the gods," Max said.

"I thought you said death wasn't necessarily relevant when you're talking about the gods," said Mont. All three heads swiveled to fix him with nasty stares. Max and Shaa, anyway; who knew *what* an expression passed for on Haddo's face, if he *had* a face, but that red thing-that-might-be-an-eye of his did look a bit more exasperated than usual. Mont didn't get it. Why were they always dumping on him? Oh, all right, he was being a little snotty, but it was an honest question and a relevant one, wasn't it?

"Truth is truth, except when is not," Haddo remarked inscrutably, and then he popped back down out of sight.

Shaa opened his mouth, perhaps to continue the exchange. Just at that moment, though, a quick shudder ran through the deck, followed by a side-to-side rocking sensation. Max slid off the roof of the cabin and landed neatly on one of the stacked crates. Instead of what might originally have been on his mind, Shaa said, "Some large river creature?"

"In the middle of Roosing Oolvaya harbor?" said Max. "Fat chance. Where's Roni?" He and Shaa locked eyes again for a brief instant, and then both of them simultaneously turned to look aft, toward Roni's temporary lab in the rear of the cabin whose roof Max had been occupying. The ship keeled over again, hard enough to make Mont take several quick off-balance steps toward the port gunwale before he tripped over a knee-high length of stacked lumber. The motion was violent enough to make even Max reach out a hand for support. The ship hesitated, its deck remaining at the extreme of its upward-canted attitude, and in the abrupt silence they heard Roni's voice say, softly but clearly, "Damn."

The brief quiet ended with the screaming hiss of what sounded like a cauldron-sized tea kettle heated suddenly to its boiling point. Then, with a crash of tearing lumber, the aft section of the cabin roof blew out, sending fragments of wood arcing through the air. In the center of the cloud of debris was a fist-sized ball of pulsing light wrapped in a lumpy, translucent, and fairly well shredded membrane, the whole structure wriggling in an organic manner. Almost as quickly as the eye could fix on this jellyfish blob, though, a sparkling meshwork column shot up after it out of the hole, the leading end expanded and split radially like the petals of a long-stemmed orchid, and then with an audible <clunk> the now scoop-shaped petals clamped shut on the flying blob. One final pulse of light leaked out through the mesh as the petals wove firmly together. Now like a small basket at the end of a short, narrow tornado, or perhaps even more accurately at the end of a thick fishing line, the encased blob danced in midair for a short moment; then, making a quick slurping sound, line and basket were sucked back down through the crater and into the cabin.

The ship flopped back to its normal attitude, sending a sheet of spray flying off the starboard side of the hull and across the adjacent dock. Small fragments of singed wood clattered on the deck. Shaa glanced at Max and raised an eyebrow.

"Looked like a supercharged paramecium," observed Max. "Roni thought she'd try to control the expression of the cellular magic bodies using some of these one-celled microbes she's been studying. The process is still at a pretty coarse level, obviously. The mid-level containment spells stopped it from getting out of hand without any trouble, though."

"Except to the ship," Shaa murmured.

"It's a small hole," Max said, clambering back up on the roof and standing over the crater with his hands appraisingly on his hips. "I might as well add some more safeguards, though," he called down through the hole.

"Sounds good to me," said Roni's voice, somewhat weakly, from below.

"What would have happened if that thing had gotten away?" Mont asked Shaa in a low voice.

"I'm not certain we'd want to find out," Shaa said thoughtfully. "I suppose the consequences might have something to do with whether the organic portion of the construct could reproduce."

Mont's sister emerged from the cabin, coughing. Streaks of black soot covered her face. Shaa produced a clean cloth and offered it to Tildamire. "The life of a laboratory assistant does have its drawbacks," he commented.

"Wow," she said dazedly. "Real science."

"Uh, Shaa?" said Mont.

"Not right at the moment, please," said Shaa. "Hold your thought. Great One," he continued, raising his voice to carry through into the cabin, "is the situation under control?"

"No problem," said Karlini, from somewhere in the thinning cloud of smoke still rolling through the door and the hole in the roof. "No injuries, just a lot of soot and some broken glassware and a busted beam or two."

"Capital," stated Shaa. "In that case, Maximillian, would you favor us with your presence on deck for a moment?"

"What?" said Max. "Oh, sure." With a somewhat distracted air, he stepped away from the hole and toward the edge of the cabin roof, dropped forward into a roll just ahead of the verge, grasped the end of the eave beam with both hands when he reached a completely upside-down attitude in his somersault, and straightened his legs above his head to go into a full handstand. After balancing momentarily, he pushed strongly off the beam with his hands and sprang upward in the air. He whipped his legs down, bending at the waist, and then straightened his upper body, effectively flipping himself end over end as he reached the top of his vertical travel and setting his body upright. His feet cleared the edge of the roof by a good six inches on his way back down. Max hit the deck with a thud and bent his knees in a deep crouch to deal with his momentum, his arms out wide to either side for balance and, Shaa was sure, for an extra theatrical flourish.

"Thank you," said Shaa. "I'll be certain to praise your capabilities when the recruiter from the circus stops by. Until then, though, there is an important question to discuss. Are you quite sure this research is safe?"

"What's safe?" said Max, straightening up again and brushing soot from his clothes. "Life isn't safe. Riding around in a boat isn't safe. Magic isn't safe. The stuff we usually do certainly isn't safe. You want *safe*, you'd better—"

"That's not entirely what I meant," responded Shaa. "I wasn't referring merely to our own personal safety, I was thinking of any larger scale consequences if the products of this research get out of hand."

"It's got to be done," Max said firmly. "Without—"

"Do I detect a note of obsession in your tone, hmm?" said Shaa. "Furthermore, you're not answering the question. Max doesn't like to be cross-examined," he added, in a sidelong aside to Tildy, who had been intently watching the exchange as though it was a tennis match, swiveling her head back and forth to focus on each speaker in turn.

"If you were anyone else," began Max.

"I'm not, though," Shaa said blandly.

"Been at it for years, the two of them," said the Great Karlini; he had appeared in the cabin doorway several volleys ago. "Usually it's just to pass the time. *This* time, though, I think Shaa's actually got a point, so don't try to change the subject, Max. I'd like to know how dangerous you think this is, too."

"This accident was nothing," Max said. "You know spellular experimentation, things are always getting loose, getting a little out of control, but it never amounts to anything. You round them up and you go back to work. Okay, every now and then you blow up the lab, but that's how things get done. That's what you call progress."

"Roni's a careful person," Karlini remarked. "She's not absentminded like me, or at least that's what people keep saying, and no one she's ever met would fault her experimental methodology."

"Of course she's good," said Max, "she *is* one of the best. That's why she's the one who's doing this work, not some hack like Umberto Iguana or even Shaa or me. If anyone can do it, Roni can."

With his own theatrically flamboyant sweep of his arm, Shaa fanned at the cloud of smoke still hanging around the cabin. "Yet suppose," he said, "a purely hypothetical case where, for whatever reason, this developmental effort reaches fruition and its products go free. I would imagine the consequences could be quite severe. Hmm?"

"Yeah," Max said, "all right, yeah. They could. I think."

"Do you mean," Tildy asked, her voice making a small nervous yelp, " 'severe' like what happened to Roosing Oolvaya?"

"No," said Shaa, "severe *compared* to what happened to Roosing Oolvaya."

"Oh," Tildy said, her voice now almost inaudible.

"Okay, so it's dangerous," said Max. "What other choice do we have? This is a great opportunity. There's no two ways about it, we've got to seize the chance."

"Of course we have a choice," said Shaa. "Status quo. Don't get apoplectic, Max. There are also other, more tactical choices. We can constrain the experimental organisms so that if they escape, they can't reproduce, or set them so they'll automatically self-destruct if they get out, or even use mutation to ensure they can't live outside of the lab dish; a matter, perhaps, of breeding them to require certain essential nutrients which only we will provide. The world is full of options."

"Good ideas," Max stated. "I'm not an idiot; I know when something makes sense. Let's do it. I'm sorry if I get a little carried away."

"Before we all get back to work," said Shaa, "I suspect this gentleman is going to want a word with someone." He indicated the leathery-skinned figure of their vessel's captain hurrying up the gangplank, his grizzled head shaking in disbelief. The captain approached the cabin, its air now largely clear of smoke, but marked still by a line of sooty vapor trailing up into the sky.

"I should have believed him," the captain said in amazement. "Meester Groot warned me about your lot, he did, and I thought it was only one of his tall stories. There'll be none of this on the river, d'you hear?"

"Captain," said Max, "why don't you and I have a word in private?"

Shaa inclined his head and the two Monts followed him up the deck, out of earshot of the now-wrangling Max and the unsettled captain. "Now," Shaa continued, turning to Jurtan, who had watched the proceedings silently, except for an occasional audible gulp of nervous swallowing, "what was it you wanted to say to me earlier?"

"Uh, ah," Jurtan said. He was disoriented; Shaa had actually remembered he'd had something to mention; he'd never expected that. How had he been going to put it?

"Pull yourself together," Shaa suggested.

"Don't be a toad," said Tildy.

Jurtan shot her a glare which she returned, in pure sibling fashion. "Ah, families," Shaa murmured under his breath. By all the signs, though, the Mont siblings had no signs of having the extreme pathology of the Shaas, fortunately for them. For one thing, neither of the Monts was out of his or her mind, and for another, their father hadn't gone out of his way to direct them against each other's throat. Their willingness to flay each other by aiming at the most sensitive spots was purely within the limits of normal variability. Jurtan left off muttering at his sister and said, "Ah, what I wanted to know before was, well, is he safe, Max I mean, I mean safe to be around? I mean, is it safe to be alone in the wilderness with this guy? Like I'm going to be?"

Shaa favored him with an appraising glance. "No," he said.

Jurtan opened his mouth, glanced at his sister, and then, with a small quick frown, apparently changed his mind about what he was going to say. "Right," he said instead. "I just wanted to make sure." He glanced over his shoulder at the spot where the captain and Max had been working things out. The captain was still there, muttering darkly to himself, but Max had disappeared. Jurtan looked around again, more wildly. Something stirred in the shadows between two lashed crates, then the something suddenly became the form of Max, leaning insouciantly against a net with his customarily sardonic grin.

"So," announced Max, "you ready to go, kid?"

How had Max snuck upon them like that? And how had he camouflaged himself so well on the spur of the moment? "What—right now?"

"You have a better time in mind?"

"Uh," said Jurtan, "I don't . . . how did you do that?"

"It's an art," Max said.

"But a teachable one," Shaa pointed out. "Have you ever heard of the Society of Masks, Jurtan?"

"Are you trying to motivate him? If he comes along," said Max, "I'll teach him stuff, but don't go promising him the whole store. We'll see how he does."

"Great," said Jurtan, in the most definite tone he could muster. "Let's do it."

4
THE FRYING PAN OR THE FIRE

Ever since I'd fallen in with Max and Shaa and the rest of them, it felt like I'd been strapped to the back of a runaway horse with my hands tied and a scarf over my eyes, facing backward; it was one change of direction after another, and the most immediate worry was just staying on and not getting stomped into pulp or flung off a cliff. As I stood there in the doorway of the tent, staring at the figure of Gashanatantra, I had the distinct impression that the horse and I had finally parted company, unequivocally and once-and-for-all. Feeling like I'd lost my orientation and my mind simultaneously was not a totally unfamiliar sensation, though, so without really planning it I found myself swinging into backup mode. I spotted another pile of pillows on a fancy rug covering the canvas floor not too far away, and before I was really aware of what I was doing I had strolled over and plopped myself atop them. The woman was still standing in the doorway, watching me with what I thought was a hint of amazement. "Come on in and make yourself comfortable, why don't you?" I told her.

"This is not what I expected," said Gash, also to the woman. "I expected you and the ring, and possibly his head or his severed hand or some other appropriate token of his demise. I did not expect the two of you, together, with all his pieces apparently still knitted into a functioning whole. I take it that you didn't get the ring, either?"

"He doesn't have it," she said, entering the tent but remaining on her feet.

"How did he convince you of that?"

"He told a plausible story, and—"

"I'm sure he did," stated Gash, "I'm sure he did. I hear that's his specialty."

"Don't take that tone with *me*, Zhardann," she said, glaring down at him with her hands on her hips. "I'm not a fool, I know quite well what he's capable of; and furthermore, I wouldn't have bothered to listen to him if the detector hadn't failed to pick up the ring on his person, too. Taunt him, yes, but listen to him, no."

"A detector," he said. "I see, a detector. How sensitive is this detector, by the way?"

"Sensitive enough."

"I see. A detector. Full of surprises today, aren't you, my dear?" Gash puffed thoughtfully on the hookah. Tight little clouds rose out of the funnel and drifted past the woman's face.

If I'd had a hookah handy, I'd have puffed thoughtfully on it, too. She'd called Gash "Zhardann," but that wasn't the first thing that had made me question whether or not he actually *was* the Gashanatantra I knew. For one thing, he wasn't acknowledging any prior meetings with me, and I hadn't read the slightest flicker of recognition on his face. He also hadn't appeared to recognize the sword Monoch in its disguise as a walking stick, yet he (Gash?) had *given* me the thing; and for that matter Monoch hadn't seemed to recognize him either. However, I had no doubt that Gash could be quite thoroughly devious enough to carry out just such an act, based on my earlier experiences with him. For another thing, then, I hadn't felt a tremor from the metabolic link Gash had left me, the one that plugged my life force into his own. I wasn't sure I *would* feel anything from the link if I came face-to-face with Gash again, but nevertheless I thought it was an observation worth making.

That wasn't all. The woman didn't recognize him as Gash; she apparently thought *I* was Gash. Her husband, Gash. If Zhardann *was* Gash, he was running a more convoluted game than I wanted to think about. That would raise a cart-load of questions. Actually, there was a good barrel-load of questions on the table in any case.

The most interesting question at the moment was still

the identity of this guy Zhardann. Was he the same person (or god) I'd dealt with before, and was that god (or person) actually Gashanatantra? In any case, Zhardann didn't seem to be talking. That didn't mean that he might not pull me aside sometime in the future in order to drop a few words of clarification in my ear, but I figured there was no reason to spend good energy waiting up for it. Was Zhardann not talking because he was the same one I'd met before but was currently up to some plot, or because he wasn't the same person and had never seen me before? If he wasn't the same person, then were the two of them related, was one a clone of the other, or was one of them wearing the other's shape for some reason?

While I was asking for small favors of elucidation, I was also hoping he'd go ahead and address the woman by name, so I could at least find out what I should be calling her. It might look odd if I was put in a situation where I had to introduce her to someone else and I didn't know what her name was, considering that she thought I was her husband.

"If he doesn't have the ring with him," Gash (or Zhardann) said after a moment, "and he claims not to be in a position to lay hands on it, just where does he say it is, and how does he say he lost—"

"I'm more than willing to sit here," I interrupted, "lounging on your pillows, but rather than hear all of this at second hand you just might want to hear it straight from me, since I do happen to *be* here, and all. Especially since we're going to be partners."

His eyebrows went up. He looked back at the woman. "How much more of importance haven't you gotten around to telling me yet?"

Glaring at both of us simultaneously, which was a neat trick since Zhardann (or Gash) and I weren't in the same line of sight, the woman stalked over to him, sat down next to him on a purple pillow with long gold tassels, and started talking to him in a low voice while keeping her back to me. I figured they'd get back to me soon enough, and I was happy not to have to actually hold up my end of a conversation right at the moment. I wasn't sure what had made me speak up when I did. There was some sense to it; if I was going to have them treat me as a partner I'd have to keep being assertive and obnoxiously forceful enough for them to continue to believe I really *was* one of them. On the other hand, I'd made the resolution to keep my mouth shut and key off what they said as much as I could until the ground rules became a little clearer. On the *other* hand, if I had some buried instinct that thought it knew what was going on better than the conscious me did, and it wanted to jump in and help, I could probably do worse than go along with it. On yet another hand, if I started listening to instincts like that I'd have to trust them more than they'd given me reason to in the past. In the past, there were times when I'd followed my instincts to the letter, and that had turned out to be just about the worst thing I could do.

The woman and Zhardann both looked up at me simultaneously, then bent their heads back together. What could they do to me, anyway? Probably plenty. My close encounter with the woman's wormball was without a doubt only an introductory lesson in what they had up their sleeves; they could proceed to torture and dismember me, I supposed, winding up with a nice slow eradication, and that would be all. Except if it wasn't—Max had implied on a couple of occasions that he thought that gods had their ways of sidetracking death. Or Death, to get personal about it. I decided to keep up the fight as long as I could. Something was bound to bounce my way eventually, and hopefully it wouldn't be the first round boulder in a large avalanche.

Zhardann looked up at me again, but this time he spoke. "Why would you give up, *you,* of all people, and after you had the ring in your *hands,* too?"

"There's giving up," I remarked, "and then there's giving up. I thought it might be interesting to stand back and watch somebody else run the fireworks for a change. Items like that ring do have a tendency to come back around, anyway, and they stir up a lot of other interesting stuff while they're doing it. After all, here you are."

They exchanged glances; apparently I'd scored a point. "I see," Zhardann said. "Then where do you think Pasook might be currently?"

"Heck, I don't know," I said. "As far as he's concerned, I've given the whole thing up, so he might not even be bothering to take precautions. We could just start with the usual places. I'll leave it up to you; after all, I was just coming along for the ride."

"I don't trust him," Zhardann told the woman. "It was a bad decision to bring him here."

"Who said *I* trusted him?" she said, being a bit huffy about it. "I brought him because he might be use—"

"For what it's worth," I put in, "I don't trust you either. Now why don't we set all that to the side and go ahead with what we're going to do?"

"You're in no position to be suggesting anything," Zhardann said. "Remember that. Something still disturbs me, something central. Why did you start all this and then drop it in the middle?"

"Who said I did?"

That was ambiguous enough to make them pause again. It had to be ambiguous, since I still didn't really know what I was talking about. My luck seemed to be holding so far, anyway. When you keep making cryptic remarks all the time, people can either think you're being deep but difficult, or a moron. At least I'd learned that they thought whoever I'd been teamed up with on the ring job was named Pasook. Now Zhardann squinted at me, as though he thought a change in refraction would improve his insight. "Are you Abdicationist?"

What the heck was *that?* I had to give some response, though, unless I'd rather court a quick lesson in having my own fat deep fried. "I haven't entirely made up my mind," I said, hoping a spot firmly on the fence rail wouldn't antagonize them too much one way or the other. "And has your own position developed at all?"

"My position is known. The divine right of gods is exact and immutable." Zhardann turned to the woman. "Do *you* know where he stands?"

Now it was *her* turn to study me again. "I think you may be on to something, Zhardann. Pod Dall did hold a checking role between the factions, and it wasn't until he got locked in the ring that things really started to break loose. That could certainly give a political angle to his decision to go after Dall in the first place. Putting Pod

Dall in play and out of action doesn't say anything about which side my husband may be on, though, since Dall did have a position in the middle."

"Not necessarily true," Zhardann said musingly. "The Abdicationists generally benefit by stirring things up, the Conservationists by maintaining the status quo. Putting Pod Dall 'in play,' as you call it, would have the impact of favoring Abdicationism."

"Only at the outset," she said, "and he'd never figure the game to be over after the first round."

"Don't forget the matter of Pod Dall's own raw power," I said brightly. "Grabbing his power would be nothing to sneeze at." Both of them swiveled their heads to glare at me. I flashed them a cheerful smile. "Don't mind me," I told them, "I'm just trying to be helpful."

"I haven't changed my mind," Zhardann said, still eyeing me but talking to her. "We'd be a lot better off with him dead, although I'd settle for melding him into a ring of his own and putting him in a jar somewhere, or better yet burying him off in the middle of a desert. Nevertheless, I'm going to yield to your point. For the moment, I think we need to keep him around."

"You'd better watch out," I said. "I have a tendency to grow on people. 'Need' may turn to 'want,' and then where would you be, all your cherished notions of who's who and what's what gone in a blaze of fraternal affection."

The woman put out an arm to hold Zhardann back. "I know," she said, "he's got a mouth and he opens it far too often, but don't forget he has his own power. He's not all talk."

"His power is a pitiful—"

"He stopped *me,*" she said, "*and* the Harmala."

At the mention of the Harmala, which I assumed must be the official name of the wormball, Zhardann's face acquired a troubled look. It sounded like warding off the Harmala was indeed a feat worth writing home about. I wished I could figure out how I'd done it, and whether it had even been my doing at all.

"You didn't ask how I compelled him to come here, either," the woman went on. "Well, I didn't. I got him *interested,* worse luck, and he decided to come on his own."

It was reassuring that she was taking that view of what had happened; the situation hadn't seemed quite that clear to me. This was no time to breathe a sigh of relief, though. "If you want to try to turn me into mulch," I told Zhardann, "go ahead and take your shot. I'd just as soon get this past us so we can settle down and cooperate like partners are supposed to, and anyway I can use the practice. If not, then let's get down to business."

Zhardann looked at the woman. She shrugged, "It's up to you if you want to challenge him," she said. "I'd advise against it. I've already had a taste of what he can do, and I'd say he's been working out seriously; he's in good form. You'd probably win, but there's no point in wasting time and energy over it just to put him in his place. I know him, remember, and so I can tell you nobody's *ever* put him in his place. You'd have to kill him to do that, and I'd have to say that's not seriously in the cards. Even for you." She flashed another one of her predatory smiles in my direction. "Catch him when his guard is down or his back is turned, though, and the situation could be entirely different."

I smiled, too. "That kind of situation can cut two ways," I said, "and *anyone* who has a back can sometimes have it turned. Heh-heh."

Her smile had turned a bit brittle, but she was still gamely holding on to it. "Very well, Jill," Zhardann said. "I will withhold the force of my righteous indignation for the present. One is supposed to listen to one's partners' advice, after all."

"That's sometimes a good enough reason to have partners in the first place," I added. "Isn't it, Jill-tang?"

Again it had happened—I hadn't known I was going to say that until I'd already gone and done it. The woman—Jill? Jill-tang?—looked like she was ready to keep the banter going, but Zhardann got there first. "Enough of this," he said. "Let us get down to planning our next move. Hopefully we'll do better than we did with our last one."

"How can you fail?" I said. Neither one of them had jumped, and they hadn't moved to mash me either. Jill-tang must really be her name; probably the longer, formal form. But, like I said earlier, I thought I'd never laid eyes on her before. So how did *I* know what her name was supposed to be? I hoped the reason was the metabolic link to Gash. If it wasn't, somebody was going to have a lot of answering to do, and I figured that somebody was going to have to be me.

Zhardann gave me another one of his dirty looks; wasn't he going to get tired of that at some point? "Where are we, Roosing Oolvaya?" he inquired. "Oolsmouth is somewhere around here, isn't it?"

"Straight down the River Oolvaan," I said.

Zhardann looked at Jill, who looked blankly back, at an apparent loss, for once. "Oolsmouth is where the headquarters of the Oolvaan Mutual Bank is located," he said thoughtfully.

"I had forgotten that," I said, trying to make my tone as insincere as possible, so they'd be left wondering if I really had forgotten it or really hadn't, but wanted them to bring it up on their own. "Oolvaan Mutual doesn't have too many offices, either, but isn't Oolsmouth the closest one in any case?"

"Why did you decide to settle in Roosing Oolvaya?" Zhardann asked me.

"I like the climate," I said. "It's out of the way, but the news gets here sooner or later. You can go fishing off the wharves. Also, I look forward to the occasional flood."

"Are you in Roosing Oolvaya *because* it's close to Oolsmouth?"

"You're not going to get anything out of him by asking him a straight question, you know that," Jill said to Zhardann.

Zhardann muttered something deep in his throat. Aloud, he snapped at her, "Stop heading me off when I'm trying to pursue a line of thought. Whose side are you on here, anyway?"

"Ours," said Jill. "As you know perfectly well. I'm just trying to show you ways to save time with him in the long run."

"Stop it, then. If your hints are worthwhile, I'll find them out for myself. And who implied there was going to *be* a long run where's he's concerned? Make sure your loyalties stay clear. Do you understand me?"

"As long as you understand *me,*" she said. "Is *that* clear?"

"Yes," said Zhardann, "very well, yes. Oolsmouth, then. Definitely Oolsmouth." He aimed a finger at me. "Only if I find out you're planning to set me up for some plot of your own, I'll—

"Yes, right," I said. "Okay. I get the message, too. Oolsmouth it is, then. You want to drink a toast or something or just hit the road? And do you want to discuss what we're going to do with the ring when we find it now, or hold that until later, too? Remember, I'm the one who knows how to control it."

I knew nothing of the sort, of course, or at least I didn't think I did, but they'd presume I understood everything about the ring whenever they got around to thinking about it. I didn't think their contemplation had taken them quite that far along the thought path just yet, though, so I figured I might as well toss it out on the table when it might still have some shock value. "I thought you'd decided you weren't interested in the ring any more," Jill commented.

"That was before you showed up," I said. "Now you've got me interested in a lot of things."

"Very well, then," said Zhardann, "we'll share the ring."

"Right," I drawled. "That was the same kind of arrangement that went sour on me last time. How dumb do you think I am, anyway?"

"We could set up a rotating escrow situation, couldn't we?" said Jill. "Zhardann, shouldn't your organization be able to handle something like that?"

"Perhaps," Zhardann said. "Perhaps. If we—"

"We could just auction the thing off," I tossed out. "For certain parties out there, having Pod Dall in their own pocket might be worth more to them than it is to us, hmm?"

Jill and Zhardann looked at each briefly, again conferring without words. I was going through this exercise not because it would actually give me a better chance of getting my share of the ring, but because they'd think something was fishy if I didn't. Whatever agreement we reached now wouldn't be worth a plugged ool, I knew. If they thought we'd dealt with the issue and I'd accepted the resolution, though, they might stop looking over their shoulders waiting for me to pull my double cross. All bets were off once we had the ring, I think we'd all agree if we were being honest, but at least we might get *that* far with reasonable cooperation. What I knew that they didn't, of course, was that the whole thing was a wild-goose chase from the start, since I'd made up the entire story that was sending us charging off to Oolsmouth on the trail of this Pasook person.

"An auction might not be all that bad an idea at that," said Jill. "I say we should tentatively plan on that for now, and revisit the question again once we're on the way. Agreed?"

"Yes," I said, "fine."

It was finally time to go. I was fully aware that our departure was another milestone that would probably reveal my total ignorance of everything the well-turned-out god should take as second nature. I'd seemed to be doing okay so far, though, and perhaps I was getting a little carried away with my luck and the feeling I was on a roll. In any case, I was sort of looking forward to finding out what would happen when we were all supposed to depart however it is gods are supposed to depart. It would be a good idea to keep trying to test the limits of the data and experience feed I was apparently getting through the metabolic link so I was waiting to see just what it was going to spring on me this time, when it thought my back was against the wall. I was particularly surprised, then, and a little deflated at the anticlimax to boot, when Zhardann whistled up a few servants, left them to pack up, and ushered Jill and me toward the tent's door-flap.

I was taken aback that we didn't fly, or zap or something fancy like that, but I guess we weren't in that much of a hurry, really, and the big flashy stuff soaks up so much energy that it's not worth using unless you have to, even if you're a god. All of a sudden I got a quick wave of the shakes, no doubt from the flood of good sense that was abruptly returning, and I decided it was just as well for another reason. If Zhardann had said, "Come on, let's zap," or words to that effect, what if the metabolic link or whatever *didn't* kick in? What if Zhardann *was* Gashanatantra, after all, and it was just part of his cruel game to cut me off cold from my knowledge of what to do next? The thought of the two of them waiting for me to do whatever it was they were doing, which of course I wouldn't have the slightest idea of how to accomplish, was not too appealing. It could have the positive result of having them disappear while I remained standing around behind, free to sneak back out the door and off into the crowd. On the other hand, the infinite variety of negative results seemed unfortunately much more probable, and I had to admit I didn't quite feel like experiencing any of them at first hand right then and there.

At the moment, though, as I mentioned, all of these hypothetical cases remained just that, hypothetical, as we strolled out into the sun and let the servants help the tent fold itself up behind us. While we'd been inside bickering, a group of horses had been rounded up outside. Zhardann swung up onto one of them, obviously a fine specimen even though I've never paid much attention to horses, and Jill boarded another even snazzier-looking chestnut and white model. "I'm certain you didn't think to bring your own transportation?" Zhardann said to me in his same sour voice.

"One of these will do just fine, thank you," I told him.

He muttered something else under his breath, probably "This is going to be a long trip" or its unprintable equivalent. I was just as pleased not to have heard his remark; I didn't know how much abuse my mild temperament was going to be able to stand. As far as I was concerned, however long the trip was going to be for them was nothing compared to what it was going to be for me. Aside from the recurring goal of just staying alive, though, I thought I also stood to gain a lot more from this than they did. After all, they knew their own identities, or at least I presumed they did. If I stayed sharp, sharp and lucky that is, and kept my ears open, I thought I might be able to go a significant distance on the way to figuring out mine.

5
ICE CUBES

The air above the surface of the River Oolvaan was frankly more humid than Zalzyn Shaa liked. He was standing on the deck of Haalsen Groot's river-ship, the *Not Unreasonable Profit,* arms crossed and leaning on the starboard gunwale, watching stands of cottonwoods pass by on the west bank of the river. They had been out on the river now for three days, having left Max and Jurtan Mont to their overland route westward, and without any of them having uncovered the slightest clue to the detective's disappearance. The departure had been a bit tiring with its flurry of activity, but since then it had been an uneventful three days. *So far,* Shaa reminded himself.

On the rises behind the bank were small areas of unpruned forest interspersed with cultivated fields. The sun was out, declining toward afternoon, and the behavior of the river was placid; all in all, it was a perfectly respectable day. Nevertheless, Shaa was not pleased. He was, in fact, in a grouchy mood, and resented the day for not giving him a convenient target to vent his spleen against.

"Excuse me?" said a voice from behind him. It was Tildamire. "I brought you some iced tea."

Shaa lowered his gaze to the greenish-brown water lapping the shore. "And what exactly were the source ingredients for this concoction?" he inquired.

"The usual—tea, I suppose, and water, and that freezer-spell thingy," Tildy said.

"Water?" Shaa said.

He was ostentatiously watching something between the

boat and the shore—oh, she got it. "Not from the river, at least I don't think so, and anyway it's been through Max's still." She moved around to stand beside him and leaned her own elbow on the gunwale, eyeing him from what might have been a safe distance. "Here." She planted a mug between them on the gunwale; protruding from its wide mouth were a sprig of mint and another leaf from Shaa's stash of his self-prescribed herbal glycoside.

"Thank you," said Shaa, making an effort to hold himself in check. She was only trying to be pleasant, after all, and there was a substantial margin between grouchy and barbaric. "I don't think I'll have any right at the moment, though."

"Suit yourself," Tildy told him. She looked out across the water herself, spotting two muskrats cavorting near the shore. "It's pretty nice out here."

"I suppose," Shaa said morosely.

"What's the matter?"

"I dislike feeling useless."

"Why should you feel that way?" said Tildy. "You redesigned Roni's experiment, didn't you, to make it harder for her animalcules to escape? And aren't you doing your own experiment with nutrients? How's that going?"

Shaa looked at her, canting his head as he brought it around so that the gaze emerged sidelong from beneath a sarcastically inclined eyebrow. "Patience is required," he responded, "as in most experimentation. As opposed to tinkering, or outright invention. Nevertheless, my investigation into obligatory nutrients is clearly a sideshow to the main event. Watching someone else do the interesting work you'd just as soon do yourself is not my idea of a spectator sport with growth potential."

"But what you've done yourself is—"

"There's no need to coddle me," Shaa said. "If I want to be patronized, I'll let you know."

Tildy frowned. "I'm just telling you what I think. Why should you be moping around? Because your curse keeps you from doing hands-on spell stuff? Because there's not more trouble to get into on the boat? Why not just think of this as a vacation, then? I mean, this *is* a trip, isn't it? A cruise down the river—people pay good money for this sort of thing."

Shaa turned his gaze back toward the water. For some reason that was not immediately apparent, an ice flow about the size of a bathtub had appeared off the bow; the boat was traveling downstream with the current but slightly faster than it, due to the effect of the sail amidships, and so the ice flow was drifting and revolving leisurely toward the stern. Surprisingly for the presence of ice, though, the water temperature was, if not downright tepid, at least well above freezing, and the nearest snow or glacier was hundreds of miles upstream and a few months removed in time. It wasn't even winter. "There is this unfortunate element of coercion involved," Shaa said abstractedly, most of his attention now concentrated on the matter of the miniature iceberg. "*Having* to take a vacation takes most of the fun out of it. A vacation is usually an internal reward for a job well done, or at least done; or even more enjoyably one takes a vacation because one just up and feels like it. Vacation under duress, enforced idleness, is a thoroughly tedious prospect."

"What about burnout, though? You've been a professional magic person, right? What do you do when you need a major recharge?"

"Sink gracefully into a light coma for a week or two," Shaa said. Tildy thought his tone sounded a bit arch. Of course, this *was* Shaa, and his tone usually sounded a bit something-or-another.

"I'm sure there are any number of things you could catch up on, reading, say? I mean, here we are on a boat on a river—you could even just sit out on deck and work on your tan."

"Accelerated dermatological aging," grumbled Shaa. "Skin cancer." Yet here he was, unquestionably sitting (or lounging) on the deck, and the sun was indeed high overhead. He pulled the brim of his hat lower over his eyebrows. "You don't have to sit around out here with me, you know," he said pointedly. "I realize my company at the moment leaves something to be desired. If asked, I'll certify that your nursemaid obligation was thoroughly and responsibly discharged."

"You don't have to be a crab when someone's just trying to be pleasant," Tildy mumbled.

Shaa wished he had a pincer on his person, or an appropriately exoskeletal piece of apparatus, so that he could produce it from beneath his shirt for ironic effect. He was not, however, prepared for every conceivable eventuality. He did *try* to be, though, and realizing that an unusual opportunity was slipping by made him even testier. "You don't have to provide me with an audience," he said, supplementing the remark by waving his hand at her and clacking his fingers and thumb together in pincer-pantomime, while making a synchronized clicking sound with his teeth. It was at best a poor alternative to the display of an actual visual aid, but then since Shaa was feeling like a poor excuse for a person of action he supposed it was reasonably fitting. The momentary look of incomprehension of Tildy's face was replaced by one of mild horror mixed with reproof. She said, "Ah, right," edged back away from the rail, and then turned and fled into the laboratory cabin.

Shaa watched as the ice floe slipped beyond the stern. He was not necessarily a person of action at most times in any case, but he did go through phases. The one he was in at the moment was certainly frustrating. Shaa wanted nothing better than to be up and around, pursuing leads, stirring things up, and generally getting into trouble, but his health had betrayed him. More to the point, his curse had betrayed his heart, which had in turn passed the betrayal on to the rest of his system. This time, no sooner had he gotten involved in enough shenanigans to get his senses keyed up than he was undercut by his body. *Now look at me,* he thought, *reduced to banter with an underage keeper on a placid river in the middle of civilized territory.* It was enough to make a grown man . . . whine.

He was the first to admit that his funk had nothing to do with good sense. He wasn't ready to out-and-out *die,* after all. If he was, he could just jump ship and strike out alone looking for someone else's business to get mixed up in. He wasn't willing to be quietly content with his present fate, either, though, so he had decided to adhere to the middle ground of being tolerably miserable for anyone else to be around until he got too bored with that and shifted to being impossibly noble for awhile, or until something worth getting excited about showed up.

Not that there was much excitement to look for from the River Oolvaan. Shaa ticked off the possibilities in his mind. The river did flood, true, but unfortunately it was now the wrong season, although there might be hope for a lightning storm or two before they reached Oolsmouth. There was undoubtedly a war on somewhere, the world being what it was, but these days the Oolvaan basin was devoted to peaceful trade, and he'd never been fond of random carnage anyway. As far as Shaa knew, the river pirates had all retired. Most of the shoreline they were passing was cultivated or lightly wooded; no interesting creatures would be found within a hundred miles, and the local nonhumans were as domesticated as the people. Well, perhaps his brother would show up.

Another chunk of ice appeared, caught up momentarily in the bow wake. Shaa's brow furrowed. He left the rail and walked aft, tracing his way amidst the tangle of lashed-down crates and awkwardly-shaped trade goods, casting an eye as he did over the river on the port side. No additional ice fragments were—no, wait, there *was* one, after all, draped with a clump of river weed. Reaching the stern cabin, Shaa leaned through the door. "Great One?" he said. "A moment of your time."

"What is it?" Karlini called back.

"Manifestations. Things are afloat."

Karlini emerged, blinking his eyes, then squinted as he followed the line of Shaa's pointing finger. "Ice?" Karlini said. "That's odd."

"Indeed. Shall we check the ice maker?"

"A resonance effect, you think? Well, maybe. Might as well start there as anywhere, I guess." The two of them went forward. The few sailors scurrying about on seamanlike tasks paid them no heed; they'd been advised before the ship left Oolsmouth that they'd be safer all around to let Karlini and his crew putter as they chose, and besides they were getting hazard pay for the trip.

"The most obvious way of observing," Shaa said, proceeding down the short flight of ladder steps into the gloomy companionway beneath the forward deck, rather than up the adjoining stairs onto the forward deck itself, "will be to stand at the bow, trying to watch the appearance of the ice; not how the ice *looks,* mind you, but where it seems to be coming from."

"Resonance can be tricky," Karlini reminded him. "You get a lot of these effects at a distance, where the additive wave crests are strongest. If the ice maker *is* buggy, it could easily be generating freezing spots in the river fifty feet away, so just trying to see where the ice is coming from might not give us that much new information."

"Indeed," said Shaa. "It's true; I can't say I've ever entirely trusted the freezer." On his right was the small galley. First taking a glance through the door to verify that no one was heading outward in his direction bearing a sizzling cauldron or a snack of pickles, Shaa eased himself through the narrow space between a heap of pots and the sacks of flour, secure against mold in their freshness-spelled wrappings.

The ice machine was perched on a cask of salt cod racked against the timbers of the hull, and was lashed for good measure to the wood. A pipe led upward through the ceiling to the water tank on the deck. Just beneath the ceiling, suspended from the joists by hooks, the pipe entered Max's purification filter. Shaa turned the stop valve on the pipe, let the water in the filter gurgle downward, opened the catch on the filter box, and carefully withdrew the differentiation sieve, a rectangular chunk of sponge mounted in a wooden edge-frame. The faint nebulous glow in the spell-guide tube leading from the filter box down to the ice maker dimmed and went out. Shaa passed the sieve to Karlini, and they both peered at it.

"Now that I take a good look," Karlini commented, "this filter is pretty low-powered, isn't it? The biggest resonant effect you'd expect out of something with this small a level of juice would be an icicle on an adjacent wall.''

''Under most circumstances I'd surely agree with you,'' said Shaa, poking at the spongy matrix with a finger; the temperature at its surface dropped abruptly to a skin-numbing chill. ''Remember who designed it, though.''

''I haven't forgotten, but you also have to keep in mind that it's not one of Max's mechanomagical hybrids,'' Karlini pointed out. ''No moving parts anywhere, just diffusion and transfer processes.''

''What do you think he might have woven into the matrix? And does it use standard first-order techniques or more of those second-quantum-level effects?''

Karlini passed a palm over the sieve's surface. ''Feels first-level to me. Max is trying to keep the second-level stuff under wraps, anyway. I don't think he'd risk blowing his big new breakthrough over something as mundane as an ice machine.''

''Trust me,'' Shaa said. ''When Max gets to tinkering on a project, he may end up using any technique he can lay his hands on. He's also assiduously solicitous about his creature comforts.''

''But we've got the ice maker; he doesn't,'' Karlini reminded him.

''He thought he was doing us a favor.''

''He *was* doing us a favor. How else do you think we'd be getting ice? We don't have space for an ice locker with all Groot's stuff on board. Heck, I like having ice.''

''So do I,'' Shaa admitted. Something thudded against the outside of the hull, sending a shiver through the deck, and then rasped along the side of the ship just at their position and halfway up the wall, a bit below where the waterline probably was. The grating lasted a few seconds, then abruptly ended. Shaa looked at the disassembled ice maker, then at Karlini. ''You know,'' he said, ''I think this device is working just fine. What do you say we shift the focus of our investigation? It sounded like that one was larger than the ones I saw before, and it was obviously closer as well.''

Before Shaa finished, Karlini had already shoved the pieces of the ice maker back together and was going through the door. Shaa followed him down the companionway and up the stairs to the foredeck. The captain was already there, accompanied by Haddo and Wroclaw, who had apparently been polishing the brasswork, judging by the pile of cloths at his feet, the vile-looking bucket of oily polish, and the half-shiny stanchion at his side. They were all gazing off the bow at the ice chunks. There were definitely more of them, and they were also without question getting larger—in fact, Shaa noted, it was not nearly as much of an exaggeration now to think of them as small icebergs. Haddo turned as they approached, an accusing expression apparent in the inclination of his hood. "Not liking am," Haddo said, "this."

"Captain Luff," Shaa said, "I take it this is not a typical phenomenon for this section of the river?"

"Never seen anything like it," admitted the captain. "Kind of nice to look at, though, wouldn't you say? Except for the fact we're on a ship, don't you know, and the blamed things look like they're aiming for us."

"Do you intend to engage in evasive action?"

"I've been considering just that very point, Mr. Shaa," the captain said, stroking his short silvery beard. "Perhaps your own opinion, or Mr. Karlini's, there, would be helpful to the situation. I've sailed the seas and rivers, as boy and man, don't you know, and the only times I've seen the like of this business there's always been some deviltry afoot. You two gentlemen, you'll excuse me for mentioning, seem to be the ranking authorities on deviltry in these parts."

"We thought it might be the ice maker," Karlini said, "but it wasn't, or at least we don't think it was. We don't know what it is, but I suspect it's not just going to go away, and by the looks of things the ice chunks *are* getting bigger. I think we can all admit that. I agree with Shaa; I'd recommend getting ready to evade them. They're solid, sure enough, not some illusion."

"Frankly, Captain," Shaa added, "I'd advise sailing your ship as you choose and not bothering to ask us for advice on it, or anyway not in the middle of a piloting emergency."

"As indeed I have been doing," said the captain. What

remained unspoken but understood was the captain's desire to avoid stepping on any toes that might lash out and bite him, Shaa thought, wincing a little as he mangled his own metaphor out of all semblance of civilized discourse. Captain Luff seemed to have reason to know that practicing magicians tend to be a dangerously prickly and unstable lot, although what he thought of Karlini in particular, and even Shaa, with their more than typically free-wheeling attitude toward matters of serious import, remained untested. "Just you gentlemen pipe on up when you have something to contribute," the captain continued.

It was apparent that the captain was as good as his word when two crewmen appeared from the stern, balancing long docking gaffs, and took up positions on either side of the bow. With a shouted "One point to port," a lookout on the mast made his presence known as well. The helmsman on the poop deck called an "Aye!" in response and the ship angled slightly to port, putting the latest ice floe on their starboard bow. The starboard gaffman caught it with his pole and leaned hard, the muscles in his back and arms standing out beneath his brief shirt, and the ice floe spun slowly around its center of mass and bore off. The captain, watching closely, said in a low voice to Shaa, "Those hunks get much larger and these gaffs won't make any difference at all; they'll just go snap."

The truth of the captain's words was evident. The icebergs were forming beneath the surface of the water and then bobbing to the top with a splash and a heave; this allowed an estimation of the mass of each new chunk to be made. Larger they were clearly continuing to become. With the ship's sail deployed to take advantage of the breeze at their back, and the force of the river's own flow added, their group had been making excellent time. "I know you folks want to make this a quick trip," the captain announced, "and it's a point of pride of my own to run the fastest transit on this part of the Oolvaan, but I don't mind telling you I'd be happier if we heaved to for a bit. With us heading downstream faster than the current, you see, the current is what's carrying the ice drifting past us.''

Slowing down, in land-side parlance, or even stopping would thus keep the ice ahead of them. *Should* keep the ice ahead of them. ''If some*one* is behind this ice visitation,'' Shaa commented, ''slowing us down may be what they had in mind. Still, captain, you *are* the captain, and happy we are to have you. Proceed as you choose.''

With an alacrity that underlined the captain's relief, he ordered the sail taken in. ''Now,'' Shaa murmured, ''we may see what is really going on.''

''You think—'' said Karlini.

''Don't you?'' said Shaa.

Haddo had again turned and was scrutinizing them both. ''Any idea have you each,'' he said, ''what about is talking the other one?''

''You are certainly one to comment,'' Shaa told him. ''Yet, somehow, communication still seems to take place. Hmm?''

Haddo, apparently having no appropriate response to that, swung back around in a huff. He renewed his scrutiny of the water ahead. ''What see I, see you?''

''Our phenomenon does appear to be evolving,'' Shaa agreed. The chunks of ice had been rising to the surface two ship's-lengths or so in front of them from a spot that continued to move ahead of them, keeping roughly the same separation between it and the bow. As the ship had begun to slow, though, the place where the ice was appearing had starting drawing inescapably closer. Their speed was now perhaps two-thirds what it had been. The distance to the ice generation zone had shrunk by the same proportion, and was continuing to shrink at the same rate. ''Captain, I trust you have been observing the same behavior as have I?''

''Aye,'' the captain said, squinting ahead in concentration.

Shaa glanced at Karlini. He was mumbling something beneath his breath and waving his hands around in tight patterns, the tips of his fingers glinting with a metallic sheen in the sunlight; perhaps it would be best not to bother him. ''I believe it is a mathematically and geometrically sound proposition,'' Shaa said to no one in particular, ''considering the rates and angles involved, that when this ship reaches stationary rest and lies-to at anchor, these ice fragments will be trying to rise to the surface from a spot beneath the keel, and approximately at the midpoint of the ship.''

''Oh, dear me,'' said Wroclaw, who had been watching the proceedings with silent alarm.

''Indeed, yes,'' Shaa confirmed. ''Not being a master mariner myself and having a fully qualified one close at hand, I hesitate to hazard an exact prediction of the outcome of such a situation, but I venture that it could represent significant morbidity, if not mortality, for this vessel.''

''Raise sail!'' the captain ordered. A brief chorus of ''Raise sail!'' echoed down the deck, followed by a few shouts of ''Raise sail, aye!'' and with an almost equally brief flurry of activity from the crew the single square-rigged mainsail was once more hoisted. The ship immediately leapt ahead again, its bow wake increasing. The place of appearance of the ice hove to in the same spot relative to the bow, stopping its inexorable advance on the ship. It did not, however, retreat back to its previous location as the ship got back up to its previous speed.

The behavior of the ice generation zone certainly cast doubt on Shaa's previous speculation that its goal might be to have them stop in place. ''Perhaps someone with an interesting sense of humor is toying with us,'' Shaa said. Karlini now had his hands on his hips, and appeared to be examining something in the air that only he could see. ''Do you have any pertinent insights to share, Great One?''

''No one seems to be running it,'' Karlini said, raising a finger to tweak a slightly curdled section of the air in front of his face. ''I've been running some tests, trying to figure out what mechanism's operating here, and exactly how whatever-it-is is keyed to the ship. Like I said, there doesn't seem to be anybody out there, at least at the moment.''

''Not unusual,'' Shaa remarked.

"Right, of course; a preprogrammed trap or other physical-effect spell doesn't necessarily need an active operator after it's been placed."

"You think this ice-business is new, not an old spell-mine left floating in the Oolvaan from some war, or something of that sort?"

"What," said Karlini, *"you're* suggesting to *me* is that all we've done is blunder into somebody's else's old business? *You're* the one who sees plots under the bed."

"That's Max, not me," Shaa said. "I am content to take the world at its word. Just let us not forget the value of an occasional reality check. Perhaps a pirate engagement took place here recently, perhaps some river creature has picked up a new skill, perhaps an arctic nereid was on the way south and we've crossed her trail. Perhaps it's one of those spontaneous manifestations one occasionally hears about, as something that someone somebody once knew had happen to their uncle."

"Pirates?" said Wroclaw, his minty-colored skin going a shade further toward wintergreen. "Creatures?"

"No," Shaa said, after a brief moment of contemplation, "probably not pirates."

" 'Tain't been pirates on the lower Oolvaan since I was a cabin boy," commented the captain. "Starboard two points, there, now!"

The ice generation zone might have remained at the same distance off their bow, but the size of the icebergs had not stopped growing. The latest one was fully the size of a small boat itself, and not just a rowboat, either. If no unexpected eddies appeared in the current, and if their maneuver to starboard was executed smartly, it would miss them. . . . And there it went, churning past off the port quarter, close enough though to feel the frosty wave of condensation off its supercooled surface. They all turned again toward the front; the hunks of ice had been appearing at fairly regular intervals, about a minute apart, Shaa estimated. The next one would be due right about now.

Or now.

Now?

Shaa glanced at Karlini. He didn't like the new look

on Karlini's face—a furrowed forehead and pursed lips. "Great One, what gives?"

"The traces I was picking up just quit."

"Do you think the spell burned out? Is it exhausted?"

"Maybe," Karlini said dubiously. "I don't know. I'm kind of worried it might have had some significant last gasp planned on its way out."

"There," announced the captain, pointing dead ahead.

"What?" said Karlini. "Oh!" A hundred feet ahead of them, a dimple had appeared in the surface of the water, as though a smooth transparent ball a double-arm's span in diameter had been pressed into it. A river swell spilled into the hole, swept around its concave side. Rather than passing out of the hole and sweeping on across the river, though, the mound of water that had sloshed in tracked around the inside surface of the pit and then kept rotating, like the blade of a slowly spinning drill bit. With a gurgle and a swoosh that were clearly audible to the watchers in the ship, the edges of the hole spread out and the water on the walls inside began to revolve in earnest as though a plug was being pulled out of a drain hole in the bottom of the riverbed.

"Have you ever—" said Shaa.

"No," stated the captain. "All hands on deck! Prepare for—what?" This last word was directed at Shaa, with a raised eyebrow and a lowered voice.

Shaa shrugged. "The unknown."

"Aye," said the captain. Then, shouting again, "Prepare for the unknown!"

People spilled onto the deck. Shaa was only peripherally aware of them. Ahead, the open whirlpool cone had abruptly started to fill from the bottom, to fill explosively, to fill and *overflow.* A mound of water, no, a *hill,* built above what had just been a hole, a surging mass of green and brown river water, green and brown except for the streaks of white inside it. Streaks? No, not streaks, but part of a single rushing shape, and the water was light green, not dark, and not just a mound but a frothing, tumbling—

The top of the water erupted. Spray flew to all sides, showering the boat a hundred feet away. Out of the mass of hurtled water burst the largest iceberg yet, not merely larger but *large* in any human-sized sense of the word, in fact fully twice as wide as the beam of the *Not Unreasonable Profit* itself. Directly toward which, of course, as it fell back onto the water, sending loose another titanic sheet of spray, the iceberg began to drift.

"Hard a-port!" yelled the captain. There was marginally more iceberg on their starboard side than there was to port, but it was still clearly a doomed gesture. There was obviously no chance of getting out of the way.

"Somehow," said Shaa thoughtfully, "I think I expected this." He braced himself for the impact, and the inevitable dive into the water. Next to him, though, there was an electric whine. Shaa started to turn his head toward Karlini.

Something clear and shiny rippled past the corner of his eye, distorting the scene behind it like an arm-thick fountain of pure water or a twisting crystal bar; it darted toward the iceberg, leaving a twinkling trail of distortion in its wake. The thing hit the iceberg a bit left of center and immediately slid like oil out across its surface. The note of the whine deepened; crunching, cracking, and grinding appeared on top of it; and the entire iceberg began to fibrillate. Fissures appeared. A cloud of snow lifted from its surface, and then the entire iceberg disappeared beneath the sudden compact blizzard with a powerful *crack.* Shaa dove for the deck and covered his head with his arms. Hail pelted down. The ship rocked, heaved, lurched, and the heavier fragments began to thud down around them on the deck. Shaa felt a smash to his shoulder and a near-miss sprayed splinters across his arms. Shaa gave it another few seconds, heard the patter begin to trickle off, and levered himself to his feet.

Ahead, waves lashed back and forth across the area where the giant iceberg had been; the ship itself had almost reached the spot. With an additional heave and a perceptible twist-and-slide to starboard, the ship bounced its way through the turbulent zone, bashing past the larger floating fragments that were the major remains of the berg. The deck around Shaa was dented and bashed and a coating of broken ice twinkled over the entire bow of the ship. Everyone else was getting to their feet as well. Next to Shaa on his right, the captain winced at him through gritted teeth as he moved one elbow gingerly around. Shaa eyed Karlini. "Looks like you were expecting this, too," Shaa told him. "That's not something you usually keep whipped up, is it?"

"All things considered," said Karlini, shaking his head vigorously, sending a sheet of icicles flying off his hair, "it looked like it might come in handy. I thought a melter would take too long, so . . ." He shrugged.

"I agree with your assessment," Shaa said thoughtfully. "Just think of the energy transfer you'd need to push out to flash-liquify that much ice. Why, it would be . . ." Shaa paused to calculate.

Wroclaw had produced another bucket, this one unsoiled by a noxious cleaning fluid, and, ever thrifty, was using it to gather up chunks of ice for the kitchen. The captain had moved to deal with the crew as they checked for damage and made things generally shipshape once again. Karlini, gazing off the bow and sunk deep in his calculations, apparently failed to notice Roni's and Tildamire's approach, even though the ice they had to crunch their way through rested as much as several inches thick on the deck. Roni directed a fondly rueful glance at Karlini. In the best of times, her husband didn't usually notice much that was going on around him without having his attention deliberately planted on it.

Shaa bent to pick up a chunk of ice. "Neat, Karlini, very neat. See—the cleavage surfaces are smooth, not powdered."

"Are they really?" Karlini said.

"What have you boys been up to?" Roni said.

"So after all this, what do you think?" Karlini asked.

"Difficult to say," said Shaa, turning the ice cube over in his hand, pausing to examine one surface more closely. "A good question indeed."

"Either someone's been trying a new recipe," Roni said, with a sharp glance at Wroclaw, who shook his head emphatically, pointing with several jabs of his finger at Karlini, "or someone's got some explaining to do."

"Free will," stated Shaa. "Random chance."

"Or deliberate action," said Karlini, gazing intently at the sky.

"Should we pay attention to them, do you think?" Shaa said to Karlini, *sotto voce.* "Or shall we prepare to get hit over the head with something nasty?"

Karlini looked wildly around. If Shaa had noticed the approach of the women and had decided to show no sign of it, Roni's husband had actually noticed nothing. Karlini was predictable, but so was Shaa, when you got right down to it; Roni had been quite careful about which one of them all she'd picked to marry. She looked at her husband, nodded her head in mild but familiar exasperation, then grabbed his shoulders with both hands and shook.

"Dear!" said Karlini. "Are you all right?"

"Yes," Roni told him. "No thanks to you. Or is it?"

"As a matter of fact—"

"What are you guys talking about?" said Tildy.

"An attack," Shaa said, "possibly."

Tildy's mouth fell slightly open, then closed with a thoughtful pursing. "You really think. . . ?"

"I often try to,"Shaa said; his difficult mood had not entirely evaporated with the iceberg's own vaporization.

"I mean, you really think somebody would try to attack us with a hunk of ice?"

"It's a significant possibility," said Shaa. He gave up studying his ice cube and popped it in his mouth.

"But who?"

"That," Shaa said, slurping the ice cube, "is usually the most interesting, not to mention salient, question."

"Could someone have been after the ring?"

"There are any number of things someone could have been after, starting with a little fun and building up from there, but I'd say the ring could certainly be on the list. Of course, it's most likely that the whole thing was nothing more than happenstance."

"Is that what you believe?" Tildy said skeptically.

"What I believe would probably have no influence on the facts of the matter," stated Shaa. "Paranoia is a survival trait, however. This ice is rather tasty, by the way."

"So you *do* think—"

Shaa opened his eyes wide and directed a guileless gaze

in her direction. "I think nothing," he said, "nothing but hypotheticals, thought experiments. Don't worry about it, the trait runs in my family."

Tildy closed her mouth and kept it shut. Without intending to, Shaa had reminded her of another trait that apparently ran in his family—stabbing each other in the back. Could his brother have been behind this attack, if it *was* an attack?

Then another thought struck her. She had never yet seen Shaa say anything without knowing exactly what message would be drawn out of his words; he was not shy about prizing his own ability with allusions. If he thought his brother was involved, wouldn't he come right out and discuss it? Unless he didn't trust her. Or unless he thought his brother might be listening. . . .

"There's another possibility," Shaa added. "It could have been a warning."

"Against what?" Roni said.

"Any number of things, I'd imagine," said Karlini.

"How do you suppose Groot is at the moment?" remarked Shaa.

"We'll know soon enough," Karlini said. "We'll be there in a few more days."

"Perhaps it might be a better idea to find out how he is *before* we get there."

"Wait a minute," said Tildamire. "If there's something going on with your friend Groot, where would a *warning* come from?"

Shaa grinned enigmatically. "There are many friends in the world beyond Haalsen Groot."

6
OUT OF THE BLUE

"I demand to know the meaning of this!" Haalsen Groot roared. On either side of him, a nattily liveried member of the Communal Police held one of his upper arms.

The sergeant in the doorway in front of him regarded Groot with a blank, officiously precise gaze. " 'Tain't no meaning here to know at all," he said. "The order is signed and sealed, as you yourself can see." He did not, however, turn the large unrolled sheet of parchment so that Groot *could* see the writ upon it, if any, or so he could view the seals, if indeed those were present as well.

"I see nothing of the sort," said Groot, dropping his volume but trying to increase the snap in his tone. He was having no trouble with the snap. Groot liked the idea of a set schedule and had put this ideal into practice for himself. These ruffians had arrived while he was reviewing correspondence in his study over his breakfast tea, still in his dressing gown. He had, however, performed his setting-up exercises upon arising, as was also his scheduled habit, had seen to the necessary ablutions, and had reviewed with his clerk Julio the calendar for the day. There had been no indication of an expected visit from any civic authorities anywhere in their itinerary. "I have seen no order, heard no charges, known no accuser. In case you haven't heard, sergeant, Oolsmouth is a free city governed by the rule of law and the guiding hand of the Council; arbitrary seizure on an unspecified charge is clearly not our policy. Not—our—policy!" he repeated, with icy emphasis.

The sergeant, a singularly stolid fellow apparently chosen for this assignment on the basis of that very attribute, gazed at Groot. "This address is 25 Rockfish Lane. You have already answered to the name of Haalsen Thelomarias Groot, and have so identified yourself. I have further identified myself as a duly constituted officer of the Civil Council of Oolsmouth and have informed you that I possess a fully executed warrant for your arrest and imprisonment. In just accordance with the law and practice of Oolsmouth, you are therefore to consider yourself under arrest, and are directed to surrender your person into my custody without delay. Failure to do so may expose you to additional criminal charges as well as the corporal power of our rightful authority. Now, please come along, sir."

Groot would have crossed his arms over his chest; it was the sort of posture that went with the defiant glower he was radiating. His arms, though, remained in the firm grasp of the other two troopers. He stuck out his chin instead. "I demand to know the charges against me; that is my right under the law."

The sergeant didn't even bother to shake his head; his expression remained placid. "I have my orders. My orders make no mention of validity of this right under the present circumstances."

"No mention?" said Groot, his mustache waving. "What is that supposed to mean? Rights are rights."

"My orders have suspended your ability to exercise this right in the present instance."

"What? You can't just—"

"The Council has spoken," the sergeant stated.

"The Council has *not* spoken, damn your eyes! I'm *on* the Council. Don't you think if the Council was going to speak, it would speak directly to me?"

"I'm certain I wouldn't know, sir. Now, please come along." The sergeant nodded to his troops. "Bring him along, boys."

"Now just a moment," said Groot, digging his slippered heels in against the wood parquet floor of the entry hall. The policemen paid no attention to his attempt at friction and merely hoisted him into the air, then carried him toward the door. "At least let me put on a suit of proper clothes, unless these almighty orders of yours prohibit that, too.''

The sergeant raised his hand and Groot found himself lowered to the floor. Unrolling the parchment again, the sergeant scrutinized it, his lips moving in silence as he made his way through its official language. ''The order does not expressly address the question of garb,'' he said. ''Thus the matter is left implicitly to my discretion. From the urgency with which the remainder of the order is phrased, and the dangerous individual you are deemed to be, sir—''

''What?'' said Groot again. ''I beg your—''

''—as I say, sir, a thoroughly dangerous individual, and one I am cautioned to take every care with lest you should gain the chance to escape, possibly causing injury, maiming, or death to myself or my subordinates in the prosecution of your desires; from this danger and the urgency of the orders my interpretation of this discretionary power would prohibit me from showing you any leniency, sir.'' Again he nodded to the others. ''Bring him along. You can bind him outside.''

They crossed the threshold more ignominiously than Groot could recall having done since he'd been living in this house, or at least since—

Groot's house servant, who had weighed the unattractive option of impalement on a pike against the hazards of letting the troops in the door when they had originally pounded for entry, appeared around the corner ahead of them at a run. He was being followed at the heels by Julio, who had left the house by foot mere moments before the police had arrived. Julio began unreeling his own tirade while still skidding to a halt. ''Julio,'' said Groot, as the troopers lashed his hands together behind his back.

Julio fell silent and cocked his head attentively, panting freely from his unexpected sprint. ''I fear you might as well desist; this functionary is firmly dedicated to his sacred orders, whatever they really are and whoever they're really from. I'd best go along with him and then try to tangle this thing apart. You round up old Snee and meet us at the prison—I assume we're going to the prison in the Hall?''

"Aye, sir," said the sergeant.

"You meet us at the prison, then, with the appropriate writs. Eelmon will escort us there."

"Yes, Meester Groot," said Eelmon, the house servant, from inside the open door. Julio took off down the street toward the office of Snee, the lawyer for Haalsen Traders, and Groot fell in with the police as they marched off after him. The door slammed behind them and Eelmon reappeared, hefting a hastily-stuffed carpetbag. Groot watched the familiar streets go past, watched familiar faces turn to stare at them in astonishment (as much for the spectacle of himself abroad in his dressing gown, he thought sourly, as for the company he was keeping, and for the fact that he'd been clapped in irons), watched as they crossed the Bridge of Bronze over the Green Canal. To their left at the top of the bridge, down the Green Canal's navigation channel, the River Oolvaan proper was visible with its usual clutter of vessels. The south bank of the Green Canal was faced with its own docks and warehouses; in fact, *Groot's* own docks and warehouses, or a major complex of them at any rate. One ship was tied up, the ocean-going *Fair Market Value*, due to finish her loading by noon for a run eastward along the coast. Instead of the expected clamor of teamsters, crane operators, stevedores, and sailors, though, the dock was eerily quiet and virtually empty. But who were those people lined up in formation on the wharf, and standing guard in front of the warehouse door?

Then Groot made sense of the scene, in the moment before they trod down the descending slope of the high-arched bridge and were lost again in the midst of the streets. More police troops had just shown up here, at the warehouse. The place was being shut down. What was going on?

Groot was not only a leading businessman in Oolsmouth, he was a good one as well. It was the soul of good business practice to participate in the affairs of one's community, to secure a local power base, and to become and remain generally well-connected; consequently, Groot had gone out of his way to do all these things. The principal reason behind this philosophy, of course, is to make sure that one can sense even subtle changes in the local climate and can position one's self to take the best advantage of them, not to mention getting advance notification of any overtly hostile moves that may be brewing aimed at one's own operations. What had gone wrong here? Groot hadn't heard a whisper of warning. How could he be taken unawares, and how could anyone else have acquired (without his noticing it) the political strength to move against him so blatantly?

There was the barest possibility that some mistake was being made; that a confusion of identity had occurred, or that someone had gone off half-cocked. The move felt too well-planned for that, though, what with his arrest and the simultaneous descent upon his commercial operations. If a mistake had been made, it would all shake out in due course anyway. Viewed from another angle, however, Groot thought with some anticipatory satisfaction that a mistake certainly *had* been made. By the time he was finished with them, whoever was behind this would fully appreciate, to their woe, just how big a mistake it had been. Groot had resources that even a well-planned raid against him would be unlikely to reveal. He also had friends.

Only what if this offensive wasn't really aimed at Groot at all, but through him *at* his friends? From the increased level of activity he'd been hearing about from Max and Shaa there was obviously something of significant import underway. And the boat on the Oolvaan would be due in soon. . . .

Ahead of them, a wide splash of sunlit lawn appeared, a spouting fountain at its center. The street they were on had widened into a boulevard, one of the seven that radiated out from the Plaza of the Bureaucrats, as Groot referred to it, and now the boulevard opened into the Plaza itself. The fountain in the civic park in the plaza's center contained several statues arranged in an interlocking tableau of local symbols—a heroic twin-masted ship with two ranks of churning rowers, a messy spiral of storm clouds and thunderbolts looming over the ship and dripping water on its canted deck, an out-of-scale fisherman swinging a full net of carp with one hand and waving a gaffed squid with the other, and so forth. A small gang of urchins were splashing around under the obligatory breaching leviathan, and they, too, paused in their free-for-all to gawk as Groot was led around the fountain and toward the block-long Hall of the People on the other side of the plaza.

Groot had been agitating sarcastically if less than seriously at Council meetings for years, when nothing else interesting was up for discussion (which in truth was most of the time), to have the name of the Hall of the People changed, since as they all knew the People had very little to do with anything significant. It was also a thoroughly unaesthetic name, the sort of name only a bureaucrat could love. Although Groot's proposals usually brought a round of nods and approving "hurrumphs" from around the Council chamber, nothing had ever come of it. The people of Oolsmouth and the surrounding countryside, which also fell under the territory of Oolsmouth Free State, while understanding that there was not in truth very much they could do to influence the course of government, notwithstanding the constant rhetoric concerning The Will of the People and their Elected Representatives, were not (for the most part) too unhappy with the general state of affairs, especially when they reflected back on the comparison with the earlier autocratic regime. It was true that the Council was filled out by the heads of the local trade guilds, a smattering of directly elected spokespersons, and even a few token nonhumans, but the unmistakable balance of control rested with the leading merchants and their proxies. All in all, though, the business interests tended to pursue a freewheeling policy of *laissez-faire* leavened with civic social benefits that were a bit on the paternalistic side.

The People might not have fully appropriate representation on the Council, but everyone was aware that they had risen in the past and could, of course, do so again. The truth was that the merchant class was not really that much more powerful than the population at large, and since there were more working people than merchant bourgeois things tended to even out. As a city based primarily on commerce rather than on manufacturing or the exploitation of natural resources, or on the production of goods and services for local consumption, the economy did not support the growth of an oligarchy or even a dramatic shift of actual power to one group or another; as a result, the basic social contract had remained in large part intact. That being so, the People as a whole figured they had better things to do than waste time grubbing around in the Council. Watching the Council in its various gyrations was a popular spectator sport, though, since the merchants liked to use it as just another arena for their typically cutthroat competition.

The Hall of the People, even for a powerful city on the leading edge of the current wave of prosperity, was an unquestionable civic extravagance. There was no doubt about its symbolism—here was a city of wealth and stability, with a government comfortable and entrenched enough to grant itself the luxury of municipal monumentalism. Even so, it was clear that the Hall of the People would not exist, at least in its present form, without a generous philanthropic contribution from the past.

People seemed to enjoy discovering the same thing over and over again. Accordingly, Oolsmouth was not the first city to take advantage of the strategic significance conferred by control of the mouth of the Oolvaan. Where Oolsmouth now stood, more or less, there had once been another city whose heyday dated back before the great Dislocation and the fall of technological civilization, and whose own descent into the swamp was probably contemporaneous with it. The chronic overflow of the Oolvaan onto its alluvial floodplain and the silting of its delta had spared Oolsmouth's ancestor from the fate of most structures of its period, or at least the fate of those structures that people could enter without dropping dead from one or another of the myriad curses of the ancients. The fate of virtually everything from before the Dislocation, not surprisingly, had been utter eradication through cannibalistic dismantling or sheer bad temper, so few discrete traces of the old world remained. There was always the tread of the suppressing foot of the gods to remember, too, as it descended metaphorically from the heavens to squash any signs and knowledge of the past, as well as those who seemed too freely interested in it. The ancients had been a crafty and cunning lot, however, so it wouldn't have really surprised Groot one bit to discover that they had arranged for this city to be swallowed by the river and covered by a swamp, awaiting a more rational time for its excavation.

Of course, Groot had hung around with Maximillian the Vaguely Disreputable, who spent a lot of time trying to commune with the ancients in one way or another, so he acknowledged that his attitude about the ancients had most likely been colored by Max's. Still, most of what the present age had pulled from the draining swamp over the past fifty years or so had been used not for study or glorification of the past, but for building materials. It was enough to make a sensible person wonder just how much the current civilization really differed from the savages of the past, especially when you saw what most of the scavenged building materials had been used to construct.

The Hall of the People hadn't *all* been assembled out of exhumed parts, of course. Much of it was built of locally-quarried stone, and the majority of the outer surface was faced with marble imported, at great but not totally unreasonable cost, by a consortium of merchants who had been on the Council at the time, when the Council itself had been an institution constituted solely for its promotional value by the government of Hugo the Autocrat. That Council had had nothing better to do than putter around with public works of marginal utility, although the precedent they had established had held through to the present modern time. Each edge of the building, including not only the four major corners and the margins of the roof but the cornices and window frames as well, had facings made not of stone but of ancient sheet metal, polished now to a slightly oxidized shine that made glancing toward the Hall on a sunny day a painful experience and would leave one walking around distracted by bright afterimages for the next half-hour. In the domed roof of the rotunda above the Council chamber, too, the large translucent panels had been cast from a slurry of crazed, opacified, and pebbled fragments of ancient glass. Furthermore, for years the building had been generating rumors of secret passages, hidden partitions, and moving floors incorporating totally unnecessary bits of old flotsam and jetsam.

By anyone's estimation, the architect had been a madman.

The Hall's front facade, which Groot was squinting his way toward now, had been outfitted with more pillars and heroic statuary than strict good taste would have been comfortable with, and these elements of modern construction sat uneasily with the dour evidence of times now gone. Which wasn't to say, Groot didn't hesitate to admit, that all the gimcrack decoration would have fit better in any other surroundings. Bad taste had a certain timeless quality to it.

The Hall was outfitted with a variety of entrances in addition to that of the grand main door, with its excessive colonnade and exhausting flight of broad stairs and long coiled drowsing-griffin balustrades. The portal on the right side just around the corner from the plaza led to the main garrison of police and, beneath it, to the prison. Groot had never been down there before, but in the typical manner of people who knew that law-enforcement activity was constantly underway but who didn't feel much personal connection with it, he'd been aware of where it was.

Law enforcement was just one of the activities that had to go on for a smoothly functioning society to exist, and it was no more of a star attraction than, say, tax collection. In the old days (not the days of the ancients, but the days of their own great-grandparents, for example) when things were much simpler all around, albeit and undeniably much more savage and brutish, law enforcement was simultaneously a more arbitrary and a more crowd-pleasing enterprise, especially in its terminal stages. Now, though, Oolsmouth was a civilized place, and these were civilized times, so the bread-and-circus atmosphere fostered by peremptory public hangings, floggings, mutilations, rackings, and assorted other tortures had been firmly laid to rest, along with many of those who had experienced them at first hand. Groot was also aware that the equipment and facilities for these various excruciations had not been destroyed, but were merely in storage somewhere in the building in front of him, stockpiled no doubt by prudent heads in the speculation of a future turn of the wheel, so to speak. Whether there were dark corners and hidden departments using these methods still was a question Groot was hoping would remained unanswered while whatever he was involved in played itself out.

After the piercing reflections from the metal details of the Hall's exterior facade, the interior corridor of the police section was a dimly-lit relief. The common area of the prison, though lit with equal inadequacy, proved less so. Long tunnels with barred gates snaked away from archways in three walls; the long narrow stair up to the ground floor, which they had just navigated, eased its way down the fourth. The jailer roused himself to produce a logbook from a niche under the stair as the troopers continued to hold Groot tightly, and between the two of them he and the sergeant noted Groot's arrival on a fresh page.

"Make your mark here," the jailer directed, pointing to a space next to their new set of totally illegible scratchings. Obviously they were used to dealing with common ruffians, Groot thought, as he instead inscribed his signature, complete with his usual intertwined loops and long sashaying underline flourishes. The jailer, a burly man with the troglodytic pallor of someone who has spent his entire working life indoors, gazed intently at the signature, then looked Groot up and down. He began absently licking his chops. "And what standard of accommodations be you requesting, yer lordship?" he said. "Two, er, *three* silver ools will get you—"

"There will be none of that here," said the sergeant. "This man is dangerous, and must be given no consideration beyond the needs of our own security; these are my orders."

"But—"

"Do you understand?"

Eelmon had dogged their steps throughout the walk and was now hanging about next to the foot of the stairs, clutching the carpetbag as though he expected someone to try to rob him of it, here in the central jail. Eelmon was a trusty sort with a good head on him, Groot thought, a sturdy man; he knew his business. Groot caught his eye and nodded slightly. Eelmon pursed his lips and nodded back.

The jailer scowled, spit off into the corner with pinpoint aim undoubtedly seasoned through long practice, and produced the traditional ring of keys from his belt. Unlocking the gate on the left with a shrill creak and hoisting a lantern from its peg just inside the entrance, he led the way off into the gloom. Groot found his nose wrinkling involuntarily. For someone who bathed unfashionably often, every day if he could, such an unwashed stench was not encouraging, not to mention its significant component aroma that indicated a total lack of concern for sanitation. Sanitation was one of the obsessions of the ancients that Max and Shaa both ardently admired and Groot had joined them as a full-fledged disciple. Well, he thought, perhaps this will be the worst they intend to do to me.

The sergeant and his troopers saw Groot securely installed alone in a small cell of perhaps three long strides in each direction before removing the chains and bonds from his arms. The new chain around his ankle, when fastened to an eyebolt in the floor, barely let him reach the intimidatingly thick wood door. Eelmon was still out there in the hall, though, and no one had made a move to imprison him as well, so one of Groot's major worries, that he would be held incommunicado in an unmarked cell with the records of his incarceration unaccountably missing, seemed to be provisionally relieved. The sergeant led his men off, hurriedly now, probably to report in to his officers or to whomever had drafted his mysterious orders, leaving the jailer to inspect the contents of the carpetbag under Eelmon's supervision. Although they were in the hall out of Groot's direct sight, he did hear the gentle clink of coins changing hands; Eelmon had taken Groot's message about the importance of giving the jailer a generous payoff, even (or especially) in the face of the sergeant's express instructions to the contrary. After a moment, the jailer entered with the carpetbag and set it on the rush-strewn floor within easy reach. "Here you are, yer lordship," he said deferentially. "I'll be getting you a bench and candles shortly." He touched his forelock and backed out.

How much *did* Eelmon pay this fellow? Groot wondered. Whatever it was, Groot had no doubt that the money would be a prudent investment in his future. Who knew, perhaps it might even help insure that he would *have* a future. Groot settled back against the wall with his legs stretched out in front of him. When the candle arrived, he would take a closer look at the cabin. In the brief glimpses he'd gotten in the light from the jailer's lantern, the links had appeared old and thick and were covered with a flaky veneer of rust. The lock on the ankle shackle had also seemed to present possibilities. Whether trying to escape was a good idea, of course, was an entirely different matter.

When the candle and bench came, they were accompanied not only by the jailer but by Julio and the lawyer, Snee. The jailer left them alone with the cell door propped open and went out to lurk in the hall. Julio and Snee arranged themselves on the bench across the cell from Groot. "To what do you attribute this incarceration, Meester Groot?" the lawyer said in a rush, eager to get the first word in.

"I had hoped that was what you were planning to tell *me,*" Groot said. "Why don't we edge backward a step or two first? What is going on out there? On the way to this place, my route passed the dock on Green Canal—all my facilities there were apparently being placed under guard."

"This is true," Julio told him. "All the Haalsen Traders assets that are a matter of official record are now under impound. From reports at the various scenes and from the single seizure I succeeded in witnessing myself, at the storehouse on Pike Street and Old Mill, the operations were conducted quickly, in a businesslike manner, but with some level of confusion on the part of the troops involved. Nevertheless, it is clear that most if not all of these forces were drawn from the Communal Police supplemented by the civic defense militia, acting under instructions supposedly issued by the Council. This was a coordinated effort to seal all buildings, intern all assets, and stop all business operations. Since the police were a bit ragged in their execution of this attack, as I said before, it's uncertain how well planned this all was—''

''Obviously it was planned well enough,'' said Groot. ''But by whom? And why? And—no, but first, was anybody hurt?''

''None of our people were significantly injured, as far as I've been able to find out, although there were a few stevedores roughed up, a few smashed doors, the temporary standoffs you'd expect when no one on either side is quite sure of what is actually happening.'' Julio hesitated. ''If I might venture a conclusion, I would say that violence or even intimidation through violence does not seem to have been the goal, just confiscation of property. No one else was arrested beside you, yourself.''

''One thing to consider is that someone may be sending you a message,'' commented Snee.

''A message may be part of it,'' Julio said, ''but my opinion is that sending a message is not the most significant point here.''

''There is clearly more than that going on,'' agreed Groot. ''You don't send a businessman a message by shutting down his whole business. When you've already tried to exterminate someone, what do you have left to say to them, and who's even left to hear the message? You haven't left yourself any room to maneuver, either. What more can you do to escalate? If you're sending messages, you build up to scorched earth, you don't start there. The way you describe it, this certainly sounds like a swath of scorched earth to me. What more can they do now?''

''You are still in good health, I presume?'' asked Snee.

''Is that just an oblique suggestion, or do you know something I don't?''

Snee ran a well-manicured hand through his thinning light-brown hair, brushing it carefully back along his temples. ''Ah, well,'' he temporized.

Groot shifted his legs, explicitly rattling the chain. ''That's not an answer, and that's certainly not the kind of thing I'm paying you for. So you tell me straight, lawyer, what's happening here? What charge am I being held on?"

"I don't know," Snee said reluctantly.

"I beg your pardon?" said Groot. This was not the response he had expected. "What do you mean, you don't know?"

"No official paperwork has been registered. I have my apprentices pursuing the matter even as we sit here, but so far nothing has come to light."

"Please explain something to me," said Groot. "I am incarcerated in an official civic facility, am I not? For this to be the case, a charge does have to be filed, doesn't it? Do we have a rule of law, or don't we?"

"It's not that simple," said the lawyer in a rather professorial tone. "You're an intelligent man, you know how things work, so don't act so surprised. In the law, there are usually quite a number of ways to get around something. If a declaration of martial law has been made, or a state of emergency or a state of civil siege, various guarantees of due process can be suspended. Beyond that, it is possible for the Council to act peremptorily, or even for individual Councillors to move unilaterally on their own if certain extreme contingencies arise."

"I didn't know that," said Groot. "Why don't I know that? I'm on the Council."

"These things are on the books," Snee said. "They're obscure, but they *are* on the books."

"What 'extreme contingencies' are we talking about here?"

"Could they be holding you for treason?" the lawyer asked cautiously.

"Treason?" Groot said incredulously. "Against whom? This is a free city!"

"Consorting with enemies, then."

"*Whose* enemies? Treason? Of course not."

"You do have many foreign contacts," Julio said.

"I'm a trader!" said Groot. "I'm *supposed* to have foreign contacts!"

"That could be at the root of your arrest," Snee said thoughtfully. "Not the seizures of property, but perhaps the arrest. If some Council member had evidence that you were in contact with hostile foreigners, they could have used that as a basis for drafting an order to hold you preemptively for the good of the state. Such an order could be kept secret for a limited amount of time, especially if there was evidence of other members of an active conspiracy still free and active. Technically, the order would have to be made official eventually, though."

Groot shook his head. "This all sounds too autocratic for my liking. What's the purpose of due process if you can get around it whenever you want? Do we have an independent judiciary, or is that just another figment, too?"

"Is that a serious question?" said Snee. "I'll be trying to get you a judicial hearing, of course, but I have to tell you that no judge is going to want to get in the way of the Council in a matter such as this, whether it involves state security or just a struggle between individual Council members. Any judge in his right mind would defer to the Council itself when it's using its own extraordinary judicial powers. And as you well know, Oolsmouth's own autocratic past is not so far behind it that there are not vestiges of it still hanging around here and there. Some of them even remain statutory."

"Damn," said Groot. "So I'm just supposed to sit here, rotting in the filth? One of the reasons I clawed after personal success and wealth was to insulate myself from annoyances like these. Are you telling me I was wasting my time?"

"The law is your friend," observed the lawyer, "except when, occasionally, it isn't."

"Thank you," Groot said. "Thank you very much. I will treasure that pearl of wisdom, alone in this squalid cell. I assume you don't know what's behind all these property seizures either?"

Snee looked at the damp ceiling, at its close-fitting stones. "Unfortunately not. I'm trying to lay hands on one of the order sheets the police have been waving about. That may give us more information, but they're obviously under instructions not to let anyone actually read the things."

Groot looked at Julio. "Who do we have who could obtain one of these sheets?"

Julio hesitated; more bad news, no doubt. "You realize, Meester Groot, that you can't actually *pay* anyone at the moment. All assets are frozen. You don't have to worry about me, sir," he added hastily, looking away. "I've been—well, you just don't have to worry about me, that's all. It's not just a matter of money."

Groot had made Julio a partner in Haalsen Traders, under terms that made it in his interest to stay with him, but Groot was willing to accept Julio's statement at face value for whatever it worth beyond that. Groot wasn't going to turn totally paranoid, at least not yet, and anyway who else did he have who was acting for him on the outside? "Who else is loyal or motivated enough, or paid up sufficiently in advance, then?"

"I'm not sure I want to hear this," stated Snee. "I don't know what means you intend to use to obtain the order sheet, but if it's not strictly aboveboard then we'll all be safer if I don't know about it. Beforehand, at any rate. If you *do* secure one of these sheets, let me know, but I don't want to know how you've done it. I'll keep on trying through my own means."

"Very well," said Groot. "How long will it take you to get to the bottom of this?"

Snee put on a cagey look. "In this case, I'm positive that evidentiary discovery will be a tricky process. There are many things we don't yet know—"

"That *is* the whole point, isn't it?"

The lawyer shrugged. "I'll do what I can. You may want to pursue your own means as well."

"Thank you," said Groot with a trace of a snarl. "Why don't you get down to it, then?"

Snee rose. "I will take my leave." He bowed to the reclining Groot, then backed out the door.

"Of course I'll pursue my own means," Groot muttered, staring after the lawyer with a dark gaze. "I'm not a fool, except perhaps in thinking I could rely on a lawyer to get me out of a mess with the law." He looked up at Julio. "We'll have to round up as full a Council session as we can get this time of year. Try to find out where the others stand first, as far as you can.''

''Dooglas?'' said Julio.

''I wouldn't be surprised. It's a much more blatant move than you'd expect, but who else is the leading candidate, anyway?''

''Indeed,'' Julio said in a dour voice. ''You haven't been spending much time cultivating your faction, have you?''

''No, I haven't, as you know perfectly well,'' said Groot. ''That doesn't look like a very good move in retrospect, does it?''

''No, sir, I have to say it does not.''

''Hmpph.'' Groot thought for a moment. ''What does Sy have to say for himself? Where has he been in all this? Why didn't he see something coming?''

''He wasn't at any of the facilities I visited, and I didn't have a chance to swing round his house.''

''Perhaps he'll show up.'' Sy Gazoont was the company sorcerer and communicator. ''We only have a few days to get all this wrapped up or our friends heading down the river may walk right into the middle of it.''

''Indeed, yes, sir. I take your meaning. If there's nothing more, perhaps I should be moving along myself?''

''Yes,'' said Groot. ''Is Eelmon still out there? You can take him if you want; it sounds like you need another pair of legs more than I need a runner on call here. Find out what's behind this and who we have to fight.''

''I'll check back with you later,'' said Julio. He vanished through the doorway. The jailer promptly reappeared, checked Groot's shackles to make sure no one had tampered with them under the cover of the meeting, tugged his forelock, and edged out of the cell again. The thick door thudded back into place.

This was a fine kettle of fish, no question about it. Groot got to his feet, clanking conspicuously, and set to examining the features of the cell, not that there were many features to be concerned with. With the exception of the wood of the door and its cast iron crosspieces, the rest of the cell was faced with stone. Even the floor was stone, not dirt—no, on closer inspection, the floor was some type of concrete. Could this be part of the foundation? Was he really that far down in the building? The light from the single candle was fairly weak, making Groot's examination not only tedious but a matter of judgment as well. Then again, he had all the time he needed to absorb the sights since he didn't seem to be going anywhere else any too rapidly.

Groot took a better look at one wall. Perhaps the regular rectangular stones making up the wall had also been cast, not quarried. Concrete was generally more crumbly than genuine native rock, but this stuff seemed quite hardy. His fingernail failed to scratch it, and the only sediment left on his finger after the attempt was not white cement dust but plain old filth. It would be ridiculous to try to tunnel out, that much was clear. The only existing exits were the door and the tiny barred ventilation shaft in the ceiling that angled who knew where; there wasn't any daylight showing through it, sure enough. Up there, though, on the outside wall just below the ceiling, that discolored area—what was that?

He carried the bench over to the wall and climbed up on it, candle in hand. One rectangular stone did indeed have a different look to it than the rest of the wall; fresher, perhaps? Less blackened with time and the soot of candle flames? Groot rapped on it, then on the next stone over. Both were apparently solid. The scratch test, however, was more interesting. He felt as though he'd dragged his finger across a coarse sandpaper or a length of pumice, but a powder of small gritty particles was left on his hand.

A new concrete block, cast in place? Surely the old one hadn't just crumbled to nothing, not with the surrounding pieces as solid as they were. Not a flaw in construction, either, most likely. Perhaps some earlier prisoner had tried to chip or drill his way out or the new block was now filling a space that had once been open. Could it have been another ventilation hole? Such a hole would have been barred, no doubt, but a window-type opening in an outer wall would have probably communicated directly with the outside of the building. . . .

Groot replaced the bench on the far side of the cell,

kicked the chain into a comfortable position, and began to pace, three strides out, three strides back. How did they make concrete in the first place?

The scrape of the locking bar on the door interrupted him again. Had Julio forgotten something? The jailer opened the door wide. With him was an unfamiliar man, in a dark sober clerical cloak and coat like Julio's, to be sure, but wearing spectacles and a full beard, not just a mustache. "Someone to see you," said the jailer.

Groot indicated the bench with one hand and retreated to the back wall. The man entered, swept a quick glance around the cell, and made a short bow toward Groot. "Meester Haalsen Groot," he stated.

"And who might you be?"

"My name is not important. I represent the Bank of the New Dawn."

The Bank of the New Dawn? Groot had no relationship with such an institution; his accounts were all at Oolvaan Mutual. For that matter, had he ever heard of the Bank of the New Dawn? "I see," said Groot. "What can I do for you? Unfortunately I am not in a position to offer the usual pleasantries of comfort and drink at the moment, although you're welcome to the bench."

"Thank you," said the banker, seating himself, but carefully keeping his cloak aloof from the floor. Groot, not to be outdone by the game of body language, settled to his spot on the floor; if he kept getting this many visitors, he'd have to think about bribing the jailer for another bench. The banker inspected the cell again, then summed up with a disapproving *tsk-tsk*. "You are perhaps wondering what brings me here for this audience," he continued, still eyeing the rude surroundings. "For that matter, you may have been wondering what sorry state of affairs has brought *you* here, yourself."

The man seemed to be waiting for some reply. Groot crossed his arms and rattled the chain. The chain was turning out to be a useful prop, underscoring the reality of the situation and Groot's awareness of it in one terse motion, sound effects included. Groot was not as great a fan of improvisation as Max, but there was still no doubt that one had to make do with what one had available.

"Well," said the banker. "I feel it is appropriate to tell you that these two conditions, that is, both our presences in this particular place, are related."

"Are they?" said Groot.

"Yes. You see, the Bank of the New Dawn, with which I believe I may have mentioned I am affiliated, has acquired the assets of the Oolvaan Mutual Bank. In fact, through this acquisition, the Oolvaan Mutual Bank has become, temporarily to be sure, a wholly-owned subsidiary of the Bank of the New Dawn. Temporarily, as I say, on a time scale most likely measured in days, at the conclusion of which the Oolvaan Mutual Bank will be totally merged into the operations of the Bank of the New Dawn. Does that clarify the situation?"

"Not in the least," said Groot. Who was this idiot? This was not at all the sort of banker with whom Groot preferred to deal. "Feel free to proceed," he added, not sure that the guy would pick up the thread again without prodding.

The banker gave a genteel little cough. "Very well. A major portion of these assets, that is, the assets of the Oolvaan Mutual Bank, as I am certain you will be aware, are associated with you and your various business enterprises. To be quite straightforward about this, the Bank of the New Dawn, in order to safeguard its investments and insure the integrity of all its assets, including those newly acquired from the Oolvaan Mutual Bank, has been compelled by good business practice to reduce our downside exposure. As the major downside risk is posed by your operations, I am certain you will understand and sympathize with our decision to bring our outstanding loans into closer balance with our tangible properties and liquidatable collateral. Accordingly, we have acted to restructure your outstanding capitalization and reduce what we have concluded, after careful examination of the records of the Oolvaan Mutual Bank, to be an overextension of your credit by the previous management."

"Are you telling me you're calling in my loans?"

"I do believe that is what I said."

It was such a ridiculous idea that Groot had never seen it coming, even with the time he'd already had to try to figure out what was going on. Like most traders and merchants, he relied on a high degree of financial leverage, borrowing to finance trade voyages and paying back with interest at their completion. He had reciprocal relationships with other traders in other locations who served as his local agents in their own vicinities. The other traders had letters of credit from him and he had letters of credit from them; Groot's credit network alone represented a significant amount of value in place. In addition, his credit was, of course, also good at the few foreign branches of Oolvaan Mutual. Oolvaan Mutual had liked him. The bank had found his cash flow unimpeachable. "All of my accounts are fully collateralized," Groot stated. "My operations have been the biggest cash cow Oolvaan Mutual has had on the books for the last five years. My credit and my bond have been unquestioned across the face of the civilized world!" This wasn't merely insane and against the terms of his contracts, it was bad business.

"In the initial period of consolidation of the Oolvaan Mutual Bank, or as I should more correctly note, the *former* Oolvaan Mutual Bank, into the Bank of the New Dawn, the management of the Bank of the New Dawn has elected to utilize conservative accounting practices," the banker expounded. "That is the most stewardly plan, at least, and the one that is being followed at present. Accordingly, we have elected to write down the value of good will, letters of credit, and other such soft negotiables, and to accept only tangible property, valuables, and other hard collateral for the liquidation of outstanding accounts. You will appreciate the prudence of our management decisions in this regard, as a businessman yourself."

As the banker might more correctly note, a *former* businessman, Groot thought, if what he thought this guy was saying was really true. "No matter what kind of internal decisions you people have decided to make," Groot said, "you can't just do this kind of the thing by yourselves, unilaterally, without any kind of notification."

"But I *am* notifying you," said the banker.

"This is totally ridiculous," Groot said, "not to mention completely against normal practice. The loans from Oolvaan Mutual were made to finance ongoing operations. If you shut down those operations and try only to realize salvage value, you destroy the value the loans were made to finance. Even so, the value of all my outstanding loans is more than adequately collateralized by the warehouses, wharves, ships in port, docking licenses, real estate, goods on hand, and so forth. There was no need to impound everything in sight even if you thought you had the right to impound *anything* in the first place, which I certainly do not concede."

"Your concession is immaterial to the reality of the situation. Your own valuation of your assets, too, is of no significance to our auditors. You, of course, will make an unrealistically high assessment of the value of your warehouses and local property, while our own rigorous investigation has put a much more appropriate evaluation into place."

"What about the independent valuations Oolvaan Mutual had on file? What about arbitration?"

The banker shrugged. "The Bank of the New Dawn makes a point of our reliance on our own trained professionals."

The value of Groot's warehouses and local property, like all such values, could be assessed either high or low. These New Dawn people were coming in at the lowest of the low, although this man wasn't putting it in those terms, with the result being that to secure its payment the bank was confiscating everything of Groot's it could get its hands on. They were grabbing property first, and perhaps (a shaky perhaps, from the look of it) they might condescend to untangle things later. They'd have had to pay off or cut in or scare off enough Council members to get the writs, to hire the police, and to all-around have the clout, and they'd have had to trample on laws left and right. This was not a simple operation or one with a low profile, and Groot was one of Oolsmouth's leading citizens. How did they expect to get away with it?

Not only had they confiscated all of Groot's property, they had confiscated Groot himself. "Why am I sitting here in jail instead of being out where I can help respond to your needs?" Groot said; he'd try to play along with the man for a minute and see if he could shake loose any useful information. "Why wasn't I notified in a businesslike fashion in the first place so we could do this thing in an orderly manner, without needing to drag in the police?"

The banker gave him a thin smile. "Your reputation for resourcefulness has preceded you," he remarked. "For our management to act responsibly, it was clear we had to minimize the possibility of circumvention." The banker leaned forward and rested his hands on his knees. "To be frank with you, our external audit of the Haalsen Traders collateral was not complete, and we felt that the liquidation value on hand would not be sufficient to cover the outstanding value of all loans. It was felt that we would have a much better chance of recovering full value if we could deal with you directly. Accordingly, we acted to assure that you would not leave the city or become unavailable, thereby leaving your debts unpaid, and the civil authorities, agreeing with our position, commissioned a warrant for your arrest."

This is the most ludicrous thing I've ever heard, thought Groot. "You really expect me to believe this concoction?"

"You are free to believe what you choose," said the banker. "After all, you will have time on your hands, will you not?"

Perhaps the banker was deliberately trying to provoke him, so they could add attempted assault or another criminal offense to the list of civil charges. "We will see," Groot said, trying for a note of temperance. "So what is your proposal?"

"Oh, we have no proposal per se at this time. This is purely a courtesy visit. The management of the Bank of the New Dawn respectfully felt you would appreciate this personal explanation."

Did they think this guy's own special touch would win them his future business? "Thank you," said Groot. "That's very congenial of you, I'm sure. Perhaps you'd also be so good as to tell me how it is that the Bank of the New Dawn came to take over Oolvaan Mutual in the first place?'' Oolvaan Mutual had been secure in its independence and apparently sound in its capitalization or Groot would never have remained with them.

For the first time, the banker hesitated. Then, reluctantly, he said, ''A dispute between the two patrons was involved.''

Oh, thought Groot. Damn. And he'd thought he'd been getting a handle on what was going on here. It made sense, though. If gods were involved, all normal rules were off.

Banks, like businesses, organizations, and people in general, sometimes adopted gods as patrons, or were adopted themselves by a god against their will. In fact, without putting too fine a face on it, it was not unknown for a god to basically strong-arm a business into giving its allegiance, thereby running what amounted to a kind of super-powered protection racket. There wasn't much you could do about being the object of such a play unless you had the right connections and were willing to go fairly far out on a limb to take advantage of them. The real mystery was why the opposite situation ever arose, why so many people went out of their way to draw a god's attention to themselves. While it was Groot's attitude that no one in his right mind would deliberately seek to get mixed up with a god, the fact remained that a lot of folks were apparently in need of such psychological therapy. As if that wasn't enough, gods had also been known to start real-world business enterprises of their own.

Which of these situations were operating here Groot didn't know. ''A dispute,'' he said.

''Apparently,'' said the banker, pushing himself to his feet. ''Those of us beneath the pinnacle of the hierarchy have hesitated to inquire too deeply.''

''Wise of you, I'm sure. Just how long do you plan to leave me rotting here?''

''I must get back to the office,'' the banker announced. ''I have already exceeded my brief time allotment here. Good day to you, then, Meester Groot.'' He fluffed through the doorway in a curl of cloak and disappeared down the hall.

When he came to lock up, the jailer brought him a lunch, or thought he did, at any rate. Groot sipped at the turgid mug of watered ale and set the coarse black bread end aside in case he had more company. While the ale set about adding its own acid to the already burning sensation in his stomach Groot tried to compose himself, and settled back for a try at a good think.

Later in the afternoon—at least, Groot assumed it was the afternoon—Julio appeared again. "There is apparently a problem with our bank," Julio said.

"I've heard about it," Groot told him. "This is the story I was told."

Julio listened silently, occasionally shaking his head in disbelief. At the conclusion, he shook his head once more for good measure. "I don't have anything to add to that account," he stated. "I hadn't even been aware that Oolvaan Mutual had a relationship with a god, nor had I known anything of significance about the Bank of the New Dawn before this man related his report to you."

"Neither had I," said Groot, "on either count. Assuming what he said was accurate as far as it went, which we may as well do in the absence of any information to the contrary, it may nevertheless be possible to make an educated guess about what was going on behind the scenes. This god who was the patron of Oolvaan Mutual has been forced to yield to the patron of New Dawn, and New Dawn's god is now calling the shots. Whoever Oolvaan Mutual's god was, he or she or whatever has clearly suffered a significant reverse." Part of the whole idea behind sponsoring a bank, if you were a god, was to lend it the weight of your own position and stability, so flopping sides and selling out depositors would be an excellent way to undermine your own credibility.

"They do say, 'Getting stuck with the gods is a one-way street,' " said Julio. "This mess would certainly seem to bear that out."

"Max will never let me live this down," Groot muttered. Once you were hooked up with a god, you were also gaffed onto whatever plots and intrigues the god was puttering around with. The downside risk that people who trafficked with the gods didn't usually consider, a risk which was considerable, was the danger of being caught up in the god's reverses. On the face of it, that was what had happened here. "Even if this story is true, we certainly don't know the part of real importance."

"You discount the rationale and motivations this banker set out?"

"Of course I do," said Groot, "and so do you, or you're not the Julio I know, but some cunning impostor."

Julio's sly smile appeared and vanished, the smile customers and most others never got the slightest hint of. When someone saw that expression for the first time, and the transformation it brought to Julio's entire face, they generally were forced into a reappraisal not only of Julio's capabilities, which had appeared competent but dull, and his sense of humor, which had appeared to be totally nonexistent, but of every transaction they had had with him in the past. "Indeed," Julio said. "I have been thinking along the same lines as you, I believe. Someone, presumably whoever is behind this new bank, wants to immobilize our operations, if not destroy them outright, and strip you of the ability to mount an active response, but all that could be a case of two birds with one stone. Do you think they're after the ship? Not only has Sy Gazoont disappeared, but I may not have mentioned that the public communicator has had his civic commission temporarily suspended as well."

"You didn't," said Groot, "but that's a move to expect, isn't it, whether they were after one ship in particular or just the fleet assets; if we are prevented from communicating with our assets in the field, we can't tell them to take evasive action. Still, I find this a suggestive move. Even if the *Profit* is only one reason among many, it is not beyond the bounds of plausibility that the *Profit* and its passengers may have something to do with the timing of this move. You said the police operations seemed disorganized, as though they'd been rushed into execution? The *Profit* is due to arrive within the next two days, ahead of schedule—that could have forced their hand prematurely."

"You would think, though, that leaving us confused

about what is going on could serve someone's aims even more. Why would the New Dawn bank bother to send this person with an explanation?"

"You would think that," Groot said, "wouldn't you? An attempt at deliberate misdirection? Perhaps our mysterious friends were merely flaunting their control of the situation, or thumbing their noses. A test to see how well we can respond to unexpected attacks? A throwing-down of a gauntlet? Or perhaps, and most likely of all, a combination. . . ." That was the way Groot would do it; there was no point in wasting three moves when they could be packaged into one. Was his opponent a player of games, or was there even a single opponent? And which was the central part of the move, here? "So who do you think would want me on ice most of all?" he said rhetorically.

Julio coughed discreetly. "Perhaps Meester Dooglas was recalling the incident concerning the *Pecuniary Interest. . . .*"

"That has been on my mind as I rot here," Groot admitted. "He's been trying to get me for that ever since." The *Pecuniary Interest,* at that time known as the *Dooglas Cloud,* had lost her mainmast and a third of her crew overboard in bad weather as she was returning, holds packed, from a voyage to Cematrilla. Groot's flagship clipper *Raging Torrent,* which had been running touch-and-go with the *Cloud* throughout the expedition, had escaped damage during the storm. With the *Cloud* about to go to wreck on a shoal and her crew loosing the lifeboats, the *Torrent* had appeared, offering rescue, and when the dust had settled the quickly renamed *Cloud* and its cargo and most of its thankful crew had ended up on the Haalsen balance sheets. It hadn't been the first skirmish between Dooglas and Groot, but it had been the kind of watershed event that shapes a relationship indefinitely into the future. "He's never been this blatant before," Groot remarked, "which means if it's him it may not be him alone; he'd have to have accumulated enough power or leverage to feel confident of pulling off a stunt like this and successfully holding off the counterattack. You did try finding out what Dooglas has been up to, I presume?"

"Of course," said Julio. "No one seems to have seen him for the last week or so, and nothing out of the ordinary seemed to be going on back then. I haven't actually knocked on his door, you understand, but I've gotten the impression that he's holed up there working on something. I left Eelmon to watch his house."

Groot lowered his voice; he had a feeling the jailer was lurking about outside the cell again. "Have you recovered the emergency stash?"

Julio actually glanced over his shoulder before responding. "The obvious one. If I was followed, so much the better. They would be expecting me to start dipping into any secret resources since everything else is frozen. I've been making a show of abruptly darting down alleys as though I'm retrieving things hidden down them, and so forth; hopefully they'll try to search them all."

"Good," Groot said, returning the pitch of his speech to normal. "As far as I know, Dooglas doesn't have particularly close ties to any gods, or at least he didn't. Let's presume for the moment that he *has* fallen in with someone new, either under his own power or because he's been recruited."

"If Meester Dooglas has been recruited, that would imply that this unknown one's agenda would be the prime motivator here," Julio mused. "That would hold even if Meester Dooglas was the one to shape the precise form of this stratagem."

"Yes," Groot said. "Even though it *is* so blatant, it would be just like Dooglas to have me thrown gratuitously in jail for the sheer annoyance, especially if he thought he could get away with it." The best way to accomplish *that* would be to have backers of unimpeachable deterrent value. If you looked at it from one school of thought, the most elegant thing to do would be to strike directly at whoever this backer was and ignore any middlemen. On the other hand, a different school might stress the indirect approach, moving first against pawns in a menacing pattern, undermining the kingpin, and then abruptly pulling the rug out from under the central figures with a neat flourish. Schools aside, though, the reality of the situation was that Groot had to think of himself first and foremost as in a state of "check."

"When your king is in check and your king happens to be yourself." Groot commented, "the most appropriate thing is to get yourself *out* of that position, and try to pick up elegance by inserting an appropriate countermenace as part of the move."

"As you say, sir," said Julio, long accustomed to apparent non sequiturs from Meester Groot. Groot had a tendency to think things through rapidly in his mind, revealing by his subsequent words that he had reappeared in an entirely different spot, with no obvious clue to the route he had taken between points A and B. Things usually made sense eventually, though, and Julio knew well enough how Groot's thought processes worked to make the jumps with him more often than not. Even when he didn't, he liked to keep Groot guessing. His voice was low again. "They will be expecting you to try *something*, no matter how well they think you've been outmaneuvered. With the remark you said the banker delivered about your reputation for action, perhaps they are expecting you to try to escape."

"Thus rendering me a free fugitive instead of a caged potential martyr," said Groot. His voice was loud, and seemed to carry deliberately. "Nevertheless, freedom is freedom, and I've never been fond of dungeons. You said Sy hasn't popped up yet?"

"No, he hasn't." Julio, with a raised eyebrow, was matching Groot's vocal projection. "You know I've never entirely trusted him."

"There's nothing to be done about it now," Groot said, "except try to find out what role he's played. I doubt there is even much left for us to do in the way of damage control, wouldn't you say? What's done is done. You're right, though—we must look to the future. What about that barbarian fellow? Now that he's back on his feet I have something for him to do. Before the barbarian, though, the first thing you do is hunt up a chemist."

7
THE SCENIC ROUTE

''Haven't spent much time on a horse, have you?''

''Urr,'' growled Jurtan Mont. Max had been acting disgustingly chipper ever since they'd left Roosing Oolvaya. Jurtan couldn't believe Max was actually much more comfortable than he was, except for obviously knowing his way around horses. Of course, the way Jurtan had been feeling, that difference alone could amount to quite a lot.

''Look at it this way,'' Max said. The small farming community they'd passed through earlier in the morning had finally slipped back into the gentle hills behind them, and they had now traveled beyond the range of cultivated fields. Prairie grasses that reached in places higher than their shoulders surrounded them on all sides but the rear, where their passage had trampled out a trail. Long slow waves rippled across the surface in the small breeze. ''Being saddlesore is commonplace. Any out-of-shape body's going to feel like it's lost a fight with a determined elephant after sitting on a horse all day, at least for the first few days. You did want to be an individual, didn't you? Well, concentrate on rising above your body, think about what makes you different.''

''I wish you wouldn't gloat,'' Jurtan mumbled.

''Who's gloating? I'm trying to help you be philosophical.''

''You sound like my father.''

''Really?'' Max said thoughtfully. ''Maybe that means I'm doing this right.''

''Urr,'' said Jurtan. All they'd been doing for days was

plod across the countryside. Oh, all right, there had been a few moments of activity that had started to look more interesting than that, but none of them had lasted. Before leaving Roosing Oolvaya, they'd checked out the haunts of the guy with no name, the Creeping Sword. Max had sniffed around the Sword's office waving his hands in strange patterns and mumbling to himself; he'd said he was running tests. "*Something* went on here," he'd stated finally. "There're still emanations leaking back off the walls."

"What," Jurtan had asked, "like a duel? Did he get blasted?"

Max scrutinized a patch of plaster near the door. "Whatever it was didn't escalate that far. I think."

Oh, don't you know? Jurtan had thought. *You're supposed to be such a big hotshot.* He didn't say this aloud, though.

"I'm sure he wasn't pulverized," Max went on; Jurtan thought he might have been thinking out loud. "Even getting ground into dust always leaves some residue." Max's nose twitched. "Why was he tangling with god-level stuff? How'd he hold it off?"

"Maybe he just talked his way out of it."

"Yeah," said Max. "Maybe." And that had been the last he'd said on the subject.

The next event that had been marginally more interesting than bouncing up and down out of synchrony with his horse had come the first night out, when they were camped out under a tree set off by a ditch from the side of the road. Max had proposed to put Jurtan through some paces with a rapier but Jurtan was already feeling too bent out of alignment, between the bruises, the flayed-raw patches, and the muscles going stiff as iron torture rods, to do more than lie flat on the ground on his back. At that point Jurtan had had no idea of the stretching-out routine Max was going to inflict on him first thing in the morning, *every* morning. It clearly wouldn't have helped if Jurtan *had* known, he realized, since he was in no shape either to sneak away from Max or to resist him while he was around. If he had known what to expect in the morning, he might have forced himself to go to sleep faster so as not to lose out on his rest from both ends; another thing he had yet to appreciate was that "morning" for Max meant the predawn gloom, at least while he was on the road. On balance, though, Jurtan was happy he hadn't realized any of this that first night. It wasn't that he thought the state of ignorance was desirable. Rather, if he had nodded off promptly he would have missed Max's activity when he thought Jurtan *had* been asleep.

Jurtan had been resting there, his eyes closed, listening to the insects harmonize with the constant background accompaniment of the sourceless music in his head. Ever since Jurtan had discovered that he could actually channel the music, sometimes, through teeth-clenching concentration, he had been working on increasing his control. There was no question that the frequency of his contrapuntal seizures had been declining as a result. Now, he often could react without full awareness of it, almost as a reflex, and before he had felt more than a slight fuzziness around the corners of his vision or a distant roar in his ears; he hadn't totally lost consciousness or fallen over in at least two weeks. The steady clip-clopping rhythm of his horse alone would have once kept him in a perpetual stupor. Jurtan had also gotten better at pushing the music into the background where it wouldn't distract him or overwhelm his thoughts on a constant basis, the way it had done before. Still, when the music wanted to draw his attention to something, it wasn't shy about making itself felt. As Jurtan rested under the tree and the stars, doing a much better imitation of a stone sarcophagus than of a limber human, he thought afterward he might even have been dozing, when a slyly insistent clatter of castanets brought his eyes open.

In the light of the big moon he could see the horses napping on their feet in the same places they'd occupied when he'd settled down. Max's bedroll, though, was empty. Jurtan raised his head. There, in the line of trees over by the stream . . . but who was Max talking to? All he could see were two vague silhouettes outlined against the moonlit shimmer of the birches. Well, it was none of his business.

Or was it? If Max was plotting with somebody to get them both in danger, that concerned Jurtan, sure enough. He creaked his way off the ground up into a crouch and headed for the stream. An attitude of care and stealth, Jurtan thought, as grass and shrubbery crunched beneath his feet, that was the ticket. As he got closer, he realized that Max's companion had a slight internal glow, sort of a will-o'-the-wisp effect, and that through his body he could vaguely see the birch behind him. The low babble of their voices was barely distinguishable from that of the brook. Gradually, though, Jurtan began to make out more than just a combination of liquid murmurs.

". . . about Shaa?"

"I've been thinking about trying to slide something past the Curse Administrator," Max said. "Try to get it annulled or superseded or even just lost."

"Tricky," said the other form. "Not to mention chancy. I wouldn't, if it were me. Jardin has . . . more active. You may want to wait until we can better see what he's up to."

". . ."

Any closer and Jurtan *knew* Max would hear him. He had the feeling they were starting to wrap up anyway. Jurtan eased gingerly back toward the campsite, trying to keep from casting too many glances over his shoulder in the direction of the stream. Just short of his bedroll, he checked behind him again. The second figure was gone—he'd had a quick impression of something like a sheet shaking itself out where the other had been, but it must have been his imagination; there was clearly nothing there but rocks and trees.

Max had said nothing the next day to indicate he knew Jurtan had been eavesdropping, but still Jurtan wondered. Jurtan had learned enough from Shaa not to want to be caught underestimating Max. If Max knew, though, why wasn't he accusing him? Maybe he didn't care. Or perhaps he didn't want to risk giving Jurtan enough leverage to get him to reveal who the other one had been, and what the two of them were discussing, by bringing the issue out in the open.

Jurtan had tried to file it away and forget it.

The only other episode of note had come the night after that. Max had been interrogating him about the symptoms of his music disorder. Jurtan had been through most of this already with Shaa and he'd said as much. "Since it's my problem at the moment, not Shaa's," Max had told him, "I want to know I have the facts straight."

"It's my problem, too, and it's going to stay my problem whether you or Shaa are around or not." Jurtan had gotten testier as the day went on and his blisters continued to break. In the middle of the afternoon he'd also been stung by a bee. Considering the state he was in, he didn't really care at that moment what nasty thing Max would say back at him.

Not for the first time, Max took him by surprise. He had one eye closed and was looking up into the air with the other one while he chewed on the corner of his lower lip. "Why didn't I think of this before?" he announced.

"Think of what?" Jurtan said nervously.

"Hold still." Max sank down next to him and placed the outspread fingers of his left hand over Jurtan's forehead, the thumb in front of his ear and the middle finger at the crown of his head. Something crackled between Max's fingertips and Jurtan's skin. "Don't move! Are you hearing music now?"

"Uh, yes." At the top of his vision, green curlicues were dancing. "Are you, uh, trying to read my mind?"

"Close your eyes. That's better. No, full telepathy's a pretty big deal; not my specialty either. Gotta match the impedances—huh!"

"What?"

"Can you make it louder? Yeah!—like a clarinet on top of a bunch of brass, is that what you're hearing?"

"You mean you can hear it, too?"

"That's not bad," Max said appraisingly. "You could dance to that."

Jurtan jerked his head back. With a <snap-snap-snap> and a peppering of small shocks Max lost his contact. "Ow!" said Jurtan, rubbing his forehead. "You going to tell me what you were doing there?"

Max scowled at him. He was shaking his hand as though he'd just pulled it back from a hot oven. "An experiment, what did you think? It was getting somewhere, too, until you ruptured the interface."

"Where was it getting? Into my thoughts?"

"I told you this wasn't telepathy, didn't I? No. I was just trying to listen in."

"On my thoughts!"

Max snorted. "No, not your *thoughts,* that's what I keep trying to tell you. I don't know what the hell is going on in that head of yours, but I've never heard of anything like it before. I don't think anyone could read your mind if they had the power of a volcano. All they'd hear is that music."

The sound of slurping cut through Jurtan's musings on the recent past. He looked down. The earth the horse was stepping into was moist; it placed its hoof again and water oozed out over it as though the beast had stamped on a sponge. "Max?" Jurtan said.

Jurtan had noted that the plain had been trending generally downward as they rode west and, Max had said, rather south. Now, Max had reined up in front of him ahead of a tongue of shallow, stagnant water broken with clumps of protruding grass and low mounds of earth. The grass had turned as much yellow as green in color; overall an unhealthy-looking tone. Jurtan had an uncomfortable feeling the stalks might glow in the dark. A smell of decayed vegetables tickled the air. There were bugs, too. Max swung himself off the horse and strolled toward the edge of the water, stretching his back, his feet making squelching sounds in the soggy earth, gazing off across the water where a maze of sluggish channels began. "There," said Max.

"There, what?" said Mont. "We're looking at a swamp, that's what's there."

"I think it's more of a bog," Max said, eyeing the terrain in a professional manner, "although you might go so far as to call it a marsh."

"What does it matter what you call it? It's wet, isn't it, and the parts that aren't totally wet are spongy." An unpleasant thought had seized him. "You don't really plan to go *in* there, do you?"

"Why do you think we went out of our way to be here

in the first place? Somewhere in there may be something we've come to find."

Find? "I thought we were going to Peridol for the Knitting, I didn't think we were out to 'find' anything."

"Shows what you know, doesn't it?" said Max. He had been probing the ground with the toe of his boot. Now, finding the surface of a low ridge that extended some way out into the water to be marginally more solid than the muck as a whole, he took first one and then another tentative step out along it, his horse reluctantly following. On his third step, the sole of his foot continued down through the surface. Mud sloshed over the top of his boot.

"That's disgusting," Jurtan said.

"Of course it's disgusting. It's a swamp."

Mont had to admit that Max didn't look terribly pleased by the prospect of sloshing through the ooze. "If you're so dead-set on going in there, why not use a boat? Why not use magic? For all we know, this stuff could go all the way to the coast."

"For all *you* know," Max muttered. "As far as *I* know, it's not that far. If this was regular ground, we'd be across it in a day."

"Have you been here before?"

"I had a reliable informant. You want to use a boat, *find* a boat."

"We could build a raft."

"I'd love to build a raft. You want to tell me where you're going to find wood?"

Mont looked around. The gentle rolling plain they'd followed to the edge of the swamp had been covered only with waving wild grain and the occasional low shrub. They'd seen a few stands of trees, true, but the last one had been an hour's ride back, and nothing came to sight now as he scanned the horizon. He turned back to the water, eyed the mud with a resigned glance, flopped off his own horse, and stepped after Max. Then Jurtan realized he was wrong. There *were* some trees in sight, twisted gnarly things though they were. The problem with them was that they were deeper into the swamp. Well, it might be better than nothing; they weren't *that* much deeper. "What about those trees?" he said. "Could we make a raft out of them?"

"Which trees? The ones we're heading toward?"

"Oh," said Mont. "You mean you've been planning all along to check out those trees and maybe use them to build a raft, only you wanted to be sure to rub in again how dumb I am not to have understood it, right?"

"Now, would I do something like that?" Max said distractedly.

"Well, okay, but what about magic, then? Is that what I'm really supposed to ask? I know you said it's usually more efficient to rely on physical means, but if it's not that large a swamp anyway—"

A large bubble burst on the surface of the water to Jurtan's left, releasing the rank smell of spoiled eggs. Jurtan's horse knocked him in the back with its head; Jurtan wished he knew how to tell it how much he agreed with its assessment. Max had paused just ahead and was looking around with an appraising manner. He sniffed the air. Jurtan had seen him do this before, usually when there wasn't anything worth smelling that *he* could detect, and so he had the general idea that what Max was trying to sense was not necessarily a physical aroma.

Max looked around again, then spoke in a low voice. "I've got reason to believe magic won't work right in this area, and even if it did it probably wouldn't be a good idea to try it. If the reports I got are right, a guy named Iskendarian used to work here."

"In a swamp?"

"He *built* the swamp. He was a very clever guy, very clever indeed."

"'Was'? Is he dead?"

"That's what they say. He hasn't been around in a half-century or so, at least not so anyone's been able to find him, and he'd probably be a hundred fifty or two hundred years old by now anyway. Still, most likely it's not a relevant question. For a sorcerer like Iskendarian, death can be a matter of degree."

"You can be *sort of* dead?"

Max turned and again began gingerly picking his way

deeper into the swamp. "Let's just say there's a continuum between sleep and total loss-of-consciousness death. Even if he *is* absolutely dead, I may still be able to get some information out of him. If he's even here."

"This sure isn't a place *I'd* want to be dead in," Mont muttered, pulling one foot free of a particularly clinging patch of ooze with a mushy slurp. "What's this Iskendarian guy have that you want, anyway?"

"Knowledge," Max said. "Maybe answers. That spell of Namelessness the Sword's wearing, for one."

"You're not thinking Iskendarian himself cast the spell on the Sword, are you? Could Iskendarian cast spells while he's dead? Is death *that* relative?"

Max grimaced. "I don't know, but I think it might be better if I did, don't you? The Sword's Spell has certain hallmarks of Iskendarian's style. There's actually another question I'd be even more interested in getting an answer to. If Iskendarian did have anything to do with this spell—a prospect I seriously doubt, mind you, but it's always important to keep an open mind—well, the question is why would he bother? When you're dead, you don't get out much. How would he have even met the Sword? Nobody's seen Iskendarian for longer than the Sword's been alive."

"You don't know where the Sword came from," said Mont. "How do you know how old *he* really is?"

Max stopped, both legs submerged to mid-hip in the midst of a pair of widening ripples, and looked thoughtfully over his shoulder at Mont, one eyebrow raised. Then he nodded once, slowly, his lips screwed up on one side in absent concentration. "Nevertheless," Max said, "Iskendarian probably doesn't have anything to do with it. Someone may have gotten hold of his notes, though, or if he was hard up enough he might have actually taught somebody the technique. Even if the spell's got nothing to do with Iskendarian, his own formula might suggest a generic mechanism that could be used to undo it. And anyway I was planning to stop off here sometime regardless of the Namelessness thing. Iskendarian planted a reasonable portion of the foundations of modern magic;

by all accounts, he is—or was—a remarkably tricky guy, so there may very well be something around worth learning from. And as long as we were headed in the right direction . . .'' He shrugged and turned back to the slow struggle toward the gradually approaching trees.

Jurtan looked at the swamp, his mind picking out rough chords for him on what sounded like a banjo. He had heard from Shaa that ruins and pre-Dislocation rumors drew Max like a dehydrated sponge drew water. Jurtan had held out what he had suspected was the forlorn hope that he wouldn't have to get too much direct knowledge of Max's peculiarities through personal experience. Shaa—suddenly Jurtan put together something Max hadn't exactly come right out and said in words. Max had implied that Iskendarian might be a master of longevity or even rejuvenation; that would have been the most natural way for him to be walking around causing trouble at an age approaching two hundred. And Shaa was certainly in need of some significant rejuvenation of his own.

Behind Jurtan, his horse was muttering again. ''Is it a good idea to be taking horses into this stuff?'' Jurtan asked. ''Mine doesn't seem to like it.''

''It's not great,'' agreed Max. ''Unfortunately, we don't have much choice. We should be coming out on the other side, for one thing, and for another if we left them here we'd never see them again.''

''But if they sink out of sight into this stuff, we'll never see them again either.''

''That's true enough. What would you do?''

Jurtan looked back at his horse. It was mucking along, probably moping a bit, but aside from the occasional snort it wasn't breathing particularly hard. One brown eye caught his with a disgruntled expression. The horse wasn't quite fed up yet, though. ''How about this,'' Jurtan suggested. ''We make it to the trees. If we can get a good enough raft out of them, we try to take the horses with us. If we can't, we let them decide. It looks like they're game if we are.''

Max took another step and disappeared beneath the surface. After a moment he thrashed back up, his hair drooping over his head as though he'd picked up a drowned muskrat for a toupee. He spit out a mouthful of water. "Game," he said. "Right. Some game."

They sloshed and floundered their way ahead, the trees beckoning them on. Max reached the grove first, having gained even more ground on Jurtan, who had been wasting a lot of his energy swinging at mosquitoes, and climbed out onto a low hillock barely awash with water. "Huh," said Max.

"What is it? Is there something wrong with the trees?"

"Forget the trees," Max said. His horse followed him onto the mound and in among the trees, and then the two of them began to drop down out of sight. Jurtan thrashed forward more vigorously and finally struggled out onto the ridge himself. The additional height let him see over the front side of the hillock and its marsh grass and down into a clear-water channel a short distance back, where Max was examining a flat bargelike boat. A mostly-decayed net of woven reeds had been thrown back onto the bank. "It looks old," said Max, "but solid."

"Whose do you think it is?"

"I wouldn't be surprised if it was Iskendarian's. At the moment, though, I'd say it's ours."

No one else arrived to question that presumption. After Max had checked the boat for traps and judged it clean, they managed to coax the horses on board by having them step straight off the bank. Although the boat rocked alarmingly and shipped water over its low gunwales, it showed no serious signs of becoming unbalanced. The attitude of the horses was not remarkably improved by the move from muck to boat. Once they were tied down and the boat had stopped lurching from side to side, however, their nervous whickering began to quiet.

The boat was really more of a raft with what amounted to a small fence around its outside edge. With the four of them on board it proved crowded. It had gotten them out of the bottom ooze, though, and when Max and Jurtan set to work with the poles they had found lashed to the deck, they discovered a similar improvement in their speed over slurping through the goop. A maze of sluggish channels among the twisted trees led them farther into the swamp.

Around the middle of the afternoon, they negotiated another hairpin turn in the channel, got hung up for a moment in the roots of one of the tentacular mangroves, as Max had taken to calling them, and then emerged into an area of relatively open water. The swamp grasses were the thickest here that they'd encountered, the height of their stalks rising toward the center of the lagoon until they were at least as tall as the tops of the mangroves. Max poled the raft toward the spot where the grass seemed most luxuriant. The grass bent reluctantly before them, occasionally lashing back with a small slap. Their sight of the landscape, such as it was, was quickly lost behind the ascending wall of weeds. Several vessel lengths farther along, though, the bottom of the barge grated along a concealed obstacle and then ground to a complete halt, the bow canted slightly upward.

The grasses had not after all mutated to ascend to gigantic heights but were planted on a low island, its surface barely out of the water. "This looks like the place," Max said.

"There's no castle here," said Mont. "There's not even a hut."

"I'll grant you it is a little surprising not to find *anything*," Max mused. "Maybe there *is* something here that we're not seeing. It could have decayed, I suppose, or gotten blown away. Or maybe there *was* something here, but it's moved." He looked suddenly thoughtful.

"You mean, like Karlini's castle? Or do you think this is where Karlini's castle actually came from?"

Max continued looking around and peering over the top of the grass line, now brought closer to his own tiptoe height since he was standing on the island. "No, I don't, actually, but it's an interesting possibility."

A more practical consideration abruptly suggested itself to Jurtan. "It's going to be getting dark pretty soon. Are we gonna spend the night here?"

"Do you have a better suggestion?"

"I knew you were going to say something like that,"

Jurtan said with resignation. "Should we let the horses out?"

They let the horses out. As the horses tried snacking on the marsh grass, dubious expressions prominently displayed, Max and Jurtan spread out to examine the small island. Jurtan headed for the center. He was heartily sick of stepping into muck and goo and so was keeping his eyes primarily on his feet and the ground around them. Still, there were enough of the tall plants around interfering with his view that at first he didn't realize what he had walked onto when he felt something crunch beneath his foot. He bent down to inspect the ground. A small beaked skull extended just beyond the toe of his boot, and the bones of a foot-long wing were outspread on either side of his heel. "Max," he said.

On his way back over toward Mont's position from the far side of the island, Max turned up half-a-dozen birds of his own in various states of disrepair. Jurtan had found a few more himself. "Why only birds?" he said. "If there's something around here that's poisonous or something, why does it only affect birds?"

"Maybe something drives ground-huggers away that birds are too dumb to notice," Max said. "What about you? Is that music of yours giving you any hints?"

Jurtan's ears had been treating him to an increasingly expectant blare of horns underlined by a rapid-paced marching beat from a kettle drum. "It thinks this place has something going on, all right."

The sun took that moment to ease below the horizon and the sudden gloom leapt out at them. "What's that other squeaking sound?" Jurtan asked. "Real high-pitched and faint?"

"I can't hear it myself," said Max, "because my hearing doesn't go that high any more, but I'd suspect it's the bats. You catch that other noise, like a few sheets of dry old paper flapping? Bat wings. I'm surprised you can hear them squeaking over the gurgling of the swamp."

The sky overhead was still reasonably bright. Max looked up into it with suddenly narrowed eyes, at the increasing clouds of bats swooping and twirling after the mosquitoes. About time somebody showed up to take care of the bugs, too. He thought about the birds. Some of those dead birds had had broken skulls, as though they'd flown headfirst into something they couldn't see. But bats . . .

"Why are they doing that?" Mont said. "The bats. I can see them kind of flopping by overhead there, but there's sort of a round place where they don't seem to go, right over the middle of the island."

The sky and the first few stars shone clearly through the area the bats were avoiding, but avoiding it they were. "The birds can't see it, but the bats can," Max said. "That's it, up there." That was whatever they had come for, suspended in the air and concealed inside a refraction zone.

8
NEWS ON THE RIVER

"Nothing new, eh?"

The Great Karlini looked up from the reference book perched open on his lap. Above the book and a comfortable distance in front of his face, in his favorite individual work-space, sat a three-dimensional matrix of colored crystalline beads, all in shades of green and blue. "Not a thing," said Karlini. "Did you bring that sandwich you mentioned?"

"I did indeed," Shaa replied, producing the snack from behind his back and uncovering it on its plate with a flourish of napkin. "I brought more tea, too," he added, moving the plate to reveal the small pitcher on which it had been balanced as well.

Karlini, still eyeing his work, picked up a neatly sliced sandwich half and took a bite. Then he pulled the sandwich away from his face and stared at it warily. "What is in this thing?"

"The main framework, I believe, is one of those onion-wheat rolls we took on in Roosing Oolvaya," Shaa said, poking at the remaining half with his finger. "The two principal internal constituent components are the river anchovies, fresh, and the chopped tomato-and-lettuce mixture, although I did take the liberty of adding some of that mashed egg-white batter stuff you like. Also, a lengthwise-sliced pickle."

"Mayonnaise," Karlini said, taking another tentative bite. "That's what Max said it's called. He found the recipe in some old scrap he was translating; turned out to be a cookbook or some kind of wrapper for a food container, I think, instead of an instruction manual. You sure there's nothing fishy besides the anchovies?''

''Reasonably certain,'' Shaa said. He went so far as to ease the top of the roll back to reinspect the contents. ''Why, don't you like it?''

''What's not to like? I just wanted to make sure nothing got transubstantiated on your way down from the kitchen.''

''It does pay to be prudent,'' agreed Shaa. ''Were you expecting something of the sort? In my experience, fish have much less of a tendency to mutate once they've landed on a plate.''

''We've already had one water-related manifestation,'' Karlini remarked with a munch. ''I thought it would be a good idea to keep a weather eye peeled for any more, don't you think?''

''I take it, then, that you're speaking from intuition and not because you've actually come up with something?''

Karlini took a swig of iced tea. ''Is it my imagination or has your mood perked up?''

''I'm always happiest when some force I don't know is trying to demolish me.''

''We still don't know for sure that anything's really happening,'' Karlini said cautiously.

''An omen, then,'' said Shaa. ''An *ambiguous* omen, if you'd rather. A sign is still a sign; whichever way you slice it, it isn't every day the lower stretch of the River Oolvaan decides to throw icebergs at you. You haven't detected a hand behind it, then? Or The Hand, I suppose, for that matter.''

''No hands, no arms, no appendages of any sort.''

''Well, that is what we expected,'' reflected Shaa. ''Any more thoughts about just mooring in the river and sending a scout down ahead in the skiff, or even overland?''

''Still sounds like overkill to me.''

''Hmm,'' Shaa said. ''I agree. Among the lot of us there shouldn't be much we can't handle. However, one does like to stack the deck.''

''It probably wasn't an omen at all,'' Karlini reasoned,

"and it probably wasn't an attack either, and even if it was it probably wasn't directed at us."

"It certainly seemed like an attack at the time. What are you trying to do, spoil all the fun? As much fun as one can get from anticipating calamity, that is."

"You *are* in a good mood, aren't you."

"I'm always in a good mood," Shaa stated. "My family is known for our equal temperament. Since you haven't found out anything about the ice-apparition itself, I presume you've been gathering intelligence about doings in Oolsmouth? It would appear prudent to do *that,* at least, as long as the intelligence collection has a reasonable overhead of its own. Judicious employment of that aerial surveillance probe of yours, perhaps?"

Karlini squinted at Shaa across the top of the remaining section of sandwich, a protruding anchovy drooping tailfirst down past his cheek. "You haven't been peeking in at me from the hall, have you?"

With a theatrical flourish, Shaa shielded his eyes with one hand. "By your answer, I take it that you have, in fact, been operating said probe in the vicinity of Oolsmouth. I will further predict that you found things to be perfectly normal. Shall I proceed to my next feat?"

"No," Karlini said sourly, "that one's quite enough, thank you. Why did I even bother to take the time in the first place if you already knew what I was going to find?"

"Well, it *is* axiomatic that aerial reconnaissance is most useful after a natural disaster, or from our point of view an unnatural one, or when one happens to be looking for an army lost somewhere in the woods, say. It takes a lot to disrupt the normal functioning of a city to an extent to where it's visible from the air. On the other hand, getting down to the person-to-person level is tedious and time-consuming, chews up energy, and leaves one open to counterforce retaliation by anti-scrutiny countermeasure shields. You are good at this, I know, and you've spent a lot of time and effort on it as well, so don't feel I'm being critical; not in the least. The world just imposes certain constraints. As you know perfectly well. You knew as well as I what your effort would probably yield."

"Yes," said Karlini, "well. I tried to locate Groot, but he's not to be found. His house and warehouses are locked up, *and* under guard, too. And before you tell me, yes, I checked the prisons, but they're search-screened as a matter of routine, so, all right, yes, I was just being thorough."

"Isn't there some way of getting hold of Groot or his people directly?" Shaa said, looking thoughtfully at the beams of the low ceiling. "Doesn't he have some kind of magician on his staff?"

"I think he does. In fact, I know he does. One of the usual mercantile specialists keeps in touch with his trading parties and ships and all those far-flung kind of things."

"Ships?"

They adjourned from Karlini's workroom, which also served as a sail-locker, and proceeded toward the bridge. While they were making their way across the main deck through the maze of lashed-down trade goods, Tildamire suddenly appeared from behind the mainmast, an exercise book in hand. "Hi," she said. "You guys come up with anything good yet?"

"Are you deliberately dogging my steps," Shaa grumbled, "or is this constant serendipity the pure result of a malign fate?" He held up his hand. "No, don't tell me; mystery is an endangered resource as it is. Dog away, if you must."

Not that she needed encouragement, thought Shaa. Perhaps if he threatened to deliver a lecture she would go away. "We are hoping to contact Groot's communications mediator," he added.

"That sounds interesting," Tildy said cautiously.

"Actually, it's not," said Shaa. "Communications mediator is a fairly tedious job and not without its wearing aspects, since many things can interfere with messages and focusing them becomes much harder the farther they have to go; the usual radiative inverse-square laws apply here. Like most other spellwork, the throughput is low because you usually need to rest up for awhile after significant communicating. It's a specialized skill requiring a lot of higher math. There's also the problem of contacting the communicator, since his or her expertise is designed around contacting *you.* You see? Not flashy at all."

Karlini preceded them up onto the quarterdeck, where the captain was staring with a sage seaman's expression down the river ahead of the ship. River traffic had been picking up over the past few hours, indicating (if any of them were in doubt) that they were fast approaching the Oolsmouth district. "A key?" the captain said, echoing Karlini's question. "Aye, a key I've got, and a key I've been using, too. Waste of time it's been. Gazoont, that's his name, Meester Groot's facilitator; not a clever sort like your lot, don't you know, but he's been regular enough in the past."

Karlini exchanged a "hmm" with Shaa. Tildamire appeared on the verge of joining them, but after a glance at Shaa she thought better of it. "We could give him the benefit of the doubt and say he's on vacation," suggested Karlini.

"Too much coincidence," Shaa said to Tildy. "Far too much."

"I'm inclined to agree with you, Dr. Shaa," the captain stated. "I don't know whether this Gazoont fellow is dead, or whether he's left Meester Groot's service, or what-all else might be afoot—"

"Communications could be jammed at the source," Karlini said dubiously, "although I didn't pick up the kind of hash in the carrier medium you expect with that."

"Next you'll be talking about atmospheric conditions being inconclusive," said Shaa. "Which is to say, it's all smoke. The important fact is that Gazoont is not answering. I find that unhappily suggestive. I would treat it as a priority to get some hard news about what is awaiting us up ahead."

"Perhaps you don't have long to wait," said the captain. He gestured with his pipe, pointing the stem out beyond the port bow. A barge was floating upriver toward them, taking advantage through its sail of the breeze at its back. "Outbound from Oolsmouth within the last day," he added. "She'll come within hailing distance in a moment."

"What was that key stuff you were talking about?" Tildy asked Shaa in a low voice.

Shaa crossed his arms and leaned on the rail guarding the drop from bridge to main deck. "If you need to contact a communicator, you generally have to have their address, which is to say their aura recognition pattern. The communicator can publish this address by imprinting it on some small object, the 'key,' which for the sake of convenience is usually a token of some sort. Creation of a usable key isn't easy, so a particular communicator usually doesn't produce too many of them. They can be fairly dangerous in the wrong hands, too, since releasing a key detailed enough for someone to contact you with can also let a properly trained person locate you in return, or even mount his own attack; this is another reason that not too many folks become communicators. Captain, does Oolsmouth have a public communicator that you know of?"

The captain cocked his head to one side, while still watching the approach of the barge. "Might be one at the Hall of the People, but if I don't mistake my own memory she works for the politicians, not free-lance or for hire. I do have to say I never did trust that Gazoont fellow. Nothing you could put your thumb on, mind you, but you'll be knowing how it is."

"Communicators do have guild associations to think of," commented Shaa, "and the endorsement of the guild requires an upstanding record of appropriate loyalty and honorable behavior, but when it comes right down to it I suppose they're as much subject to bribes or suborning as anyone else."

Cupping his hands around his mouth, the captain took aim at the barge and let loose with tremendous volume. "Ahoy, *Pilodar!*"

A much fainter reply came back. "Ahoy, *Profit!* Have you heard you're under new ownership?"

"What was that? New ownership, did you say?"

"Aye, most likely! You're a ship of Groot's, aren't you?"

"Aye, that we are!"

"Groot's run hard aground!" said the man on the *Pilodar.*

The barge was close enough now for the captain to quit flaying his larynx. Shaa tentatively released the muffling palm he was holding over his ear. "On what shoal?" called Captain Luff.

"The Powers-that-Be," the *Pilodar* said ominously.

Captain Luff exchanged a glance with Karlini and Shaa. Shaa shrugged. "I thought Groot *was* one of the powers-that-be," he said.

"Aye," said the captain. He cupped his hands again. "What more can you tell us?"

"It be wiser not to be discussing it at all!"

"Captain Moore, is it? When we're in port together, I'll stand you a round!"

The two captains exchanged pleasantries, but soon the ships had begun to draw apart and there was clearly nothing to be gained by continuing. "The *Pile-o'-Dough,* that's what she's called on the river," the captain said, watching the barge retreat.

"The contrast between the high-technology of modern sorcery and the low-tech ways of the world is always remarkable, don't you think?" said Shaa. "On the other hand, hollering back and forth may be crude, but there's no denying it works."

"Just because I couldn't find out what was happening is no reason to—" Karlini began.

"Just so you know," Shaa told him, "I am not pleased to find my earlier vague suspicions confirmed."

"There's deviltry afoot, sure enough," said Captain Luff.

"Aye, there is," agreed Shaa. "Perhaps we should consider bypassing the Oolsmouth port altogether."

"Oolsmouth docks and levees control all passage south to the sea," the captain pointed out. "The several channels of the Oolvaan delta don't start until the other side of Oolsmouth."

"Are there any turnoffs between our current position and Oolsmouth? Any side channels?"

"Not a one, Doctor Shaa, not a one."

"Hmm," said Shaa. "We could turn around and return to Roosing Oolvaya, or anchor in place here and wait for things to play out in Oolsmouth, or disembark passengers for an overland trip. However, all these options would waste time and, more significantly, wouldn't necessarily solve anything.''

''Meester Groot's troubles could travel toward us on the river,'' the captain suggested. ''If these Powers-that-Be decide to send forces after us, if indeed for some reason someone is looking for this very ship—''he directed a hard gaze at Shaa, which Shaa returned with a pleasant and guileless one of his own—''aye, as I say, a writ of seizure from Oolsmouth might very well be honored in Roosing Oolvaya.''

''Or even if it wasn't, we might still be impounded until things settle themselves out,'' added Karlini.

''One could consider the old plague-on-the-ship trick,'' Shaa said.

''Do you know,'' said the captain, ''I myself have seen plague ships burnt to the waterline by dock wardens, or blasted completely to smithereens. Plague ships, aye, and even one that had only the rumor of it without the slightest boil or fever in anyone aboard. Perhaps the legalities were consulted afterward, perhaps not.''

''It may be reasonable to leave that particular stratagem in reserve for a later time,'' agreed Shaa.

''We could just turn ourselves over,'' the captain said. ''Perhaps Meester Groot has the wrong of it, and this new owner Captain Moore spoke of has the right.''

Shaa raised a skeptical eyebrow, Karlini resorted to goggling his eyes, and Tildy dropped her jaw disbelievingly.

'' 'Twas only a suggestion,'' said the captain, eyeing them. ''I didn't mean nothing by it.''

''We thus return by the process of elimination to our central course,'' Shaa said, ''which is to continue on in to Oolsmouth, handling problems as they arise in the manner we have evolved through long practice. After all, we are at least forewarned, and forewarned *is* forearmed, which brings one halfway to octopod status, not an unhelpful place to be at all.''

''Yeah,'' said Karlini, making a sour face, ''but it sounds like we may have to face one of the worst menaces in the civilized world—a bureaucrat armed with some official document.''

''Ah,'' Shaa said mysteriously, ''but we are not without useful documents of our own. Nor is this all the preparation available to us. Come, let us reason together craftily.''

9
A TINCTURE OF LIVERWORT

The power of a strong arm, Haalsen Groot had always thought, is less than that of a strong mind. Like all aphorisms, this one had situations where it was likely to fail, such as the one where the strong arm was facing down the strong mind in close quarters in the same room, with the strong mind's mouth gagged and its arms lashed behind its back. Things are rarely perfect. Nevertheless, in the past he'd taken the attitude that he'd rather fail while trying a stratagem than succeed through a *coup de main*. Groot thought it did put things in perspective, though, to remember that his previous philosophy had been adopted in the abstract, without any foreseeable expectation of actually having to test its validity, rather than from the vantage point of a thick-walled cell in a jail with his leg chained to the floor.

Which was not to say that Groot had a philosophical objection to empirical methods. He was keeping the candle on the far side of the cell from him in case the door began to open suddenly and he needed to take advantage of the additional gloom to try to quickly conceal his work, which meant he was operating as much by touch as sight; on the whole, he thought the final effect would be much superior if he wasn't interrupted before all the pieces were in place. He finished spreading the first coat of solvent across the face of the concrete block of variant composition he had spotted earlier; the newer, more crumbly one at the junction of ceiling and outer wall. Julio's reconnaissance and a bit of triangulation had revealed that Groot's guess concerning the nature of that particular block had been more or less correct. Barred ventilation holes that had been part of the original construction in many of the cells had indeed been subsequently blocked off. As Groot had estimated, these now-vanished windows had opened onto the outside air, that much was true, but the openings had not been at ground level, or not exactly, anyway. The prison section of the Hall of the People was surrounded by a deep trench dug into the ground around the footings of the building as a sort of a dry moat. Unlike the more usual objective served by moat-building, that of keeping unwanted visitors out, this one had, of course, been designed to help keep unwilling visitors in. Although there would have been a two-story drop from the window to the bottom of the trench, some prisoner had apparently managed to navigate the hazard at some heroic time in the past, for the openings had all been obliterated by rock fill and new concrete and the top of the trench had been closed off as well by a grating of iron grillwork.

Even before Groot had finished covering the surface, the pasty solvent had begun to foam. He dipped the spatula into the wooden pot once more, used it to neatly square off the one remaining corner of block, hopped carefully off the bench, and moved the bench back against the opposite wall. The solvent, based on a tincture of pressed liverwort in an alkaline broth, was both well-tested and fairly nontoxic, at least if you weren't made of concrete, or such had been the claim of the chemist Julio had found. Still, Groot didn't particularly want the stuff dripping on his head or down his back, so he was content to watch it work from across the cell. The solvent had filled a shallow reservoir at the bottom of the large dinner pot; Groot estimated he'd used about half of his supply thus far.

Another implement had been concealed within the pot as well: a skeleton key. Groot inserted it into the lock on his leg chain, and after creaking to itself and shapeshifting its outline in a quick blur and a tingling vibration against his fingers, the key found its match. The lock clacked open.

Groot replaced the key in its slot and lowered the large

crock of stew into the pot after it, concealing key and solvent alike beneath its false bottom; the crock locked itself into place with a small click. The solvent had all been present when the dinner had been delivered although the level of stew had been a bit low, no doubt due to some judicious taste-testing on the part of the jailer as he made his inspection, but that was, after all, his prerogative, even with the bribes that Groot made sure kept coming his way.

Julio had used a runner hired off the street to deliver the meal. Hopefully, that would insulate him from immediate implication if the scheme failed, and both Julio and Eelmon were nowhere in the vicinity at the moment. Still, Groot thought, there are times when risks must be run, and since those who were holding him were obviously expecting him to try something to the sort, it would be best not to disappoint them.

The foam was letting off a small sizzle as it worked its way through the cement matrix. It was not dripping down the wall, as Groot had anticipated; instead, the solvent was sticking firmly to its area of application and was, in fact, sinking with alacrity deeper into the block. He heard a small clatter of pebble against rock as a chunk of embedded gravel fell free onto the solid block below, the cement around it turning to goo and then to slush, followed by an irregular patter as the rest of the material began to slide free as well. At one upper corner daylight suddenly peeped through. Groot squinted his eyes just in case, but when no stab of pain from seeing the sun after a day in stygian dungeon gloom resulted, he shrugged to himself and opened them again. Of course, he *had* had a candle, and the new light from outside wasn't exactly direct sunlight spilling down into the dry moat, but rather a fuzzy daytime glow; there was surely no need to get histrionic about this thing, Groot thought, frowning. "Stygian gloom," indeed.

Trying to keep a tighter grip on his sense of proportion, Groot crossed back to the rapidly vanishing block. It looked much less like rock now and much more like a chunk of almost-melted ice. On the other side of the opening by the side of the outer wall, a length of rope dropped into view. "Hello?" Groot hissed carefully.

"Who calls?" answered a deep rumbly whisper, followed by a short round of muffled coughing.

"Groot," he confirmed.

There was no need to ask who was on the other end. Once indoors and away from the clinging river air, Max's friend Svin had quickly thrown off his shakes and chills and had proceeded to eat steadily for the better part of a week, rapidly filling out much of the mass he'd shed and beginning to look less like a sheared seven-foot sheep and more like the barbarian fighting machine of prototypical legend. The cough remained, however, although now it seemed to be triggered mostly by speech and exercise. Svin hadn't been talking much, but he *had* been spending most of his time working out, so the top floor and screened roof-deck of Groot's house where Svin had been staying in seclusion and out of sight had been rattled alternately by the thud and thump of his exertions and the rack of his booming catarrh.

Using the thick cloth that had swaddled the stewpot, Groot pushed the slurry of foaming gravel that was now all that remained of the concrete block away from him over the edge of the wall, wiped the facing surfaces clean, and rolled the cloth over the side after the goo. As his earlier estimation had implied, the revealed open space was big enough for a tight squeeze through to the outside. Groot stretched one arm ahead through the opening, grasped the outer edge, boosted himself headfirst into the breach, and wiggled carefully forward. A quick glance down over the rim showed that the cloth and the remains of the block had already merged into the expanse of leaves, branches, mounded dirt, and assorted litter that lined the bottom of the moat. He twisted enough to crane his head upward.

The rope rose another ten feet to terminate in a hook which was looped over a stout iron crossbar supporting the local section of grating. Perched on the low retaining wall on the plaza side was the figure of Svin, his back toward the moat, sitting with the contained menace of a lolling jungle cat, his hands clasped around his knees and his back leaning backward over the screened moat. "What about this grating?" Groot asked softly.

"Rust," said Svin. "It is rotten and will snap under your weight. Grasp the thin part next to the rope."

"Very well." It was credible, which was what was required. "Proceed to your diversion now, if you would. Remember, no killings—are you clear on that?"

"It is no task for a warrior born," Svin commented, "but I am getting used to that sort of thing."

"Good, as long as you are clear on it. Contact Julio when you're finished."

Svin grunted. "I am a barbarian, not an infant; I can remember instructions." He unfolded himself to his feet and strode off.

Groot grunted for good measure. The man had done his task. Using the arm he had left outstretched behind him, Groot took hold of the inner lip of the wall and drew himself backward. As his chest emerged from the passageway back into the cell and his weight dropped him back toward the bench, his grip on the outside slipped at just the wrong instant and his head lashed up and bashed itself against the rock above him. He gritted his teeth and paused for a moment until the wave of pain eased.

Guilt by association, that's all this is anyway, he thought to himself. *Maximillian and the rest of them like this kind of nonsense, fighting with guards, sneaking in and out of buildings, amusing themselves with feats of daring, but not me; give me a back room, an account book, and a well-filled pipe any day.* If it hadn't been for the money and his investment, he never would have gotten involved with them in the first place. And look what it had brought him to now. Fah! How he had gotten a reputation as a person of physical action himself, why they had felt it necessary to lock him up, and why they nonetheless expected him to try some miraculous escape, was beyond him. Irrational, not to mention . . .

His mind caught up in thought, Groot eased himself the last inches backward, felt for the bench with his toes and then let his weight fully down onto it, stretched out his back with a satisfying lumbar pop, stepped off the bench onto the floor, and started to turn, with the intention of seating himself where he could catch the sluggish air now circulating through his new window and trying to freshen his environment. Instead, his turn brought with it its own surprises. The cell door was standing open and a familiar face was framed in it. "What do we have here, now, then, your lordship?" said the jailer.

There was still no reason not to make himself comfortable, at least for the moment, so Groot resumed his motion and lowered himself to the bench. "What does it look like?" he said crossly.

"Why, an escape, your lordship, that it does."

"How can it be an escape if I'm still here?"

"An escape *attempt*, sir, then, if you please. You shouldn't do this sort of thing; you know that. I'll have to report this, surely I will."

Of course you'll report it, you nincompoop, that's your *job*. Instead of that remark, though, Groot said, "How can I be trying to escape if I was coming *back* into the cell?"

"You got stuck, couldn't squeeze yourself through, then, could you? One too many steins of the stout, was it?"

"On the contrary," stated Groot. "If you will investigate for yourself, you will clearly see that this ventilation shaft is quite wide enough for both of us to pass at once. I was merely having a look at the weather and wondering where that bit of wall went to while I was dozing."

The jailer was looking a bit smug, and not a little reassured. "Checking the lay of the land, then, were you?" he chuckled. "Well, no matter." He had crossed the cell and was examining the hole for himself. "What's this, then—a rope?"

"That's what it looked like to me. What do you think it's doing there?"

"Perhaps you'll be telling the magistrate that yourself, then, won't you. You may think you're something, sir, but you're no match for the likes of us, now, are you? Hah!—and what's *this?*"

"This" was the loose chain and empty leg manacle.

"If you please, sir?" the warder proposed. Groot allowed himself to be shackled again. As the jailer straightened, a muffled pounding came to them from down the hall, along with someone shouting inaudible words. "What's this, then?"

"Perhaps you've been ignoring some other prisoner?" Groot suggested.

"Not that racket, sir; that's coming from the entrance hall. You mind yourself here, sir, I'll be back with you right away. And I'll be taking this, too, if you don't mind," he added, carrying the stewpot with him to the door. Groot watched from his bench, arms crossed over his chest. His hand on the door to close it, the jailer paused. "You're a gentlemen, sir, of that there's no doubt."

"Oh? Why is that?"

"A strong fast one like you, not trying to cosh me and grab my keys while there you were, free of the chain. A smart move, though, I'll have you know. You might have made it through to the door, but after that, then, well . . ." He shrugged. "There might just have been a small detachment loitering about out in the front who wouldn't be as kindly disposed toward you as a pleasant fellow such as I." The jailer touched his hand to his forelock.

"My man will show you our appreciation," Groot told him.

"You stay put now," the jailer warned, securing the door behind him.

Of course I'll stay put, thought Groot, *that's the whole idea.* Now that he'd found what they had expected and had easily headed it off, they could feel they had everything under control. That in turn should give Julio and Groot the freedom to concentrate on some real preparations. He settled back to think and wait.

He didn't have to wait long, as it turned out, for it wasn't more than a minute before Warder Clang was back. The jailer's shoulders, though, were hunched, as though he were unconsciously trying to protect himself from an ax-blow in the back, and his face was set in a deep frown. Pushing open the door, he said, "These visitors would speak with—oof!"

"Out of our way," snapped the first of the men behind him, unnecessarily, since his contemptuous shove had already sent the jailer reeling off to one side. The man raised a gloved finger as Clang recovered his balance with a hand against the wall and wheeled to confront him. "Quiet," the man said.

The three visitors filed slowly into the cell and arranged themselves in a line facing Groot. They were dressed identically, all in black, black breeches, black tunics, black gloves, and black masks pulled over their heads and stuffed down their necks into the shirts. Oval cutouts lined with filmy black gauze outlined their eyes and mouths. The men on either flank were carrying small black satchels. "I thought the Council had the last of your lot disbanded years ago," Groot told them.

"No," said the one who had already spoken. "Obviously not. Public consumption to the contrary. You must know why we have come."

"Why don't you explain it to me?" said Groot dryly. Inside, though, he felt anything but calm. Could this have been what the lawyer Snee had been concerned about, with his allusions about the remnants of Oolsmouth's autocratic past?

"Very well, let your dread increase," the man said. "You are Meester Haalsen Groot. We are who we are. We have come to put you to the question. The key to his chain, please." He stretched out a hand to the jailer, but did not move the direction of his gauze-hidden gaze from Groot.

"What's the need of that, then?" said the jailer, his attitude surly.

"To unlock the chain," said the man, "so we can remove him without first removing his foot." The lower part of the hood stretched as he smiled beneath it. "Each thing in its time and place. To advance prematurely would be scarcely professional." His two companions added a "hear-hear" in agreement on either side of him.

"No, sir," said the jailer. "Begging your lordship's pardon—"

"Be still," the man told him. "We could take both of you as easily as one. Now, the key."

The jailer stared back at him, undecided, and the man in black raised a hand to strike him.

"Just a moment," said Groot. "You are obviously making some mistake. My incarceration here is purely a civil matter. Even if 'the question' was still legal or even standard procedure, which it clearly is not, you—"

The man, his attention diverted from the jailer to Groot, but obviously not wanting to waste an already uplifted hand, swept it down into Groot's face. Groot rolled to the left with the slap as the man's fingers scraped down his cheek and spun his head heavily around. Slightly too late, Groot realized fuzzily that there was more beneath the glove than just a hand, that under the glove the man was wearing an appliance giving him the force of heavy mass and a raw flaying surface studded with the hooks or tiny barbs that had just ripped their way through his flesh. He could clearly feel the warmth of blood as it trickled down toward his jaw from his mauled skin. Rather than concentrate on that, Groot unscrewed his eyes and looked back up. The man was standing with his arms crossed. "It is ordered," he said.

"By whom?" said Groot mushily.

"By those who give such orders."

"Look here," Groot said, trying to drag his thoughts back into focus; he wasn't entirely sure what he was saying and what he was merely thinking. "This situation is totally unnecessary," *not to mention unexpected.* "Whatever questions you have, why not just ask me? No one's asked me anything," *have they?*

"As in many such undertakings," the man admitted, "the interrogation portion of the question is scarcely the point. Yet our orders are clear. There is no mistake."

"I'm being held to guarantee my bank loans," muttered Groot. "That's what I was told. I'm here as part of an extended business transaction. To advance from that to this attention from you is completely uncalled for."

"You are hardly in a position to—"

"It would unbalance the stability of Oolsmouth," Groot said, reeling on. "I'm a citizen. I'm a member of the Council! If *I* can be imprisoned, stripped of assets by thieving decree, and put to the question just because some gods choose to have a squabble, then what rights and expectations does *any* citizen have?''

''I know nothing of these things,'' said the torturer, apparently enjoying the writhings of his prey, ''and furthermore, I care even less. We have a job to do, a task has been set us, and—''

''A question of the social compact is at stake,'' Groot snapped. ''There is always a tension between the prerogatives of gods and the rights of people, but this is without question an egregious breach. How can business continue on a rational basis if a bolt like this can strike from a cloudless sky? And furthermore, I challenge your legitimacy to be here—your kind was banned years ago! I demand to see your orders! Who—''

As he threw words at them, the three torturers had scrutinized Groot from behind their masks as though he were a small bug due for dissection. He had realized he was wasting his voice as far as they were concerned, but they weren't really his intended audience. The jailer, who had begun edging backward as the men in black shifted all their attention to Groot, had now reached the hall. The heavy thump of the closing door brought their focus back to him in a hurry. The torturers wheeled in astonishment and stared at the door.

''What are you doing?'' shouted the head of the delegation as they heard the thud of the locking bar dropping into place outside the cell. ''What is the meaning of this?''

''Meester Groot speaks aright,'' the jailer said, his voice emboldened by the intervention of six inches of iron-bound wood. ''Show whichever documentation you've got, your warrant and your charter, for—''

''Open that door this instant or I will personally flay the meat from—''

''None of that, then, sir, if you please,'' said the jailer. ''My own father was dragged away by a crew like yours; never saw him again, did we, not a piece. Now these days I can vote, and I do that, don't you know, and one reason is to stand for the rule of law, as Meester Groot makes the point, and against your kind. Now, your documents, please, sir.''

"If you don't open that door, Groot and his points will be moot," the torturer said.

That was, of course, from Groot's angle the major shortcoming in the jailer's move, but it was the best opportunity that had presented itself. Would the jailer take the next step, though?

There was a pause while the three torturers examined Groot, waiting for the jailer's response. "Where are you?" yelled the first man in black after a moment. "You haven't gone and—"

"Begging your pardon, your lordship," the jailer said, his voice faint but growing louder again. "Here we are. It's rather a bit bulky, don't you know, so I haven't been lugging it about before this, never could see the need, but after this business it will never be far from my hand, I can assure you that, sir. This, you see, sir." In the light of the jailer's lantern Groot caught a flash of brass outside the barred hole in the door; the torturers, though, could probably see it better. "There's a troop on station just outside waiting for the call of this horn," explained the jailer. "Now, then, shall I blow, or will you produce your bone feedays?"

"What?"

"I suspect he means 'bona fides,' " Groot said under his breath. No one paid him any heed, which suited Groot just fine at the moment.

The man in black glowered at the door, then reached his decision. "On your head be it!" He raised his left hand and snapped his fingers. Along with the snap, his hand gave off a slight metallic clang as his concealed appliance jangled. The man on his left set down his satchel and neatly folded the lid panels away to either side. Groot got a brief glimpse of shiny metal implements stowed away in compartments or lashed to each visible surface; something that incorporated a vise-clamp with needle-razor jaws and a hollow vacuum tube drew his attention as though the metal and his eyes were both complementarily magnetized. Instead of an instrument, however, the man withdrew a rolled parchment of official-looking cast and passed it to his leader, then closed and re-latched his case.

"This is our warrant," said the leader, raising the parchment to shoulder level.

"Show it to Meester Groot," the jailer told him.

"He has nothing to say in this—"

"This window is scarcely large enough to pass such a grand document without shredding it into rags," said the jailer patiently, as though imparting a lesson to a child, "and I will not be opening this door so it can be handed to me more conveniently. Show it to Meester Groot." He displayed his horn again behind the tight bars.

The torturer stood motionless for a moment before turning stiffly to half-hand, half-throw the document toward Groot. "Thank you," said Groot. "The candle is over there on the floor, if you don't mind?"

To Groot's surprise, one of the assistants actually brought it over. Between the candle and the glow from the hole in the wall, the writing was easy to make out. "This is a rather curious memorandum," he said after a moment, starting to read it a second time. "It is indeed a warrant for the 'extraction of substance through the procedure of the Question,' as it states here in so many words, from Haalsen Groot, presently incarcerated in so on and so forth. It gives no statutory authority except in effect the recognizance of the executor, whose signature is unclear; however, it is a signature I recognize, that of a certain Dooglas who serves with me on the Council. For some reason, Meester Dooglas seems to feel justified, in this instrument, in speaking in the name and on behalf of the full Council, which is, of course, absurd. However, the most curious part of this document is where Meester Dooglas states that this warrant is commissioned at the behest and in the name of the patron of the Bank of the New Dawn, who is identified here by name as the god Sapriel."

"A god, you say, then?" asked the jailer.

"That is what the document states."

"Sapriel?" mused Warder Clang. "Can't say where I've ever heard of a god by that name."

"Do you wish to add blasphemy to your—" the torturer said.

"Be quiet, if you please, sir, while Meester Groot and

I are conferring. Does this paper show any seals, countersignatures, or tokens, Meester Groot?''

"Only the personal stamp of Dooglas himself, with which I am familiar. It appears, given the poor lighting, to be legitimate.''

"I don't know about this,'' said the jailer thoughtfully. "There's a problem with jurisdiction, you see, that goes beyond the question of these other gentlemen themselves.''

"Dooglas is clearly exaggerating when he talks about acting for the Council,'' Groot said, "since I am on the Council and he obviously is not acting for *me*. Knowing Dooglas as I do, I think it quite probable that he was acting alone, by himself, in creating this order, as part of a long-standing enmity between us; not, as the document claims, in the name of a god, and especially not in the name of the Council. Even if we grant him the power of attorney for this Sapriel and say that this warrant is indeed rightfully commissioned in his name, Oolsmouth, as a matter of practice under the Charter of Rights, does not recognize the magisterium of gods over civil government. I presume that is the problem of jurisdiction you referred to?''

"What—'' sputtered the lead torturer—'' what? This is beyond blasphemy, beyond mere disobedience to divine will, beyond—''

"Yes, well, there it is,'' stated Groot. "Your orthodoxy is not well chosen in this instance. The operative passage of the Charter of Rights clearly states that Oolsmouth does not submit itself to the sovereignty of any—''

"When we get our instruments on you, I will enjoy—''

"It is true that it is difficult to say no to a god whose determination is set on a particular path,'' said Groot, the pain in his cheek goading him to more feistiness than he usually displayed. "The gods are like the hypertrophic mountain ape of the proverb, which goes where it chooses rather than where society would have it; admittedly, then, that paragraph of the Charter of Rights is more a matter of general policy than blanket writ. If there were no gods there would still be earthquakes, volcanoes, calamities of all sorts against which legislation would similarly fail.

Nevertheless, we still must stand for some things. If this Sapriel is so committed to this course of action, let him come and prosecute it himself; if not, let us follow the procedures imposed by the consent of the governed."

"If you listen to this argument," the torturer told the jailer, "I will personally see to it that any children of yours are—"

"In truth, there is something to be said on each side," interrupted the jailer. "On the one hand, as Meester Groot has it, the rule of law; on the other, as you yourself put it, the force of fear and power. As Meester Groot stated aright, you yourself and the other gentlemen there have no official standing, you and your 'question'; in fact, you are outlaws, if I might be so bold. You are also, at this moment, behind bars."

"We will set to work on him," said the torturer.

"I will summon the reinforcements," said the jailer.

"Wait a moment," said Groot. "I do not understand why Meester Dooglas, known throughout Oolsmouth for his suspicious and devious attitude, would be so open about issuing such a controversial and ill-grounded order or involving himself so unambiguously with *any* particular god, since gods are so notoriously fickle and unreliable. I did not understand this and I still do not, but another explanation has presented itself. I have discovered just now that this signature is not actually in Dooglas' handwriting."

"Do you mean to tell us that you claim this document is *forged?*" said the torturer.

"Look for yourself," Groot said, holding it up. "Whoever is behind this is toying with you just as you are toying with me."

"This is absurd," the torturer declared. "You'd expect him to say whatever he could in his futile attempt to escape."

"Are you sure, then?" the jailer asked Groot.

"Absolutely," Groot lied.

"This is a suspicious business," said the jailer, "a very suspicious business indeed. It is too much for the likes of me to decide, of that there is no question. I will not yield Meester Groot without the approval of my superior."

"Now you just—" shouted the torturer.

The jailer rolled stolidly over him. "I reckon that my superior would require more proof of this order you have here. I'd reckon that he'd require a personal appearance or some other proof from this Sapriel, or enough convincing from this Meester Douglas, and I know my superior well enough to be sure he'd need a good quotation of the right municipal codes. Then you can have him."

"By rights," said Groot, "the full Council should convene for discussion, since the name of the Council has been brought into this. An individual Council member does not have the authority to act against another citizen, let alone another Council member, let alone in such an underhanded way as this, and especially using the name of Council as a whole, so you can clearly see the necessity for a full debate."

"As you say, sir," said the jailer. "This is my decision. Since Meester Groot is under my keeping, I will not have you mutilating him before reinforcements can arrive. Since you have made threats against me, I will not let you go free to mutilate *me* without reinforcements at my side to prevent that. What I will do is this. I will blow this noisemaker to summon the troops outside. Right then, I will unbar this door and retreat quickly up this hall away from the exit. If you hurry and do not pause for any mutilations whatever, you will have just enough time to escape from this building before the troops arrive to capture you."

The lead torturer had been sputtering and trying to break in, without success. Now, he had just managed to insert, in a shout full of menace, "Don't you *dare* blow—" when the clear tone of a hunting horn burst on them at close quarters—"oo, OOH; oo, OOH; oo, OOH!" The torturer's curse was buried under the echoes, and then under the creak of the door being dragged open by his two assistants as they almost tumbled over themselves in their haste. "Damn!" yelled the leader, following the other two through the exit at a dead run.

A short moment later, the jailer poked his head back into the cell.

"Thank you," said Groot.

"I may be just a plain man, just a turnkey, as you see, but I know what my job is, not to pat myself on the back, don't you know, and sometimes I even know what's wrong and what's right. Now, after I check with the captain to make sure they caught up those three characters on their way out, I'll just get back to what I was doing before, then, which was moving you to a cell without a passage straight through the wall, and if you don't mind I'll fetch you something for that cheek of yours, too."

"You are a prince among civic officials," said Groot as the jailer barred the door again from the outside and took off. Groot spread out the warrant, which he had retained, and had another careful look at it. So, it *was* Dooglas, after all. Groot regretted the exaggeration concerning the forged signature; on the other hand, at that point it had still seemed possible for the matter to swing either way. Now the situation was clearer. There would be no more of this pussyfooting around. Dooglas had thrown down his gauntlet. It was time to see he got it back.

10
ON THE OOLSMOUTH STREETS

The trip down to Oolsmouth was a total bust as far as answers were concerned. Zhardann and Jill-tang and I rode horses all day, stopped for an occasional meal, and let the servants pop open the baggage train for a peaceful fire and the raising of Zhardann's mobile pavilion when we dug in for the night. I didn't sleep in the pavilion, don't get me wrong, and whatever Zhardann and Jill were up to in there was fine with me; she may have thought she was my wife, but that didn't mean I had to agree, and if she thought she could tick me off by hanging out with Zhardann I was perfectly willing to let her waste the effort. I was happy enough that she wasn't trying to put the make on *me*. I didn't let *her* know that, of course. If she discovered anything that made me happy I figured she'd immediately set about removing it from the scene, and anything that drove me up the wall, well, I didn't particularly want to think about that.

I'm not complaining. It was a pleasant enough excursion as long as I didn't dwell too deeply on my fate if they discovered I wasn't who they thought I was. For that matter, lazing around with the gods was not nearly the transcendental experience I might have anticipated. They didn't wear their power on their sleeves, so to speak, and the grass didn't turn greener (or blacker, which I guess would have been equally probable) when they walked across it. In fact, you'd have been hard put to find any difference between the way they traveled and the habits of any normal rich person with a retinue to wash the dishes and pick up after them, if you'd be willing to call *that* normal.

We made reasonable time; not the kind of pace you'd set with a winged horse or a sky-chariot or even a steered balloon, but we sure didn't dawdle either. When you got right down to it, the only differences that sprang to mind between the trip I'd expected to have and the one I was getting instead were the direction I was heading and the company I was traveling with. Of course, those weren't exactly minor differences either. Although I was sure Max could be a difficult traveling companion if he wanted, at least I didn't have to watch my every step with him, with the penalty of a wrong move being instant annihilation.

We didn't talk much, just bounced around on our horses during the day and sat looking cryptically at each other over our plates in the evening. As a result, I didn't find out anything more on the road about why we were heading for Oolsmouth, or what it was about the headquarters of the Oolvaan Mutual Bank that would justify the trip once we'd arrived. There was no disguising Zhardann's priorities, though, for when we reached Oolsmouth late on the morning of the fourth day after our departure from Roosing Oolvaya, Zhardann sent the retainers off in one direction with the baggage and immediately led Jill and me out into the city on another course entirely.

Compared to Roosing Oolvaya, Oolsmouth was a real city decorated conspicuously with the signs of genuine wealth. Not that Roosing Oolvaya is anything to sneer at, you understand, but Oolsmouth did make its smaller cousin to the north look a bit shabby by comparison. With its wide streets and public statuary and big fancy buildings, the block-sized palaces of the merchant trading houses and their adjoining temples festooned with stone carvings and stained glass and long paneled frescoes, the parks with their rolling green lawns and pruned trees and civilized squirrels, and the unmistakable absence of a city wall, Oolsmouth radiated an aura of smug gentility mixed with ostentatious opulence. It was a place that was secure enough in its affluence and stature that it had to fear neither invasion nor the restraints of good taste and didn't care who knew it. We even passed an opera house, of all things, complete with a grand colonnaded entrance lined with statues of musicians waving their various flutes and woodwinds and strings toward the heroically proportioned woman at the center, her stone wings upraised, arms outstretched, eyes uplifted, and throat distended in a mercifully silent stratospheric wail; at least they'd stopped short of having some specialist sorcerer animate the statues, although maybe they saved that for the opening night of the season. A block down from the opera building, in front of the open gate of another three-story wood-frame complex, my skin prickled and the air turned abruptly cool and fresh as we entered the leakage zone of an air-conditioner field pushing back the muggy breezes off the river. I immediately tried to think of a good reason to visit whoever lived inside the place, or at least to stroll in the door, since their air conditioning was the most pleasant sensation I'd felt all day. Even my horse turned its head and glanced longingly through the gate, but Zhardann, in the lead, never wavered. I gritted my teeth and urged the horse on. Five paces later the humid river air came rolling back over us.

We turned the corner at the end of the block. Amazingly, the street just ahead even had a stone sidewalk separated from the thoroughfare proper by a neat row of shrubs. Traffic was as bustling and purposeful here as it had been anywhere else around the center of town. Over on the right, though, where another major building occupied the center of the block flanked by a two-story structure on each side, I could see an obvious gap in the traffic. People were edging away from the entrance to the bigger building, making long curves in the street to keep from getting too close and taking a detour that was too self-evident to be anything else. A few men were loitering around in front of the place, men with pikes and swords who were all wearing the same outfit, a yellow tunic with a green cape draped over the left shoulder and balanced with a rakish dangle off the right.

Zhardann reined up. "Hmm," he said. Then he urged his horse ahead again and trotted toward the cleared area, making for the locked gates at the entrance to the building's courtyard. Jill and I followed. As we broke clear of the street traffic and it became apparent what our destination was, two of the uniformed men moved to intercept us, holding their pikes at the ready. One of them raised his free hand to block Zhardann and said, "Halt! What is your business here?"

"Why?" said Zhardann, letting his horse continue straight toward the man. "Who are you?"

The man held his position, dropped the butt of his pike to the ground, and lowered the sharpened metal tip toward Zhardann's face. "Halt, I said. What are you, deaf?"

Zhardann looked at the pike. Judging by the look in his eyes, he was apparently weighing exactly how to go about pulverizing it. He pulled the horse to a stop a hand's-breadth before he would have impaled himself in the eye. "And *I* said, who are you to be asking me anything? I have business with this establishment."

"No, you do not, sir," said the guard.

"Oh?" said Zhardann. "And why is that?"

"Because this establishment is closed, sir."

The gate was not only closed and locked, it had a thick chain looped through it, and the chain, too, was locked. The driveway under the third-story overhang and the interior courtyard I could see beyond appeared empty and deserted. A person-sized street-entry door next to the gate was also closed and sealed shut with a chain. "Just why is this establishment closed?" Zhardann demanded. "This is a bank, is it not, and the idea of banking is to deal with customers, of whom I am one, so what is the problem here?"

"The establishment is closed. Sir."

"So you said. Why?"

"Because it's not open."

Jill, who'd ridden up next to Zhardann, leaned over and put a hand on his shoulder. I was a little surprised to see that her palm wasn't burned; Zhardann was obviously getting pretty heated up. "When *will* the bank be open?" she said.

"I don't know that I can say, ma'am."

"Is the bank still in business?"

"That most likely depends on how you define things,"

said the guard, who was either the Oolsmouth champion straight man or who was having a very good time without a sign of it showing on his face.

"What do you mean," shouted Zhardann, " 'define things'?"

"I think you'd best be moving along now, sir." The guard waggled his pike suggestively.

"Do you have any idea who I am?"

"Wouldn't make no never mind if I did."

"Wait," said Jill, tightening her grip on Zhardann. "This is the Oolvaan Mutual Bank, isn't it?'

"Again, ma'am, that mostly depends on how you define it," said the guard.

"How would *you* define it?"

"It's surely not my place to say, ma'am."

"Who could we see to find out more about the situation, then?"

"I'd have to think about that, ma'am. Don't rightly know that there *is* more to find out."

The score was now (at best) Guard 2, My Side 0, so I figured I might as well step up and take my chance. "Who hired you?" I asked him.

"I don't know that that's any of your concern, sir."

"Look," I said. "You've heard we're here to do business with a bank. You're telling us we can't do business with *this* bank, right? Do you have any suggestions about another bank we should take our trade to?"

"That would be the Bank of the New Dawn, sir."

Zhardann and Jill turned in unison to stare at me. I crossed my forearms over the pommel and leaned comfortably forward over my horse's neck toward the guard. "Any particular reason you make that specific recommendation?"

"Of course, sir," said the guard. "I don't take the affairs of business lightly, I can assure you."

He wasn't going to continue until I asked the right question. "I'm sure you don't," I said. "Neither do we. Let me review the situation for you. We need to accomplish a transaction with a banking establishment. You tell us that this one, the one we had planned to use, the Oolvaan Mutual Bank, is unavailable, and you suggest we take our business instead to this Bank of the New Dawn. If we're going to change our arrangements, though, we could just as easily pick a new bank at random or consult with our colleagues for their referral, so unless you have a particularly convincing justification for this New Dawn place I doubt we're going to bother visiting it. Why should we consider the Bank of the New Dawn?"

"I surely wouldn't insult you by stating the obvious, sir," the guard said.

"Go ahead," I told him. "I can take it."

Finally the guy's mouth quirked; he knew I had him. He could just refuse to say anything, of course, but I didn't think that was the game he was playing. He thought about it for a second or so, though, before responding. "Although it's not rightly my place to say, I believe the Bank of the New Dawn will be taking over the accounts of the Oolvaan Mutual Bank. If you and your colleagues are already customers of the Oolvaan Mutual, I'm sure the Bank of the New Dawn will be in touch with you soon."

"Thank you," I said. "That's very helpful. Zhardann, why don't you tip this helpful fellow?"

"You must be—" said Zhardann.

"I agree," Jill hissed. "Do it."

Zhardann dug in his belt and came up with a few coins which he extended toward the guard. The guard touched two fingers to his forehead and reached out his hand for them, although he didn't move his pike from its position in front of Zhardann's nose during the process. Before the guard could grab the money, though, Zhardann lifted his hand out of reach. "What about the patron of the Oolvaan Mutual Bank? I have dealt with him corporeally in the past."

"I'm sure I don't know, sir," said the guard. He eyed the money but kept himself from out-and-out licking his lips.

"You could guess," I suggested. "I'm sure my colleague would be content with a guess."

"I don't think that would be very prudent, sir."

"The patron's name is Pasook," said Zhardann, "Soaf Pasook."

The guard shook his head. "Can't say I can help you, sir. I'm a guard, sir, not an information agency."

"Hand it to him," Jill told Zhardann, "don't throw it in his face."

"Thank you very much, sir," said the guard, finally pocketing the coins.

"It must have been busy for you," I remarked to the guard in a conversational tone, "dealing with all the other customers coming up here, wanting to know what's happened to their bank."

The guard looked at Zhardann. He may have stiffened his shoulders, but he still took the hint and went again for his coin-bag. The new coin in his hand, Zhardann narrowed his eyes and tried to stare the guy down. "Don't know if I can rightly say," the guard repeated thoughtfully, absently letting the pike slip so that its point rested gently between Zhardann's eyes. Zhardann carefully handed him the coin.

The guard straightened up and adjusted the pike backward away from Zhardann's face. "I beg your pardon, sir. This midday sun and all these questions, don't you know, and perhaps a touch of the sunstroke. Your party must be new to the city, I wager."

"What makes you say that?" I asked him.

"Why, only because you're the first ones to inquire about this establishment all day."

"And why wouldn't the locals be doing the same?"

"I'm sure I don't know, sir," said the guard, "but because of the sunstroke perhaps I'll venture a guess. Perhaps it's only that they've heard about old Groot."

Groot? I thought. "What about this 'old Groot'?"

"Only that he's in prison, sir, and some speculate on the coincidence, seeing as his company had its dealings with this very establishment."

"Are you saying—" said Zhardann.

"Was I saying something?" the guard inquired. He shook his head. "It must be that sunstroke, damn it; can't rightly remember from moment to moment what I was talking about. No telling what nonsense might be slipping from my mouth in an instant of confusion."

I glanced around at the other three guards. They had

edged in smoothly to surround us but had otherwise kept their own mouths shut. "Perhaps one of your fellow sentinels could help in your time of incapacitation?"

"As you can see, sir, this entire post is exposed to the full force of the sun. My men and I suffer together in experiencing its effects."

"Then my friends join with me, I'm certain, in wishing you all a full and prompt recovery," I told him. I turned to Zhardann. "Shall we leave this poor fellow in peace?"

"I—"

"Yes," said Jill, "let's do that."

I jockeyed my horse around and let her drag Zhardann after me as behind us the other guards converged on their spokesman to help him split up the loot. After a moment, Zhardann trotted up level with me on the left and Jill matched him on the right. "I thought that was interesting," I said. "Didn't you?"

"What's so interesting about a disrespectful mortal?" said Zhardann sharply; he was still fuming. "There are ways of dealing with that kind of useless—"

"Yes, there are," I said, "and if you were paying attention you will have noticed that I used one of them. To digress for a second, you don't want everybody in the city to know there's an unhappy god stalking the streets, do you?"

"It achieves results."

"It also sends folks into hiding under the bed, them and their valuables. Like their rings. On top of that, there's no reason for us to reveal our hand until we absolutely have to." If Zhardann was honestly thinking the way he was talking, no way could he really be Gashanatantra in disguise; from his reputation Gash was spinning off stratagems and intrigues even in his sleep. "Let's keep the advantage of surprise, why don't we?"

"Oh, yes," Zhardann said caustically, "surprise. For beings of our stature, there are worthy tactics and unworthy tactics. Power is meant to be used for domination, not hidden away for—"

"It's the difference between an army with broadswords and a trained assassin with a knife," I said. "They each have their uses. You may be the master of one, but I'm the master of the other, and we happen to be playing my kind of game at the moment. Don't worry about it; you've got potential, I think you'll do just fine."

"What did you think was so interesting?" Jill said quickly.

"It's a strange coincidence," I remarked, "wouldn't you think? Somebody else making a move on Pasook just when we've arrived to search him out."

A wagon loaded with crates and drawn by a pair of morose oxen moved slowly across the intersection in front of us and we stopped to let it pass. "Could someone else have discovered the connection between Soaf Pasook and the ring?" Jill said.

"It does make you wonder, doesn't it," I said. "I haven't talked about the ring to anyone else but who knows about Pasook himself; maybe he let something slip, or maybe somebody had something on him that made him slip. And, of course, we all know there are other ways as well."

"Hmph," said Zhardann. "This is all quite improbable."

"Nevertheless," Jill said, "something more is going on here than we anticipated."

"All we have to do is cut through it, then," Zhardann announced, digging his heels into the horse's sides; the horse jerked into motion, shoving people out of the way to a chorus of yells and curses. "Let's visit this Bank of the New Dawn and get them to—"

"Stop that," said Jill. She urged her horse level with Zhardann's again, knocking another knot of people aside on her own, and grabbed his reins. Both horses ground to a halt. "He's right. There's no reason to be unnecessarily conspicuous. If nothing else, creating a bad scene here could get back to the Abdicationists and bolster their case."

"Wait a second," I said. "You don't intrigue against gods this way, do you, Zhardann?"

"Of course not." Zhardann was the picture of resentment, shoulders tensed, arms folded belligerently across his chest, face locked in a scowl. "What does that have to do with anything? These aren't gods, these are people. They are as dust beneath our feet."

"That's not a helpful mind-set. Try thinking of these people like they *were* gods. Never underestimate your adversary, right? Treat them as if they were worthy of your subtlety, even if they're not; you'll be able to get a lot more done with them in any case if you don't look at them like squirrels. I'll grant you it may be more fun to eradicate a few here and there, but that's not what we're here for, as I recall. Unless you've changed your agenda?"

"Very well," he said after a moment. "What is your plan, then?"

"We'll want to visit this New Dawn place eventually, but I'd rather not go directly there until we know a little more about what's going on. The guard mentioned this Groot person they've thrown in jail—perhaps there's something useful he can tell us."

"Yes," Zhardann said slowly. "That might be a worthwhile course."

"Why don't you go to our rooms and start arranging things there," Jill said to Zhardann, "while he and I find Groot. As he said, this is his element."

"Indeed," said Zhardann, with another sour glance at me.

"Indeed, indeed," I added for good measure. I could have suggested I go alone, but there was no point in wasting my breath; Jill had volunteered to accompany me not to help me out but to keep me under her thumb. I might be able to make that cut both ways, though, and in any case I was feeling enough of a sense of relief at the moment that a little matter like a homicidal nursemaid dogging my steps wasn't enough to ruffle me.

Soaf Pasook hadn't been around, and from the sound of it there was a decent chance he was gone from the scene for one reason or another. As long as he wasn't available, I wouldn't have to confront him. If I'd had to come face to face with Pasook, who, of course, wouldn't have the slightest idea who I was, the jig would most probably have been up, since my erstwhile partners would have immediately realized I'd never been teamed up with

Pasook at all and that he'd never heard of the ring that was at the center of our present shenanigans.

There was a disturbing side to this situation, though, that I couldn't ignore. What was the real story behind this bank war and why was it happening at this particular time? It couldn't be connected with the story about Pasook and the ring—or could it? Jill and Zhardann had put that story together with my tacit prodding. What if there was someone else who knew about me and my connections (or rather about the god they thought I really was) and had come to the same conclusions as Zhardann? If this hypothetical someone had pieced together the same story, but a little earlier than we had, they could have pounced on Pasook first.

Well, whatever the background, I was the natural person to take the lead in digging out the answers. Even Jill and Zhardann should be able to accept that. After all, they figured that even if I was really Gash I *had* been masquerading as a detective, and since I'd done a reasonably convincing job of it I had to be at least competent in that role. Of course, they didn't know I really *was* a detective, but for the purposes of this discussion that didn't necessarily matter. Unless . . .

Another disconcerting thought struck me. What if the detective bit really was a masquerade, except *I* was the one who didn't know about it? I hadn't been dwelling on the Spell of Namelessness, but that didn't mean it was completely out of my thoughts. No, I decided, that thought was just a little too paranoid, even for me. Wiping out my memory with some fancy curse was one thing, changing my entire personality was something else entirely; it was clearly too improbable to swallow.

Without another word, Zhardann turned his horse and headed off down the intersecting boulevard. "He's in a touchy mood today," I remarked, "isn't he now."

"You should treat him with more respect," said Jill. "*You* know who he is, even if these vermin infesting us don't."

"Vermin infestation, that's a nice turn of phrase. Do me a favor, though, don't use it as a form of address when we're with these folks, okay? Trying to talk somebody into doing something they don't think they should do isn't made any easier by calling them Your Verminship.'' That wagon had finally cleared the intersection and we rode on through in the same direction in which we'd already been proceeding. Ahead of us a few blocks down I could see an open space that looked like a park, with some kind of overgrown stone fountain in the middle. ''By the way, do you have any idea what direction the main jail's in? I don't remember visiting Oolsmouth before.''

''I thought you were supposed to be a detective,'' she said, amused. ''Well, detect it.''

''Thanks a lot,'' I said. ''You want to see me jump through a hoop, fine, I'll jump through a hoop.''

''Why did you say the 'main' jail, though? Groot could be incarcerated anywhere.''

''The guard said he'd been arrested, so that implies he's being held by the city, not by a private force in some private lockup. If he's really as important a businessman as it sounds, or at least as important to the Oolvaan Mutual Bank, they'd want him in the principal facility.''

''Is that kind of reasoning all a detective has to do? It's so simple it's embarrassing. Anyone could do it.

''Thought is thought,'' I said. ''That's all it is and that's all it takes, that and a willingness to talk to people, get lied to, get beaten up occasionally just like a regular person, spend a lot of your time frustrated and bored, and ultimately find out things you didn't really want to know in the first place. I never said it was anything special. You want to give it a try, be my guest.''

More of that plaza was coming into view down the boulevard in front of us. Either Oolsmouth was even richer than I'd figured, enough so to afford more than one big useless civic loitering yard, or that was the center of town; the jail had to be around there somewhere. As we got closer, all doubt vanished. Facing us across the plaza was a stone, glass, and metal building that was so large, so lumpish, so overhung with architectural doodads and geegaws, and so lacking in style or taste that it had to be where the Oolsmouth bureaucrats hung out when they weren't in the streets fleecing the public or generally making life difficult. They'd know where the jail was.

The building's horse park was around the side, which was where we stumbled across the entrance to the jail as well. "You see?" I told Jill confidently, pointing it out in case she'd missed it. "Here it is. Does that restore your faith, or what?"

"You can't restore something that never was—"

"Fine," I said, "thank you, I appreciate the compliment." I cantered ahead to the fenced-off corral at the rear, swung off the horse, took a numbered chit of wood from the stable attendant, and walked back across the yard toward the city hall building's side entrance. Over in the street, a group of prettied-up workers were gathered around a small bazaar of street vendors, wrapped in clouds of steam from fat-fryers and the aromas of heaped fish; I guessed it was already lunchtime, at that. A gaggle of supplicants, mendicants, transients, and other loiterers were loafing around the scene or working the passersby in one way or another, and a line of bored-looking folks stretched out of another side entrance and off down the street.

"What makes you think we'll be able to get in to see this Groot person without revealing something important?" Jill asked, having caught up with me where I'd paused to survey the crowd.

"Part of the art," I said. "Keep your voice down."

Actually, her volume hadn't been that loud, but it had been loud enough to attract the attention of a man who had been crossing the courtyard going in roughly the same direction as us, toward the jail. At the mention of Groot, he had paused in his tracks and looked straight at us. More for his ears than hers, I said, "You realize, before we can convince Groot to talk to us we may have to promise to help get him out."

"What do you mean by that?"

The man had taken an uncertain step in our direction. He was dressed in a black banker's robe and wore a sandy-colored mustache, that much I could see out of the corner of my eye. Since Jill hadn't noticed him at all and I was apparently still looking at the stall of a fruit vendor, he had no idea he was being observed. I turned toward him, locked eyes, and crooked an index finger in the standard come-here gesture. He gave a momentary start, followed by the typical reflexive glance over his shoulder to make sure he was really the one I was aiming at, then firmed his shoulders and looked back at me again. I nodded at him, yes, and he came to his decision.

"Wait a—" Jill said, as she followed the direction of my gaze and saw the fellow strolling toward us. "What's going on here?"

"This is something else detectives do," I told her. "Watch, you might learn something."

The name of Groot wasn't a new one to me, of course; I'd known that somebody called Groot who was a big-time trader in Oolsmouth was connected with Max and the gang. I'd never met Groot and I didn't think he'd know who I was, unless Max or Karlini had put something into one of their communications; the basic plan I'd settled for on the trip down, though, was to try to sneak away from Zhardann and Jill once we'd arrived in Oolsmouth long enough to make my own contact. Having the mention of Groot dropped into my lap by the guard had changed that plan quickly enough.

I figured that anything that affected Groot badly enough to land him in jail was important enough to know about sooner rather than later, and not only because of the game I was running with Zhardann and Jill, either. I knew the boat with the Karlinis and Shaa was on its way down the river to Oolsmouth and was due to be showing up reasonably soon. It stood to reason that any unexpected attack on Groot could easily extend itself to enwrap them, too. At the moment, events might actually have placed Jill and Zhardann on the same side as Groot, Shaa, and the rest, and me too for that matter. The juxtaposition of causes that had created this situation probably wouldn't last long, however, and I wanted to make as much hay as I could out of it while it existed.

"Good day," I said to the man.

"And to you, sir, good day," he responded, with a small bow in the direction of Jill for good measure.

"You are a resident of Oolsmouth, I take it?"

"Yes, I am," he said cautiously.

"Ah," I said. "That will explain it, then."

"I beg your pardon?" said the man.

"Have you eaten?" I asked him.

"I am in something of a hurry," he said, glancing across the yard at the jail door. "If you will—"

"We are also not merely standing around for the sake of our health. Yet perhaps we have matters worth discussing together."

"And what matters might those be?"

I raised my eyebrow at him. "To start with, the matter of a particular incarcerant in the municipal jail over there, a particular incarcerant by the name of Groot."

He fixed me in return with a cool, appraising gaze. What he saw, of course, were clothes that were somewhat the worse for recent travel, a clean-shaven face, somewhat thin in the cheeks, and a shock of brown hair streaked with blond. "What is your business with Groot?" he said.

"That may depend on you."

I could see wheels turning behind his eyes. His face was pale from underexposure to the sun, and against the light skin tones the smudged rings around his eyes from lack of sleep were quite apparent. A slight squint and the tension lines in his forehead filled out the appearance of considerables stress. "Who are you?"

"I will give you the opportunity not to have asked that question."

"Nevertheless," he said, after a momentary pause, "I have asked it, and I will ask again, who are you?"

"The potential exists for us to be a variety of things," I remarked. "Potentially we are friends. Potentially we could also be the messengers of trouble; all these potentials are there. Potentially we are the answer to your prayers."

"You mean that in a metaphorical fashion," he said, "of course."

"I do?" I said. "Are you sure you don't want lunch?"

"What is your name?"

I sighed. "Why this insistence of identities? Any name I told you, whether true or not, you would be very unlikely to recognize; and if you did know it you would probably be much happier if you hadn't heard it spoken. You're obviously an intelligent fellow. I would think that at this stage you would at least be open-minded where the possibility of help is concerned."

Jill had backed off a bit and edged over to the side where she could watch my expression and that of the man simultaneously without being in the guy's direct line of sight herself. Her expression was one of patient confusion. Nevertheless, she was giving me room to make my play. It would be a bad moment for my credibility if my intuition walked out on me now. "Help?" said the man. "What help?"

"Why, for you and your employer, of course."

"I believe we have never met before," he stated. "You are not from Oolsmouth. What do you know about me and my affairs?"

"You are the principal clerk for the businessman Groot," I told him. "As he is now confined in that dungeon over there, you are his main link with the outside world and so you are attempting to manage his affairs in the face of the current reverses."

"Perhaps a bit of smoked cod would sit well at that," said the clerk.

I indicated the location of the fishmonger's stand with an outstretched arm and he started toward it. As I turned to follow, Jill grabbed my arm. "How did you know all that?" she whispered. "Who he is, and what's his connection with Groot?"

"Omnipotence?"

"Don't be ridiculous," Jill snorted. "You know better than I do that there's nothing to that old fable."

"Very well, then," I said. "The clerk part was easy enough—you did notice the ink-stained index finger and the writing case under his arm? He's well-dressed, his clothes are fairly new, and if that sable collar is any indication they're expensive, too, so it's reasonable to presume he's not just some interchangeable bookkeeper but high-ranking in his own right; hence, a chief clerk or principal manager or something on that order. He initially stopped and paid attention to us before when you mentioned Groot, but if you remember what that guard said back at the bank, your basic person on the street isn't eager to be connected with either the bank or Groot right at the moment. That made it likely that a significant connection to Groot was present. Either this guy was one of Groot's accusers, jailers, creditors, or employees.

"I made the surmise that he's one of Groot's people. By the looks of the situation at the Oolvaan Mutual Bank and our conversation with that guard, this whole deal was sprung on the victims by surprise, and only in the last day or so. If Groot was locked up without any advance notice, that would be a messy situation; somebody would have to be trying to untangle his affairs on the outside and reporting back to him, as well as trying to react and get him released. From this fellow's face he's been working long hours; probably even been up all night. He's clearly under stress and not for a pleasant reason, either. He's been rushing around, but hearing what we were talking about was enough to stop him in his tracks. When I mentioned how we might have to get Groot released, that decided him—that's when he started to come over to us."

"He could be an informer or an agent of the police," Jill commented. "Or he could be one of those responsible for Groot's imprisonment."

"It doesn't fit the rest of the facts," I said. "In the abstract, yes, it could be, but if you put it together with everything else it doesn't make sense. For that matter, you might think that as long as they were locking up Groot they could have swept up his staff, too, but even then there'd be *somebody* left walking the streets, and when you get right down to it that kind of major grab is probably more than a democratic city like Oolsmouth could get away with unless there's an insurrection or some other crisis going on at the same time. Still, I'm willing to admit I may have made a bit of a leap, based on the available facts and my reading of the situation."

"You mean you didn't actually know all of that, you only guessed?" said Jill. "I thought deduction was a pure science with no chance involved; just follow the facts and interpret them as appropriate."

"What kind of ivory-tower world do you think this is, anyway?" The clerk was looking over his shoulder at us from his position at the fishmonger's, so I crossed over the yard and joined him. I paid his bill and picked up a small bucket of ale and an apple while I was at it, then led him to one of the stone benches arranged in rows next to the street. Jill reappeared with a roasted chicken. The clerk had also gotten an onion bread and a sliced tomato to go along with his cod and after a moment of fiddling he had the various ingredients stacked to his satisfaction. "So," I said. "Tell us about it."

The clerk chewed and swallowed. "I am Julio," he said, "and as you know my master is Haalsen Groot, who now languishes in municipal captivity. You also know, I take it, about the Bank of the New Dawn, the Oolvaan Mutual Bank, and the freezing and confiscation of the Haalsen Traders assets?"

"Somewhat," I said, "but presume we don't know whatever is most interesting. I'd appreciate hearing anything new you have discovered beyond the obvious."

"I don't know you," Julio repeated. "Thank you for the lunch, and I compliment you on your perspicacity, but these things don't explain why I should tell you anything. I don't know who you are, where you come from, or what your interest is in this. How do I know you're not in league with those who seek to destroy us?"

"What point would there be in sending us around to try to be sneaky when your enemies have already gotten everything they're after through a frontal assault?"

Julio shrugged. "Gods are involved."

"Yes," Jill said. "We know that."

"Oh," said Julio thoughtfully. "*Oh.* Yet when, ah, gods are, ah, ah—"

"Go ahead," I said. "Speak freely. We won't bite you. Sure, the rules of reason sometimes go out the door when you get mixed up with gods, but that's all the more reason to share your burden with us."

"I'm not certain I understand why that makes any sense," said Julio. "May I have some of that?"

I passed him the bucket of ale, which I had really bought for that specific purpose in the first place. "It makes sense because you'd have access to expert advice and a vantage point that would otherwise be closed to you, and the possibility of a strong arm raised on your behalf. And in any case how much worse off could you be?"

He finished his swig and wiped his mustache. "There is that, I suppose. I just don't know."

Jill had apparently gotten bored with the conversation since it frankly appeared to be going nowhere, and at the moment she had her whole concentration on dismembering her chicken. I decided to go for it. I raised my eyebrow on the side away from Jill and said, "It's not like I just walked off a riverboat and claimed to be an old friend of Groot's, but you will admit that he might have friends who have not yet revealed themselves, eh?"

Julio narrowed one eye as if the squint would let him see better and pursed his lips, then glanced quickly at Jill. I frowned at him and gave a small shake of my head, no. He gazed off at the street traffic; then, apparently reaching his decision, he nodded slowly to himself. "Very well," said Julio. "I will confide in you in the hope that—well, I will confide in you. Everything about this matter is quite irregular, you understand, unreasonable seizure without due process of state and so forth. We feel that there was absolutely no justification for arresting Meester Groot or confiscating his assets. We feel, and our legal adviser agrees, that this was done in outright contravention of the laws and practice of Oolsmouth, as well as of valid commercial sensibility. Our lawyer has been attempting to unearth the authority and pretext behind all this, unfortunately without notable success. With slightly more promising results, he and I both have been meeting with Council members in an attempt to convene a full Council session. As you know, Meester Groot is a member of Council himself."

"What do these other Councillors have to say for themselves?"

"To a person, they've been quite surprised and distressed. A few of them have also been concerned for their own security. Even more so, they are troubled at signs the gods may be meddling directly in the affairs of Oolsmouth. They feel that would mean nothing but trouble."

"That's certainly a prudent way to look at it," I said. Coming from me, for some reason that remark didn't seem to reassure him. "Why hasn't the Council put an immediate stop to these goings-on, then, especially if as you say it's been accomplished against the law?"

"Politics," said Julio. "Meester Groot is one of the stronger voices on the Council and his incarceration shifts certain groupings and the entire internal balance. Councillor Dooglas, who opposes him, is another pole of the Council, yet he has not made himself available over the past day to any but his closest intimates. And then there are the gods."

True, it was the soul of wisdom to tread softly when the gods were mucking around in your vicinity; just look at me. "You have to admit these Councillors aren't necessarily idiots," I said. "There is a fine balance that is useful to maintain between directly confronting a scheme that the gods may be wrapped up in and finding some clever way of turning the tables. Still, your Councillors' natural instinct to hide under the porch is clearly not what you're looking to them for at the moment. Another thing that is sometimes helpful, sometimes disastrous, and always risky is recruiting another god to oppose the designs of those who are on the other side, if there aren't more of them involved already.

"I see you shudder," I went on. "I take it that's not a course you prefer to pursue. There's also a perfectly natural tendency for people to consider how they want to deal with those folks who are already tied in with the gods, whether they want to give such folks a clean pass or get closer to them, or even whether to go for an out-and-out alliance. Even the gods themselves build coalitions. Or so they say."

"My master," Julio said, speaking carefully, "as a matter of philosophy, prefers to avoid troubling the gods on his behalf, either directly or through intermediaries."

"That's very noble of him, I'm sure," remarked Jill sarcastically, diverting her attention from the chicken.

"Ah, yes," said Julio, "thank you. We do feel, nevertheless, that we have the situation well in hand, and our preparations are advancing—''

''Right,'' I said. ''Save your voice; we've seen how well your preparations are advancing. What have you discovered about the other forces involved here?''

''There is the Bank of the New Dawn, but I assume you know all about that.''

''Don't assume. As I said, we're interested in your perceptions. What about this bank?''

Julio washed down a thick slice of cod sandwich with a healthy swig of ale. ''I had never heard of the Bank of the New Dawn before this started, but until I began to investigate I had no idea how new it actually was, or in fact how old.''

''What are you talking about?'' said Jill.

Jill was a natural for the good cop/bad cop game, as long as she always got to play the bad one. Julio swallowed, this time without any food in his mouth. ''You *didn't* know? Ah, well, 'New Dawn' is a new name for an old institution, the Oracular Treasury Trust.''

Jill drew her breath in sharply. Out of the corner of my vision I could see her glance quickly toward me with an expression that mixed surprise and, I thought, some fear; a roasted chicken leg hung momentarily forgotten in her hand. ''Indeed,'' I observed, and took a thoughtful munch from my apple.''That *is* interesting.'' Now that Jill had had a chance to recover her composure, I looked over at her. ''I think we should bring friend Julio a bit more into our confidence, don't you? You see,'' I said, turning back to Julio, ''our interest lies primarily in the area of banking, including financial transactions, negotiable securities and their exchanges, and various considerations relating to business relationships in these areas between the divine and mortal populations. My own principal area of specialization concerns mergers, acquisitions, and takeovers, both amicable and otherwise, in the institutions involved, and, of course, in the nuances of the patronage relationships brought into play.

''While you might have presumed that these institutions and their patrons could freely prosecute whatever commercial dealings they choose,'' I continued, warming more to the topic I was making up from whole cloth as I went along, a habit I seemed to be falling into more and more of late, "working out any differences or disagreements through negotiation, guile, or, ahem, force, there is in fact a certain level of, shall we say, *status quo* that must be maintained. The patron element is not, as we all know, all-powerful, and so the restraints of good sense are also the bonds of prudence. If one party to the social contract grows too obnoxious, to put it plainly, the other party might feel forced for its part to resist, and there is also the possibility of dissension within the party itself. Our role, then, is to monitor events, and if necessary to intercede when a specific situation appears to be getting out of hand." On second thought, maybe I *hadn't* been making all of it up from nothing. That stuff about the Abdicationists and Conservationists I'd heard from Jill and Zhardann—if that wasn't dissension within the ranks of the gods, what was it? It had sure sounded like more than just a debating point.

"You don't say," said Julio. "Do you think that *this* particular situation appears to be, ah, getting out of hand?"

"It does seem to have that potential. Don't you agree?" I remarked to Jill.

She was looking at me with an expression of unpleasant astonishment. "We will have to discuss it," she told me.

I had been keeping an eye on the people in the courtyard while we talked, just on general principles, and so I had seen a young man emerge from the entrance to the jail and stride off toward the street, glancing anxiously around him. Now, his gaze fell in our direction. At the sight of our little group, he turned and made his way vigorously toward us, arms pumping at his sides, halfway between a fast walk and a slow jog. "Are you expecting someone?" I asked Julio.

He peered over his shoulder in the direction I was looking, then set the remains of his cod to one side and rose to his feet. The man skidded to a halt next to him. "Excuse me, sir," he said in a pant, "I was sent to find you. I work at the prison, for Warder Clang, he's the one who's—"

"Yes, yes," said Julio, "I remember you, go on, what is it?"

"There's been a spot of trouble, you see, sir, trouble with your Meester Groot, not his fault, mind you, but trouble nevertheless, and—"

"Get yourself together, man," Julio said, his voice rising. I handed Julio the ale bucket; I figured there was enough still sloshing around in the bottom to make a useful impact. The messenger took a deep guzzle and wiped his mouth with the back of his arm.

"Thank you kindly, sir," the messenger said. "The warder thought you should know that a party came to us to take away your Meester Groot, to put him to the question, so they said. Warder Clang—"

"They *what?*" said Julio. "Where is he now, where did they take him? I must—"

"Don't be getting yourself in such a state, sir," said the messenger. "As I was trying to tell you, Warder Clang sent them away. He didna have orders, and even though their warrant was signed by Meester Dooglas for the Council, when your Meester Groot said the paper was forged, well—"

"I'd best be off," Julio said to me.

"I think that's a sound idea," I told him. "Perhaps I, and perhaps also my associates, will pursue certain matters with this Meester Dooglas, as well as this Bank of the New Dawn or whatever else it's calling itself by now. How shall we reach you if necessary?"

Julio dug in his writing case and withdrew a small card with an address already lettered on it, then quickly scrawled another on the back. "You do read, don't you?" he asked as an afterthought as he handed the card to me.

Seeing as the matter was as much his responsibility as mine, I took a quick glance at the card; the penmanship was legible enough, but after all he *was* a clerk. "It won't be a problem," I started to say, but by the time I looked up Julio was already out of easy earshot, crossing the yard with the messenger from the jail.

Jill was staring at me. "I don't believe you!" she said.

"Nevertheless," I said, "I still seem to exist. What's the problem? You don't believe I can really read? Or is that not what you're complaining about this time? You still have some problem with my methods? We found out some pertinent—"

"That's completely immaterial, next to your nonexistent sense of judgment! Airing secrets to a *person,* and in *public*—you're close to the edge, and if you don't realize it then you're already *over* the edge, whether you really *are* an Abdicationist or not. Even I didn't know you had that much gall, I'll grant you that."

"Look," I said. "We're clearly up against the patron of this New Dawn group, or more accurately the Oracular Treasury Trust; we need all the information we can get. If there's a problem with this Julio fellow we can always eradicate him, and how many other people is he likely to mention anything to? We can certainly exterminate a few more if we have to. But I don't think it's a concern in the first place, especially when you consider the misdirection."

"I'll give you this much, too," Jill said. "That agency you invented isn't such a bad idea at that, the one we're supposedly part of. Pure audacity, but that always was one of your strong points. Although how you'd imagine that anyone with a mind would be taken in by a fable like that. . . ."

"I chose my audience."

"I suppose you're right; he was just a man, after all, doesn't know the least bit about anything important. *You* should know full well, maybe better than anyone, how difficult it is to get cooperation on anything, especially without immediate payback. Much less toward the idea of any kind of centralized authority. A *de facto* hierarchy is one thing, but regulation is quite another." She shook her head. "How the Abdicationists think anyone would ever agree to a proposal like this is absurd. And they call themselves *moderates*—hah! You're not *really* an Abdicationist, are you?"

"What," I said, "and have you think I'm absurd? You know better than to draw an inference about my true thoughts from some remark that happens to drip from my mouth, surely. Expediency, prosecution of a plot, and truth are quite different, it should go without saying; altogether different. Are you quite finished with that chicken?''

A pile of gnawed bones sat in the pool of grease in the midst of the wrapping paper the chicken had been served in; very little meat, if any, remained, but for all I knew she liked to devour her food down to the skeleton. Jill stood up and moved away from the remains, folding her arms over her chest. ''Very well, yes,'' she said. ''Is it now time to visit Groot, O Great Detective?''

Oolsmouth so far had been a remarkably clean city; part of their civic ostentation, no doubt, was to employ a refuse disposal squad. There was even a designated trash container too tall for the roving dogs over on one side of the courtyard. As much to annoy Jill as to assuage my own sense of order, and to eliminate the attack on my aesthetic sense mounted by a heap of ragged bones on an otherwise undisturbed marble bench, I carefully took up the garbage by the corners of its wrapping paper and brought it to the trash area, which was only a few strides away. Jill followed me, unbelievingly. ''Your mind has rotted,'' said Jill. ''There is clearly no doubt about it.''

''Fine,'' I said. ''Then go away.''

Her sigh was more of a ''humph.'' ''Groot?'' she said.

''No,'' I said. ''Julio was enough for now, and he'll be busy enough himself with Groot for the time being. Let's check in with Zhardann.''

''First Groot, then no Groot—why don't you make up your mind?''

''The one that's rotten?'' I said.

She snarled at me and headed for the horse park. If I was trying to annoy her, it appeared I was succeeding. Actually, I *was* trying to annoy her, at least a little. I didn't want her to start feeling happy I was around, or worse yet, comfortable. As long as she thought we were married, I didn't want her to get the idea that maybe whatever was wrong between us was on the way to being reconciled.

We redeemed the horses and she took the lead; Zhardann had told her where he was setting up shop but hadn't bothered to clue me in. I waited until Jill's concentration was firmly on the twisting of streets and intersections before I asked her, "What do you want to tell me about the Oracular Treasury Trust?"

"Nothing," she said, "I don't know a thing." The expression that flipped across her face, though, told me something else.

What was she hiding? Probably something having to do with the Oracular Trust's patron. Was I supposed to know the identity of that god? No, I didn't think so; *she* knew something that she didn't expect *me* to know. But if I heard the name of the patron, I bet she thought I'd recognize him or her, or more to the point that the god Jill thought I was would know who this other god was. The way things were going, though, I'd find it out eventually. Either she hadn't thought that part through or she saw some value in keeping the information from me as long as she could.

Zhardann had found lodgings in a predominantly residential section of the city not far from the central plaza we'd just visited, or for all I knew he may have actually owned the place. The three-story house sat solidly on the corner lot of the Lane of Wealth, a street lined with similar houses, each with a neat gentrified garden out front that was fenced off from the cobblestone sidewalks by a chest-high stone wall topped with an iron grating. The gratings all had clever designs worked into them, coats-of-arms and heraldic beasts and long trailing vines and whatnot, but their vertical bars ended with sharp polished spear-heads; if I knew Zhardann, that detail alone would have been enough to close the lease for him. One of the servants who'd accompanied us down from Roosing Oolvaya unbolted the side gate and Jill and I rode down the carriageway toward the stables at the rear of the house. "See to the horses and freshen up, why don't you, and then we'll meet in the house," Jill told me, swinging to the ground under an awning that stretched from the back door.

"The last thing any horse in his right mind would want is me seeing to him," I said, easing myself out of my saddle as well. The servant had relocked the gate behind us, and he now took both sets of reins to lead the horses away. Jill gave him a dirty look.

"Just freshen up, then," said Jill, "or do you have some moral objection to cleanliness as well?"

"I wouldn't say that, not in the least." A line of round stepping-stones led from the dirt driveway across the lawn and through the flower beds around the side of the house; a gardener was working his way along it, clipping at shrubs with a pair of shears. A trail of cut leaves snaked behind him all the way to our own position. I stretched out an arm to indicate the gardener. "The mere sight of cleanliness in action, of order arising from chaos through the artistry of skill and hard work, brings a smile to my lips and fills my heart with gladness. But, as you well know, I take nothing to extremes, and I must say I'm feeling remarkably energized, not to say downright chipper, at the moment. If you feel no need to 'freshen' yourself, as you put it, I can't see how I can do less than follow your example. Shall we check in with Zhardann?"

"Ooch, you're impossible," she said. She did, however, appear to give up the idea of trying to decoy me away while she talked with Zhardann first without me being around. We scraped off our boots and entered through a sunroom that led into the kitchen, where I could see the cook stowing vegetables in a cupboard. The cook raised her head when she heard us stomp in, jerked her head toward the front of the house, and said, "Upstairs, in the study." Jill had already headed straight in that direction, into a hall lined with portraits of somebody's ancestors that led past the entrances to a pair of rooms on each side and then to the entry hall and front door. One side of the hall was taken up by a straight staircase with an ornate banister carved from some dark wood; by the shine of it one of the servants had spent the morning moving up it with a barrel of wax. Up the stairs we went, past another row of portraits and a detailed mythical battle scene, full of dragons chewing on sky-carriages and dodging lightning that rained down from the heavens onto the muddy conflict below. The staircase continued to the top floor, but we departed at the end of the first flight, walking about the well in the floor to reach the room at the front corner on the right. Jill eased the door open, peered around the jamb, and then quietly entered.

Windows filled out the two outside walls, overlooking the middle branches of a tree on the right side and the front lawn, spiked fence, and street on the other. The ceiling was paneled with squares of the same dark wood as the staircase. The ceiling panels were separated by rails and hanging bosses, but since the second story was high there was still enough headroom to move freely beneath them. Zhardann sat in a comfortably overstuffed armchair in front of an unlit fireplace topped off with a marble mantle supporting a loudly ticking clock and an array of stuffed birds. The picture over the hearth showed a whiskered man dressed in forest greens brandishing a bow against a backdrop of trees; he was surrounded on a patch of meadow by heaps of bloody birds, an arrow protruding from each, and two more were still falling limply from the sky, one directly above his head. I didn't recognize the man in the picture, and for that matter I didn't exactly recognize Zhardann either. The top part of his body, from above his head to his waist, was shrouded by, well, a *cocoon,* or at least the kind of cocoon that might have resulted if a battalion of silkworms had been using wisps of cloud-cotton instead of silk for the job. The windings of cloud actually continued down his legs to the floor, now that I took a good look, but they were wispier, letting the outlines of his legs show through.

Jill sank silently into another armchair next to the fireplace and facing Zhardann's while I stretched out on a small sofa. I'd initially thought Zhardann might be in a trance. Now I saw that was clearly less than the whole truth, for the shape inside the cocoon was moving, stretching, and apparently gesturing as though he was talking without making a sound with someone who wasn't there. The sight didn't bother Jill, though, so I saw no reason to let it bother me.

I watched Zhardann's gauze-wrapped antics carefully all the same. I didn't have to watch all that long, as it turned out. After a few moments, Zhardann sat back and stopped his writhing, and the cloud enveloping his body began to spin as though caught up in a sudden wind. Then, like a magician grabbing a sheet and pulling it upward, making a point from the center, letting the loose ends flutter behind, and causing the sheet to vanish point-first into a hole in the air, the cloud sucked itself off Zhardann, rose into the air above his head, and disappeared in a rolling puff.

The newly revealed Zhardann was seated at ease with his arms folded across his chest, apparently none the worse for the experience and rather pleased with himself into the bargain. "Guess who's behind this New Dawn business?" he said to Jill.

"The Oracular Treasury Trust," she told him. Myself, I thought her tone of voice was a bit too firm and a bit too strained, as though she was trying to warn him of something, but he didn't seem to be paying as much attention to her as usual; maybe he was still under the aftereffects of the spell of the cloud. Frankly, I had taken the cloud to heart, too. Just because I hadn't seen much sorcerizing over the past few days didn't mean it wasn't there, at least in potential. It wouldn't do to lose track of the fact that where magic was concerned these two were heavyweight masters. Events might have been conventional enough so far in our relationship, but that didn't mean they'd stay that way.

"Of course," said Zhardann, "of course. You've been busy, too, haven't you? I can't say I expected to find his hand in this, but then it's not entirely a surprise either, is it. Focasti thinks there may be an additional operator here, but even she agrees it's really his play. Well, he may have carved off more than he can handle this time. I've been in touch with some of the others who have an interest in these things, and they're responsive—the setup even looks strong enough to mount an up-and-down challenge. With the right preparation, we may be able to maneuver him into submission without actually having to use a frontal assault. Wouldn't that be something? Sapriel on the defensive for once."

I'd been looking at him but watching her as well, so when Zhardann said the name "Sapriel" and Jill gasped, shot him a dose of eye-powered venom, and immediately turned her gaze on me to capture my response, I'd already prepared myself. I'd been ready for something of the sort; the fact that I didn't know Sapriel from Haddo was completely beside the point. "Sapriel," I said, letting the syllables ooze from my mouth like they'd been steeped in the savory juice of malice. "Indeed, Sapriel. I wouldn't at all mind getting Sapriel in a situation where he was at someone's mercy, myself." Jill presumably thought that Sapriel and I had had encounters in the past, and my guess was that we were supposed to be enemies. "This may be more fun than I'd anticipated. What do you bet that this guy Dooglas is his local front man?"

Jill was a trooper, though; she rolled with it. "Ally, front man, dupe, what does it matter?"

Zhardann, who finally seemed to be returning to earth, said, "Dooglas? Who's Dooglas?"

"I'll explain in a moment," Jill told him. "The obvious plan is for you to continue developing what you've begun while my husband moves ahead with the mortals, starting with Dooglas." She turned to me. "Stay away from these banks, and especially from the Trust. If Sapriel sees you—need I say more?"

"No," I said thoughtfully. "No, you needn't, at that."

"If Soaf Pasook turns up, we may be able to use him, too," she continued, but by then I was being overtaken by my own thoughts. As if it wasn't already bad enough worrying about the sticky situation I'd be in if I did run across Pasook, now I had to worry about this Sapriel, too. With luck, if I was going to meet either one of them, I would . . .

The problem with trying to plan that way was that I realized I'd been relying way too heavily on luck; I was clearly overdrawn in that department. My luck couldn't hold out forever. When it turned, I just hoped—

Aw, hell, I thought. All I could do was keep playing it bounce to bounce.

But who *was* Sapriel?

11
IN THE AIR

The sun had yet to make its appearance, but the sky had lightened enough with its advance-guard radiance for Jurtan and Max to get to work. "Have you ever seen anything like this before?" asked Jurtan, craning his neck upward and squinting his eyes at different angles in a vain attempt to catch a solid glimpse of the object hanging invisibly overhead.

"Not enough like this, no." Max was back at the edge of the low island in the middle of the swamp, holding his thumb up at the end of his outstretched arm and sighting past it in various directions. "That has to be an internal refraction unit up there; nothing else makes sense. There was a case once where a cache of something-or-other was hidden by a refraction setup, only that one was slung by a cable from the underside of an overhanging cliff. Once you'd figured it out and managed to get to the top of the cliff, you could theoretically slide down the cable to the thing and get into it from there."

"Couldn't you use the cable to pull it up? Or just cut the cable and catch it from underneath?"

"Sure," Max said, "if you wanted to set it off. Of course you couldn't see the cable itself either. There was about a thousand-foot drop down the face of this cliff, too, as I remember, and you had to hack your way to the top through the ice while hanging from pitons."

"Why would anyone be crazy enough to hide something like that in the first place?"

"So it wouldn't get found; what do you think? Or do you mean why would they put themselves through all the overhead they'd need to actually get it there?'' Max began to stroll clockwise around the island, shoving his way through the tall grass. ''A lot of the problems go away if you can fly.''

''People can fly?''

''Not usually,'' Max admitted. ''You've got your levitation spells and so forth, but there you're talking truly exorbitant energy costs, and there are more ways to do them wrong than you can—well, let's just say there are good reasons they're not very popular.'' He reached the first of the island's gnarled mangroves, its roots trailing off into the water, bent over for a close look at its bark, carved a small scraping off with his knife, and launched himself up the trunk. He disappeared into the maze of branches. The tree shuddered, twigs and leaves cascaded down, and then Jurtan saw Max's head pop up out of the top of the canopy. After glancing around, he disappeared again, only to quickly reemerge at the bottom in the midst of another cloud of leaves. He set off for the next tree. ''The person doesn't have to be the one who does the flying, of course,'' he remarked.

''Like that big bird of Karlini's, right?'' Jurtan said. ''You think that's how you're supposed to reach this one?''

''It's a possibility. If I'd built it, though, I'd have made sure it could recognize me, say with an amulet or an acknowledgment code or something of that sort, and would just lower itself to the ground when I showed up. I wouldn't want to go through some ludicrous gyrations ever time I wanted to come or go.''

''Do you think *your* amulet. . . ?''

''Hasn't seemed to do much since we've been here,'' Max said, ''has it? Anyway, that's not one of its functions, at least not as far as I know. Another possibility is there's a ladder hidden around here someplace. It'd have to be an awfully tall ladder from the looks of it, though.''

Jurtan now had to shade his eyes against the first direct glow of the sun. He walked around so the sun was at his back and stared upward again. ''What holds it up?''

''What do you think holds it up?'' Max was on his third tree now. This time, though, the trunk resisted the cut of his knife, and even gave off a small thunk when he jabbed it with the point. He pulled down a branch and peered intently at its leaves.

Was this a trick question? "Uh, magic, right?"

"You have any idea how strong a field spell you'd need to keep a couple-ton object hanging in the air indefinitely? Damping instabilities alone would drive you crazy. Let's just say I sure wouldn't want to try it."

"But I thought this Iskendarian guy was even smarter than you."

"That's not the way I would have put it, kid." Max's voice came from midway up the tree. "You say something like that to most spellcasters and all of a sudden you find out you're facing the rest of your life as a kumquat or some kind of squishy amphibian."

"I'm sorry," Jurtan said, "but didn't you tell me—"

"I don't think even Iskendarian could have pulled it off. In any case, he didn't. Those tests I was running last night not only confirmed this isn't a real healthy place to be doing spellwork, they would have gone off the scale if there was a field like that around."

"*Something's* got to be holding it up. A big magnet under the ground?"

Max eased himself carefully out of the leaves at the top of the tree and felt around him in the air. "Ah-*hah!*" he said after a moment. He leaned over and began to trace out a flat surface in pantomime with both hands.

"Okay," Jurtan said thoughtfully. "Not a magnet. What about—"

Max rapped on the air with the hilt of his knife. The air clunked. "A pylon. It's grafted into the tree. Probably swings over like an arch. Most likely we'll find two more of them at equal intervals around the shore."

"Hey!—that's pretty neat. You going to climb up it now?"

"Too slippery," said Max, running his hand along the invisible surface. "Could be a side effect of the refraction field." He retreated back into the tree.

"With all this swamp gas, you could lift a balloon, couldn't you? Or a kite! What about a kite?"

"You feel any wind?" Max dropped to the ground from

the lowest branch and shook off the leaves. "I'll admit I was thinking about a kite myself, and I've always been fond of balloons, although we don't have nearly enough fabric between us to build one big enough." He reached their small camp next to the beached boat and began rummaging through the packs. One of the grazing horses ambled over to gaze dubiously over his shoulder.

"I could run across the island dragging the kite," Jurtan suggested. "Or we could use one of the horses. The kite doesn't have to stay up, just hop up high enough for the rope to go over the—oh."

Max had come up with his machine-crossbow and was winding its spring with the footpedal. An arrow in place, he clipped the reel of line to the hook at the back of the fletching, walked back toward the tree with the pylon, sighted, and fired. The arrow sprang into the air, nosed over in a neat parabola, and plunged down, dragging behind it the light rope humming out of its reel. As the arrow embedded itself upside down in the soft ground the rope hesitated, still keeping to the line of the parabolic trail, fluttered, and began to fall, then suddenly paused in the middle and grew taut. "Now we'll see if that column's got a razor edge," Max commented, just as the line parted into two segments at the very top. Each one flapped separately to the ground.

"Not surprising," said Max. "I'd have done the same thing myself. Anyway, it was worth a try."

"So what now? We try the kite?"

"No, the arrow again, only this time I aim for the center where the pylons meet, now that I know approximately where it is from the curve of the column." He rolled up the loose end of cord, detached it from the arrow, wiped off the mud, loaded and sighted, and again let fly.

The arrow was still heading upward as it passed the center of the island when they suddenly saw it stop in the air with a small thunk and bounce back. It had barely tumbled five feet before it hit something else, fell flat, and started to slide down a smooth curve, dragging the cable behind it. The cord was outlining the surface of a sphere that curved away to Max's left. Heading toward the right, he broke into a run, still carefully holding the crossbow, as above him the rope drooping across the invisible suspended sphere paused in its slide. The arrow dove into the ground. The rope, though, was remaining up.

Max completed a complete circuit around the hanging rope, passing the embedded arrow partway around his path. The cord hovered in the air, apparently unsupported by anything solid. On one end the arrow held it down like a tentpeg. From the arrow, the cable angled up in a straight line to a point perhaps forty feet overhead, bent over the curved top of a spherical surface, looped once around itself, outlining a circular space two feet in diameter, and then led downward again in the same manner, displaced a third of the way around the sphere from its entrance. It terminated in the crossbow reel Max still held. "Let's get that net," Max announced, carefully setting the crossbow down in the grass.

They unloaded the decrepit net they had originally found camouflaging the boat. "You're actually going up there?" Jurtan asked with a note of incredulity.

"You want to do it instead?" Max adjusted his resorted knapsack on his back. "That is the whole point of this exercise, in case you weren't paying attention along the way."

"You really *enjoy* this stuff."

"Regular storehouse of rhetorical questions, aren't you," Max muttered. He hefted a coil of heavier rope over to the upended arrow and tied one end of it around the arrowhead. "Watch that it pays out smoothly," he told Jurtan.

"What's the matter with the rope that's already up there?"

Max began pulling, carefully winding the slender cord back onto the crossbow reel. "See how thin it is? The stuff's strong, but it's a pain getting a good climbing grip." The heavier cable rose into the air, navigated the loop, and sunk back down into Max's grasp. One of the wizened trees had dug in not far from his position; after disengaging the thin cord from the new thick segment, he pulled the free end over to the tree and tied it securely around the trunk. Then he crossed back to Jurtan.

Jurtan was looking across at the knot around the tree. "What am I supposed to do if you lose your hold and—" The rope jerked at his feet. Where had Max gone this—

Max was already halfway up, his hand-over-hand grip backstopped by the loop of rope slapped around his waist and dropping loosely between his feet. He scurried up another ten feet, then slowed. Just above his head, the cable curved over across the invisible sphere. Max slowly reached out toward it.

"Huh," he said, again running his hand along a pantomime surface. "Looks like it *is* a full ball. I thought it might be flat on the bottom." At least it wasn't rotating, and it hadn't zapped him, either. Of course, those had been the safe odds. It hadn't fried the birds, they'd only bashed into it.

"What if the door's on the bottom?"

Max slithered his way up the slope, ignoring Mont. He'd been in a lot of odd situations, but for sheer disorientation value this one was no slouch. Even with his nose up against the surface it was thoroughly transparent—he was looking down at the ground through an unsupported drop in apparent ignorance of the law of gravity. But then he'd reached the top and was outright sitting on air. It felt more like polished ice than air, though. Supported by the loop around his body, he locked his legs around the lower rope and let loose with his hands.

This promised to be one of the trickiest parts of the whole enterprise. Before leaving the ground, he had cut a short length of free cable. He fished it out of his shirt now, passed it around the other rope where it crossed itself in its ring around the central support pillar, and made several knots using both hands, which was the only way to do it unless you were going to pull some old fakir trick. Then he flipped another, longer length of rope around the first one, sat up against the pillar, and knotted the rope around his waist.

"That looks weird," called Mont.

"Tell me about it." A glance down told Max that, regardless of his kibitzing, Mont had gotten ready with the net. Max hauled in the dangling length of rope and the net came up tied to the end.

Although its tails were certainly ratty, a closer inspection had revealed that the camouflage netting was in hardier shape than the initial once-over had implied. On the ground Max had sliced it halfway through from one edge to its center. With this slit eased around the central pylon, the net draped itself over the sides of the sphere and hung free at its lower hem. A moment more of tying loose ends together across the long slice, and Max had an actual visible surface to work on. He cast loose from his roped-in perch and started creeping across the scaffold.

Max was certainly hoping the door *wasn't* on the bottom, and not only because he didn't want to give the kid the satisfaction of having called it. The door could still be reached even in that position, but it would take some tricky rappelling that Max was not excited about at all; it was really too early in the morning for that sort of thing, not to mention a bit gratuitous to boot. In any case, bottom entry would have presented the designer with some significant problems for the layout of the interior if he or she didn't want things rolling out every time the door was opened. The ball wasn't tiny, but with a diameter of ten or twelve feet it wasn't exactly built for entertaining either. Then again, the use of an appropriately suspended lower deck and a guard rail could have . . . ah!

The hideout didn't use second quantum level spellwork; Max had learned that much from the absence of the characteristic emission spectrum during his investigations of the previous evening. He hadn't been able to learn much more with his nose pressed up against it. True, he could now feel the refraction zone matrix. The fact that the optical discontinuity was standing an inch or so out from the actual underlying surface on which his weight was resting was a disconcerting effect in its own right, if not a totally unexpected one. The underside of the netting where it came closest to the surface fuzzed out as it dipped through the discontinuity and tried to vanish, as did Max's own hands and other body parts.

With his face pressed right up against the interface, the clear view of the ground took on the blur of a cloudy crystal or the reflection of a mirror tarnished enough to show its own silver on top of the image behind.

With his restriction to manual means or at the most to passive, receptive spellwork, even Max had had a smidgen of doubt about his ability to figure out a way into the sphere on any sort of near-term basis, not that he would have mentioned it to the kid; he might not have even mentioned it to Shaa. Too, there was the barest chance that the whole thing was a decoy. It wasn't until his fingers running carefully across the surface felt a slight ripple, a ripple that on further investigation could actually have been a fine crack, that Max started to feel a bit more confident. The crack outlined a circle just the right size for a hatch. Its top edge was perhaps two feet down from the base of the suspension pillar, which would put it in an appropriate position as well. He tugged open enough of the netting to expose the area.

Of course, another slight hurdle remained to be overcome. He was unable to feel any other surface features either inside the circle or in its immediate vicinity. He decided to risk one or two low-energy revelation bursts, but when these had soaked in through the refraction field nothing had changed; no runes had appeared, no instructions had fluoresced, no locking mechanisms had materialized. To be sure, Max again pressed his face up against the surface and squeegeed it around in a search pattern. Through the refraction haze, he could see Jurtan Mont standing beneath him on the ground, his neck uncomfortably contorted. "Why don't you hit it?" Mont yelled up.

The last two search spells were still circulating. Max closed his eyes and let himself feel the ebb and flow of field lines. It *was* a door, that was clear, with a compound-configuration recess that was waiting for some kind of key to catalyze its shift to its other state of stability . . . no, there were more than just the two states, now that he looked more closely. The closed-and-locked state was easy, that was the one before him now, and "open" was a matter of logical deduction, but then for that matter so were the two—no, three—trap states whose activation hooks seemed precariously close to the sequence that seemed likely to lead to unfastening. Max would have to concentrate, but he had no doubt he could handle it. It would take awhile, though.

He lifted his head off the ball to get himself into a more comfortable position. Something seemed to retard his movement, tugging his chest back toward the surface. A small tented shape was drawing his shirt outward. Something under his shirt?

The amulet?

Max pulled it out. The central gem was glowing blue, and it was *warm.* When he let go, the amulet swung out on its chain and clinked against the surface like one half of a magnet pair. It began to turn, clockwise, stopped, counter-rotated half a revolution, then—

Max grabbed it back. It resisted him more forcefully this time; he actually had to yank it away. It came free with a sudden jerk. He had had an unpleasant vision of the door suddenly swinging open into the sphere, the amulet stuck to it, the amulet's strong chain drawing tight around his neck and dragging him abruptly after it with the choke of an unexpected garrote. Max turned the amulet in his fingers, probing at it. It ignored him. It had been ignoring him since he'd first obtained it, during his last visit to the Imperial Thaumaturgical Archives. Not for the first time, the thought that this particular piece had not come to his hands through total accident was in his mind. If so, the thing's personality was no less than he deserved. It liked to treat him the same way he treated others.

He'd never had a hint that the amulet was useful as a key, though. Given that it *could* be a key, it was more likely that it had the action of a skeleton key against a particular class of lock than to presume it had specifically been designed to fit *this* lock. The latter possibility was certainly the more intriguing, reeking as it did of murky plots, nameless intrigues, and hidden stratagems. That sort of thing was improbable even in the midst of an improbable life-style, but the improbable was not the same as the unheard-of. Still, this was scarcely the time to be pondering the mysterious when more evidence might be available close at hand.

Max slipped the chain off over his head and gingerly inserted the amulet into the guide-path he'd felt earlier weaving its way through the lock matrix. Actually, the amulet had its own clear idea of where it wanted to go. This time, it hit the invisible sphere with the protruding curve of its big gem, a jewel that in its resting state was clearly a diamond but that at the moment was the spitting image of a large sapphire. The jewel wobbled once, then hung there twisting back and forth in apparent insubordination to the standards of earthward motion. Then the jewel, trailing its chain, sank downward into the air and disappeared from sight. Max's hand, outstretched after it, encountered no resistance of its own, and similarly faded out. He lowered his head into the empty space.

After a short distance, the space wasn't empty at all, which was scarcely a surprise. The view of netting and ground dimmed and suffused into mist. Instead, there was the hatch, swung down and back, its surface now revealed to be metal polished to a light matte finish. His amulet still hung outward from the hatch with its gem just touching the surface. Just beyond the hatch in the middle of the sphere and dangling on a tripodic chain from the roof, a large wizard-light globe was in the process of igniting itself, its color pulsing back and forth between green and purple and finally settling for an atmospheric pale solferino. It lit up a ball-shaped room of the right proportions to match the volume draped by the netting outside, a flat peg-and-groove floor covering the lower bilge curve. Bookcases bent around the wall and outlined a small desk across from the hatch. In the center of the floor was an ornate rug, and on top of the rug was a comfortable-looking divan.

The divan and its head-pillows bore the imprint of a human-sized body. Not, however, the *recent* imprint—someone had spent enough time there in the past to dent the springs, but they didn't seem to have been around any too lately, judging from the quantity of dust and the number of drooping cobwebs. Either Iskendarian hadn't wanted to spend the effort to set up a perpetual cleanliness spell or he just hadn't cared one way or the other about housekeeping. Or, possibly, he hadn't planned on coming back. From the number of books on the shelves and the height of the stacked manuscript notebooks and loose pages by the desk, though, that last guess seemed less than apt. Now, how much of the stuff could Max carry? Maybe it would be better to settle in for a few weeks and just read everything.

The manuscripts were the logical place to start. The only problem, Max realized as soon as he started paging down through the sheets from the top, was that Iskendarian had exhibited good paranoid technique by using his own writing code. Max could recognize equations interspersed among the text; it was difficult to disguise their form but much easier to obscure their contents. Here he had a whole transformational derivation stretching through five—ten!—pages. Something about that one looked a bit familiar . . . communications, that was it, *that* term had to be a carrier-wave modulator, and that one . . .

"Max! Max!" broke in on his concentration some time later. He mounted the ladder and extended his head back out into the world.

"What is it?"

The sun had shifted positions in the sky; instead of rising, it was already starting to descend. "Are you okay?" Jurtan called up.

"Yeah," said Max. Something more than the usual was bothering the kid. Mont hadn't been yelling; he'd been speaking almost softly. "What's up?"

"I thought it might be you, thought you might be in trouble. The music—something doesn't feel right." Jurtan looked nervously over his shoulder back in the direction they'd come from. "Could somebody be following us?"

"Damn!" said Max. He leaned farther out of the hatch, knife in hand, and slashed at the knots he'd tied to hold the net in place. It slipped free and headed for the ground. Mont hopped back in a hurry, and the net just managed to miss his head.

"What are you doing?" Jurtan said.

"I thought we shook them." Max was still busy with the knife. "Cut that knot! Go!"

"Shook who?" Jurtan reached the tree and hacked once at the rope with his own knife. The loose end began to whip upward.

The other end wasn't falling, though; Max was hauling the whole thing in. He'd cut loose the cross-tie that had held the cable in place around the pylon. Max's body still vanished into the empty air at the level of his waist—his torso and head were clear enough, although he was balancing on nothing, but below them was—well, it was weird. The rope was disappearing into the same place his legs would have been. "Them," said Max. "The Hand. Get down! Can you tell how close they are?"

"You mean someone *was* following us here? This Hand guy?"

Both ends of the rope slithered upward and popped away into the air. Max withdrew from sight after them. "The Hand isn't a person, it's a group," he hissed. "They're—"

"We know you're in there, Maximillian!" The shout came from somewhere across the water surrounding their island. "You might as well come out!"

"Like I said," Max muttered. "The Hand."

"I wish you wouldn't keep springing things on me like this," Jurtan said morosely, face down on the ground beneath the level of the marsh grass.

"Things get sprung on you one way or the other, kid. You get them from me or I can stand out of the way and let life pitch them at you direct, take your pick."

"We have the island surrounded, Maximillian! Please come out and save us all some trouble, eh, my old friend?"

"Who's that talking?" whispered Jurtan. "What are we going to do? What are *you* going to do?"

12
DIFFERENT PERSPECTIVES

"Can't you hold this thing any steadier?" said the Great Karlini.

"Bird is," said Haddo. "Not is machine." Karlini had never been nearly as fond of flying as Max, who enjoyed the freedom of clear skies and open air and rushing speed. Not that Karlini disliked all of it—he didn't mind smooth air, or a straight and level glide, or even high altitude above a totally unsupported free-fall drop. Max was blessed with a thoroughly unflappable sense of balance, though, and the cast-iron constitution of his inner ear let him actually enjoy the swoops, banks, rolls, stalls, and crash dives of the large scavenger bird that Karlini had, after a fashion, inherited. Haddo—well, who knew what kind of sense of balance Haddo had, anyway, but at the least he seemed to have a solid rapport with the bird, and if the skin beneath his ever-present fuligin black cloak ever turned green (or whatever passed for the color of nausea in Haddo's circle) he had never given the slightest sign of it. Karlini screwed his eyes shut again, took in a slow deep breath, and tightened his double-armed grip around Haddo's midsection, conveniently located just ahead of him on the tandem saddle slung across the bird's shoulders at the base of its long wattled neck. "Constrict not my lung," Haddo grumbled, but he didn't actually try to pry Karlini loose from his death-grip hug.

Along with whatever mutation and environmental shift had let the subspecies grow to such a hypertrophic size that they were capable of carrying two fully-grown humans (or a human and a something-else-of-roughly-human-mass-and-shape), and on top of them a limited amount of cargo at the same time, the birds had acquired a different attitude toward the aesthetics of flight than their dwarf ancestors and cousins. Rather than just looping idly around the sky, drifting on updrafts and generally lazing around while they waited for some groundhugger creature to do them the favor of turning itself into carrion, the giant buzzards now seemed to enjoy executing more strenuous aerial calisthenics. That was paradoxical on the face of it, Karlini thought, because the stresses on the birds' skeletons and musculature would have increased out of proportion with their increase in size.

Shaa had once described to him the results of a rare necropsy on one of the giant birds. Although Shaa had not actually been present for the event but had instead heard the story from a medical acquaintance, he had illuminated the scene as though he had been the one manning the saw, mentioning the hydrogen-filled buoyancy spaces in the hollow bones, tendons with the tensile strength of old-world bridge cables, and a supercharger affair on the high-efficiency heart. Max had nodded sagely at the last point; he was the only one of them who seemed to have the slightest clue of what a supercharger actually might be, but typically enough he hadn't been talking. Sinking into his reverie, which had looked to be a clear sight more comfortable than his current situation, Karlini's innards suddenly all leapt at once toward his left shoulder, revolved around his chest until they were plastered against his right side, and then caromed smartly off his backbone. "Blech," said Karlini.

"Grouse you not," Haddo snapped.

"You can't tell me you actually enjoy this?" asked Karlini. "Can you?"

"Not to enjoy for me is," said Haddo. "Is for me command of Karlini. 'Fly bird,' is of Karlini the word, and of Karlini are both the servants, I and bird both, so choice have we what?" The bird might indeed have been listening; no one who might legitimately know had been willing to say how smart the birds really were. It executed a particularly vicious side-slip, nosed over, and launched itself in a tight spiral toward the ground. Haddo squawked at the bird and hauled on the reins; the bird hollered back and reluctantly flattened out into a long glide, and then a slow smooth climb. "Always with bird Haddo is," he continued. "Did sign up not to manager of aviary be. Not—"

"Not is in your contract, yes, Haddo, I know," said Karlini with half a mind, "and I assure you we all appreciate the sacrifice you're making."

"Also not job is to run of operation air the freight," Haddo added, but that was just his mouth slowing from its momentum, Karlini figured; Haddo knew he'd made his point. For only the first time in over half an hour.

"Quite an outstanding job you're doing with the bird, too," Karlini commented. "I don't know where you've been keeping it, but I hadn't seen it around since before we left Roosing Oolvaya. Was it out foraging? How did it know when to show up?"

"Arrangement have we." The bird whooped once in agreement.

Karlini cracked one eye cautiously open and looked around. Their altitude still let them look down across the broken-mirror glitter of the moonlit Oolvaan off to the left, snaking back and forth in its sullen meanderings and gradually spilling open on both banks as it entered its delta out toward the horizon far ahead. Much closer, though, the urban center of Oolsmouth was clearly apparent. The bird banked right again and began to lose altitude, at a much more civilized rate this time.

Haddo and the bird had obviously worked out a deal that gave the bird a certain amount of autonomy over its own schedule; frankly, Karlini figured that was just as well, since the problem of where to house the bird otherwise never seemed to go away. As it was, letting the bird hang out on its own avoided a lot of hassles, especially since the bird seemed willing enough to make itself available when needed. If you could reliably reason from the scant evidence, it would appear that the bird liked its job with Karlini much more than its old one, for the Death who'd ended up in the ring, and was willing to compromise to keep its employers happy. "Do you think you've got enough of a rapport with this thing,'' Karlini said in a low voice, ''that it'll let you know in advance before it decides to take its leave of absence to visit the ancestral breeding grounds?''

''It better,'' Haddo said, ''if knows for itself good what is.''

Well, what more could you want from a bird, anyway? Karlini thought. Their decision to use the bird to ferry him to Oolsmouth had been reached early enough in the day that Karlini had actually had enough time to force himself to skip two meals. As a result, the visceral warfare hadn't taken the same toll on his stomach that it otherwise would certainly have done; in fact, he'd even managed to keep himself from retching outright. That was something to be thankful for, sure enough. The bird was willing to drag them around, but it did this under some sufferance, and Karlini didn't want to test its level of forbearance by throwing up all over its pinfeathers. He kept his teeth firmly gritted as they dropped lower; then, all at once, the landscape below was no longer an abstract picture disconnected from them, but an expanse of rushing trees almost close enough to touch, their crowns and branches monochromatic under the white-splashed moon.

Actually, they weren't really close enough to touch, not yet, but the bird was coming in steadily as Haddo looked for a space big enough for a landing-strip. A road ran through the trees—surely it was too narrow? . . . yes, Haddo had let it pass. The trees abruptly ended in a neat line and yielded to fields, the torchlit sprawl of Oolsmouth conspicuous on their left. The ground skimmed past, they hopped a fence, and then the bird reared up, stalled, and settled gently in with a fluff of wings.

''Whoof!'' said Karlini, letting himself slide to the ground. One foot landed on soil, but the other leg embedded itself in a brambly shrub. Certainly that wasn't the only plant around? No, the entire field was filled with even rows of them. He disentangled his foot, glad that he'd worn his heavy pants for the ride on the bird-saddle . . . but now his entire leg was covered with bits of fluffy white, almost glowing in the moonlight. They'd landed in a cotton field.

Haddo had tossed down his pack. Karlini hefted it and turned back to the bird to have a final word with Haddo before his departure, but the pilot seat was empty. "Come," hissed Haddo. His glowing eyes were already some distance down the row of cotton plants.

Karlini weaved toward him. Just as he reached Haddo, he heard a flap and a *whuff* behind him and a gust of air blew against his back. He turned around just in time to see the bird take a final step off the ground and soar off over the field, flap its wings again, and fade gracefully into the night. "I thought you were just dropping me off," said Karlini.

"Thought apparently you wrong." Haddo turned and headed purposefully across the field.

Now, wait a minute, Karlini thought. The plan was for him to sneak into Oolsmouth, try to find out exactly what was happening with Groot, and with luck resolve the situation—but what did Haddo intend to do? Karlini caught up with him. "Where do you think you're going?" Karlini said. "You're not just doing this to go shopping, are you?"

"Business have you. Business have I, too," Haddo told him mysteriously but in a tone of definite purpose; a tone that made it sound like Haddo knew more about what he wanted to accomplish and how he intended to do it than Karlini did himself.

Maybe I should try to talk him into taking me along on his *errand first,* Karlini thought.

"Coming are you?" Haddo said impatiently.

Karlini got himself moving again and trailed Haddo to the edge of the field and over a split-log fence onto a dirt road. Without the merest hesitation, Haddo turned left and scuttled off down the lane with the air of a being who knew exactly where he was going and what he was about.

For some time, Karlini's curiosity about Haddo had been growing. If he watched closely, this might be a useful opportunity to find out something worthwhile. Haddo's recalcitrance and cryptic nature easily outpaced even Max's level of cussedness, though. The fact that he was not only letting Karlini accompany him on his "business" without being harangued for half an hour first, or being wheedled into it, but had out-and-out told Karlini to hurry along with him, was enough to give even a normally impetuous person pause. Karlini didn't think of himself as impetuous in the least but really rather more the stay-at-home type, so the situation was all the more glaring in its stark contrast to their usual routine.

The side road they were on soon met up with a larger one. They turned right at the intersection, clearly aiming toward the outskirts of Oolsmouth across the gently sloping land. It had been a number of years since the last time Karlini had visited Oolsmouth and with the continuing pace of the local pastime, public works projects, he wasn't sure he'd know his way around. If he remembered correctly, though, they were heading toward what had been the shantytown area on the northwestern edge of town. Wandering around in the post-midnight gloom, even with a good moon still up, was not exactly the best way to renew a connection with unfamiliar geography, but Haddo still seemed to know where *he* was going, sure enough.

"Uh, Haddo? Is this side of the city still the, uh—"

"See you will," said Haddo. "Quiet now be."

"If that's where we're going," Karlini muttered, "I'm glad I'm with you."

"Glad should you be."

Ahead of them, a clutter of ramshackle buildings, some little more than lean-tos, marked the edge of Oolsmouth. *Don't look like a victim,* Karlini reminded himself. *That's what they always say.* But you weren't supposed to call attention to yourself by being too forthright, either. There was a spell-sequence for turning yourself invisible, but it would have taken a several-hour session to set up even if Karlini had the right references at hand, and in any case it was most effective against straightforward humans. The street was still deserted as they passed the first buildings. Down the block on the right, however, he could see a fairly solid-looking two-story timber-frame structure with open glassless windows on the second floor. Something drifted past one window, something luminous and wispy, like a person-shaped cloud or a gauze manikin. It didn't look tough, and things wrapped in gauze usually had a hard time being menacing, but then it was probably only a lookout.

On the other side of the street, protruding from a deep pool of shadow between two houses, Karlini spotted a pair of legs. The feet, clad in old ratty sandals, were resting in the rubbish-heaped gutter, and the bare legs stretched back away into the darkness, disappearing from sight just above the knee. Each of the two legs was as thick at its calf as Karlini's waist and their length from knee to ankle would have measured Karlini from floor to hip. A rumbly snore rasped from the alley. Karlini was not relieved to see that Haddo gave the legs a wide berth, but he locked his jaw shut and followed Haddo's path. *It doesn't matter,* he thought. *They're still pretty basically like us.'*

At the next corner, though, the figure sitting on a flat perch nailed halfway up that building, and leaning backward against the wall with his arms folded over his chest, appeared human in all particulars, at least to the limit of visibility provided by the moon and the few firelit windows. The head swiveled to follow them down the street, the silver color of moonlight glinting in its eyes. Karlini kept himself from rushing his pace as they went past. There *were* some people who had extensive congress with their more outré cousins, whether out of business, philosophy, or various emotional hangups, but since cross-species fraternization was more of a vice than a mainstream activity, and a tawdry vice at that, those folks didn't advertise it around too loudly; they were in a sense as much of a silent population as the nonhumans themselves, the kind of people whom one saw standing on a streetcorner shouting hoarse-voiced manifestos from beneath a mane of scraggly hair, or giving lectures on "My Life with the Folk of the Field." *Rather tedious, really,* thought Karlini. On the other hand, anyone who spent the night perched on an outer wall watching the street could be more than odd, he could be downright dangerous. *You're a sorcerer,* Karlini told himself, *and a leading one, too. You can certainly deal with a single weirdo.*

It wasn't reassuring. The guy could have friends. The guy could know the whole district. And the only backup Karlini had was—Haddo?

Where he had gone?

A sharp hiss came from the right, where another narrow alley would off between the buildings. Karlini tried to steady his breathing and went into it. Haddo's glowing-coal eyes glared up at him. "Attention pay," Haddo snapped. "Lost get not."

"How much farther are we going?"

"Until get there we." The eyes disappeared as Haddo swung around. Karlini heard the small sound of feet crunching through the usual ground-garbage. The sound began to retreat again from him so he followed once more.

It was much darker in the alley, which wasn't a real surprise. He didn't like using spells in this gods-forsaken place, but did he remember anything for night vision? What about—

Gods-forsaken?

"Haddo," Karlini said in a low voice, "do you folks have any gods?"

The crunching ahead of him stopped. "What mean you?"

"All the gods I've ever heard about have been human, in appearance I mean, and in temperament, too. Are there any gods like you?"

Haddo said nothing. Maybe it was a sore subject; he probably should have thought more before bringing it up in the first place. The answer could have significance, though, to someone at sometime somewhere if not obviously so at the moment. "Personal, question is," Haddo said slowly.

"Oh, I don't know. It's more—"

"My word, take."

"Well," Karlini said, "don't you have gods leaning on you and looking over your shoulder the way we do?"

"Without representation, taxation still is."

"I'm not sure I—"

"Maximillian, ask should you. Expert on gods is he." Haddo turned and crunched hurriedly away.

Was Haddo just trying to distract him with misdirection? He knew Max wasn't anywhere Karlini could reach him for a question at the moment. No, it probably wasn't misdirection at all; it would be just like Max to have wormed something interesting out of Haddo and not have mentioned it to anybody. Around the next bend, his thoughts still churning queasily, Karlini almost tripped over Haddo. Haddo for once didn't bother to mention this, He was scrutinizing the apparently blank wall of a building, hands on what were presumably hips. "Haddo izney tu," he said to the building.

Nothing happened. After a moment, he said, in a louder and more aggrieved voice, "Haddo izney *hala*-tu!" Then he kicked the wall for good measure.

A concealed door separated itself from the wall and opened inward. Haddo, abandoning his usual scuttling gait, strode into a dark hall. Karlini squared up his shoulders and trailed him in. The door closed after them. "With doors tricks more," muttered Haddo. "Always with doors tricks. Think you up with something new come they would."

A voice spoke out of the gloom deeper down in the hall and from a higher level, as though the speaker was hanging from the ceiling; the character of the voice was a sort of contralto buzzing whine, the kind of sound a person with a few bees caught in their throat might make. "Nobody said you had to come here," the voice said.

"Haddo am I," said Haddo.

"Are you now?" buzzed the voice. "And who is this—person?"

"With games stop," Haddo snapped. "Door open."

"You can go in," the voice said reluctantly, "but your man waits outside."

A sudden glare of red slashed across Karlini's dark-adapted vision. His own barely stifled yelp went totally unheard under the twin sounds of an electric-arc zapping and the frantic buzz of a beehive abruptly kicked off its tree branch. In the seared-white afterimage Karlini could see the figure of Haddo just ahead of him, one arm at shoulder level, backlit in silhouette by the core of the light-burst pouring out from his hand. The buzzing ran down the scale with a gulp and a pant. Without another word, though, a new door opened ahead and to the right. A staircase led down. "Word say not," Haddo muttered back over his shoulder. "Cool be." He headed down the stairs.

Ahead of them spilling up the staircase were the jumping lights of candles and lanterns, quite a number of candles and lanterns at that, and as they descended a large fireplace came into view as well across the room, its piled wood in full roar. Karlini had given up trying to seriously figure out what Haddo was leading him into, but he'd expected perhaps a small room illuminated by a single low candle in the middle of a table, with various dimly-glimpsed beings arranged around it making secret signs and behaving in an obstinately enigmatic manner. Instead, the sprawling basement room that greeted them was clearly a tavern, or more properly an establishment of cosmopolitan iniquities, and by the looks of it quite a flourishing one at that. It was plainly not, though, a place particularly catering to humans, of which species Karlini found himself to be the sole member in attendance.

For the most part, the major nonhuman breeds differed only in size, skin color, number of joints, and facial features from what humans liked to think of as the norm. Nevertheless, there wasn't usually a lot of social mixing. For the most part, the nonhumans congregated in their own districts when they were in cities. Whether this happened under their own pure volition or because of pressure from the human citizens (or directly from the coercive power of the cities themselves) was for most purposes a moot point; as long as they were out of sight, people were happier overall. The happiness of the nonhumans was a matter few people troubled themselves with. To be more precise, Karlini reminded himself, not much else about nonhumans troubled people either. People as a whole couldn't care less about what the nonhumans did in their part of a city, or what they did when they weren't in cities, for that matter. Well, okay, that was a gross generalization, but then lumping all individual differences in a common pot was the kind of thing people are good at. Shaa had told him he thought there was a significant case of societal myopia at work, if not outright amnesia, but then Shaa had always held himself to be a social critic.

Ahead of them, a party of stout waist-high folks with the generally rough-and-tumble air of roustabouts were gathered singing off-key choral rounds around the hearth; they turned to look Haddo and Karlini over as they came down the stairs, and a few other assorted patrons raised their heads to eye the two of them as well. Karlini found himself trading stares with the large purple eyes of a white-furred face topped by a coordinating lilac beret; a thin rope of glowing smoke wound upward from the cigarette perched in an ivory holder in the red-lipped mouth. Karlini held her stare long enough to demonstrate his security of character but not long enough to mean anything by it, and then swung his gaze around the room with a feeling of relief. He'd found the proportions and the color scheme of her face vaguely distressing, but she was a far sight better than the out-and-out distasteful looks of her companions around the table. One had something more than vaguely snakish about him, and the one with his leathery arm around the smoker's shoulders, well . . . Karlini's foot came down on something more solid than the thick but slippery stair risers, and he realized they had reached the main part of the floor.

Haddo twisted his way off to the left, Karlini carefully threading along with him. The bartender, a thick-set humanoid about three feet taller than Karlini and perhaps twice his bulk, watched their progress with pursed lips, or more correctly watched Haddo's approach and ignored Karlini altogether. The guy took a final appraising look at Haddo, then disappeared into the stockroom behind the bar. Karlini noticed that the center portion of the bar was set at a comfortable height for the average-sized human, which seemed to be around the average for the folks around the room as well; the left end of the bar, though, had a series of risers set along the floor, and the right end had a trench dug down into the ground beneath the uprooted planking. Haddo sauntered up onto the middle part of the short-beings' section and turned to look over the crowd again. Karlini edged next to him and whispered, "Did we really have to come here? I mean, Haddo, this bar stuff is such a cliché."

"For you to meet is someone," said Haddo, peering into the murk of the far corner of the room. "To meet, go must where one is."

"I haven't been in a place like this since, well, since the time I met you."

Haddo mumbled something unintelligible. The bartender reemerged from the storeroom, ducking beneath the door sill at the back of the bar with a wooden crate the size of a valise under his arm. He set the crate down in front of Haddo, took a firm hold on the lid, and worked it back and forth. Nails let loose with drawn-out squeaks. Setting the lid aside, the bartender probed around in the crate with a hand that seemed almost as large as the interior itself. Wood shavings spilled out on the bar. Then, with a grunt of triumph, he withdrew a cylindrical parcel wrapped in fuzzy cloth. Haddo straightened. "Imri naj?" he said.

The bartender tugged loose a corner of the cloth and flashed Haddo a glimpse within. Karlini, off at a different angle, got an impression of dark heavy glass containing the sparkle of active lightning. Haddo reached inside his cloak after his purse, but the bartender held out his other hand, palm out. "Your name Haddo?" he said.

"Haddo am I," Haddo said.

"Then it's paid for," said the bartender.

Haddo paused a second, then shrugged, took the intoxicant, hopped off the riser, and headed for a table.

Karlini looked at the bartender, who ignored him and turned away. He took two long steps and caught up with Haddo. "Why didn't you order something for me?" said Karlini.

"Not would like your system the menu," Haddo said.

A path was opening in front of them as Haddo weaved his way through the room. A being about Karlini's height whose features were concealed by the hood of a forest-green cloak was walking from one table to another with a foaming mug protruding from his sleeve, his head swiveling loosely about. Then he caught sight of the form of Haddo bearing down on him with Karlini at his heels, abruptly straightened, and reeled back out of the way. Behind him and off to the back, Karlini spotted the empty table Haddo evidently had in mind as his destination. Another table of patrons turned away, sniffing the air as though something noxious was drifting toward them. Haddo bent his path and headed in their direction.

Karlini grabbed Haddo's shoulder and leaned over him. "Uh, Haddo?" he whispered in as surreptitious a voice as he could manage under the circumstances. "Don't you think it would be better if I waited outside? I don't want to set anything off, but these folks seem kind of jittery with me around."

"Not are they because of *you* upset," Haddo told him. Haddo shot another glance at the table of supercilious gnomes, said, "On you, all *feh!*" in their direction, turned his shoulder on them, and scuttled again toward the empty table and its beckoning chairs. As they reached the back, Karlini noticed that he had been holding his breath. "Inhale you can," said Haddo dryly, having noticed it too.

Karlini wedged himself into the chair behind the table and found himself mashed up against the wall. Had the Haddo he knew changed places in the dark with a ringer? Their table was back toward one corner of the room and the room's main illumination spilling from the hearth was shadowed by the stone side of the fireplace itself where it protruded into the room. Mounted on the stone front of the fireplace next to the fire was a dartboard; a small humanoid creature with bare furry feet and a nasty attitude was standing five paces back from it on top of a table, preparing to throw. He threw and hit the board, threw and hit, causing the few hangers-on to murmur approvingly. A smirk appeared on the short guy's button-nosed face and he said, in a cloyingly high-pitched squeak clearly audible across the intervening patrons, "You bums think that was good? Well, watch *this*." He threw again, underhand this time. The fletching on the short dart grazed the pointy ear of the elvish-looking fellow slouched in his chair at the front of the table, and as the elvish guy shot out an arm to grab the furry-footed one by the throat, the dart went corkscrewing off-course into the fire. The thrower started to backpedal out of the way but put his foot into a tray of salad. The salad promptly shot out from under him. He landed back-first on a pitcher of ale, which smashed, and then hit one corner of the table going down as the elvish guy hit the other side of the table on his way up; the table, predictably, flipped, and all of them went sliding to the floor. "Do you usually hang out with these kind of friends?" Karlini asked Haddo, still keeping his voice low. "Why are we here, really?"

"Time it is some things you should hear," Haddo said, taking a swig from his container. A small bolt of lightning rolled out of the jar mouth and crackled down into his hood. "But nothing trust," he continued, raising an admonishing finger. "Explain will I later."

"Hopefully more than you've been explaining until now," Karlini grumbled.

The floor shuddered. An earthquake? No, earthquakes didn't make that kind of low, gritty, scraping sound, like something was rasping long stone fingernails along the underside of the foundation of a building. Except for the clatter of chairs being knocked about and the crashing of the upended table, which was now being rapidly demolished, and the huffing, grunting, and cursing of the dartplayers where they were rolling around beneath it on the floor, all other activity had hastily ground to a halt. The same long grating noise came again, this time even causing the fighting dartplayers to pause. They'd stopped beating at each other with their table legs and were no longer gnawing on each other's elbows, and their mouths were hanging thoughtfully open as they listened with the rest of the crowd, but—they were still moving. The table top slid off them and fell flat with a bang. They were moving, because—

The floor underneath them had started to revolve.

Suddenly the bartender was there, shooing the bystanders away with a sweeping gesture and a firm kick, reaching into the pile of hesitating fighters and coming up with the short nasty one held upside down by one furry foot. The bartender slung him backward along the floor toward the stair, sliding him after the rapidly thinning crowd.

The short guy's elvish friend scurried after him on hands and knees, trying to rapidly make headway and gain his feet at the same time. Another kick here and a shove there, and the hulking bartender had cleared the moving section of floor of the pieces of table and the upset chairs, and the few adjacent but still right-side-up chairs as well. Then the bartender knelt down and rapped on the floorboard in the center of the revolving circle.

The circle stopped turning and the screeching died. Rap rap, *whack* came back at him from the underside. The bartender knocked a few more times and stepped back. The floorboards rotated another quarter turn, the rasp changed into more of a screech, and that section of floor swung open into the room.

Something moved in the passage beneath the trapdoor. Darkly gleaming and round, like the top of an upside-down cauldron, it couldn't be *alive* . . . but it *was* lurching up into the air. It was the small top part that was round like a cauldron, Karlini realized, and somewhere in its innards there might be a fully spherical shape about half his height, but as it rose into the room the mechanism—for it was certainly a mechanism—seemed so festooned with clanking, whirring, spinning, and huffing pieces of strange apparatus, arranged in so many intriguing lumps and modules, that there was in truth no telling what might have been inside.

Karlini was accustomed to seeing the latest small assemblies of illicit or contraband machinery that Max had dragged home, or whatever his latest target for tinkering happened to be, but he had never seen anything like *this*—such a conglomeration of cogwheels and jeweled gears, pulleys and linkages and belts, sprockets, cams, cables, and cranks, pneumatic bellows, and panels of lights. Gusts of vaporous air were emerging in spurts from the thing's flared base; each new gust sent the contraption rising up farther from the floor, only to see it settle slowly back down again before the next gust puffed forth. The cauldron-lid on the top of the thing—no, it was really more of a *dome*—was faced around with what looked like a strip of hardy windows; it spun slowly around, eyeing the retreating crowd and then the bartender, who eyed it silently back. The dome continued to traverse the room. Finally, it caught sight of Karlini. ''Eyeing'' was exactly the right word to describe what it was doing, Karlini suddenly thought, as blinking back at him from the blackness behind the windows in the dome were two apparently organic eyes, equipped with the usual pupils and lids and shaded a delicate light green. Standing next to Karlini, Haddo waved at it.

The mechanism tilted slightly over on its left, a trio of vanes like metal grouper fins flapping in the midst of the gears, and another gust of vapor emerged from its rear. Of course, Karlini realized, what else?—the thing was making its way over to their table. It hopped over the last intervening set of chairs and drifted to a halt. Clanking again, three sucker-tipped struts slid out from its underside and it settled gingerly toward the floor. One at a time, the suckers slurped hold of the floorboards. The mechanism wobbled back and forth, getting its footing so to speak, and the whirring, clicking, clanking, and wheezing activity on its surface quieted down substantially. The dome tracked around again and faced Haddo, who was leaning back in his chair with his arms folded over his chest under his dark robe. A small hatch flopped open on one side of the dome and a tube topped with a flaring, tulip-petal horn rose out. It, too, pointed itself at Haddo. In tinny tones, the speaking tube said something totally unintelligible.

''Lower Pocklish not use,'' said Haddo.

The tube blew air with a flatulent honk. Then, in a slightly less fractured pitch, it said, ''Haddo, with you how is?''

Karlini tried to stifle a groan. It was bad enough trying to communicate with Haddo by himself—now he was supposed to deal simultaneously with something else with the same variant syntax? ''With me all is fine, Favored One,'' Haddo said to the tube.

The dome ground to the left again, to get a better view of Karlini. ''This one Maximillian is not,'' the machine said.

''You right are. Introduction to make is time. Great Karlini,'' Haddo said, ''Favored-of-the-Gods meet.''

"A pleasure," said Karlini, making an abortive handshaking gesture toward the mechanism that left him waggling his fingers in midair.

"Hmph," said the machine. The dome glanced around them. Karlini, glancing around, too, noticed that the crowd had thinned virtually to nothing. Two of the thickset short miner types were still hanging around at the top of the stairs, out of earshot from their table, obviously keeping watch. Across the room, the bartender nodded once at the machine and gave a thumbs-up, then ducked out of sight into the storeroom. "To me looks situation stable," Haddo said.

The speaking tube snorted again and withdrew back under its hatch. A metallic clang came from deep in the machine, following by the *snickt*ing sounds of clamps unclamping and the squelch of screws unscrewing. The dome shook itself, then lifted up off the rest of the machine with a soft *slurp* and rotated back. A pair of pointed ears rose into sight, followed by a rag-mop of hair and a small elongated face. The ears swiveled to point at them, one at Haddo and one at Karlini, and the rest of the creature hoisted itself out of the interior onto a new perch on the rubberized seal of the dome's mounting ledge. He was all of three feet tall, even shorter than Haddo. "Are you some kind of elf?" Karlini said.

"That's one way to put it, I suppose," Favored-of-the-Gods snapped, "and not the way I'd prefer it if you'd like to know the truth."

"I see," said Karlini, not seeing at all. "I beg your pardon. A gnome?"

"Now, wait just a minute here," said Favored-of-the-Gods. "Wait just a damned minute!" He waved one hand in the air. "I am not a gnome! You got that?"

Karlini threw his own hands up. "Excuse *me!* I didn't realize it was a racial slur." The guy did look like a gnome, though, at least if he wasn't some breed of miniature elf. Was there some newer, more politically correct way of referring to them?

Favored frowned at Haddo. "*This* is the one latched by the trap of Pod Dall?" he said, pointing incredulously at Karlini.

"Correct are you," Haddo said. "Karlini it was."

"Who's Pod Dall?" Karlini asked.

"Remember you of castle the trap? Remember you your vision, of Death the god, of by ring the capture? Pod Dall that god was. Castle of Pod Dall was it where trapped were you. Owns Pod Dall castle that moves."

"Now, *you* wait a minute, Haddo. I thought nobody knew *who* that god was," said Karlini. "It's nice of you to mention it now, but I don't understand why it had to wait all this time. Why didn't you bring this up before, when we were all busting our necks trying to figure it out? It's important information, and—"

"You just watch your tone of voice, you big clodhopper," snapped Favored. "Where the hell you come off talking to Haddo that way? You better give him some more respect, you hear me?"

"What are you talking about?" Karlini said. "I thought Haddo was *working* for me. It's starting to look like I was wrong, isn't it, Haddo?"

"You didn't think a guy of Haddo's stature would waste his time hanging around with the likes of you if there wasn't a very good reason, did you?" Favored said.

"Uh," said the Great Karlini. "As a matter of fact—"

"Ego has he," Haddo said to him, patting Karlini reassuringly on the hand. "Attention pay not."

"He damn well better—" said Favored.

"Touchy always acts Favored," Haddo said, chopping him off as he was just getting underway again. "Habit is. When short you are, difficult can you become."

Karlini fought against a rising attack of apoplexy. "What is this guy, Haddo, your agent? A labor lawyer? What is this, he's going to sue me for treating you wrong? And what 'stature' is he talking about, anyway? When did *you* turn into a sorcerer?"

"This guy's nothing but a hedge wizard," Favored muttered. "Nostrums and love potions and no more science than you can—"

"Now just a—"

"Quiet!" hissed Haddo. "Of you, both!" He glared at the creature perched on the hatch of the machine. "Of you ashamed am I. Always pick you fights, must?"

"He's a *human,* goddamit," Favored said sulkily. "You know better than to expect me to roll out my manners for a hulk like *him.*"

"For purpose are we here," Haddo said slowly, enunciating each word with a deliberate slap, still keeping his gaze on Favored. The eye-sparks under the hood of his cloak seemed to grow sharper, brighter, hotter, until they were visibly lighting Favored's face with an angry yellow smear. Karlini could see Favored's pupils contracting along their vertical slit edges. A wisp of steam started from Favored's left eyebrow. "Is greater Karlini's curiosity than Karlini's manners, but does not in Karlini mean rudeness meanness. If manners keep will he, manners keep will you? Shall meet in middle, we?"

Favored kept on trying to stare Haddo down for another second. Then he abruptly closed his eyes and swung his face away. "All right, all right," he said, "but it's only because you're insisting so much. I still say you've been spending too much time with big idiots like him; you shouldn't be away from your own people."

"For absence reasons are; news to you is not." The searchlight glare from Haddo's hood faded. Afterimages of Favored's face danced in Karlini's own eyes; he was glad *he* hadn't been on the receiving end of that bit of stagecraft. Haddo glanced over at Karlini, who was happy to see he was able to keep himself from flinching. "Excuse of Favored behavior," Haddo said. "Walks he tightrope. Difficult is world."

"That's for sure," Karlini said appeasingly. Walking a tightrope was probably a fair description of Favored-of-the-Gods' life, even if he had been *floating* rather than walking, per se. Karlini couldn't get over the amount of machinery Favored was moving around with. "You really *must* be favored by the gods," he said to Favored. "Anybody I know who'd try to put together that much technology would find themselves catapulted into the nearest lava pit, or they'd come home to find their house gone and no one in the neighborhood admitting to having ever seen them before, or they'd look down while they're out in the street to find that a bottomless pit had just opened up under their shoes, all of which I guess really amounts to pretty much the same thing all around."

"Hmph," said Favored.

"Appears it that here must do talking I," Haddo said, glowering at Favored. "Help give you whenever urge you feel. Random is not name of Favored," he continued, turning toward Karlini. "Description is of job."

"You mean you work for the gods?" Karlini asked Favored.

"Yeah, yeah, I do some jobs for the big guys," Favored said reluctantly. "One of them in particular, really. They been keeping me on the hook."

Karlini drummed his fingers on the table top and wished he had a drink. "You're a technologist?"

"A Fabricator, I like to call it."

"But the gods prohibit—"

"Oh, all right," Favored-of-the-Gods said with a note of resignation. "You'll never understand anything if Haddo tries to explain it, anyway, and even if you could figure out what he's saying he always gets it wrong. This is the deal. Sometimes the gods need mechanicals, and some of them just plain like the stuff, for recreation. You know, like some of them collect art or buildings or jewels or stuff, or some of them collect people; most of 'em have got what they call their aesthetical amusements. You're about to say they mash down technology out in the world, right? Well, they do, but that doesn't mean they make themselves play by the same rules. Haddo says you're not an idiot so I guess you've gotta know the gods don't play fair."

"I won't tell you it's news," Karlini said.

"Right," said Favored. "They like a mortal population they can control. I don't know if they really think the fruits of engineering can upset their cart, but they like to play it safe and anyway they're in charge. So like I said, some of them go for mechanicals on their own time. As far as they're concerned, for themselves, mechanicals aren't taboo, they're not what you'd call appalling, but they're sort of risqué for those who swing that way."

"Technology is a guilty pleasure?"

"Yeah, that's right, you could say that. It's frowned on in your polite company, if you can say there *is* polite company with the gods. Most of them turn up their noses at this stuff, call it lowbrow, quaint, that kind of thing. Those gods who *do* go for that kind of kink don't really know much of anything about how to actually build the things, though, so they've got to farm out the work."

"No god's ever contacted Max about doing work," Karlini said to Haddo. "He must be one of the best technologists alive. He wouldn't *do* anything about it, I'm sure, but no one's ever asked him. For that matter, I've never heard of anyone who's been on retainer to the gods. Maybe it isn't the sort of thing you're allowed to talk about."

"Your pal Max is a different kettle of fish altogether," Favored said, "although I don't know why you're so certain no one's ever come after him. You want to kick in anything here, Haddo?"

"With exposition continue," Haddo said.

"Have it your way," said Favored. He adjusted his perch on the edge of his hatch. "Your name's Karlini? Okay, Karlini, you can't be too surprised you've never heard of this stuff before. The gods aren't fools. They don't like using humans if there's any way to help it; humans are too much trouble. They're too much like the gods themselves, sneaky and nasty and you can't trust them worth a damn, if you ask me. You can drive yourself crazy trying to reason with a human, too, and they're all goddamned busybodies, they won't just do a job and leave it at that. On top of it all they talk too much. Even when they're not out broadcasting to the world, they've got a hellish gift for thinking up new ways to cause problems. You hear what I'm saying?"

And he was calling *me* a racist, Karlini thought. "I assume you're building up to some point," he said.

"Through underbrush," said Haddo, "what saying Favored is, when want done job gods, call gods human not. Call gods Favored."

"The best Fabricator in the business," said Favored, "that's me, and I don't mind being the one to tell you."

"Okay," Karlini said, "now you've told me. Why?"

"Don't put a cramp," Favored said. "I'm getting there, I'm getting there. Like I was saying, along with the jobs I've done I've been able to spring myself some slack to do stuff on my own."

"Such as your vehicle there?"

"Yeah, like old Flotarobolis. What do you think of it?"

"Looks a little small for me," Karlini said cautiously. "There's no denying it's got character, though, and you had to have put an awful lot of work into it. The fact that for most anybody on the planet, building that elaborate a mechanism would draw you an immediate sentence of eradication from the nearest god adds a certain something, too."

Favored frowned. "You may be a human, but what you say is sure true enough. I'm in kind of a tricky situation. They may like me, but that doesn't mean I can just do whatever I want. It's hard to know where their limits are. I mean, I've got a lot more room to maneuver than most, but like I said . . ." He shrugged his shoulders.

"But your—whatever you called it, Floater-mobile?—your god friends think that's okay, right?"

Favored glanced around him, then leaned over to peer down into his craft, apparently examining some indicator device. He straightened up and checked over his shoulder again before saying, "Actually, they haven't seen it yet."

"Oh?" said Karlini. "On the face of it, since you're under the thumb of the gods, so to speak, doesn't that mean they'd also have you under their increased scrutiny? After all, they wouldn't want to risk you spilling all their secrets, would they? Wouldn't they be unhappy with you for sitting around discussing this stuff so freely in public?" Why *were* they discussing this stuff, anyway, other than out of general comradeship and tale-spinning curiosity?

"This of the matter crux is," Haddo said. He took a last sizzle out of his tumbler and slurped at the rim, then peered longingly down into its depths. "Vintage of excellence, was. Try you sometime should."

"Not for me," said Favored. "I don't have natural grounding like you do; it'd fry my innards to a crisp. But anyhow, Haddo's right. I've come up with this, ah, *misdirection* technique that defeats the probe of the gods; seems to work pretty well as long as you don't use it too much. I'm running it right now, in fact.'' A soft beep-beep, beep-beep from the depths of his vehicle interrupted. Favored leaned over and fiddled with some controls out of sight, and the beeping died off.

''Technology that can outwit the sight of the gods,'' Karlini said. ''That's exactly the kind of thing they're worried about.''

''You're right again,'' stated Favored, making one last adjustment. He settled himself back against the flipped-up hatch. ''I haven't been doing this stuff just for the heck of it. It's not worth it to risk getting pulped over some no-account puttering, even *I'll* say that. I'm doing it 'cause the time is right. You know about this business the gods have going on with their politics? This Conservationist and Abdicationist thing?''

''Some,'' Karlini said slowly. Haddo looked at him, his hood tilted at an incredulous angle. ''You're not the only one's got your own little secrets,'' Karlini said to him.

''Job description change must,'' announced Haddo, ''trusted confidant from, menial laborer to.''

''Don't start that again, will you please, Haddo?'' said Karlini. ''Why don't we just say we're even for the moment, okay?''

''See will we,'' muttered Haddo.

''If you two are quite finished?'' Favored said. ''The Abdicationists and Conservationists, right? From what I've been able to find out, it sounds like they're not just debating any more, their squabble's starting to spill over into outright action, like with this Pod Dall thing. There's still talk, but things're getting too intense for talk by itself. Like Karlini here put it, I don't like being a bug under the thumb of the gods for the rest of my life, and I think that by playing things right I might be able to help the Abdicationists come out on top; and if that means the gods decide to abdicate their control, well, I wouldn't be a bug anymore, would I?''

''We,'' said Haddo.

"What?" Favored said.

" 'I' not. Said you 'I'—'I like don't,' 'I Abdication help,' 'I' and 'I.' Not should say 'I,' should say 'we.' Are here we not for 'I,' are here we for 'we.' "

Even Favored looked a bit flustered after that one. Karlini was getting the idea, though, finally, of why Favored had wanted to meet, or at least he thought he was. "As you probably realize," he told Favored, "the crew I'm involved with, and especially Max, whom you obviously know, or know of anyway, also have the same long-term goal of breaking up the gods' hegemony over everybody else. I think we definitely may have something to talk about here, but before we get into that, I've got a major question I need an answer for." Karlini swung around. "Haddo, where do you fit into all this? Have I been paying good money to a spy, somebody who's plotting to stab all of us in our backs? Don't tell me you're just a loyal servitor, either—you've plainly got more going on than you've been willing to share. Well?"

"How say that can you?" said Haddo in his most aggrieved tone. "Have not been I in faithful extreme?"

"I don't know. Have you?"

"Disappointment have I with you," Haddo grumbled. "Think you—"

Favored had been watching the two of them with his sculpted eyebrows raised and the corner of his mouth curled. "You know, Haddo, I thought your pal had a point."

"Enemies from all corners have I! Mournful is world! To corner will slink I, to there pine and die. Okay! Okay. Generous will be I. Can understand I why might think old comrade Karlini this. Okay. Reasonable is question. From mind furthest was thing to in back stab friends. Okay?"

"That's not a bad start," Karlini said, "as long as it goes on to something more substantive."

"Box nit sassafras," muttered Haddo under his breath, or words to that effect. "Well very. In conscience good cannot say I that false completely is, charge that own plans have I, but did ever ask you me? Never ask did you."

"I *did* ask if you were loyal."

"Loyal am I!" Haddo said, throwing his arms in the air over his head. "In contract nothing is, prohibit that would own interests to pursue at same time as performing of job for you responsibilities of. Since are aimed us both at goal same, especially not prohibit contract would. Than this have done I nothing more, than to work on own time for same ends. Did not think you that gang of your only one was, to dethrone gods trying were?"

"It's technically true that your contract gives you a large amount of personal freedom," Karlini said, "I'll admit that much. When the two of us executed it, though, I thought we had a clear understanding about conflict of interest."

"Is in conflict interest not!"

"All right," said Karlini, "all right. I'm willing to let that pass." He had to acknowledge, to himself at least, that he was more intrigued than upset, anyway, and he didn't really want to choke off the conversation. "I just want you to know that Roni and I would have appreciated the extra help it looks like you were in a position to give us, if what I've been hearing here is any indication."

"How know you extra help gave I not? Glad am I brought you that up. Significant more is question than realize you. Alluding are you to talents of magic mine?"

"You're not going to tell me now that you ever gave any hint you were a sorcerer, too?"

"Not am sorcerer I," said Haddo. "Not am sorcerer I, in sense same as are sorcerer you. Did learn I not magic by study, work I not magic by symbol. Innate are talents. Magic of Haddo part is."

Karlini glanced at Favored. "Am I hearing this right? Is Haddo really saying that that old common folklore wisdom stuff about you guys having natural magical abilities is true? I mean, sure, elves and such and useless forest magic, everybody knows about that, but magic that's good for something?"

"Don't spread it around," said Favored, "but, yeah, you big galoots don't have a monopoly on magic users. Only you might as well know Haddo's still not giving you the whole story."

"On side which are anyway you?"

"On the side of not being a bug, pal. It's like this, Karlini. Haddo here'd have you think he was born doing magic, that it's built in, and I won't lie to you, some of that's true, but it's not the whole deal at all. He's studied, too, learned magic in the way it's been set out and lined up by gods and you people, with all that symbolic logic and rigorous math you all've saddled it with. Stop sputtering at me, Haddo."

"Not is public, this. Quiet this must keep."

"You're the one who thought it was time to tell some human, you wimp," said Favored. "Karlini was your idea. If you don't think he's trustworthy enough, don't you think it might have been a better idea to bring it up before all this?"

"Trust I Karlini," said Haddo. "To do something have to, we, still agree I. Difficult to change habit is. Easier to cute be."

"I think I missed something there," Karlini said. "You want to translate?"

"We're set up to feel like animals that broke out of a zoo, or'd do better to stay on some nature reserve," said Favored, "but that does have its good side. A tiger's a threat because it can chew your leg off, not because it can beat your spell with one of its own, or because it can out-scheme your power play. Things with real human-type power aren't cute, things that don't threaten you can be. People think of folks like Haddo or me as quaint little adorable darlings—" Favored made a disgusted face and spit toward the floor "—well, it may be annoying as hell, but it hasn't necessarily been a total loss."

"Protective coloration, isn't that called?" Karlini said.

"Yeah, right."

"So Haddo's made a point of keeping his abilities under wraps," said Karlini, "and you nonhuman folks need to be taken seriously, but you don't want anybody to know it. That's all very nice, but, again, why are you telling all this to me if you don't want anyone to know about it, and why now?"

"If will patient be Karlini," said Haddo, "get there we will. As have heard you, same goals share all we, and reasons for roughly same. Yet have differences means about, we. Thinks friend Favored, dangerous is work of Roni.''

''That's right,'' said Favored, directing a sharp stare at Karlini, ''I do. I've never met your wife and I'm sure I don't have anything against her, personally, at least no more than just because she's one of you big oafs, but that's beside the main point. The point is this stuff she's working on. If it gets out of control, there's no telling what could happen, and even it it doesn't get out of control it may be more power than anybody knows how to deal with.''

''But we've taken precautions,'' Karlini said, ''and—''

''I'm not finished. Take a look at Haddo over there. You ever seen him without that cloak? You ever seen anything under that hood but those two glowing red things? You think that's natural?''

''Pardon beg you I?''

''He may be too embarrassed to mention it,'' Favored said, ''but I'm not. He's got magic woven into his makeup. You start tinkering with the roots of magic, you might stir up things that're gonna be hazardous to his health. And it's not just Haddo, either, it's an awful lot of us. It may even be a lot of you people, too, even if you don't realize it.

''And even *that's* not all. For myself, I think that lot would be quite enough, frankly, thank you, but since I can tell you're gonna be a hard sell, I'll give you the clincher. None of that research your wife's up to is even necessary. If we play things right and just do a lot of keeping quiet over on the sidelines, I think this political stuff going on with the gods will settle things our way. We're not gonna have to fight them outright, we're not gonna need this goddamned arms race you're starting, all we've gotta do is be smart.''

''You *think,''* said Karlini. ''What if you're wrong? If you're wrong, we've got no fall-back position; we're back at the beginning, or worse. Even if you're right and we don't need to use the new stuff to fight the gods or undermine them, it's still new knowledge and it's still valuable. There'll be no end to the ways we'll all think of to use it. We've got extra precautions coming out of our ears, I told you that; nothing's going to get out of control. The research is moving so promisingly, too, it would be silly to stop it all now, which is what I presume you'd like us to? I presume that's the real subject of this little meeting?"

Favored-of-the-Gods sighed. "I'm not surprised that's your reaction. I've been in enough contact with Haddo to know what you were likely to say. I also know you've only got Haddo to vouch for me; you've never seen me before and don't know who or what I really am. I realize all that. I'd be happier if you quit your fooling around where you shouldn't be, you understand that well enough, but I suppose you're not going to do that just on my say-so. I'm a Fabricator, too—I know what it's like not to want to give up a neat line of research just because somebody you've never met tells you to. I'll even admit there's something to what you say about not putting all the eggs under one hen."

Favored scowled. "So I'm gonna be a wimp, too. Keep working on your own front, see if I care. But do me a favor? Do yourself a favor, do *everybody* a favor—go as slowly and as carefully, and as quietly, too, as you possibly can. And pay attention to what Haddo has to tell you."

"Haddo?" said Karlini. "Of course I listen to Haddo's input, when he says something that's not a complaint or a contract grievance. If he's got comments or suggestions, of course I'll listen to them."

Haddo snorted. He tilted his hood back and to the side, and his red eye-things combined to shoot Karlini an "oh, come on now" kind of look. "With subtleness been trying have I, to your impression of me change. Of time waste has been it. Blind even to obvious are you."

"That's not true!" said Karlini. "It's not fair."

"Think you of what say would Roni," Haddo told him.

"Well," Karlini said, "all right. Maybe. So why aren't you talking to her instead of me?"

"Look," said Favored. "Don't change the subject. If your image of Haddo the faithful sidekick hadn't been blown apart here, you'd still keep plugging him into the role you'd already carved out for him; he'd be a supporting character in your life with a no-negotiation predefined role. Right? Now you just take this and chew on it. Haddo represents himself and a whole bunch of us, too, and you've just got to accept that.''

''You should be having this meeting with Max, not me,'' Karlini said. ''After all, he's been the one who set this plan up; he's the prime motivator, he's the main plotter in most everything we're all doing. The research was his idea in the first place, based on *his* concepts.''

''Petulant now sound you,'' Haddo pointed out.

''Don't *you* change the subject,'' said Karlini. ''Why me and not Max? When he finds out the work's slowing down again because of *more* safety quibbles, you know he's not going to like that. Don't tell me about dangerous, I've seen Max mad.''

''Uh,'' said Favored, exchanging an unreadable glance with Haddo, ''okay. Here it is, then, straight out on the table, since that's the way you want it. We don't exactly trust your pal Max. *I* sure don't. He's a little too gung-ho about this whole game-against-the-gods things to make me comfortable. He could . . . get carried away with his plots and his plans and kick off something really nasty someday. Okay, there it is.''

''. . . I see,'' said Karlini. ''I don't agree with you. I think you're wrong.''

''I'm sure you do,'' said Favored. ''Will you do this much, anyway? Keep this conversation to yourself? Don't blow it all to your friends.''

''I don't know. What about—''

''Of *course* don't blow it to your wife.''

''I don't like it,'' Karlini said reluctantly, ''but I'll do it. For the time being I won't talk to anybody about this, not even Roni. Are you satisfied?''

''You're not a bad sort, guy,'' Favored said. ''I think we may end up meeting again. Right now, though, it's time for me to get out of here and get to work; we've been pushing our luck as it is.''

''But what about—''

''Catch you later.'' Favored finished lowering himself down into his vehicle and slammed the hatch shut behind him. The legs retracted, Flotarobolis chugged and lifted off, executed a turn-and-bank that would have done credit to Haddo's bird, and swooped toward its hole in the floor.

"All night wait will you?" said Haddo. He was standing impatiently by the table, making a tapping noise beneath his cloak against the floor.

Karlini rose and followed him toward the stairs. "How am I going to deal with you now?" he said, half to himself; he was a little shocked to hear how plaintive his own tone sounded. "I always had the impression you *enjoyed* working for me, even if you *do* like to complain a lot. Were Roni and I just convenient tools for you, just a means to an end? We always liked *you*, and we thought you liked us, too."

"In the world more than liking is—" began Haddo.

"How do you expect me to believe anything you tell me now?" Karlini said heavily.

Haddo didn't really have an answer for that. They walked out onto the street and angled toward the human core of Oolsmouth. After awhile, Karlini said, "Did this meeting at least have anything to do with the immediate problem of Groot and the boat?"

"Is connected everything," said Haddo. "Only out to figure have to is which connection which."

"Was that remark supposed to be helpful?"

"Is not in general useful philosophy?"

"Not as useful as some straightforward help would be, no."

"In your soul no poetry is," Haddo muttered darkly. "Left turn we here."

They had almost reached the river, by the smell of it, and by the glimpses of empty space opening up at the ends of some of the cross streets. "What does my soul have to do with anything?" said Karlini.

"My point, this exactly is," said Haddo.

"What point? Are you planning to tell me how my soul is supposed to bail out Groot? Wait a minute—doesn't Groot live somewhere around here?"

"Could be," Haddo said dryly.

Karlini suddenly noticed that Haddo was no longer leading him straight down a street, but rather up to the side entrance of a block of flats, up to it and through the door, in fact, into a dark inner hallway. Doors and stairs to the individual apartments opened along the hallway's length in the dim light from the street. Haddo, as always, displayed his ability to proceed without hesitation in the gloom. At the third door on the right, or perhaps it was the fourth, he knocked softly. After a moment they heard a creak of floorboards from behind the door, and a voice said, "Who is it?"

Karlini, waiting again for Haddo for handle this, was surprised to feel a kick against his shin. "Tell him," hissed Haddo.

"The Great Karlini," Karlini told the door. "And Haddo."

Bolts clanked back and the door eased open, so they slid inside. The man who'd spoken finished fastening the door shut again before unhooding his lamp.

"Julio?" said Karlini.

"Yes, of course, Meester Karlini," said Julio, tramping barefoot in his bathrobe into the room. "Thank you for coming; I must say I'm glad you're here. I was surprised when I got your message that you were on your way—you must have had the devil's own time tracking me down, with all the excitement there's been. You and your sorcerous ways, I suppose."

"I guess," said Karlini, staring at Haddo, who was making a show of examining the tatty wallpaper coming down at the top and peeling open at the seams.

"This hideout isn't being watched as far as I've been able to determine, so we're free to talk and plan here. Might I get you some refreshment?"

They settled down with mugs of coffee, or Julio and Karlini did, at least, and traded stories. Actually, the story was mostly Julio's, since Karlini felt Haddo's eyes on him whenever he so much as thought about the enigmatic session with Favored-of-the-Gods. That wasn't all Karlini had available to talk about, though.

"An *iceberg*, you say?" Julio shook his head. "We didn't have a thing to do with that. Perhaps those two strange characters from this—no, *yesterday*—afternoon, perhaps it was their doing. I thought they might be gods, but then one of them, the man, said something that made me think he might be one of you. Blue eyes, clean-shaven, a bit sharp-tongued in manner, carrying a walking stick, of all things."

A walking stick? "He didn't give you his name," said Karlini, "did he? No, he wouldn't have. You're right, he is one of ours, sort of." Maybe. "You said he was doing most of the talking? Did the woman he was with seem to be holding him prisoner?"

"I don't know," Julio admitted. "It wasn't the first thing on my mind, you understand. There did seem to be something a bit odd between them, but I thought it might have to do with their being gods, if that's what they were. So you say they weren't?"

"*He's* not," Karlini said, "but for all I know she very well might be. Maybe they'll help out and maybe they won't, but I wouldn't count on seeing them again. I'd put my focus on this Council meeting tomorrow. You still don't have any idea what this Dooglas is going to try to pull?"

"No. Dooglas is still in hiding in his mansion. I've spoken to his usual compatriots on the Council and even they haven't heard from him. At least that was what they told me, those I was able to meet with, but I believe they were telling the truth. They seemed as confused and curious as any of us."

"With so much curiosity around," Karlini said, "they probably have a full house at the session. Is that good for Groot?"

"With the evidence of the torture warrant and Dooglas' signature on it, you would have to say so. Except for Dooglas' behavior. That concerns me."

"Of himself sure is he acting," commented Haddo. "Perhaps ally has he."

"Yes," Julio agreed. "That god Sapriel the warrant mentions. And there was that delegation of torturers—no one knows where they came from, and somehow they managed to give the police squad the slip. Dooglas has quite an unusual number of men-at-arms at his property, too. If it was up to the Council, yes, I think they'd shut this nonsense down, but Dooglas worries me."

Karlini adjusted his posture, balanced uncomfortably as he was on the front edge of the sagging couch; he didn't know what might try to climb down his pants if he put more of himself in contact with the cushions, and especially their back recesses. "Well, you may not have that communicator magician of yours, Sy Gazoont, but I'm here, and Shaa's on the way in, too. I'll tell you about that in a minute. And—wait a second. Does the Council still meet in that Hall of the People place? The one with all the scavenged pre-Dislocation stuff, with that round meeting chamber and the metal floor?"

"Yes," said Julio, "exactly so. Why do you ask? Do you have something in mind?"

"Maybe," Karlini said. "I think I do. Look, Haddo, can you get back in touch with Fa—with that other fellow you know?"

"Could be," Haddo said cautiously. "Idea what is?"

"Okay, listen to this . . ."

13
THE RAPTURE OF THE GODS

So there I was.

Squirm as I might, and I'd been doing a lot of that, I can assure you, my alternatives still looked as limited as they'd been all along. There was no doubt I'd been getting a little carried away with the current skullduggery, and especially with the luck that had continued to roll my way since we'd arrived in Oolsmouth. True, Soaf Pasook hadn't turned up yet. The closer I got to roping him in, though, the closer I got to the problematic moment when Zhardann and Jill confronted him only to discover he didn't know anything about the ring or his supposed collaboration with me in my presumptive role as Gashanatantra; when that happened, the jig would be up. Even if they merely managed to catch up with Sapriel, the god who was apparently behind the raid on Pasook, my story would be blown as soon as he told them his attack had had nothing to do with some crummy ring.

What *was* the alternative, though? I could just try to bug out, leaving Oolsmouth and Jill and Zhardann. I wasn't sure I could; it wasn't clear that they'd let me. Also, the time hadn't been a total loss in itself. I'd been finding out some very interesting new details about the gods, and potentially about my own situation. After all, Gashanatantra had to be involved here one way or the other, either through Jill, his wife, Zhardann, his look-alike, Pasook, his supposed associate, or Sapriel, whose raid on Pasook could theoretically have been an attempt to get at Gashanatantra himself at second hand. For that matter, if you wanted to think deviously enough, in a sufficient haze of double-back stratagems and tricky schemes, the motivation behind Sapriel's strike could have been aimed at Gash through his contact with me.

I realized there was a chance I'd been hanging around these folks too much. Their own reflexive double-crossing and check-behind-your-back mentality was certainly rubbing off.

Still, that didn't change the fact that my involvement with Zhardann had put me in a position to have a chance at helping out Groot, and by extension Karlini, Shaa, et al. But the closer I came to Pasook or Sapriel, the closer things were going to be cut. The significant danger, of course, was that the things to feel that blade were going to be extremities attached to my own body.

Not that I had a choice, really. The way to play this out was to keep on moving along with them, doubts and questions or not, on the trail of the ring, or to be more precise, the wild-goose chase after the ring I knew wasn't there. It was *somewhere,* that much I *did* know, but it sure wasn't in the corner of the woods we were looking. In the midst of my own fancy footwork, danced in reaction to the steps I'd been confronted with, my basic hope was that I hadn't outsmarted myself and left myself in the process of tripping over my own pair of left feet. The more twists this thing took, the harder it was getting to remember who'd heard which story and how I was supposed to act with them, and who-all I had to worry about actually showing up on the scene.

I'd convinced Jill and Zhardann that I (whom they assumed to be Gashanatantra) had been in league with a partner, and that the partner had double-crossed me and now had the ring we'd teamed up to obtain. I'd let them decide for themselves who this partner actually was, trying to seem cryptic as part of the process, and now here we were, struggling to track them down. The main thing that could happen to get me off the hook would be to encounter the real person they thought I was. Coming across the authentic Gash could be a mixed blessing at best for me. Not only could he blow my assumed cover if he wanted, but knowing him even to the superficial extent I did, he'd probably take immediate and dire remedial action for my hubris in impersonating him in the first place, even though it had been done involuntarily and by default. The same could be the case, of course, if the new guy I was now involved with who looked identical to Gash, the one I knew as Zhardann, turned out to have been Gash himself all along; in that case, though, I would probably turn out to have been part of Gash's ongoing scheme myself anyway. There was simply nothing I could do about it.

"This is the address," I stated.

It had been close enough for an easy walk from Zhardann's place. Zhardann or his agents had done well in choosing the house on the Lane of Wealth as the site for his base of Oolsmouth operations; not only was it convenient to the city center, it had turned out to be agreeably close to several other locations I could see myself having the need to visit. The first of these had been the home of Meester Neville Hanglebord Dooglas, erstwhile Councillor and adversary of the incarcerated Groot, in front of which Jill and I now stood.

I'd already been around Oolsmouth seeing the local sights, of course, and between Julio and Zhardann's local contact, who was now on call back at the house, I'd heard enough about Dooglas himself to formulate some idea of what to expect, so I was not exactly rocked back in astonishment to see where the street address and the directions had actually brought us. The wall around the block was stone, and what we had been able to see of the main building as we approached, before we got so close that the looming bulk of the wall shielded it from sight, was hacked from rock as well; rock, and a lot of it.

"How do you propose to get in there?" Jill asked, implying by her delivery that she was humoring a fool, and that a minute from now she'd step in to sweep me away and tidy things up the way a competent person would have arranged it in the first place; not to be catty, but this was frankly looking to be her usual tone.

"Not by breaking and entering, if that's what your question had in mind."

"Isn't that what detectives do?"

"Sometimes," I said, walking on down the sidewalk

toward the guard booth I could see protruding onto the sidewalk where the driveway entered the compound from the street. Jill lengthened her stride to match me. "Detecting isn't a one-trick affair," I went on. "You have to have a whole repertoire of possibilities."

"You're not planning to *ask* them to let you in?" she said mockingly.

"Why not?" I said. "I washed my face." I'd also borrowed a fancy cloak from the stock of clothing that had come with the house, royal blue with a crimson lining and a fur-trimmed ruff; not what I think of as my best colors, but it had a certain overstated touch of flagrancy about it that I thought was well-suited to the prevailing Oolsmouth style. "If you want, though, I'm willing to let you pull your part of the weight, rather than hogging all the pleasure for myself."

"I'm having my own fun watching you squirm," she told me.

"I hate to be a spoilsport, but would you rather have your fun," I responded, "or the ring? Partner? Just to know for the future, let's say?"

"Why choose? Being one of us means having it all, don't you remember that?"

"You're being shortsighted again."

"Am I now. Tell me then, O Husband, teach me the proper attitude for success with these grubby little people you like so much."

"Watch again, then, and learn." I hadn't really had my mind on the discussion, to be honest, and had been responding mostly out of rote; I was getting thoroughly fed up with this superior-class-dumping-on-the-scum-of-the-earth repartee. I was hoping I wouldn't get so disgusted I'd inadvertently lash back and break my cover. There were bigger things to worry about at the moment, though.

"Planning to unleash your power against them, then, are you?" she said. "And after you counseled us to avoid revealing our true selves, to refrain from—"

"Some judicious escalation may not be out of proportion for a place like this," I murmured. We had just come abreast of the main gate and its standing platoon of goons, albeit well-manicured, liveried ones. Each was wearing a matching orange jacket bearing on its back another one of these junky insignias; probably the Arms of the House of Dooglas, or some such nonsense. The only element of the design I could make out was a stylized sailing ship embedded in a fluffy cloud. Ahead of us was the wide carriageway leading ahead to the house, which from this angle was clearly more of a small castle. Between the two of us and the castle door, though, was that goon platoon I mentioned, and the gate, and a few dogs who had obviously been cross-bred with hippopotami and hadn't been fed since they'd emerged from the vat, and the tingle of some unquestionably nasty sorceries wound into the wrought-iron of the fence grating and spread for good measure around the grounds. No way was anybody getting me to sneak into that place, unless a convenient secret underground passage came to light and all the dogs got hit by some incapacitating canine plague. "All right, then," I said to Jill, "shut your stupid mouth and let someone who knows what they're doing handle this."

I wasn't even looking at her and I could still clearly feel her begin to seethe with menace; I could just imagine the look on her face. Three more steps took me face-to-face with the gatekeeper. "Dooglas," I said.

He was looking at Jill, and he couldn't take his eyes off her. Not that he seemed to be struck with her beauty, which was not insignificant, although his lids *were* opened unnaturally wide and the eyeballs had protruded as though he'd come down with a sudden attack of thyroid fever. I'd seen that look on sightseeing men before, but it generally went along with a touch of slack-jawed drooling, rather than the kind of picture the rest of this guy's face was presenting. With the blood drained from his face, his tanned skin had gone the kind of white you usually find on the boneless mollusks that hang out under the rocks in a swamp. He gulped, and said, "No one enters."

"No one but us," I stated. "Dooglas has been treating with our associates. Now we have arrived ourselves. Open the gate."

"He has, at that," said the guard, in a voice that was

barely audible, perhaps because he seemed to be in the process of swallowing his tongue. He backpedaled, revealing behind himself as he retreated the small walk-through gate at the side of the big one.

I wrinkled my nose and gave him a little sneer as I passed; I would have looked down on him except he was about a hand's-span taller than I was. At the moment, though, he gave the impression of a man who'd been bitten by a paralyzing adder and on dropping over had found himself in a pit of quicksand. The word went out ahead of us, I was happy to see, and so their handlers kept the dogs from leaping for our throats. Still, it wasn't until we'd gone all the way up the driveway into the central courtyard and were through the two-story arm-thick front doors cooling our heels in the entry hall that I started feeling solid relief; the dogs were outside, but we were in. I could hear the hum of distant voices down a corridor that snaked off around the inside of the castle paralleling the lines of the courtyard and figured that was probably the direction of the building's business office section. Where Dooglas himself would be found, though, I wouldn't have ventured to guess.

"That was a cute trick," Jill commented; she had simmered down on the way in.

"Thanks," I said. "I thought you might like it."

"You haven't lost your old style." She was studying a pair of glowering life-masks that hung on the wall, her back toward me. The masks, of a man with fiercely angled eyebrows and a dour bush of a mustache, and a woman who was his double for expression, all deeply etched lines and hard jagged thoughts, had been beaten from metal and annealed black. "That was what drew me to you, did you know that? Originally?"

"Was it, now."

"Of course. That dark flair of yours—oh!" She gave a small shudder of remembered delight. "That deft twist, your arabesques of deceit and betrayal, the way your victims found themselves manipulated without any idea of how it had really come about, and for that matter how badly they'd been screwed. And that cool thin smile as you watched your designs play out. I wasn't the only one to fall for you, you know."

"I would hardly have guessed," I said. "Anyway, that's all gone and done with now."

"Is it?" said Jill. "Is it really?"

"Trust me."

"Style," she said musingly. "It *was* more attractive to watch you use it on others, I will give you that, but still to be the object of your attention was an interesting sensation in its own right. When you did it to me again just now, though, it did bring back a touch of that old magic, just for a moment."

"Call it one for old times' sake, then," I said, trying to flash her a cool thin smile, aloof and sardonic at the same time. She was still turned away from me, but verisimilitude in a role looked like a—

"This way," said another man from the goon crew, from the end of the entry hall.

He led us just around the corner into a sitting room. It was only early afternoon and a pleasant day outside, and in contrast to the usual for stone castles, with their drafts and chills and dank rock walls, the interior of this one was actually comfortable, if not exactly cozy. The sitting room, though, had a totally unnecessary fire roaring in a large hearth. A row of plants across the room in front of the closed courtyard windows were wilting, but the man staring into the fire with one hand outstretched on the mantle had his smoking jacket firmly belted and buttoned all the way up. The way he was focusing on the fire, I wasn't sure he was even aware we'd entered, but then he abruptly said, "You're not Sapriel."

"I never said we were," I told him.

He turned from the fire. In the strong red firelight hitting his face from the side, pulling out the creases and lines around his eyes and stretching down from his nose to the corners of his mouth, the relationship to the mask in the hall outside was apparent. The mask could have been that of his brother, or his father, or for that matter of the man himself at a different stage of his life, or perhaps merely under different circumstances, but that the mask was the image of a close relative was clear.

Dooglas was older than I'd expected, possibly in his late fifties or even later. "What do you want, then?" he demanded.

"A talk," I said. "A few words."

"What significance are your words to me? My time is not yours to waste; I am a busy man." By "busy," he clearly meant "important," but then he hadn't moved to throw us out, either.

If that was the way he wanted to play it, though, fine. "You have abandoned the bounds of prudence," I stated. "You have attracted attention."

From his smirk, Dooglas seemed to find that funny. "So? What business is that of mine, with my enemies at my feet? And who are you to say so?"

"Sapriel may have been fool enough to treat with the likes of you, but that doesn't mean you should draw any blanket conclusions about your importance."

"Or his," added Jill.

This time he *did* laugh, throwing his head back and "heh-heh-heh"ing at the ceiling. "He said your kind would be around, yapping at heels like curs after scraps." Dooglas took two quick steps toward me, stared me square in the eye for an instant, and then jabbed an extended finger into my chest. "*This* for your prudence," he announced. "*This* for your attention." He exhaled in my face, a breath of old garlic and a few rotten teeth and a heavy dose of something that had been rancid for at least six months, then stepped back and folded his arms. "Touch me if you dare. *He* has given me his favor, his favor and his protection."

"Well, la-di-dah," I said. "Since you obviously have nothing to worry about, how about sharing your side of the story with us?"

"All in its good time," said Dooglas, "all in its time." He giggled again.

"Shall I strike him down?" Jill murmured in my ear.

"Don't bother," I said, speaking as much to him as to her. "His comeuppance will dawn soon enough."

"Like curs," Dooglas repeated. "Like beetles, like vermin of all sorts."

"Right. You *are* Dooglas, Councillor Douglas, aren't you?"

"Oh, yes," he said, "for this moment at least, oh, yes."

"Just making sure," I told Jill.

"This is obviously a waste of time," she said.

"You know, I agree with you." I took another look at Dooglas, preening himself by the fire, rising up on his toes and then sinking back down, watching us with the shining eyes of somebody who's just found true religion. "Ask yourself this," I said to him, "if you've a mind left to do it with. Where will you be if Sapriel's power runs out, or even Sapriel himself? We are not the only ones interested in him. Do you think he will waste a thought on you? Where will you be, you and your business? You are not exactly leaving much to the imagination, are you, and you have not left yourself anywhere to retreat. Is this what a leading merchant renowned for his perspicacity would do?"

That didn't ruffle him; nothing was going to ruffle him. He hadn't even been listening, so why should I bother wasting my voice? I jerked my head at the door and Jill preceded me without another word. We didn't have any more trouble with the dogs on the way out than we had on the way in. Dooglas' small army of goons was probably following the same guidelines that had gotten us into the house on our arrival, that and the intimidating effect of Jill, but the way they melted away from us on our exit could possibly have had something to do with the expression on my own face.

"Somehow that didn't sound like normal senility," I said when we'd reached the street. I'd heard of god-rapture, but I'd never actually seen a case up close. Not every person could handle the personal attention of a god; all that power and temptation right there, staring you in the face, and its wielder dealing with you as one person to another. Maybe it was some side-effect of projecting a god's aura, something real gods learned to use as a weapon, but whatever the cause, the effect could be enough to make a previously rational man take leave of his judgment. Delusions of grandeur had nothing on it, especially if you lost track of the fact that there was always a price and listened instead to the rhetoric that gods were so good at, about gracing you with their favor or rewarding you for your devotion or needing something only you could provide. "Not much doubt about what was going on there."

"You didn't ask questions," Jill said. "I thought we were there to find out what his role was."

"I *did* ask," I reminded her. "He wasn't answering. But that doesn't mean we didn't find out anyway."

"Oh, we did, did we?"

"Sure we did, as you know very well. There's no reason to act dense with me. He's Sapriel's front man on this Groot thing, which means he was in with the bank deal, too, and in return Sapriel promised him backing for whatever he plans to do; probably take over the city, that's what these guys always seem to have in mind. By the sound of it, Sapriel may have even promised he'd elevate his stature in the world."

"Or out of it," said Jill.

"Yeah," I said, "you're right. But our real interest wasn't in Dooglas; it never was. He's just a flunky. No matter how much goo he's got in his brain, though, he'd have to be a total idiot not to let Sapriel know we were sniffing around. That'll stir things up, maybe even flush Sapriel out into the open."

"It could also send him into hiding. He'll certainly have more warning to prepare his response."

"Maybe. He had to expect someone would show up asking questions, so I'd suspect he already had some plans of his own to deal with it. I don't think it'll matter. Anyway, I believe in the value of stirring as a general token of principle."

There was more she could have said, but she didn't, and so eventually we turned onto the Lane of Wealth and arrived back at the house. Jill eyed me again as we climbed the stairs, but she didn't even bother to try the freshening-up ploy again; we'd check in with Zhardann together. Or at least I thought that was the plan, until I pushed open the door of the study.

Zhardann was still there, having changed into a comfortable lounging robe in the interim. At the creak of the door he looked over to me in the entranceway, and then glanced back across the room, to the other man over by the window. The new man was about my height but stockier, with a shock of straight black hair combed carefully to the side over his ears and flopping over his collar at the rear. His dark eyes were bloodshot, as was his nose, frankly, but his outfit was fine, all black with silver trim and a brocade neck ruffle, if a bit the worse for apparently having been worn around the clock for at least the last few days. Whether he'd really been sleeping in his clothes was a toss-up, since he was another character who didn't look like he'd been getting a whole lot of sleep lately in *any* position. Although I'd been repeating the observation enough to make even myself doubt it, I was sure I'd never met him before.

He nodded to me across the room in recognition and pleasant acknowledgment, and said, "Good to see you, my man."

I nodded to him in return, and touched the handle of my walking stick to my brow as a quick salute. As I did this, Monoch gave off a gentle tingly vibration, like a tactile purr, then quickly subsided again into silence. Rather than remain standing in the doorway, I went over to the mantle and leaned back against it as though I were at ease. "So," I said.

The newcomer coughed gently, not in a catarrhy sort of way but as a bit of opening punctuation. "As I was saying, I do regret that events have evolved in the manner you know. Even if the point is obvious, it must be stated that I failed to realize the ring would be so difficult to handle, and so popular an item as to make it difficult to hold onto as well." He gave another little cough. "One is sometimes forced to eat one's words, or to face an embarrassing situation of one's own making. One is never happy about this sort of thing, but we are all mature here, we all know how the game is played."

Good gods, I thought. Could this be the missing Soaf Pasook?

Who else could it be?

But why was he validating the details of that made-up story I'd told Zhardann and Jill?

"Indeed we do," I said in a noncommittal tone.

"The situation is different now, of course," he continued, "and I for one am looking forward with no little anticipation to assisting your new group in the matter of Sapriel. I have no doubt that in the process we will succeed in recovering the ring, and who knows what else may—"

Jill was still in the doorway. "*Another* partner?" she said.

"Not just a partner," Zhardann said. His fingers steepled in front of his face, a pleasant smile of the sort I hadn't seen any evidence he was capable of displaying on his face, he was radiating an aura of, well, outright *warmth.* Even I knew him well enough by this time to see he was trying to focus all his faculties on buttering up the new guy. Pasook. My own stomach was doing flipflops. "From what we were discussing when you came in, it is clear that he has significant grievances, grievances of substance, grievances, even, of general significance. With his willingness to issue a formal complaint, my own empowerment is such that I may convene a statutory tribunal of arbitration. An *enforceable* tribunal."

From the way Zhardann was staring at Jill as he expounded, I thought he was telling her to follow his lead and he'd explain everything later. She wasn't buying it. "I don't know if that's such a good idea," she stated. "Tribunals have a way of getting out of hand."

Zhardann waved his hand as if clearing away a stray wisp of smoke. "Nothing that can't be handled, and the battleground would be ours. This would be a first-class chance to force Sapriel to a confrontation of our own choosing."

"Are you sure you want the question of the ring brought up in public forum?"

"Scarcely *public*, my dear."

"*Semi*-public, then," Jill snorted. "Airing the real story—even *part* of the real story—don't tell me you don't think that's dangerous. If—when—the ring's current owner gets identified, everybody in on the debate is going to take off after him or her."

"That risk can be mitigated," said Zhardann, a little of his customary irritation poking through his sunny demeanor. "What are we here for, tell me, if not to take that risk?"

"What indeed?" I contributed. "Well put."

Both Zhardann and Jill swung toward me with a startled flinch, as though they might have forgotten for a moment that I was there. The new guy had never entirely taken his eyes and his small smile of internal amusement off me. Jill opened her mouth to lash back at my contribution, no doubt, but then paused, narrowed her gaze, looked more closely at me, turned and directed the same scrutiny on the new guy, and then glanced back and forth once again. "Are you two related?" she said.

"Related?" said the guy, aiming his pleasant smile at her. "Aren't we all?"

"Do you really think so?" I added. I thought I'd been doing a good job of maintaining my air of know-it-allness and I wasn't about to cash it all in over one out-of-the-hinterlands remark, but I would really have liked to be able to ask her just what similarity she felt she'd detected. I didn't find any obvious correspondence in physical appearance between the two of us, but at this stage of the game I knew that was no evidence one way or the other. Reasoning from the way my own situation had evolved, these gods were used to changing bodies, or at least to changing the way their standard bodies appeared, so Jill must have thought there was some other familial relationship that would remain constant between physical redos. Probably she was looking at whatever characteristics she had recognized me by in the first place. Something in our auras?

She flashed me a sharp-edged grin with a few too many teeth showing. "My husband never liked to discuss family," she said to no one in particular, "even when our relationship was such that we discussed *anything.*"

"Family is relative," I said, a bit lamely, even for me.

"It's not a *strong* similarity, at that," Jill said finally. "One can occasionally get some degree of aural overlap merely from close collaboration,'' the guy said in a helpful tone. ''When the two of us were examining the opportunity of Pod Dall—''

Pasook, I thought. No question about it. Or someone who thought he was Pasook. Or someone who thought it was in his interest to think he was Pasook.

''—and particularly later, during the engineering of the ring-well, there was a certain bidirectional flow, wouldn't you say?''

He was talking to me, I realized with a start. ''Well, yes,'' I said, ''the ring itself, being fairly tricky, and not of merely incidental interest from a purely technical perspective, did require more than the usual level of effort.''

''Yes,'' Pasook said, ''quite. After all, the design did have to be robust enough to suck up one of *us,* and a leading Death, at that. A nice piece of work. Nontrivial, if I do say so.''

''You never *used* to be that adroit a technician,'' Jill said to me. ''Was your old behavior just a pose? Did you distrust me that far back?''

''Some of us can learn,'' I commented.

''What do you mean by that?'' she snapped.

''Why, nothing,'' I said, ''nothing at all. I thought learning was supposed to be one of those virtues with no downside, something we were all in favor of as a matter of principle. At least among ourselves, *for* ourselves.''

''He *is* good, though, you know,'' said Pasook. ''The system that stabilizes the confinement matrix, for example—what did you call it?''

''I thought we agreed those were all trade secrets.''

''Oh, come, come,'' he said. ''We're all associates here now.''

I realized now what he was doing. He was trying to force me to reveal how much I really knew about the ring, like whether I knew enough to have actually had my hands on it. Both Pasook and I knew that the storyline he was holding to was a fabrication. Neither of us could tell that to Jill and Zhardann, of course, so he was able to use my reluctance to risk blowing my own cover story to lever me into helping him with *his* hunt for the ring. At least that was the way it seemed to shake out, lacking a stray inconsistent detail or two. I didn't know how much *he* actually knew, but in any case I was trapped. He'd backed me into a corner; I had to say something that sounded plausible or I'd raise serious suspicions. Fortunately, I had hung around with Max and Shaa enough while they were analyzing the ring to learn something about its matrix construction. "The parasitic catalysis shunt," I said. "The power of the ring's occupant is synchronized with the on-board master-wave and used to boost the circumscription field. It's like one of those woven puzzles made of straw, the kind where you stick a finger in each end and then can't pull them back out again—the occupant's own power is used to immobilize himself. That's also the reason the ring looked so innocuous while it was empty, before the trap was sprung; so innocuous that a notoriously sneaky victim could actually be convinced to pick it up. In its primed state, the confinement matrix was folded in its unpowered quiescence mode with virtually nothing protruding, especially above the countermeasures clutter. When it was triggered, though, the feedback expansion let loose along with the—"

"Rather diabolical, really," said Pasook, his voice filled with admiration. He was trying to butter *me* up, now, or at least to make Jill and Zhardann think he was. On the other hand, he might have been genuinely impressed with my clatter of jargon. If he knew anything solid about the ring, though, more than deduction or speculation, he'd understand that my exposition had been the authentic article. Up to a point. "But you will appreciate—indeed, it goes without saying—that the technicalities of the hardware were less important than the target."

Jill had taken a seat on the chair by the hearth, in all probability concluding that we might be there for a while. "Are you saying that the power boost the ring's wearer gets is beside the point? You *are* saying that, of course."

"Of course he is," said Zhardann. "There's no need to play games with him. He knows we know the importance of Pod Dall."

"Nobody ever turns down a little extra power," I said, "especially when it's really somebody else's, but if it was just that, we wouldn't have gone after as dangerous a target as Dall.''

''And you wouldn't be who you are,'' added Soaf Pasook. ''Capturing Pod Dall was a clear move of 'check' on the big board, not that the game is nearly that simple, you appreciate.''

Zhardann grunted and squirmed around in his chair, searching for a new posture of maximal comfort. ''The game has as many sides as players,'' he grumbled. ''Still, the move was elegant. Dall was as well-pleased as anyone. From that strategic position of his, he could maintain a virtual lock-down hold on the Abdicationist and Conservationist factions, both. By snatching him and penning him up, the whole power structure is thrown into disarray. All that from the loss of a swing vote.''

''Scarcely,'' said Pasook, a bit superciliously. ''The strength of Dall was partly political, as a matter of the swing of the coalition vote, as you say, but it was also partly positional in a much more physical manner, and a question of raw might.''

''Of course, of course,'' said Zhardann, being conciliatory again. ''It is amazing, though, is it not, to contemplate the possibilities that Pod Dall as a commodity presents that Pod Dall incarnate did not?''

''Hmm, yes,'' said Pasook, as if the matter was of academic interest to him. ''Some would like to see Dall freed and restored to action, or ransomed into their own custody or control, while some would just as soon see him disappear forever, never to be seen again.''

''And you?'' said Jill. ''What did *you* want?''

Pasook made a guileless expression coalesce from the combination of his dramatically opened eyes and the gently opened ''O'' of his mouth. Then he closed his mouth and merely looked thoughtful. ''Perspective,'' he said slowly. ''Many of us have lost that, you know. A restoration of perspective, a forced reexamination of tenets and positions—is that not to the general good?''

''My husband never did anything for the general good,'' said Jill.

''He is a complex fellow,'' said Pasook. ''What is this political struggle that has us all so polarized based on in the first place, though? At its root there lies the philosophical question of Abdication: the Abdicationists want to relinquish power and let the world get on with its own affairs, while the Conservationists, on the other hand, say, 'What are you, idiots?', to put it kindly, and to paraphrase the coarser element among us. The Conservationists like things the way they have been and think it would be the height of bad management to throw themselves out of office and privilege, but still they exhibit a spectrum of thought. There are shades of opinion within the Abdicationist community, too, ranging from a radical extreme of those who would hie us back to the Age of Stone, in fact who would return us all to a mere mortal state, and from that nihilistic fringe all the way to those centralists who would make changes only in slight degree, merely loosening the yoke of dominion by a notch, or perhaps two.

"Then there is the religious aspect. I shy away from religion, myself, and especially questions of theology," said Soaf Pasook, "since lack of certitude on the part of someone in our position is to my mind irritatingly paradoxical, and I dislike dwelling on either irritations *or* paradox, let alone both together. Instead—"

"Certitude?" I said. What the hell, I was interested.

"What does godhood *mean?"* Pasook said, with some heat. Then he looked a bit abashed at his own outburst. "If we have no firm answers, who does? Some have gotten uncomfortable with living the self-made life when there may be those who . . . *outrank* us actually around somewhere. This faction thinks that any deitical beings who exceed us would probably be quite annoyed with our carryings on. Another subgroup thinks, in line with certain ancient and presently suppressed scriptures, that regardless of hierarchy or deitogenesis those who wish to be more than human should aspire to higher standards as well, rather than just behaving like more powerful humans, and gangster humans at that. Harsh words, indeed, but of course I merely quote, in an attempt to fairly represent a position."

"There are those," Zhardann said carefully, "who

would call this kind of talk heretical, and would call for punishment.''

''What is the point of being what we are if one has to toe an ideological line? Practicalities, yes, there are certainly reasons for those, but restraint of discourse among ourselves? No, I think not. Who can afford to abandon the search for wisdom?''

''This is just a lot of talk,'' said Jill disgustedly. ''What does another search for wisdom have to do with Pod Dall? The only wisdom he understood is the wisdom of power. Look at him now, without it—that pretty much proves his position, doesn't it? You were talking about perspective. What's Dall's perspective?''

''You can ask him, if you want,'' Pasook said, ''when we recover the ring.''

''Let me get this straight,'' said Jill, pointing a finger at him. ''You wanted to make people take a new look at their politics by turning Dall into a trade good. That's it? What then? No,'' she shook her head, ''it doesn't wash. This wasn't some high and mighty act of philosophical nobility, you're not going to get me to believe that. You'd be the kingpin, you'd be the one in charge. You'd be the one who'd profit.''

''Yes, of course,'' said Pasook, as though amazed that the issue should be any less than obvious.

''Harshness doesn't suit you, my dear,''Zhardann said to Jill. ''Philosophy is interesting, of course, we all have our hobbies, but there's nothing inappropriate about combining axiology with business; quite the contrary. Especially with the stakes so high. There's nothing that says that even a search for wisdom has to be free, that no one should benefit.''

''Just so,'' Pasook agreed.

''So as you say,'' Zhardann continued, ''the two of you—'' he nodded coolly in my direction, ''—had intended to play the role of pivotal middlemen and dealmakers between the Abdicationist and Conservationist factions without actually declaring for one or the other, on the grounds that those who hold the balance—the kingmakers, if you will—will wind up with the most important role in continuing affairs whichever side wins out in the end. If neither side has an out-and-out triumph, of course, your value would be even greater. Accordingly, your real interest would seem to have been concentrated in seeing the struggle continue. All this is moot now, of course, but it is always helpful to understand where one's associates have come from.''

''As you say,'' said Soaf Pasook.

''So, to be blunt about it,'' Zhardann said, ''why *is* all this moot now? Why are you before us now, rather than wielding the ring, with or without your former partner?''

''I would think it would be obvious.''

Zhardann tightened up his tone, letting a bit of his usual peevishness loose into the room. ''I have had quite enough of things that should be obvious. For once, I would like to see something laid out on the floor in front of me in unambiguous detail. Shall I restate the question?''

''No,'' said Pasook, sounded a bit wounded himself, ''no. That won't be necessary, I'm sure. A break with normal etiquette; but these are not normal times, are they, if indeed they ever were. Yes, well. As you know, the two of us broke our collaboration—'' I raised an eyebrow at Pasook, which clearly caught his gaze since he had been looking with a contemplative manner directly into my face ''—when I determined I could make better use of the ring alone than the two of us could together. His own power and, one must say, his vigilance, were drained from managing the operational aspect of emplacing and retrieving the ring, as well as the ring engineering task, of course, and so he had left himself in a vulnerable state.''

''Hmph,'' I said, hoping for a menacing tone. Why hadn't they asked *me* all this stuff? Well, actually, they had, sort of, only I'd squirmed out of answering because I wouldn't have known what I was talking about. Pasook, though, was being forthcoming to the point of exsanguination. Why lecture us on stuff we all presumably knew?

He had to buy his way in, that could be part of it. I'd come into the game on my own terms. At least that was how they'd interpreted it; even so, I'd made them treat me as an equal rather than relying on their favor. Pasook, on the other hand, was a supplicant. He wanted their help, although Zhardann was willing to treat it as a two-way street when it suited him. He would also presumably want their protection from *my* wrath; after all, he *had* double-crossed me, or so the story went. Now that I was hearing it from someone else, maybe even *I'd* start to believe it.

"I came down here to Oolsmouth," Pasook went on, "and thought that would be the end of it. Then—"

"Why?" said Jill. "Why did you think that would be the end of it? Why didn't you think he'd come after you?"

Pasook looked straight at me and said, "He's not what he was. He has gone soft. He's due for retirement."

That rocked them back in their chairs. Me, too, even though I'd been expecting something of the sort eventually. All heads swiveled toward me again. "That may have been the case at the time," I said in a steady, almost-pleasant tone, an almost-genial smile on my lips, "but softness is not an irreversible condition."

Perhaps they saw the suggestion of something hard and noxious cross my face then; I certainly tried hard enough to send it there. I thought of adding a line about ignoring the implications at their peril, but it would have been less than subtle and, more than that, gratuitous. Instead, I contented myself with saying, "Jill-tang can attest to my present temperament."

The heads swung toward Jill. She merely screwed up one corner of her mouth and scowled out at nothing in particular, and let the heads ultimately drift back to fix on Pasook.

"That was the situation then," he said finally. "The strong deal with the weak, that is the way things go. If the weak become strong, well, that is a different matter." That was probably as much of an apology as I would ever get out of him, especially considering that none of it had ever actually happened. "When I arrived in Oolsmouth, there were certain matters requiring my attention at the bank, so—"

"The Oolvaan Mutual Bank?"said Zhardann.

"Yes, quite. After attending to business and after a

judicious interval, I turned my consideration again to the ring."

"This 'business' you mentioned," I said. "What was its nature?"

"Loans," said Pasook. "Capitalization. Strictly questions of mortal commerce. I understand you've been interesting yourself in my customer Groot—yes, some of this activity concerned him, but not to any degree out of the ordinary; issues of extending credit for new trade voyages, that sort of thing. It was not until—"

"Did he learn about the ring?" I asked. "*Could* he have learned about the ring?"

Pasook tipped his head to one side and seemed to consider the proposal seriously. "No," he said. "No. Even when I began to deploy feelers, gingerly of course, which was later, and even from looking at it from the current vantage point, I don't see Groot's direct hand in what transpired. Why do you ask?"

"Confirmation, that's all. Groot's reverses seemed to be a byproduct of the thing between Sapriel and you, not a deliberate stab directed at him by Sapriel. A direct stab, yes, but by Sapriel's stooge."

"What is this?" said Zhardann.

"Let's hear my old friend out," I suggested. "If the question remains unanswered, I will address it myself. Please proceed, my old friend."

"Yes," said Pasook, swallowing. He was certainly playing his role all the way through. "As I said, I began to carefully send out word about the ring, about Dall. The first I realized Sapriel was even in Oolsmouth was when he attacked. That time, where he was strong, *I* was weak. My precautions were insufficient. In retrospect, I was mistaken to try to do this thing on my own. At that moment, though, I found myself Sapriel's prisoner."

"And the ring?" I said.

"The ring, yes, the ring; well, that was another matter. I didn't have the ring with me, of course, you understand. To pressure me, Sapriel began to dismantle my operations; in particular, the Oolvaan Mutual Bank. He had recruited a local agent—"

"Douglas," inserted Jill.

"—yes, quite, Dooglas, which of course complicated matters, since Dooglas had his own ends to satisfy as well. Among those of us in this room, that pressure probably would have been enough, but Sapriel chose to apply more direct force as well." He raised the edge of his tunic. Scabbed welts punctuated by jagged flayed strips and the spot-punctures of thorns covered his skin. He *had* been holding himself rather stiffly in the chair, now that I thought about it. Gingerly, he eased the fabric back down. "Finally I capitulated. The ring was hidden some distance out from the city. While Sapriel was engaged in collecting it, I was able to win free. And so here I am."

What was his game? To my way of thinking, he was playing to the story I'd established too obviously for any element of chance. Pasook had to know more than he was letting on. But why, what were his motives? To get back at Sapriel for raiding Pasook's own bank, for one; that was a no-charge given. To toy with Gashanatantra? That possibility was more interesting. If Pasook really had been Gash's associate in the ring bit, if that much had been accurate deduction rather than invention, he could have had a plan in mind where he would show up here, encounter the real Gash, and horn in on his new action. Surely Pasook could tell that I wasn't him. Jill, Gash's wife, hadn't known the difference, but then she hadn't seen him in a long time; Pasook, though, would have been hanging around with Gash much more recently.

But Pasook was obviously a sneaky customer in his own right. If he'd been surprised to find me instead of Gash, he could have smoothly rolled with it and decided to play along, at least until he could get me alone and find out why Jill and Zhardann thought I was Gash, and where the real Gash really was. He'd have enough threat hanging over my head to back me into a corner and make me *his* tool. I could see him thinking that way, in any case.

What if Pasook *hadn't* been Gash's associate, though? What if we'd all guessed wrong? Still, there *was* a Pasook, who could have heard about our speculations and decided to live up to them, again fitting himself into our ongoing plot. Again, in that scenario he could be out to get a piece of the action against Sapriel, or to use us to help him get back at Sapriel for raiding his bank. Also again, if he knew I wasn't Gash, he'd figure I was in no position to contradict him. Under this construction, though, where Pasook hadn't been in partnership with Gash, he might have no reason not to think I wasn't Gash after all.

There was another outside possibility, but I figured it was so loopy that it couldn't be true, even in the middle of an admittedly loopy state of affairs. He couldn't be *that* devious, could he?

Downside risks and all, I dearly wanted to get Pasook alone for a one-on-one. I doubted that was in the offing, or that it would have been a good idea even if I could arrange it, but it was entirely possible that here was someone who actually knew the answer to *something*.

"Torture, you said," stated Zhardann.

"Yes, there was that," Pasook admitted with a bit of embarrassment. "It was not, shall we say, an overly pleasant experience. I had not been keeping up my personal protection as well as I might, but then who would expect one of us to break with normal practice so violently? These things just aren't done."

"No," said Zhardann, "no, they are certainly not. Shocking. All the more reason to put him in line. We are all together on this?"

We were. "We must confer further," Zhardann continued, "but I, for one, would like to take a break." He pushed himself out of the depths of the armchair cushions and turned solicitously to Pasook. Pasook, though, had managed to rise from his own chair, if a bit gingerly. He walked carefully toward the door. Then, as he came abreast of my position, he paused and gazed at me, which was only fair since I had been gazing at him. He approached me a few steps and stuck out his right hand. I looked at him, and it, and then extended my own. As our palms met, I felt an electric tingle in my knuckles followed immediately by a sharp lancing pain in my palm, as though a large nail had suddenly been pounded through the center of my hand. Blue sparks arced out from between our fingers. I thought I heard a low sizzle, too, but before I could even jerk my hand away Pasook had closed his own fingers in a tight grasp around my wrist. Before I could get out a yelp, either, the pain was gone as abruptly as it had descended.

Zhardann was talking with Jill over by the doorway, their faces averted. They appeared to have noticed nothing. Soaf Pasook was grinning at me, but it was a different, craftier grin than he'd showed us before. He pumped my hand once, then released it. "We must speak," Pasook said, "my old friend." He turned to the door and was gone.

My hand wasn't smoking. The skin over my palm appeared completely normal—no scorch marks, no holes, no rush of blood. I felt exhausted, as though I'd just finished running down from Roosing Oolvaya carrying the horse on *my* back, say. The odd part was that, in a strange way and at the same time, I seemed to be more energetic, as though the zap had sent a transfusion of lightning through my heart and off into my limbs. Long hours, poor eating habits, and maybe the raw power of the zap itself; I couldn't imagine what else it could be. I'd never experienced anything like it before.

I squared my shoulders and headed for the door myself. At least Pasook had sounded interested in talking to me. For some reason, though, the thought seemed to have lost some of its appeal. Life is just dangerous, I guess, unless perhaps you're somebody like an accountant. No, that wasn't right, either; Julio was the next thing over from an accountant, and he was in a mess, too. At least I had now had a better idea of how to help him and Groot, and of where matters were going.

It was sure going to be interesting if Sapriel actually had the ring.

14
A CAPTAIN AND HIS CREW

"Mind that skiff, now!" called Shaa.

"Aye," said the mate, apparently paying not the slightest attention to him. The coxswain continued to pound his drum at the front of the quarterdeck, the crew kept time with their oars, with surprising gusto, Shaa was happy to see; in short, everything was as it should be, even with the wind gone and the ship now moving across the current as it headed through the maze of ships toward the main public dock of Oolsmouth. They cleared the skiff Shaa had mentioned in his warning with a tidy expanse of empty water to spare and headed in the direction of a barge plodding slowly at a right angle to their path, on a converging course. While Shaa was considering the appropriate instruction for that situation, Tildamire appeared at the head of the stairs, followed by Roni. They were both wearing cloaks with hoods.

"These things should be banned," Roni muttered, flapping a long sleeve out of her way.

"Are you acquiring a particular taste for fashion, after all these years?" Shaa asked, diverting his attention from the needs of the ship. The crew, ably led by the new mate, could obviously take care of themselves for a moment or two.

"Don't give me that 'all these years' nonsense," she told him. "The most ridiculous part of these carryings on has always been the disguises. I mean, look at *you.*"

"Yes, don't you like it?" Shaa took off his cap, polished a dust speck off the insignia on the sleeve of his jacket, and replaced it, with perhaps the barest inclination toward a rakish tilt. "Just a slightly different way of viewing truth."

"Are you sure you should be doing this?" said Tildy. "Your heart . . ."

It was time to nip this in the bud. That was what Roni was supposed to be there for, but she had turned away, ignoring them; he would have to do it all himself. "Are we married?" Shaa asked.

"What are you talking about? Of course we're not—"

"Are we betrothed? Do we have a relationship other than that of two people who happen to be on the same boat at the same time?"

"Why are you—"

"Look," said Shaa. "You're a nice girl, a very nice girl. I like you—you're a nice girl. I don't want to be rude, but if that's the way you take it, then my conscience will just have to figure out an appropriate way for me to do penance. Nevertheless, there it is."

"There *what* is?"

"My business, my choices, my freedom of action, however limited, on the one side, and your solicitous-bordering-on-meddlesome attitude on the other. By which I mean to say, if you need to hear it another way, thank you for your interest but please leave me alone. Hmm?"

"All I was doing was—"

"*I* know what you were doing," Shaa told her. "Do you?"

"But what if things get out of control? It could kill you, couldn't it?"

"You are persistent, I'll give you that, but the last time I checked, persistence was not one of the cardinal virtues. As far as for dying, well, everyone dies eventually. Well, almost everyone," amended Shaa. The mate gave him an are-you-crazy-or-do-you-just-sound-that-way look over his shoulder, the space on his jaw where until very recently a tidy beard had rooted showing fish-belly pale against the weatherbeaten leather of the rest of his countenance. "As you were," Shaa said to him. The mate shook his head and examined the sky, but then shrugged himself and turned back to his steerage.

"When you say you like me," Tildy said slowly, "just

what do you mean by that? What do you mean I'm a 'nice girl'?''

She seemed to be lagging a sentence or two behind him, Shaa noted. Yet another case of bad timing. ''Why are you interested?''

''Well, there's your curse . . . I mean my brother told me you, ah, well, you said that it said you'd, ah, fall, ah, in love while on some adventure, and, well, I was, ah, wondering . . .''

So that *was* it. Shaa had known he would rue the day he had picked Jurtan Mont as someone who needed his help. Actually, he recalled, he had known it immediately, a knowledge that hadn't let up on him yet. ''Let me give *you* a piece of advice, for a change. Don't get mixed up with a curse. Don't get mixed up with anybody with a curse; don't even *think* about it. It's bad for your health, and it could be bad for *their* health.'' Shaa deliberately stared out ahead, at the sailing vessel that was crossing their bow, at the dock beyond it. ''Let's do this smartly, now, men,'' he called to the crew.

''Urr,'' said the mate.

Tildy had grabbed his arm. ''Now wait just a second, you! Why are you always pushing people off, you with your cute turns of phrase and your changing the subject and your, your *attitude?*'' Her comprehension had apparently caught up with Shaa's warning of impending rudeness. ''What is it—your curse, right? You're just going to blame everything on this curse?''

''To be logically consistent,'' said Shaa, ''I should point out that *you* were the one who was blaming my limitations on my curse a moment ago, and *you* were—''

''So what—you're just going to let the curse rule your life?''

Was the ship passing through a zone of logical plasticity? ''If I recall correctly, I was arguing for free will in the face of destiny's control, manifested in this case by the curse, and you were arguing in favor of not pushing the issue. Now you seem to be trying to reverse—''

''For once in your life, answer a question, will you?''

Shaa had not been facing her; now he turned to do so. Under the shadowing hood, she had exactly the look of determination he had expected. "Very well," he said. "I recall doing something like this with your brother, so I suppose it's only fair. What question do you have in mind?"

Her teeth clenched even further; if she kept this up, she was going to make some dentist who liked crown work very happy. "Are you going to let the curse rule your life?" she said, squeezing each word through her lips like a spurt of batter out of a tight dough bag, and chopping off the end of each syllable with the verbal equivalent of a sharp cleaver.

"As a matter of fact, yes," Shaa said, "I am, at least up to a point. That's what you do with curses, that's what they're for."

"What about happiness?"

"It's difficult to be happy when you're dead," said Shaa. "I have this on solid authority."

"Then why are you deliberately putting yourself in danger again?"

The dock was approaching quickly; they'd have to wrap this up soon. "The danger should be minimal, it shouldn't involve much physical exertion, and in any case I never said I don't intend to keep on challenging the curse envelope. At the moment I have certain boundaries; there's no getting around that. Everyone has boundaries; mine are more limited, that's a downside, but I know where they are, which is generally a plus. Nothing doesn't keep me from being creative about working with them and trying to push them out. I hope you're satisfied, because that's all you're going to get."

The mate and coxswain between them had been managing their advent at the dock. "Very neat," Shaa told them, "very clean, all very shipshape."

"Urr," the mate said again, followed by a reluctant "aye."

"So who do they think they are?" Roni said. "There, on the dock?"

"Police, do you think?" said Shaa. "Militia, perhaps, in those numbers." A troop of perhaps thirty men were drawn up in ranks on the quay where they'd been directed to moor by the harbor-pilot's vessel crisscrossing the river at the head of the harbor. At the head of the troop was a loose group of five more men—the troop's commander was clearly distinguishable through his polished breastplate, serious-looking olive beret, and swagger stick, and a second man wearing oilskin coveralls, thick boots, and a professional manner was confirmed by the mate to be the dockmaster. This man, his arms planted impatiently on his hips, was looking distrustfully at the third member of the party, a purse-lipped sallow-faced fellow with a plumed hat and a satin-lined off-the-shoulder cloak, and a rolled-up document of some sort under his arm. Behind him on either side were two fellows with the look of personal guards, their swords loose in their hands; one was large, but the other was larger. "Avast, there," Shaa said absently.

On a barked command from the coxswain, oars were raised and shipped, the ship lost headway, the mate twirled the wheel and the stern of the ship swung smartly to starboard, and then they were creeping to a dead halt not three feet from the wharf. Lines were tossed and secured and the gangplank was lowered. The crew stood back, silent; they had their orders. On the dock, the official bearing the document was in the midst of a hurried consultation with the dockmaster, the official jabbing his arm toward the ship while the dockmaster alternately shook his head and shrugged his shoulders. Then they appeared to resolve something, or perhaps they didn't, for the official was stalking officiously up the gangplank, followed immediately by the two guards and after them by the commander of troops, and trailed at a distinct distance by a clearly displeased dockmaster. Shaa drifted toward the front of the quarterdeck and observed their passage over the gunwale and back toward the bridge. The official had a moment's hesitation on encountering the steep stairs, which usually demanded a double handhold on their railing if one was not to tumble backward onto the deck at the slightest swell, or even sideways, encountering on one side the lower stair into the cabin or on the other a barrel of pitch. The man clearly did not intend to be trifled with, though, least of all by a staircase, so he jammed his document more firmly between his chest and shoulder and took hold of it with the same hand, a feat mediated by a dramatically contorted elbow and forearm, and continued his march up the steps, his gait almost unbroken. He popped off the top stair riser like a spring-loaded toy, looked around, promptly culled Shaa out from the group, no doubt by his natty nautical outfit, as the one in whom he was most immediately interested, and fixed him with the pallor of his gaze.

"I applaud you," Shaa said, touching a finger to the brim of his cap.

"Cawp-whopt?" said the official, his own words stumbling in his mouth as they encountered his reaction to the unexpected greeting. "What is this?"

"I didn't believe the promise was serious," Shaa told him, in a confidential tone, draping an arm over his shoulder and down his back, "but my pessimistic anticipations have clearly been proven wrong. My vote is secure for the next election, I can assure you."

"What are you talking about?" The man's voice was rising.

"It is so rare these days to redeem from local government the trust one has placed in it. We were promised a civic campaign to maintain order on the waterfront, though, and by the gods that is surely what we have here before us."

The official finally squirmed free from Shaa's friendly grasp and reeled back. "Seize that man!" he ordered, pointing with his entire arm outstretched. The two guards, their faces impassive, moved toward Shaa and reached out to take hold of him from either side.

"Ah," said Shaa, "a personal demonstration of the firm-rootedness of your measures—what a graphic example of outreach to build solidarity among the loyal constituents! Nevertheless, the exhibition most properly should be made on the dock, since as your companion the worthy dockmaster will testify, the captain of a ship is inviolate upon his own deck. It would be an unfortunate precedent to attempt to set, I'm sure you'll agree, as you are so obviously a gentleman of some authority and repute yourself, regardless of the benefits of the civic promotion or other gains that may accrue through—I beg your pardon!'' Shaa glared at the guard holding his left arm, and then turned a matching glare on the guard to his right. To his right, and *up*—the man was at least a head taller than Shaa, and the mass that had seemed so well proportioned from the distance of ship-to-dock was more reminiscent of a small foothill when pushed up against it at shorter range.

The dockmaster cleared his throat reluctantly. ''We are part of the civilized world, as you know, Lord, and therefore the rule of law and practice is a code we all bear witness to. It is true that a captain on his own ship—''

''Thank *you*, sir,'' said Shaa. ''You see, this man speaks the matter right. The breakdown of custom is a terrible thing, a terrible thing indeed, leading to abrogation of the law, rioting, agitation; breakdown, in short, of all those enlightenments that separate us from the savage, from the life of the barbarians. Present company excluded, of course,'' he added, in an aside to the guard on his right, whose hand had wrapped itself easily around Shaa's entire upper arm.

''I—'' said the guard in a deep throaty rumble, but then he broke into a spasm of coughing. The sound of the cough was even deeper than the voice, and more forceful; Shaa felt himself rattled as if by a close peal of thunder. The cough, though, was also damp, if not out-and-out wet.

Shaa took another look at him. ''Are you well?'' he asked solicitously. ''In my travels, I have been fortunate enough to acquire a smattering of medical wisdom which I would be pleased to place at your disposal.''

''Thank—''

''Stop that!'' The official was now waving the unrolled sheet of parchment, revealing it to be indeed at least as overwrought as he himself. He had also, somewhat surprisingly, taken to yelling himself, to boot.

''This man could do with some attention,'' Shaa told him. ''It is less than one would expect of a city such as Oolsmouth, a great city the likes of this, to fasten for its support and succor on the infirm, no matter their, shall we say, undeniable stature. I feel that—''

''Now you listen to me!'' The official snapped his

parchment in the air. "I am the duly constituted and jurisdictional representative of the Municipal Authority of Oolsmouth. This document impels and requires—"

"Did you say the 'Municipal Authority' of Oolsmouth?" asked Shaa.

"I most certainly did," the official preened. "Do not interrupt—"

"Not the Authority of Ports and Tariffs?"

"I said, do *not* interrupt me wh—"

"That's interesting," Shaa said loudly but conversationally, again overriding the official's momentum. "I was not aware that the Municipal Authority had any hint of magisterial prerogative over affairs of the harbor and its traffic. Now, if you had identified yourself as a direct functionary of the High Commissioner of Rates and Tithes, say, here on an excise matter or a question of customs duty, or indeed a delegated diplomat of the Oolsmouth Representative Council, your presence might be more amenable to straightforward understanding. Under the situation, though, I fail to see what significance your appearance here would present to any one of us, or indeed the reason for your detaining us in own prosecution of business. Accordingly—"

"Your ship and goods are hereby impounded under peremptory decree!"

"No, no, no," said Shaa. "You surely have this all wrong. Orders of fiat are clearly proscribed by the Waterborne Edict of Pollison, at least without the Seal of Imperial Cognizance to override the routine procedures. Please show your—"

"Here is my writ, here is my warrant," snarled the official, again waving the document out of reach.

Shaa ostentatiously cocked an eye in his attempt to follow the moving sheet. "I see no seal here," Shaa stated. He had always been confident that his time on the Roosing Oolvaya docks as Waterfront Health Commissioner would come in handy again someday, not that he'd had the slightest idea how this was to come about. It was all becoming clear now, though. "This document, whatever it might charitably be called, plainly contains no Writ of Judicial Attainder, either. The value of your attempt at preemption is thus nil and moot. Even if it was validly executed, this ship is covered by the Concordat of Water-borne Enterprise, not by some extraordinary regional declaration. According to the River Commerce Measure of '93, as promulgated by O'Rinn and Finebold during the reign of—''

''All issues of river commerce are overridden while in port by the jurisdiction of the local municipality!''

''But clear precedent, for example that of Wisenfeller, Groth, and Knee-mare in the case of Craven Shipping Associates, states that a ship is not considering to be 'in port' until it has officially docked at a designated moorage site *and* registered with the appropriate harbor authorities—''

''Established Oolsmouth practice is that all vessels within the greater Oolsmouth harbor zone are considered to be 'in port,' '' the dockmaster inserted mildly. ''Furthermore—''

''I will concede that much temporarily, for the sake of argument,'' said Shaa with a small bow toward the dockmaster, ''and in recognition of your own stature and erudition, sir. Nevertheless, as captain of this ship—''

''You're not the captain of this ship!'' the official shouted.

''Don't be absurd. Certainly I am.''

''Is this ship not the *Not Unreasonable Profit*, registered to Haalsen Traders and the property of Haalsen Groot?''

''Not the last time I checked,'' Shaa said blandly. ''What name did *you* see painted on the stern, at the area with the various identifications and symbols?''

The dockmaster, standing behind the official and out of his line of sight, had been eyeing the mate. Each time he did so, a grin appeared about to break out on his face, and his mouth contorted into a grimace as he tried to keep himself from an involuntary vocalization. Now he looked away from the mate again and said, in a voice that sounded as though someone was choking him gently about the throat, ''The name I saw was *Perfidious Stranger.*''

''*Not Unreasonable Profit*, did you say?'' Shaa responded. ''I believe we did pass her upriver, now that you mention it; they were putting about and heading back to Roosing Oolvaya by the looks of the situation. We hailed them in case we could offer some assistance, but her master, a stout fellow by the looks of him, said all was well, they'd only just discovered they'd forgotten something important back in the last port."

"No," the official said, glaring at the dockmaster, and then whipping about to accuse Shaa again, "no! You're all in league together, that much is obvious. I will hereby take possession of this vessel and throw the lot of you in—"

"Fetch our papers," Shaa told the mate. The mate bent, opened a small sea chest at his feet, and withdrew an oilskin-wrapped parcel, which he handed to Shaa.

"Capital!" said Shaa, busying himself with untangling the contents. "First-rate crew, don't you know, fully prepared for every eventuality, anything from a standard port call or a mere routine inspection—ah, here we have it. Them." He held out a battered logbook and a small seal-spattered parchment.

The official grabbed the items out of Shaa's hands and gazed at the parchment in disbelief. "Lies, more lies!" His tone, though, was a bit less sure of itself. Was he starting to hedge, perhaps even to doubt? "According to this scrap, this ship is, is—"

"You see?" Shaa said, leaning over to indicate one section with his finger. "*Perfidious Stranger*, as this good man stated."

"Yes!" the official said. "No!" He stared at his own parchment in sudden distress. "The description is exact, the cargo manifest complete, the—"

"What cargo manifest?" asked Shaa. "How would anyone know *what* cargo we've aboard? Excepting myself, of course. We concluded our own contracts upriver, a few particularly good sessions of dealing if you must know, and I don't mind if you do, and what with an extra spot of trading on the dock no one could possibly predict the contents of our hold. This is all very irregular."

Shaa suspected the official knew he had overstepped in his eagerness. He was, though, an obvious bureaucrat, and was clearly not about to let a small matter like an untrue fact put him at a disadvantage. The man swung on the dockmaster. "You are here to assist me in impounding this ship and its passengers. Now issue your orders! Is that clear?"

"May I see those?" said the dockmaster, indicating Shaa's documents. The official thrust them at him. Chewing idly on his lip, he looked closely at the parchment of registration, then thumbed through the smudged, splattered, and sea-stained book. Shaa continued his pose of nonchalance, hoping nevertheless that the man wouldn't decide to rub at the gold leaf of the seals; the black ink he knew was dry, and of course the signatures, but the decoration-work had not had quite enough time to fully set. However, it was apparent that the dockmaster recognized the newly-demoted mate, or thought he did, and found at least that part of the matter seriously amusing, and when that was coupled with his obvious distaste for the official and the whole nature of the proceedings, there was a reasonable chance that even if he found some irregularity he would be inclined to overlook it.

"Seems quite in order to me," the dockmaster said finally, handing the papers back to the mate. "Furthermore, I am familiar with the ship you are looking for, the *Not Unreasonable Profit.* While there are overall correspondences between that ship and this, since they are of the same class laid down in the same shipyard, with similar if not identical measurements of beam, freeboard, and so on, this ship has been customized quite differently in its upper works. We have these extra mid-deck structures, for example, this awning over the quarterdeck, a mainmast *and* a mizzen rather than just the single-mast fore-and-aft gaff rig." He leaned forward over the quarterdeck rail and rapped on the mizzenmast, producing a solid *thunk.* Shaa was glad he had insisted on verisimilitude in their utilization of the onboard supplies for camouflage; accordingly, Karlini's image-work didn't start until an arm's length above the deck. As a result, the base of the mast was solid, but its continuation overhead, as well as the furled sails and the revised rigging, were all refractive illusion. It had been a calculated risk, to be sure, but with Roni's lab packed away and disguised as well it had looked like a calculation well-balanced in their favor, and since the ring wasn't on board either, any reception party wouldn't have been able to get them by detecting *that*. Perhaps it might work out yet. . . .

The official nodded slowly, his lips tighter than ever. "If that is how you choose to declare yourself, so be it." Without turning, he raised one arm and motioned the troop commander forward with a wave of his fingers. "Lieutenant, deploy your men. Secure this ship and place these two under arrest. My men—" he nodded at the two guards on either side of Shaa "—will assist you. Let no one else on or off this vessel. Some violation of order is underway here, and we will soon get to the bottom of it. We will soon decide who is in league with whom. We—"

"Are you quite finished?" Shaa said. "For if you are, or even, let us be frank, if you are not, I wish—no, I demand!—to lodge a protest. I have been quite patient with this nonsense, quite patient indeed, but you have clearly exceeded the bounds of civil procedure and even, shall we say, the codes of law, not to mention those of rationality and good sense, but let that pass. Is the Oolsmouth Council of Representation in session?"

"Yes, Captain," said the dockmaster, "it is."

"The Council is in *special* session," the official snapped, "and the meeting is closed, and in any case the Council would never wish to be troubled with the likes of you, whatever your—"

"To the contrary," Shaa said. "I represent the executors of the trade base of this great city, those who work responsibly under the rule of law to build the wealth and power of Oolsmouth and to increase its stature among the many municipalities; in short, this case stands for the ability of honest, hard-working folk to pursue valid employment and assist the growth of capital. That is exactly the business of the Council, is it not, and the direct interest of those who sit upon it? I wish—no, again, there are no two ways about it, I *demand*—to lodge my protest formally and in person before the Council, to lay this harassment at their feet, and to submit to their wise judgment for the resolution of this annoying matter. Such an unfounded interference in honest business must be of central importance to them! Furthermore, after this already significant waste of time, I demand to deal with superiors, and with the superiors of superiors until (if necessary) the very top, and to cease frittering with underlings and flunkies. Enough is enough!'' He folded his arms over his chest, drew himself up, and tried to project a solid, immovable demeanor. The demeanor was fine; no problem there. His heart, though, was pounding. He hoped there was a breather in store soon.

''Very well,'' the official said after a moment; he too appeared to be breathing hard, although probably not for quite the same reasons. ''Fah! Let someone else deal with you and your nonsense. Lieutenant, you will still secure this ship. My men and I will escort this troublemaker to the Hall of the People.''

''Thank you,'' said Shaa, ''a firm example of good sense and—''

''It might be appropriate for me to join you,'' said the dockmaster, ''given the circumstances.''

''I was just about to suggest that very thing,'' Shaa told him approvingly. ''Shall we go, then?'' He offered his arms to the guards. The giant one on his right grasped that side again, with surprising grace for his obvious barbarian ancestry. Shaa took another quick glance up at him. How closely might Max's description of his recent caravan-mate, the northerner Svin, fit this fellow? There were not all *that* many barbarians roaming the south, surely—there weren't that many barbarians left *anywhere* these days. Perhaps the chance of him showing up here, in this particular situation, was not as remote as it might objectively seem. Max had said he intended to ask Groot to look out for the fellow—could Groot have actually *found* him? Well, one way or another, between Karlini and Shaa, himself, and with the barbarian or not, perhaps they could finally settle this nonsense Groot had gotten himself mixed up in, and get back to what they had set out to do in the first place. ''Well, what are we waiting for?'' Shaa said to the official, who had paused by the head of the stairs for no obvious reason. Now that he had set matters into motion at this end, Shaa had to admit he was looking forward to whatever Karlini had put together somewhere up ahead.

15
THE HAND AND ITS GRASP

The afternoon was wearing on. The Hand did indeed have the island surrounded, more or less. It wasn't a very large island, so the five detachments of The Hand, each with their own cobbled-together raft, were able among them to maintain full surveillance of the entire shore, at least to the limits imposed by the marsh grass, which marched straight off the island into the water, still waving. The beached boat was clearly visible, though, as were the two grazing horses, so The Hand had to know they were in the right place. The right place for what had not yet been established.

Jurtan Mont had become more closely acquainted with waterlogged earth and its myriad tiny creatures than he had ever intended. An egret had even strolled past him once earlier in the day, lifting its stick legs fastidiously over his reclining chest. From the quiet that had descended on the area, most of the other waterfowl had fled the scene, although an occasional honk or the farther-off call of a loon did help to break the monotony.

According to the brief description Jurtan had managed to pry out of Max while he'd still been willing to talk, The Hand was a free-lance mercenary troop. At the moment, they had deployed forty men around the various rafts. All three principals were present as well, the triumvirate known as the Vees.

"You are not being cooperative, Maximillian!" shouted the speaker. "If you do not give yourself up, we will fire the island and shoot you down as you attempt to emerge!"

Up above, Max was still considering how to proceed. He had the hatch open, since they clearly couldn't see any part of it from the ground, and it gave him an easy way to eavesdrop on what was going on below. From The Hand's lack of interest in the sky, Max had apparently gotten rid of the ropes and concealed his presence in the air before they'd caught sight of anything. It had been a close thing, though.

Occasionally, Max had eased the small mirror from his pack up through the door to assess the lay of the situation. Gadol V'Nora, the one who'd been talking, was in Max's experience of The Hand almost *always* the one who was talking; he was The Hand's negotiator and interlocutor. Max remembered that curly black beard and overgrown hair-mop well; from his present vantage point, however, he could see that the area on the top of Gadol's head had begun to thin significantly. In the course of his remarks Gadol had been gesturing freely with his left arm. Either he'd gotten better care than The Hand's medic had been in the habit of providing, or Max had broken the arm more cleanly than he'd thought at the time of their last farewell.

Still, Gadol wasn't actually holding a weapon. Most of the other assorted men-at-arms spread out across the rafts had that covered; they were hefting nocked bows and had their swords at the ready. The one who radiated the greatest air of menace, though, was the man at Gadol's side. Max had asked him once if he'd had his aura spell-doctored to make him emanate so convincingly. Romm had just grunted at him, which from him passed for a substantial conversation, before he'd punched Max in the stomach again. Romm V'Nisa was master of troops and militance expert.

Romm would have been responsible for The Hand's careful deployment. Max was always happy to make a tactical problem of himself, and Romm was certainly one to appreciate the difficulties. He would much rather have moved his men directly onto the island and combed the ground from the shore in, Max figured, leaving a maneuver reserve with their bows on the rafts at the rear. However, he also figured that Romm wasn't about to underestimate Max's personal capability for close-quarters combat again. Giving Max the chance to close with even a half-dozen of his men, especially in the muddle of the tall grass, was not a break Romm would be willing to give. Hence the threat to smoke him out.

Iskendarian's hideout was being remarkably unhelpful. He had to have equipped it with the means to detect and manage intrusions in his neighborhood, but Max hadn't been able to turn up the slightest clue to the scheme of control. It was quite probable that Iskendarian had left the defenses on automatic, but if so, Max had yet to discover what provocation would set them off. Maybe Chas would help him out.

On the other hand, maybe they'd just give up eventually. He'd faked them out before; maybe they'd think he'd done it again. Of course, there were the horses and the boat to consider. Knowing The Hand, too, they'd blast the island before they left just to make sure they'd hadn't been missing something. Now, though, the men were getting ready with fire arrows. "Maximillian, this is your last chance!" announced Gadol.

"Max?" he heard Jurtan Mont gasp.

"Keep your head down," Max said. "Don't worry, I'm on it."

"You leave us no choice! Fire!"

Arrows arched into the grass, trailing flame and soot. A chorus of hisses arose as many of them plunged straight into the mud and were immediately doused. Others caught up in the few small shrubs on the marginally higher ground, two thocked into trees, and perhaps half a dozen lodged themselves in protruding tangles of grass. Small wisps of smoke rose up here and there around the island, and one of the grass clumps started spouting low flames of its own. Gadol turned to Romm, who was watching the lack of spectacle with arms folded and a sternly disapproving expression. Romm listened, shrugged once, and pointed at the water. His message was clear, Max thought. What did Gadol expect in the middle of a swamp, anyway? Of course everything would be waterlogged.

Max angled the mirror downward. There was the kid,

still hugging the ground, clear of the arrows; the closest one was almost five feet away. A clear miss. As Max watched, Mont rolled over and stared up accusingly at him. When are you planning to do something? the kid mouthed.

He thought Mont would rather not learn he had been considering giving himself up. That would give him the best chance of finding out why The Hand had suddenly taken an interest in him again, and was willing to send the whole team into a swamp, of all places, to try to get the drop on him. If The Hand was serious about this, they were sure to pop up again, though, so Max would have other chances. Of course, Max tried his best to assume the most steadfastly paranoid attitude possible. It was always safer to assume someone was after you, and for the worst of reasons, too, so it was a shame to dilute such nefarious potential through the application of facts.

A romantic attitude, Max thought, if a less than practical one. Well, if Gadol didn't go to Chas now, he'd try to think of something . . . ah. Ah-hah! One raft clockwise of Gadol's, a tall man with the archaic tonsure of one of the Kreelmon monkish sects was getting up from his seat on a wooden chest, stowing his pipe in a belt-pouch, shrugging back the sleeves on his light robe, and raising his arms. Chas V'Halila, the team sorcerer, was getting ready for action.

Chas liked flash. He also liked his own personal comfort and safety, but what he didn't always like was groundwork. In the old days he'd been a little too slothful about checking for atmospheric conditions and other potential sources of problems; his spells were direct and to the point. He'd always been one to shoot first and mop up any mess later.

He was too far away and the angle was too weird for Max to see what Chas was launching, but he could guess. A puff of white smoke obscured Chas' hands as out of them appeared a blurred globe of sun-yellow fire. It soared toward the island, breaking into chunks, each dragging its own bright afterimage trail, and then they started to touch down in a flurry of *whoosh* and *whoomp,* getting fires going for real this time. Max felt a swirl of force around him in the sphere. It was too quick to get any kind of fix on; as soon as he noticed it, it was already focusing and collimating and vectoring itself directly toward—

Chas lit up like a fireworks display, his aura fluorescing a swamp-toad green and sparks spraying off his outstretched arms, his skeleton burning electric red behind the pasty shadow of his flesh. His robe went up in soot. Then Chas himself fell over backward like a lock-jointed statue into the murky water. A much larger cloud of steam fizzed up from the surface.

Same old Chas, Max thought. Through his own introductory examination of the swamp, Max had gotten the hint that Iskendarian hadn't wanted anyone running magic in the vicinity, the hint that Chas had obviously missed. What Max hadn't been able to determine was the form the backlash would take. Now that—

A small mountain kicked the outside of the hideout sphere. Max separated from his perch at the hatch, hit the bookcase, and fell to the floor, a pile of books cascading onto him and the sliding divan aiming for his chest. Then the room lashed back in the other direction. It wasn't being kicked, no, but with that amount of motion, what about the island?

Max grabbed the ladder as it swung past, boosted himself up to the open hatch, and leaned over the side. Below him, water was rushing in from all sides of the island, its leading edge disappeared behind the billows of steam and smoke boiling off the patches of Chas' fire as they got drenched and went out. The boat lifted off the shore and floated toward the center. The two horses were looking wildly around as water foamed in their direction, then over their hooves and forelegs. A tree fell over into the wave. The island—

The island was sinking.

The rafts of The Hand were vanishing into the fog. Below him, Max could see Jurtan Mont, now on his feet but reeling from side to side as the island continued to shudder on its way down. "Try to get the horses onto the boat!" Max called to him. Had he heard? But there he was, lurching toward the horses, his arms wide but his voice soothing. And here came the boat.

Max dropped down the ladder to the floor and looked for the rope. He'd gone to the trouble to coil it up while he'd waited, but where was—oh, there, under the cushion from the couch, and there next to it was the bulging oil-cloth sack, too. He grabbed them both, shook loose the end of the rope, and tied it around the neck of the bag. Pushing the sack ahead of him out of the hatch, which was a lot more difficult than when he'd brought it up empty, he finally popped back up into the air. Around the invisible pylon once with the rope—pause for a quick wobble from the island—then again, with another turn. Max passed the end with the sack twice around his body and cinched it with a quick slipknot in front. Taking a firm one-handed hold on the other end of the rope where it emerged from its double twist around the pylon, he boosted himself up, swung both legs out of the hatchway, snatched his amulet away from the hatch with his free hand, dropped the chain over his neck as the hatch began to ease itself closed, and let himself slide backward along the drop-off curve of the sphere.

The sack dangled below his feet. From the sack, the rope went around Max's waist, up to the pylon, and back down to his now double-fisted grip as he rapidly paid it out. Fog and smoke still covered the scene; the only evidence of The Hand was a large shouting from all directions. Grass came up with water beneath it, and then he was down. A strong tug on the rope end around his waist sent the loose bit whipping up into the air, around itself, and then back down toward him in free-fall.

Mont had somehow gotten both horses up onto the barge. Everything was wet and covered with mud, the kid perhaps most of all. The water had stopping coming in, though, leaving a table-sized patch of ground above it in the center of the island. Max slogged as fast as he could toward the barge and flopped on himself. "Good work," he told Mont. "Now hold on."

"Hold on? But—"

Max had one of the poles in his hands and was heaving at the earth behind them. The barge had grounded itself on the mud when he'd climbed aboard; now, with a lurching slide, it began to move free. A bob, and they were clearly out on the water. Behind them, though, the edge of the water was foaming, pulling away from the small center of ground. Pulling?—no, *rushing*, and the barge was starting to *lift*, as the island surged powerfully back to the surface, hurling the water in front of it.

All of a sudden the barge was riding the white-capped crest of a wave. Max had his legs planted wide, one in front of the other, with the pole held out over the bow of the barge. Ahead through the mist and tall grass, the confused shouts of The Hand grew louder, although the creaking of the island and the roar of water in motion were growing louder still. Then, off to the right as they broke through the fog, in front and below, a quick glimpse of standing men with open mouths and upturned faces, men leaning away and reeling back, a cascade of water, a jumble of waving arms and tumbling heads. A wooden barrel bounced through the air ahead of the wave. The maze of trees and channels that faced the lagoon was approaching.

"Sloppy to let them sneak up like that; maybe I'm getting old," Max said, shaking his head, looking behind them at the turbulent lagoon still filled with splashing men. "Shaa would never have let this happen. He's a lot better about these things than I am."

". . . Shaa's better at this than you are?" Jurtan was hanging frantically onto the horses, an arm around each one's neck. The horses, though, seemed to be having a surprisingly good time.

"He went to school, he's had formal training. I haven't. I came up from the streets. A damned urchin, that's what I was."

"Then Shaa's curse. . . ?" Jurtan gasped.

"Yeah, Arznaak knew exactly where to stick the knife for the best effect." The barge slid smoothly around a clump of trees and into a channel, still surfing along the rapidly dying wave. Max had his pole ready and fended off from a root-choked bank. "Shaa might have been in line to be Chancellor of the Imperial Institute; that's how good he was. Don't let him fool you."

"So did you at least find anything while you were up in that place that'll help him?"

"I don't know," replied Max. "Maybe. If I can get this stuff deciphered, maybe." He nudged the sack on the deck with his foot. Paper crunched and rustled inside; he'd been able to fit in most of Iskendarian's manuscript material while he'd been hanging around in the sphere waiting for The Hand's move. "There's a lot of stuff left back in the ball that might be useful, but we'll have to write that off. I don't know when I'll be able to get back here."

"You're not planning to wait until this settles down and go back up?" Jurtan felt his footing was solid enough to try letting go of the horses; the barge was still jumping and shipping water over the sides, but he could surely handle little things like those, couldn't he?

"That wait would probably be long enough to make us miss the Knitting; this area's gonna stay hot for awhile, it looks like. Also, I don't want to give The Hand any more of a clue to the place than they already might have, which means I sure don't want them watching while I climb up again. I'd like to try to dump them, this time for good, and that means getting out of here while they're still putting themselves back together."

"Those guys have been after you for a long time, then, haven't they? Why didn't you kill them? You had the chance."

"Shaa doesn't like it when people get slaughtered."

"He's not here."

Max shrugged. "He rubs off. He's either a good influence or a bad one, depending on where your own stance started. You could say I may have been spending too much time around him."

Mont managed to get the last horse tie-down secured and took up the other pole, by his intent expression apparently planning his next rhetorical foray. "You have any more detours in mind you want to tell me about?"

Max gave him a sidelong glance. "No."

"Do you mean I should rephrase that? Okay, do you have—"

"No! As far as I'm concerned, the next scheduled stop

is Peridol." Max eyed the sack with Iskendarian's manuscripts. There would be help available in Peridol, perhaps, if he was careful; untangling Iskendarian's code looked to be a nontrivial task. A nontrivial task, but a worthwhile one. Max very much wanted to know if he'd identified the equations properly, and correctly intuited their meaning. The thought that Iskendarian had figured out how to decode the communications system of the gods was worth the price of admission all by itself, but that was by no means the only topic of interest. It would very tantalizing indeed if Iskendarian had actually been the original creator of the Spell of Namelessness.

16
THE HALL OF THE PEOPLE

"Aren't you ready yet?" the Great Karlini hissed into the hole in the floor. "They're coming." He was answered only by another dull clunk of metal on metal, followed by the careful tapping of a small hammer.

"I must go," Julio told him from the doorway; he'd been dancing from foot to foot with totally unconcealed impatience for the last five minutes, ever since he'd darted upstairs for the final time to say that the Council Guard had at last arrived to check Groot out of his cell and escort him to the Council chamber for the debate on his case.

"Go, then," said Karlini, getting up off the floor, "go. Oh, and good—"

"Gone is he," Haddo said. "Ridiculous is this, think you not?" He had pressed himself up against the side wall in the tiny alcove, little more than the size of a broom closet, really, to keep his cloak from being snagged as the secret door revolved again on its circular base. From the outside, the entrance was no more than another semicircular niche with another heroic statue on another landing off the staircase that curved its way up the outside of the Council room toward to the observation deck at the base of the Hall of the People's dome. To operate it, you actually had to perch yourself on the statue's back, contorting past its extended marble elbows as it leaned forward with both hands on the guard of its sword, which was positioned point-downward in the suggested flank of some gigantic and most likely allegorical beast. After navigating the elbow, it was necessary to wedge oneself between the niche wall and the statue's flowing cloak of battle, and to activate a lever concealed up against the base with one foot, whereupon the springs of the mechanism would twirl wall section, statue, and passenger alike through a half revolution into this dark little cabinet.

"Give me the light, will you?" said Karlini. Haddo unhooded the lantern and passed it over.

"Good for you is not present Roni," Haddo observed.

"Why is that?"

"Filth," said Haddo succinctly. This place had obviously not been visited in years. Dust had covered every possible surface, as well as the tube that led down through the gap in the floor into the bowels of the Hall. Of course, much of that dust was now in the air, and most of the rest was covering Karlini.

"Who cares about a little grime? Did you finish rewinding the door mechanism?"

"As told you I when last time you asked, is still answer yes." Once they'd packed themselves into the room and cast around with the lantern, the first feature they'd discovered was the windlass crank on the floor just in front of the revolving door element; its function had become clear when the door had begun to slow significantly and make sproinging sounds after its third trip around.

"What's keeping him down there?" Karlini mumbled, sliding the small panel on the inner wall aside again and applying his eye to the peephole. Ahead of him and below, the circular Council hall beneath the domed rotunda was beginning to fill. The buzz of aisleway conversation was clearly apparent.

"Without Favored," Haddo said, "would be none of us here."

"I had something to do with it, too, if you'll remember."

"If had not known Favored Fabricator who this building built—"

"Yeah, all right, but if he doesn't stop that banging, he may have gotten us here but we're not going to *be* here real long either." Karlini closed the viewing panel and flopped down to the floor again. "At least hold down the noise, will you?" he muttered into the vent.

The voice of Favored-of-the-Gods floated faintly out of the duct. "Give me a break, will you? I've never even seen this stuff before, and it probably hasn't moved in the last thousand years anyway. Where the hell's that motor oil?"

"If they hear you out there—"

"Shut up already—I told you I'm working on it!"

"Quiet!" Haddo hissed at Karlini. "To this listen!" Karlini held his breath. From outside the hidden door, he could clearly hear the tramp of feet trudging up the stairs. Toward their position?

Toward them, yes, but then without a hesitation past them as well. The steps faded out above, still tracking around to the right. "Didn't Julio say no one ever came up here?" Karlini said. "The only thing higher than us in this place is supposed to be that observation deck."

Haddo seemed about to say something but was superseded as a clatter of parts echoed up the tube, followed by an incensed "Yeouch!" Karlini winced, and not in sympathy either. "He's not finished and they're starting out there," said Karlini. "They're not just going to think it's rats."

"Busy will be debate. Over talk nothing will they hear."

Karlini clasped his hands behind his back and tried to pace, but one step brought him face-to-face with the farther wall. "We can't just sit here doing nothing," he grumbled to it.

"Know you spell of soundproofing?" Haddo suggested.

Haalsen Groot had made his share of dramatic entrances into this august hall and flamboyant gestures on its floor, but for him this was a whole new category. The members were not yet at their seats along the curved benches surrounding the central Pit of Debate, but they had arranged themselves in their habitual clumps in the aisles, around the punch bowls and water barrel, in the Pit itself, and along the entranceway, and a few small clusters were still hanging about in the corridor outside, too, having yet to straggle through the door themselves. The loiterers were thus the ones privileged to catch the first sight of Groot and his escort, of whom there were a generous ten: four before him and four after, and one on either side holding the chains to the closest arm and leg. Between their police sashes, their tall caps, their swords, and the four halberds just surrounding him to front and rear, the escort made its own statement of power coercively applied and officiously maintained; this much Groot had expected. The challenge that had confronted him was which statement would be best to make for himself.

He had been initially of two minds. One approach, certainly the mainstream one and perhaps also the safest, would have been to appear meek and innocuous, neatly groomed and conservatively garbed, as one who could present no threat to the smallest creature, let alone a great city such as Oolsmouth; in short, to remind the members of the Council before a word was spoken that he was one of them, torn unfairly and most heinously from their midst. Julio's politicking on his behalf and that of the lawyer Snee, though, had already made those points. Further, Groot in his time had been many things, but meek and innocuous had not typically been among them. Donning that particular mantle of martyrdom, then, might have seemed a little too ingenuous of him. His fellow councillors were a tricky lot themselves, whether merchants, citizens' representatives, or ruffians-at-large—the last thing he wanted was to have them think he was trying to hoodwink *them.* On the other hand, the other principal approach, while none the less histrionic in its own right, held out the attraction of the power of shock appeal.

Accordingly, he had uncovered the gash on his cheek for the occasion, and had let more than a hint of the dried blood remain smeared on his face as well. His clothes were torn and grimy. His hair showed that although he had tried to comb it, the circumstances had been unfavorable, and he had also managed to miss certain areas of filth when washing his hands and face. The effect was hopefully that of someone trying to make himself presentable through adversity that was not his fault, someone who has been dramatically and unrightfully put upon. He had been pleased to discover that he harmonized quite appropriately with the picture cut by his escort. The group of them, then, presented in one easily captured image the quintessence of man caught up by the wheels of rogue authority. Or at least that was the idea.

Faces turned toward them, conversation stilled, jaws opened or lips pursed, as the bunch of them marched through, Groot clanking in his chains. When they came out of the anteroom into the Council chamber itself and started down the aisle, Groot saw that an area had been set aside in the Pit next to the central lectern of the presiding Speaker, an area with an elevated display box for him to stand in, surrounded by enough space for his entire troop of guards. After a quick consultation with the Doorkeeper, the commander of the guard detachment led them out into the Pit and installed each one in their assigned place.

Actually, Groot's escort had really numbered eleven: the ten guards from the police, and Eelmon, who had been drifting along behind them dogging their steps and generally keeping his eye on things, not that there seemed to be much he could do if anything went sour but run for help. Julio, too, had been waiting in the corridor as they'd passed. He'd pulled Eelmon aside for a brief consultation, after which Eelmon had disappeared down a side turning and Julio had followed Groot and the guards into the Council chamber.

As the members left their eddies of conversation and filed into the benches, Groot made a point of trying to fix as many of them as possible with his gaze during the moments when they glanced in his direction. Those Councillors Julio had tallied for him during their last consultation session in his cell all appeared to be present—there was Darkan, of course, and Penn Galtick, and Queeling the Procrastinator, and even old Caloot, but where was Dooglas? Snee the lawyer had his head together with Julio's, the two of them punctuating their deliberation by nods here and there in the direction of certain Council members. Then Snee nodded reassuringly to Julio himself and made his way toward the Speaker, who was mounting his pulpit. They exchanged their own few words before Snee crossed over to sit at a small table next to Groot's compartment as the Speaker called the session to order.

"It is always better to start with a spiritual message," the Speaker said, after the vocal hum had subsided to the level of a few scattered whispers, "before we get down to the serious business of ripping each other to shreds." That occasioned a ripple of nervous laughter, which the Speaker allowed to run its course. "Yumun Pondwater has been nominated as the chaplain of the day. Let us all give him our attention."

The invocation was innocuous enough, with a brief parable saying allegorically that things usually work out, at least for someone, under the divine inspiration of the gods; Groot rated it as neutral for his side. Then the Speaker rose again.

Set into the base of the Speaker's cylindrical lectern for its occupant to stand on was an axle-mounted footplate disk, which this particular Speaker sometimes liked to use for dramatic punctuation. He employed it now, letting himself revolve around through a full circle to cast his gaze across all the Councillors who surrounded him. Then, with a <click> Groot was close enough to hear, he engaged the brake and came to a sudden stiff halt. "We are convened today," he said, "on a matter of gravity." They were off.

The Speaker himself ran through a quick prècis of the basic facts: Groot's arrest, the seizure of property, his request for a hearing in Council; an evenhanded presentation. After this preamble he moved directly to the issue. "Who stands to accuse?"

The man who had visited Groot as the representative of the Bank of the New Dawn rose, looking somewhat ill-at-ease. "This is not a matter of accusation per se, your honor," he said. "We firmly protest against this proceeding on—"

"Identify yourself," said the Speaker.

"Mark Lizzard," the man said reluctantly, casting a look over his shoulder toward the entrance door.

"Are you representing yourself, Meester Lizzard?"

The burst of laughter brought a slight cringe out of him. "The Bank of the New Dawn," he said. "As a question purely of the conduct of business, this—"

The Speaker rapped the Mallet of Presidium sharply against the lectern surface. "Thank you, sir. Will Meester Groot speak for himself?"

Snee rose smoothly, dapper in his outfit of sober responsibility. "Meester Groot, beset by privation, has requested my assistance. I am Sunworth Snee, of the firm of Snee, Ruffson, League, and Gatling. Meester Speaker, we question the absence of Councillor Dooglas from these proceedings, since we will demonstrate how he was truly the principal in this vicious and unprovoked attack against Meester Groot."

"The Chair, too, questions the absence and activities of Councillor Dooglas, Meester Snee," said the Speaker, in a tone shading a surprising distance toward the dire. "Nevertheless, we will ask that all available facts and players be set before this assembly, and perhaps Councillor Dooglas will grace us with his presence before we have concluded."

Snee inclined his head toward the Speaker, flashed Groot a reassuring nod, and sat, as the Speaker called on Mark Lizzard to say his piece. It was the same thing as Groot had already heard from him during their earlier meeting. Groot looked out across the room, still looking for Dooglas, trying to gauge the tenor of the crowd. The chamber had a different feel from this close to the center, both of the room and of the debate. He gave up watching faces and followed the concentric swirl of the parquet outward beneath the benches toward the door. The metal floor of the chamber was almost completely covered by the parquet, which had been commissioned by the Council of seven years before, and the new rugs atop that concealed much of the new wood as well. By the entrance, though, the parquet sloped down to match the level of the door sill and ended there; the small gap between the shiny old metal and the doorframe itself was apparent enough if anyone was interested to look for it. Nowhere in the place, though, was there any sign of Dooglas, neither on the floor itself, nor in the doorway, nor in what was visible of the antechamber.

Lizzard finished, and then Snee rose to begin dismantling him. Although Groot had engaged Snee initially for his reputation in the guidance and litigation of the matters of business, he was pleasantly surprised to find him rising to the demands of the present occasion, displaying the full armamentarium of the prototypical barrister: the sly innuendo, the dramatic punctuation, the delicate control of "spin," casting the available facts to provide the best reflection on Groot while gracefully weaving through them the odd supposition or outright conclusion he wished the audience to appreciate. He had reached the story of Groot's visit from the would-be torturers and their reluctant revelation of the warrant signed by Dooglas when a commotion began in the anteroom. A door slammed, heavy footsteps were heard, a gabble of voices rose. Snee broke off as the members craned their necks to try to glimpse what was going on. "Order in the cloakroom!" the Speaker was shouting as he bashed away with the Mallet.

"Order?" a voice floated back, cutting through the hubbub with its maniac edge. "Oh, yes, I'll give you order." A quick high-pitched laugh that was almost a giggle followed the words, and then following the laugh in the chamber came a man; Dooglas. Behind him, though, the disturbance in the entry hall continued.

"Councillor," said the Speaker, his neatly pointed gray beard waggling with accusation, "I charge you to restore the composure you have so wantonly violated."

"You are wanton in your own demands, you old moppet," shouted Dooglas. "First you want order, then composure—well, which is it? Perhaps I'll give you order first, and then the composure will take care of itself, heh?" He spun around, his ermine cloak flapping and swishing and his jewels clanking and clattering; he really was horribly overdressed, Groot realized, and he was actually wearing a powdered wig. "You heard the

Speaker,'' he yelled through the door. ''Quiet out there. Order!''

Surprisingly, the commotion did die down, with a last couple of thumps and a metallic twang; a rather ominous silence replaced it. ''There,'' said Dooglas, striding down the aisle to the front row. He struck a dramatic stance, his feet planted strongly, one hand on his hip and the other raised with a flourish, and swept his eyes around the room. ''Order is restored. Shall we proceed with the show?'' He dropped into the seat the current occupants of the bench had prudently opened up for him, then concluded his entrance with another surprising titter.

''The second childhood, is it, then?'' said a voice across the Pit from Dooglas; old Caloot, who, from the scraggly white-maned creased-skin looks he'd affected throughout living memory, most likely had more than a passing personal familiarity with the subject himself. He got his own small scattering of laughter but no more than that. Dooglas, for all his new-found eccentric flamboyance, had the members spooked.

The Speaker employed his Mallet again. ''Will someone step into the cloakroom and bring out the Doorkeeper? Councillor Toomey, I see you by the aisle, will you be so good . . . thank you.'' Just as Toomey reached the top of the aisle, the door to the anteroom slammed shut in his face. A voice spoke indistinctly behind it.

Toomey listened closely, then turned to address the Council, displaying his own look of puzzlement. ''He says it's rather a mess, but he'll have it cleaned up in a moment. Not to worry, he says, there's the guard of honor out there with him.''

''Captain,'' the Speaker said in a low voice to the head of Groot's personal escort, ''would you mind having your men assess the situation in the cloakroom?''

''My orders are clear,'' said the man indifferently, with perhaps the barest glance toward Dooglas. ''We are here to guard this dangerous prisoner, and guard him we shall.''

''Stop this vacillation!'' called Dooglas. ''Get on with it!''

The Speaker looked at Snee, who shrugged, then out

at the Council. "Very well. We will proceed for the moment. Meester Snee, please continue."

Snee rose again, cleared his throat, and raised the warrant of torture signed by Dooglas. "As the learned Councillors will recall, we were discussing this most irregular document, most irregular and thoroughly illegal, violating as it does—"

"And in whose name is this worthy document executed?" Dooglas interrupted loudly, springing to his feet.

"Councillor!" said the Speaker. "You will have your chance in good time. Meester Snee now has the floor."

"The god Sapriel! I just want you all to remember that," Dooglas added. "The god Sapriel," he repeated, this time almost to himself, as he lowered himself back to the bench.

"Meester Speaker?" said Snee. He approached the pulpit and the two of them began to whisper together. The Council had been growing increasingly restive, and now a group of the back-benchers got up, apparently after mutual consultation, and headed toward the door. The lead one pushed on it, but it was still quite securely locked. He began pounding on the top panel with his fist.

Dooglas had roused himself again, too, but he had sauntered out into the Pit and was making his way over to Groot's box; in the general disorder, no one paid him much heed. Groot noted that his guards certainly did not. Dooglas leaned closer and told him, "I swore I'd get even with you, and now I have, at last."

"You've done nothing of the sort," Groot said. "Everyone can see already that you've overstepped the bounds of propriety and good sense. You're rampaging around like a rogue elephant. First it was me, but now you're mocking the whole Council."

"What Council? I see no Council. An artifact, perhaps, a rabble, a fossil, a creature soon to be extinct." He laughed his high-pitched laugh. "Very soon."

"Why are you being so blatant about all this nonsense?" said Groot. "We have laws in this city, in case you haven't given thought to them lately, and more than that we all have to live together in the same small patch of land. It would be much more convenient if we could do it without turning that land into a field of battle."

"We don't *all* have to continue *living*, my old friend. Hah! My old friend. Field of battle indeed. You're right! Enough of this." He fished out a whistle on a chain around his neck and blew. Its tone was loud and shrill, but not nearly as loud as the slap of the suddenly flung-open door or the shouts of the Councillors gathered around it as they were shoved and punched back. One fell to the floor, clearly revealing the band of fully armed soldiers crowding through the door into the room behind him. A trooper paused to kick him out of the way as they spread out around the chamber.

"Councillor!" the Speaker was shouting at Dooglas. "What is the meaning of this?"

"Why, you asked for order and decorum, did you not?" Dooglas said. "You saw how difficult a request that was. I am merely providing the means to ensure your needs, once and for all." His mirth bubbled over again.

The red of the Speaker's face was beginning to contrast alarmingly with his silver beard. He raised the Mallet, hefted it, and then swung it with remarkable alacrity toward Dooglas' head. Suddenly a muscled arm was in the way, grasping the Speaker by the wrist with a grinding of bone.

"None of that," said the sergeant of Groot's guard. The Mallet fell to the floor. The sergeant gave a yank and the Speaker came out of his pulpit liked a leaping marlin. Then the soldier opened his grip. The Speaker sank down, his back against the lectern, his hand cradled to his chest, his complexion the reddish-purple of volcanic sunset.

"Thank you," Dooglas told the sergeant crisply. He bent and retrieved the Mallet, gazed at it fondly for a moment, then roused himself and straightened. "Order," he said. "Time for order." He opened the Speaker's pulpit and mounted within.

At the familiar banging, heads turned toward the center; when they saw who was present, conversation froze. Into the silence, Dooglas said, in a conversational voice, "Order."

A few Councillors began shouting at him. Dooglas bashed the podium again with the Mallet and yelled back, "Look around you!" As they did, and their voices again trailed off, Dooglas added, "Now sit down, all of you!"

"Yes," he went on, after giving the members a chance to sort themselves out, "I control the forces you see about you. Yes, subversion can still succeed, even in this place and time. Yes, unhelpful forces can still be locked in barracks by one's own private troops. Yes—"

"The last time this happened was about 'aught-five," said old Caloot in his white-haired civic eminence, a bit irritably. "Or was it 'aught-six? It's all back there in the Council books, one way or the other. I hope you've been taking good notes," he snapped in a sharp-tongued aside to the Council secretary, still seated in his writing position at the desk before the front bench. The secretary hurriedly held up his transcription book, turning it so the pages faced outward toward Caloot, and indicated the furious runs of new ink he been frantically scribbling. Caloot gave him a curt nod and told him, "Carry on." He then returned his gaze to Dooglas. "These things never work, you know, and they're bad for business, too. Don't you boys ever learn anything?"

"Silence him," Dooglas said to the sergeant, not taking his eyes off Caloot.

Caloot didn't take his eyes off Dooglas, either. Ferocious eyes they still were, too, given additional fire by the maze of inflamed blood vessels and the eagle-crag cant of his sunken eye sockets. "Just try it, sonny," he said.

Perhaps Dooglas shrank back a bit, and perhaps he turned the barest shade of green. He cackled once, though with a bit less glee than he'd been exhibiting, then said, "Out of the old sentiment and respect of a one-time apprentice, this time I will—"

"Put a lid on it," muttered Caloot. "If you'd been an apprentice of mine, I'd have drowned you in the discard ale." Caloot was the major Oolsmouth brewer and distiller, and a leading importer of foreign spirits as well.

"I will let you live," Dooglas said determinedly, as

the sergeant returned to his side, "to choke on your words as you see me master of Oolsmouth."

"A case of my Old Stout says he doesn't last the day!" said Caloot. "What, no takers? You're all a lily-livered no-account—"

"Do not push me too far," stated Dooglas, "or you will leave me no choice."

"What *are* you talking about?" the Speaker mumbled from his position on the floor.

Dooglas banged the Mallet. "Let us proceed. Send in the inquisitors!"

One of the goons at the doorway leaned through it and yelled, "Boss wants the inquisitors!" Three figures garbed all in black—three figures who seemed quite familiar to Groot—immediately filed in; they must have been waiting on call only steps away. A collective gasp rose up around the chamber.

"Come to me!" Dooglas called to them. "It is time to continue the hearing. However," he continued, turning to Groot, "the rules have changed. In a moment—what is it now?"

Loud conversation had again broken out in the anteroom. "He'll gab the government to its knees if he doesn't get his hearing, by the gods he will," one voice said in a particularly aggravated squeal that cut through the rest of the talk.

"An exaggeration to be sure," said another voice, "but when set upon and misused, not to mention maltreated, by the forces of misguided, misinformed, or even, shall we say, mistaken officialdom, what is an honest merchantman to do but to seek clarification, at the least, from—"

"What is going on out there?" Dooglas shouted across the room.

That was a question whose answer Groot was eager to learn as well. He had recognized the second voice, which was well-nigh unmistakable. The three torturers, now apparently promoted to inquisitors, had paused halfway down the aisle, and had turned with everyone else to view the new spectacle at the entranceway as a familiar man in a nautical outfit plowed through into the chamber like a manic rod-puppet, dragging behind him two reluctant guards, each with a tentative hold on one of his arms, and behind them a gaggle of at least half-a-dozen assorted officials of increasing rank, every one of them gesticulating vigorously and simultaneously babbling. Behind this rabble came another fellow in oilskins and dock boots, and an aloof but amused expression.

"What is this?" said Dooglas. "Who is this ragged sea-captain to disturb the decorum of the Representative Council?"

"I *told* him he couldn't come in here," said one of the bureaucrats, "but he wouldn't accept—"

"So did I," said another, and then they all started yelling at each other again; they had thus far been too busy, it appeared, to have noticed the troops standing guard around the chamber, and the three inquisitors ahead of them in the aisle. The inquisitors began padding toward them with a menacing glide.

"Who is responsible for interfering with my ship?" Shaa demanded loudly, his captain's jacket flapping. "Some excuse for a commercial center this Oolsmouth has become. You people of the Council should be ashamed of yourselves—obstructing an honest trader just trying to do a good day's work. I am not unknown in the Maritime Guild, no, not unknown at all, and I will make the strong recommendation—"

"Shut up!" said Dooglas. "We have no time for this! Inquisitors, shut him up."

"Are you in charge here, sir?" said Shaa, aiming an accusing finger down the aisle at Dooglas. "Well, then, *sir,* I would advise you that you have no more important matter before you than this. I will have you know that I represent the firm of Crumwald, Twist, and Loop, and I can assure you that they will not be pleased, not pleased in the least, with the way you now choose to do business in your jurisdiction. Words will be said, I can promise you, words indeed. When all is said and done—in fact, without exaggeration, I will venture to state that by the time not more than *half* has been said and done—you will rue well the day that—I beg your pardon?"

Two of the three inquisitors were facing Shaa; the third

had kneeled on the floor to open his case of instruments. Shaa glared at each of them in turn. "You heard Speaker Dooglas," the central one said. "Shut up. Please hold his arms more securely," he added to the guards who had accompanied Shaa in. "We are all professionals here." He raised his hand, flattened his palm, and moved it toward Shaa. Then the black-covered arm seemed to shrink as a truly massive hand appeared from the side and clasped it with an almost gentle ease. The gentility might have been deceptive, though, since the man let out a small shriek and fell to his knees next to his assistant who was still fumbling for their equipment.

"He will speak." The gigantic fingers opened. Its arm was raised. Arm and voice were attached to the same body, that of the big barbarian guard, the *big* barbarian one. The voice had been big and deep, just the sort of voice you'd expect from a barbarian, in fact, and the floor under his feet and the framed plaques on the wall behind him hadn't yet stopped rattling. The barbarian raised his eyebrow and looked around him. The members of the wharf delegation were looking at him with their mouths open. *Everyone* was looking at him with their mouths open. Groot, from his perch in the Pit, had a look of satisfaction on his face; the look of a businessman who has just appreciated that a transaction of his was working out even better than he'd anticipated. Even Shaa had craned his neck around and was eyeing the barbarian with surprise. Clearly the barbarian had the floor.

"Where *did* he come from?" mumbled the original leader of the wharf delegation, the duly constituted and jurisdictional representative of the Municipal Authority of Oolsmouth who had challenged Shaa on the deck of the disguised ship. He and his delegation had been waiting on the wharf for the ship when the big guy had come walking up, claiming to have been sent by the Captain of Police as a reinforcement in case of trouble. He'd had some kind of token he'd claimed was from the Council, too. Now that he thought about it, though, the official didn't remember ever having seen the barbarian around the city before.

Svin coughed; the catarrh had eased enough for him to

start getting back in shape, but his throat still spent most of its time being clogged. Still, it had deepened his already subterranean voice and added to its resonance, so that when he spoke it was like blowing through a low-register organ pipe. He thought perhaps he should remember to get sick more often. "It has been a lot of trouble to bring him here," Svin said, when he was sure he had everyone's attention. "He is very annoying." For good measure, he rested a hand on the hilt of his ax. "He will speak."

"Thank you, sir," Shaa told Svin, inclining his head in a bow of acknowledgment. "At least one man here has the right of the matter. Now, Meester Speaker—Dooglas, I believe this fellow said your name was?—now, Meester Dooglas, then, I have—"

"Enough of this!" Dooglas shouted. "An end to this, I say! Won't any of you subdue this man?" Some of his goons grunted, some stood still as though they hadn't heard a thing, and one or two out-and-out shook their heads; some of them had had experience with big barbarians before, and the others had no desire to find out if the stories they'd heard about berserker ferocity or the strength of ten or the bullheadedness not to know when you were beaten were even half true. "Be that way, then!" Dooglas told them. He tilted his head back and looked up at the rotunda dome. "Gazoont! Are you up there?"

A hand appeared over the edge of the railing of the observation deck and waved. "Here, master," a voice echoed. "Shall I rain fire upon him?"

"Yes," said Dooglas. For the first time, some of the Council members started to take cover, sinking down out of sight beneath their benches. "Why don't you do that?"

A sudden sizzle and a swelling orange glow came from the balcony. Svin let go of Shaa's arm and launched himself down the aisle, one foot coming down neatly onto the outstretched hand of the head inquisitor where he had placed it on the floor for leverage in getting himself back up on his feet. The inquisitor wailed again and collapsed, then hollered yet another time as Shaa's other guard, who had somehow found himself propelled forward using the leverage of his firm hold on Shaa's arm, only to be thrown cartwheeling over Shaa's hip, fell full onto the inquisitor's back. Shaa dove out of sight under the nearest bench. A pillar of flame reached from the observation deck toward the aisle. The gaggle of bureaucrats scattered.

The end of the flame-coil from the balcony paused, lashed around like a snake looking for the best target, then looped around in midair and headed down the aisle after Svin. Svin had reached the central pulpit. His knees flexed and sent him into a tremendous leap up over the lip of the lectern, across it, then down into its interior, his weight jamming Dooglas up against the side containing the entry gate. The latch to the gate came free with a rip of wood, the gate slammed open, and Dooglas tumbled out of the lectern to fall flat on the floor next to the Speaker.

Above, a slender sparkling-blue thread had appeared two-thirds of the way up between the floor and the observation level, reeling itself apparently out of the blank wall in the midst of the wrap-around mural of civic forefathers painted around the rotunda. Whiplike, it wrapped its tip around the trunk of the flame pillar and yanked tight. The lower section of flame, now disconnected from its umbilical, roiled angrily, expanded, and whooshed out in a singeing cloud, embers raining around the room.

"That's it!" said a very faint voice that rang with a metallic twang, seemingly from just underfoot. "I've finally got it!" Something coughed like a freshly heated boiler and a shudder ran through the circular metal floor.

"Don't you think events are going beyond the need for your presence?" Groot said to the commander of his own guard escort. Amazingly, the ten members of the escort had remained at their stations surrounding his box.

"I have orders," began the sergeant. The remains of the flame coil overhead had begun lashing about like a serpent now in its death throes, its head permanently severed. It grazed the wall where the blue lasso had come from and a ten-foot expanse of mural exploded out into the air. Revealed behind it was a jagged section of stone and beams, and part of a small room. A man was standing in the room, or more precisely, he was reeling back from the new open brink, or even more precisely, he was being *dragged* back by what appeared to be a waist-high heap of rags. In the Pit across from Groot, Dooglas was getting a wobbly leg under his body. Svin came out of his battle crouch and sprang through the flopping lectern gate toward him. Just at that moment, though, the floor began to move.

The circular floor was, of course, massive and ponderous, between its own bulk and the combined magnitude of Councillors and furniture. Even with its opening jerk, though, as it lurched through a full hour's position on a half-day clock, if in a counter-clockwise sense, causing Dooglas to be yanked out of the way of the airborne Svin's convulsive grab, the floor was giving a clear signal that it was not about to be trifled with, or to be impeded in its course by any practical considerations of power and drag. Dooglas lurched forward and grabbed hold of the trailing edge of the pulpit's swinging door. Behind him, Svin hit the floor on a rug, which promptly slid out from underneath his feet, and as the rest of him tumbled toward the floor he skidded into the railing that fenced the Pit off from the front bench. The railing burst and Svin's hurtling bulk went straight through it into the bench itself. The bench and its half-dozen members predictably flipped over backward. Groot's box groaned against the floor and began to glide outward toward the wall.

Amidst the great creaking and grinding of the floor itself, and the smashing of collapsing furniture and the hollering of the chamber's occupants, a large bass chuffing noise in the middle of a humming whine was making itself felt from *beneath* the floor as well, centered approximately under the Speaker's lectern. Perhaps not coincidentally, the lectern (being at the center of the room) was the point around which the floor was revolving, now with clearly increasing angular momentum. Groot braced himself against the edge of the judgment box; he probably should have dropped to its floor for additional protection, he thought, but he never liked to miss an interesting spectacle. Dooglas had managed to lever his upper body back into the lectern, his legs trailing back onto the floor but his feet scrabbling for purchase. One shoe slipped against the slick surface and lashed back, directly into the knee of one of the troopers who had been guarding Groot. The trooper and four of his squadmates had finally broken ranks and were making for the lectern themselves. Now, as the one Dooglas had kicked tumbled backward, his feet shooting out from under him and his arms outspread for unforthcoming purchase, it was plain that the lot of them were going nowhere but down. The man caromed into first one, then another of his colleagues like a rogue set of flailing tenpins, and the knot of them began to roll and slide outward toward the wall.

From the observation deck, Sy Gazoont, Groot's former communications mediator, was leaning over the intact section of the balcony rail, watching the spinning floor as he chewed anxiously on his cheek. "Blast the floor?" he muttered. "No, too dangerous, might hit Dooglas. Main force? How much could I muster? How much would I need?" Getting the flame pillar under control before its lashings destroyed his entire perch, instead of merely blasting away three-quarters of the railing and a jagged chunk of the adjoining floor, had been trickier than he'd expected. It had looked so straightforward in the book, too. He'd always looked down his nose at those brute sorcerers who wasted their time with attack magic; after all, any fool could throw raw power around and burn things down, couldn't he? A communicator, though, needed a more refined talent, a delicate sense of control. He would still beat them at their own game, and with his own flair. "Inhibition field, that's the ticket. Shut down the motivator spell, right."

Over the racket from below and the sound of his own voice, and through his rapt train of thought, tightly focused as it was on the problem at hand, Sy was paying not the slightest attention to the balcony door behind him. There was certainly no need. He had removed it from consideration by sliding the latch and blocking it from the inside with a chair. Accordingly, even if he had heard or noticed the door as it began to ease open, he might have dismissed the observation as an attack of nerves, unless he had realized that with the damage the observation level had already taken the door jamb had been sprung and the chair moved. Then, too, it might have occurred to him that anyone who really wanted to get in might not have hesitated to smash the door down. But, then, they still would have been too late, since his inhibition spell was almost ready to go. It would soon shut down the sorcerous engine powering that madcap floor, Dooglas' henchmen would restore order, and he, Sy Gazoont, would have saved the day. What kind of reward would be most appropriate?

"There!" he said. "On the way." Even the spell matrix was neatly crafted, with its multi-faceted green surface and all those glints and highlights; as his course of study had stressed, the aesthetics of spellwork are as important as the function. The matrix dropped away from him, directly on target for the center of the Speaker's pulpit, darted past Dooglas' face where he was just pulling himself erect once again within the lectern, hit the floor at his feet, and released. Any second now . . . any second.

Now?

The floor was still spinning, and apparently even gaining speed. Sy frowned down at it.

"Not a *bad* spell," said a man at his shoulder. Sy Gazoont looked up wildly. Next to him, peering over the railing just as he had been doing, was a guy totally covered with soot and plaster dust. "Just the *wrong* one."

"What are you talking about?" Sy heard himself say. He brought his hands up into his casting position, trying to remember the other offensive spell he'd learned.

"Not too bad a guess at that," the stranger said, "at least if you didn't have the prudence to actually check out the details of the situation. How could you know antimagic wouldn't work?"

"Wouldn't work?" said Sy, pausing out of curiosity before flinging the spell that would destroy this upstart. "Why?"

"Because the motivator isn't magic, of course," said the Great Karlini. "It's mechanical." He looked past Sy Gazoont's shoulder. "Haddo?"

"Hah!" began Sy. Karlini took a step toward him. Always keep a working distance, Sy had been taught, so he also took a step back, and fell neatly over the upended chair Haddo had placed.

"Amateur," Haddo said. "With communications stayed should he."

On the Council floor, perhaps the only one who had noticed any part of this exchange had been Dooglas. Whatever Gazoont had been up to with his green gem-thing, though, it had obviously not led anywhere useful. "Fah!" he shouted. Enough of this. Balancing himself precariously in the center of the whirling pulpit, with a bracing arm extended to the lip at his side, he dug underneath his shirt, past the whistle, and found the small rune-covered disk on its heavy chain. Dooglas pulled the chain over his head and held the disk up in his clenched fist. "Sapriel!" Dooglas called. "Hear me!"

Svin had shaken clear of the tangle of troops and cascading benches. Most everything movable, including pews, desks, rugs, loose sections of parquet, and, of course personages, had made their way outward to the wall, either sliding, tumbling, or hurtling, where they had now piled up in a long mixed-media heap. The single door had become clogged almost immediately by the two bureaucrats and a back-bencher who had reached it simultaneously, being followed immediately after by the back bench itself; the resulting agglomeration had eliminated the doorway from useful consideration as an exit. Svin, however, had managed to keep hold of his ax, and was using it to make his way against the centrifugal pull toward the center, like a mountain climber working his way against gravity up the ice. A straight line of ragged gouges in the parquet traced his path radially behind him. Now, he jammed the fingers of his left hand into the space cleared by the ax on its previous chop, clenched his teeth, drew himself ahead, and then in a smooth motion jerked the ax free of the floor and swung it out in front with a convulsive fling. It bit securely. Only two more rounds of this and he would be at the lectern.

Shaa shook his trailing foot clear of the policeman who had been hanging onto it and pulled himself more securely onto his perch. He had reached the ledge that circled the chamber ten feet above the floor and served as the take-off stage for the ornamental pillars of the rotunda by immediately scurrying toward the wall when the floor had started to turn, keeping a careful eye out for newly arriving passengers and debris, and making his way up the growing pile. This was scarcely the diversion he had hoped to cause. If it worked, though, he would be more than happy to claim credit later. He rose and carefully inched his way around to the left, then leaned down and extended his hand. Haalsen Groot had just arrived at the wall, riding his box of judgment like a saddled battering ram. Out in the center of the room, a volume of air above Dooglas' head was starting to coagulate.

Groot finished clambering out of the box onto the ledge. "Did you think this was going to happen?" Shaa asked him, nodding with his chin at the developing manifestation.

"What?—oh! No, surely not. I certainly would have never thought this Sapriel would take an active role even if Dooglas *was* involved with him."

"Hmm," said Shaa. "Well, unless yon barbarian is able to wind this up quickly, we look to be seeing an active role, and then some."

"Send me your power!" Dooglas was saying. "Back me in my moment of need! Invest me with the aura of your greatness!"

"A bit excessive on the rhetoric," Shaa said critically, "wouldn't you say?" A shaft of coiling vapor with a distinctly orange tinge was reaching down from the area of curdling air toward Dooglas. Dooglas' head and upraised arm began to scintillate.

Like the scraping of giant fingernails across slate, a large shuddering screech appeared, setting teeth on edge across the room. The hum and chug of the engine under the floor faltered. The floor shuddered, rocked, hopped up an inch and wobbled back down. Oily black smoke sifted up through the newest holes Svin had chopped; he drew a deep breath and narrowed his eyes, trying to see ahead through the sudden fog. He got a hand on the sill of the flapping pulpit door.

A deep voice spoke in the midst of the crystalline zone above Dooglas. "Go *away!*" it said.

"Lord," Dooglas said perplexedly, his head tilted back to stare upward, "I beg your pardon—"

"I'm right in the middle of—" the voice continued. Then the voice was overtaken by a large sound of sucking, and the swirl of sparkling air began to collapse inward like a deflating balloon. Above the ebbing slurp, a distant deep howl was briefly heard as the air rippled a last time and became smooth.

"Sapriel!" shouted Dooglas. "Sapriel? Where are—" Beneath his feet, the floor heaved again, settled, visibly canted over at a slight angle, a spray of parquet and a jagged coil of torn metal leapt into the air at the edge of the Pit, and the floor ground to a sudden halt. Svin had just set himself into motion. With the centrifugal resistance unexpectedly removed, he hurtled forward like a boulder out of a siege catapult through the open gate of the pulpit and into the still-twinkling Dooglas, the flat of his ax chewing a wide splintery track through the decorative hardwood siding. Dooglas and Svin hit the opposite side and kept going. The sparkle that had covered Dooglas' upper body came loose like a suddenly-molted skin; firefly motes danced for a moment in the air before winking out in small delicate puffs.

Svin brushed a pile of punched-out wood off his arms and began to get off the flattened Dooglas, who was looking at nothing in particular with his eyes crossed. The logjam at the doorway heaved and fell free in a jumble of waving arms and bench legs. Behind it was Eelmon, and behind *him* was a press of new police troops. They began to push their way into the chamber, the lead policeman shouting, "Traitors! Lay down your arms!" Then he looked around, saw the heaps of furniture and persons piled up against the walls, and the lack of remaining armed insurrectionists, and his voice trailed off.

People began to separate themselves from the wreckage, sorting out the bruises and puncture wounds from the occasional broken bone. Groot spotted the Speaker being extricated headfirst from a mound of rug, smiling weakly, and then noted the figure of old Caloot bounding across the floor toward the recumbent Dooglas. Dooglas watched Caloot come toward him with glazed eyes and a loose-jawed drool. Groot eased himself off the ledge and across the judgment box and went to join them.

"You boys never do learn, do you?" Caloot was saying, one hand on his hip and the other on the hilt of his walking cane, and his gaze turned downward. "You thought you could move against Groot here and not be taken down for it, and maybe you could have, you never know. Oh, maybe the Council would have given you a slap on the wrist if you'd left it there, but with the number of members you started off controlling and the others who wouldn't have had enough guts to actually line up against you if you hadn't forced them, you didn't have anything serious to fear. But you wanted it all, miscalculated and played your whole hand, didn't you, except you didn't have as much to build with as you thought, eh? Well, at least you got headed off before you caused too much harm, before it got too far out of control." He waggled his finger. "Let this be a lesson."

Caloot turned away and started limping out, then paused once more to look around him. "Why does everybody always want to take over a city? You take over a city, you've got to actually *run* the place." He shook his head. "Some folks are just plain crazy."

17
THE HALL OF THE GODS

"Is everyone ready?" said Zhardann.

"Sure," I said heartily. Jill, Soaf Pasook, Zhardann, and I were once again in the second-floor study of Zhardann's place, sitting around the unlit fireplace with our armchairs in a half-circle.

"Ordinarily," Zhardann said, addressing all of us, "I support the principle of separate arrivals. Certainly the individual entrance reveals the least detail concerning one's affiliations and confederations, allows the greatest ambiguity about one's intentions, gives one maximum flexibility for maneuver, or those tastefully yet dramatically timed shifts of direction, and so forth; all worthy goals to be cultivated, we all agree. Anything else is a bit . . . jejune, shall we say. Nevertheless, the bold stroke, the dramatic gesture, the small slap at accepted propriety do have their place. The sheer shock value of an unexpectedly explicit statement can make its own message unmistakable."

Both Jill and Pasook looked impatiently placid, as though they were waiting for Zhardann to get past his rationalization to whatever conclusion he was leading us up to, but were willing to give him the space he wanted. Whenever Jill got restless, I'd noticed, she usually broke in with an unexpectedly explicit remark of her own. From the fact that she was keeping her mouth shut here, I figured she knew what Zhardann was aiming at and had decided to go along with it. For Zhardann's part, too, I caught from him the feeling of an orator warming up, doing his knee-bends and short sprints, and generally giving himself a running start, as it were.

That was fine with me, too. As far as I was concerned, Zhardann could take all the time he wanted. When he got to the end of his spiel, we'd all have to zap ourselves off to the tribunal of the gods. That feat would give three out of the four of us no problem at all, but of course the three weren't my immediate concern. The fourth, however, certainly was.

"It is no secret that those of us who aspire to the higher levels of intrigue must be flexible," Zhardann was saying, in his most convincing and crowd-pleasing voice. "I believe this is a case where the direct application of these maxims is appropriate. I will be specific. In this case, it may be important to impress the gathering with our solidarity and unified purpose right from the outset. Accordingly, we will utilize—that is, I *propose* a modified group field transfer. Are there any objections?" He glanced around the circle.

He was obviously trying to put himself in a conciliatory frame of mind instead of just going with his usual high-handed peremptory style. If that told me anything about what was coming up, it was that he'd be trying to sway others by force of persuasion rather than telling them dictatorially what to do. That much I'd already guessed, though. I nodded back at him to indicate my own assent, telling him through my offhand manner that the trivial question of means didn't matter to me one way or the other. Inside, however, I was hoping that *group* transfer meant Zhardann would be doing the work and I'd just be pulled along for the ride.

"I do say *modified* group transfer," Zhardann reminded us. "As I will be the one called on to perform any major work that arises during this synod, it is appropriate not to dilute my strength through extraneous extension. To that end, I will provide the synchronization carrier, but each of us will separately power his own jump. If we *are* ready, then, let us be off." He raised his hand and drew it down over his face, waggling his fingers rapidly.

I had barely enough time to say "Ulp" beneath my

breath before the cloud appeared above Zhardann's head. As though spilling out of an invisible box a hand's-breadth above his hair, a coil of fluffy grayish white dropped down like a python, coiled around itself at the level of Zhardann's forehead, and spun out into a plump disk. If it was not the identical effect I'd seen him use before, when Jill and I had come upon him in this room shortly after our arrival in Oolsmouth, it was surely a close relation. He'd been using it then for communication, but his body had apparently never moved from the room.

Pasook and Jill were now wearing their own hat-clouds, too, but I had to squint to see them since for some reason my vision had begun to fog and someone had tossed a shade over the lights in the room. No, I realized, that wasn't it at all! To my surprise, I suddenly became aware that at the top limit of my vision, a fourth cloud was hovering above my own head. I brought my hand up in front of my face as the others were doing and flailed my fingers, as usual not having the slightest idea of what I was really trying to accomplish.

No, that wasn't right either—and this time that comprehension brought with it a long rolling chill that started at my neck, tracked down my spine, and then flowed over into the pit of my stomach. It wasn't just that my fingers were not moving randomly at all but with purpose, although that was the case, and it wasn't that I felt no more in control of events than at the other times when magic had occurred around me, although that was the case, too. The disconcerting realization was that it felt *familiar.* It felt as though I might have actually done this before.

With all my experience of Gash and his metabolic link, I'd never had a sensation like this before. Could the throughput of the link have somehow been increased, to the point where I was getting perceptions piped in from Gash, too? The cloud dropped down over my eyes and the scene went gray, then darker, almost to black. I felt the clammy whisper move lower on my face like the breath of an anesthetic gauze—my smell faded away, my taste, even the caress of air upon my skin. My head was turning—was it?—well, it *felt* like it was turning, anyway, *orienting* itself, as a tendril of soft sound eased itself into my left ear, like a conversation heard across a stadium field in the fog. A silvery construction of thin unsupported wire swam vaguely through the cloud around my head. I lifted my other hand—the first was still making its gestures of power, although I couldn't see it in front of my face, and the grayness had slid over it like a velvet cloud—and tried to pinch the skin on my chest. Had I dematerialized? But I could feel my chest there in the right place; I'd grabbed hard enough to hurt. Instead of pain, though, I'd felt only a dull pull-and-twist.

This was sorcery on a fairly high level of sophistication, I was sure, although Zhardann's synchronization coordinator—the silver wire thing—had two obvious extra loops as well as a subtle glitch that on closer examination might turn out to be an actual bug. He was guiding us to one of the standard meeting-grounds, that much was straightforward, and I could feel the four of us deploying into a line—Jill on the left, then Zhardann and Pasook, with me holding the right flank—with the arrival zone he'd picked coming up fast. The imminent-arrival warning went out ahead, and then, and then . . .

What had I been thinking about?

My mind lurched after that flickering sense of competence, the momentary feeling that I understood something that was going on . . . but whatever it had been, whether my own imagination or something else, it was gone. I felt solidity beneath my feet. The gray nothingness before my eyes lightened and grew transparent, not as if it was actually blowing away as a normal fog might, but more like one of those trick panes of glass that are dark and opaque from one orientation yet become clear when rotated a quarter-turn. I heard conversation and the clink of crystal around me. We had arrived.

I was on the right end of my party, with Soaf Pasook to my immediate left. We were standing on the roughly flat-topped surface of what appeared to be a cumulus cloud, fluffy billows rolling slowly around us and towering above us into the brilliant blue sky. Perhaps two paces to my right the edge of the cloud dropped off, revealing a small meadow of waving green twenty seconds or so of free-fall below. Steep walls of ice and snow-dusted rock ringed the meadow on three sides. The cliff-sides—for so they were—mounted toward the altitude of our position, the central peak in fact overtopping the cloud by a gut-wrenching leap. The whole sight had me by the stomach, to be frank, and the gaps that were opening and closing here and there in the surface of the cloud, showing other aerial vistas of rock and glacier through them far below, did not help to relieve that one bit. Neither did the other mountain ridge toward which the cloud appeared to be drifting in a straight line.

None of these features of landscape appeared to faze the others in the least. When I say "others," I don't mean only Zhardann, Jill, and Pasook, either, although they were certainly surveying the scene with their own aloof calm, Pasook saying by his folded arms and Zhardann by his erect but easy posture and his quick politician's grin that scenic details meant no more to them than the idle amusement of a clever party trick. If that was the game, I'd be damned if I wouldn't play along. After all, *I* wasn't afraid of heights, not really, not in the least. But even if they *were* out of their minds in this way, as in the several others I'd already suspected, they were clearly not alone.

The ballroom-sized expanse of cloud was already occupied by thirty or so other people—gods?—*beings* was probably the safest category to use until I could get the situation clarified. Gods, yes, probably, but all the gods I'd met so far were at least humanoid, if not outright human, in aspect. Here, although humanoid body plans were still in the clear majority, the range of diversity was striking, especially for a guy like me fresh from a backwater neck-of-the-woods kind of place like Roosing Oolvaya. Ahead of me across a slowly closing gap in the cloud base was a group of three. One was human, wearing a metal-foil cape full on both shoulders, and one was a sparrow fully as tall as the first, but the third looked to my untutored eye like a series of intermeshing spheres rolling smoothly and silently within each other. I presumed the thing was an attendee and not some kind of accessory since hanging in the air in front of it was a brandy snifter that would occasionally tilt and pour an amber-colored liquid into a retractable spout in its front, and the other two were matching it tot for tot. And the sphere-bubbler wasn't the oddest personage there, either—almost, but not quite.

Another striking feature of the crowd was how relaxed everyone was acting. I'd spent enough time myself with the gang to be sure it *was* an act, and that each being present was certainly keeping the appropriate organ peeled to watch their back and to be vigilant for a convenient opening to use against someone else. An occasional head had turned and not a few eyes had twitched at the sight of our arrival, with the four of us standing together shoulder-to-shoulder as a clear faction, so Zhardann's goal of making an immediate line-in-the-sand statement had apparently been met, but aside from that no one seemed very impressed with our presence one way or the other. Or they were just playing things thoroughly cool. I found myself listening in on a conversation a short distance away on my right, next to a punch bowl perched on a graceful curl of cloud.

"Have you heard from the Yaws lately?" the first one was saying.

"Zimrat and Ozzie? No, I understand they've dropped out of sight." This speaker appeared to be a male ocelot standing on its hind legs and wearing a toga. Balanced in one forepaw was a china plate covered with miniature eggrolls, complete with a small finger bowl filled with red sweet-and-sour sauce. A pair of speckled orange-and-brown-frame sunglasses were pushed back on top of his head. "Even when they were connected, they never liked these little get-togethers, you know. Always had other things they'd rather be doing."

"Those look quite good," said the ocelot's companion, a woman with a cobra wrapped turban-style around her hair, the snake's hypnotically waving head positioned like a tiara in front of her forehead. "Do you think I might have some?"

"With my compliments," said the ocelot. An identical plate appeared in the woman's hand. One eggroll flipped end-over-end and dipped itself in the sauce, then floated up to her mouth, where it crackled appetizingly. She took a hefty bite.

"I'm going to grab some of that nectar before we start," Soaf Pasook said beside me, strolling forward toward the open chasm in the cloud between us and the sphere-guy, forward—and out across it. Strolling placidly across the open air. But if he could do it, could I? And why would I possibly want to try?

The issue of meandering over the edge of cloud could wait until later. In the meantime, I decided to mingle, too, since it didn't seem we'd be getting started on business right away. My first step forward, though, was odd enough to make me pause there, one foot planted in front of the other, coils of cloud-stuff washing gently over my boots. It wasn't that I felt I was falling through the vapor; no, the cloud surface was quite firm enough, rather like a thick carpet on top of a pile of rubber. It was my leg that felt strange. I had felt it operating as I took the step, its muscles contracting and relaxing and the lower portion swiveling at the knee joint and the ankle stabilizing to take up my shifted weight, but at the same time, almost like a phantom resting behind the forthright sensations of movement, it felt to me as though I was still sitting in the armchair of the second-floor study back at Zhardann's rented house on the Lane of Wealth.

Now that I concentrated, I could detect a vague pressure in the seat of my pants and up my back and along the undersides of my forearms; exactly the sensations I'd have had if I was really was propped in a chair rather than standing and walking on a cloud, as my eyes and ears and the foreground messages of my muscles and skeleton would have it. It was easy enough to ignore the sensations that were more vague, the ones that didn't seem to fit, and something was tugging at me like the hand on the business end of the leash from a querulous dog, enticing me to do just that. Not that it was unpleasant. Instead, I felt the peculiar heightened texture of a dream, where you may seem to yourself to be completely mobile even though your body is giving off, at most, an occasional twitch. This was no dream, though, or at least not one of the standard default sort, especially when you considered the fact that I had already witnessed what this phenomenon looked like from the other end to an outside observer.

When Jill and I had come in on him after our arrival at the house in Oolsmouth, Zhardann had been seated in one of the chairs, his body wrapped in fog like a fluff-trimmed mummy. He hadn't been moving while we watched, but when he emerged (or the cloud-cocoon retracted) he'd had the air of someone who'd just been engaged in conversation, and had the new information to match, too. What if he hadn't merely been conversing, though? What if he'd been *transported*, in effect, to *meet* the other party, with all his senses telling him he was present there in the flesh? "What if," nothing—I had no doubt that was really what was going on. We were really still lazing around back in Oolsmouth; or our bodies were, anyway. We only *thought* we were somewhere else.

But did that mean that this place didn't exist, either? That this whole cloudscape was really some kind of simulation, a virtual but not physical reality?

I didn't immediately see how to test that hypothesis. It seemed safer not to, in any case, so I moved slowly forward after Pasook, snagged a long-stemmed glass filled with honey-colored liquid from atop a conveniently circulating service-tray cloud-puff, and tried to project the image of a person who was looking around for somebody he knew. Apparently I did a convincing job. Off to my right, someone broke away from a group of four and waved in my direction. I bent my path toward him and he moved forward to meet me, a normal-looking guy with rakishly wavy blond hair, a buccaneer's mustache, a small neat scar on his left cheek, and a dangling earring in his left ear, dressed in gilt-trimmed scarlet with a number of tasteful jewels clinking here and there. "It's certainly been a while, hasn't it?" he said, studying me.

"Has it?" I said. "I suppose."

"The last time was that thing out in—well, you remember that place, the one with all the ivy? With that fellow who thought he was hero material and the Steadman crypt, wasn't it? Of course you had the poor taste to be on the opposite side from *me*, poor fellow. I was never quite sure what your interest in the sarcophagus actually was. Or were you really after the idol? Surely it couldn't have been the *hero?*"

"You know how it is. No hard feelings, I hope." I took a sip from the glass. The stuff hit my palate like flambéd honey, but when I swallowed nothing seemed to actually move down my throat. "Didn't you know? I've got a collection."

The guy twinkled an obnoxiously clear blue eye at me. "Touché. You must come sometime and see my own. I have the manuscript copy of the Second Iskendarian Codex, you know."

"No," I said, drawing the word out with a dollop of incredulity. "You don't say. So that's where the thing's been all these years. You wouldn't consider letting it out on loan, now, would you?"

"Put together a museum tour, you mean? That *is* an interesting idea. Perhaps I should speak to the Imperial Archivist. Most likely the logistics would interfere, not to mention the inadvisability of giving anyone else a chance to read the words and have their mind jellied."

"The world's a dangerous place."

"So it is," he said, "so it is. And a good thing, too, or the lot of us would be out of our jobs as soon as the word got out. A toast?"

"Why not?" I clinked glasses with him. "To living dangerously."

He seemed amused by that, but tossed his drink straight back. Wisps of smoke coiled out of each ear. "Nice touch, that," I told him.

"Flamboyance," he said ruefully. "It gets in the blood. Speaking of which, I've been hearing the oddest stories about you and Pod Dall."

"Have you?"

"Of course, I didn't believe a word of it."

"Prudent of you, I'd say. There's no predicting some people's imaginations."

He threw back his head and gave a hearty, surprisingly authentic-sounded laugh. "Right you are," he said, "right you are." The guy gave his eyes a wipe with a monogrammed lace handkerchief whose monogram, unfortunately, was in a rune I didn't know, then stuffed it back into his sleeve before I had enough time to memorize the swirls so I could show them to someone else or try to look them up in a book. "Quite seriously, though, we should get together sometime. Our interests may be congruent."

"You really think so? Yours and mine?"

The chuckle continued. "Oh, yes. Oh, yes, indeed." A stunningly beautiful woman drifted over from the group my new friend had just left. For that matter, it hadn't escaped my notice that all the human-looking folks around the cloud were unnaturally striking, and that even the odder characters radiated a well-groomed glow of attraction. Just before she reached us, the man leaned closer and said, "I've been in touch with a friend of yours, I believe. A fellow named Max."

"How interesting," I said, more faintly than I liked. "A friend of *mine,* you say?"

I got the sly smile again. The woman rested her side against him, draped an arm over his shoulders, and tickled his earring with her finger. "Am I?" the woman said to me.

"Oh," he said, to both of us at the same time. "Have you met?"

"Quite possibly," I said. "If so, though, the exact circumstances momentarily escape my mind. That is quite an intriguing dress."

The woman's gown had been drifting in and out of consciousness on an irregular schedule. Each time it reappeared, it had changed color and style, but in between, when it was off making up its mind, it apparently forgot all about her. "Does it run off the principle of Conservation of Imagination?"

"I beg your pardon?" she said. "Phlinn, do you know that one?"

"I'm sure he spends much more time on research than I do. Come now," Phlinn urged, "you must elaborate." That's what his mouth said, but his arched eyes and the permanent half-smile were clearly anticipating a punchline.

"Well," I expounded, "the theory is that there is only

a fixed amount of imagination around in any closed system. If we consider you, my dear, and your outfit as the system—you see?'' Of course, I'd never heard of the principle of Conservation of Imagination, I'd only just made it up. With my recent track record of having the fruits of my own imagination reveal stories that everyone around me was all too eager to treat as the truth, though, it was obviously a habit I'd be a lot better off breaking. In this case, unfortunately, as in the previous ones, I was stuck having to reel it through. ''While the outfit is imagining its new incarnation, there's no slack left in such a closed system.''

''No slack?''

''For leaving your own underlying form to anyone else's imagination,'' I finished helplessly.

The woman looked at me as though I were out of my mind, if indeed I had ever had one, as the dress reappeared around her pink nubileness, this time in lavender with ruffles down the front and out one shoulder, but Phlinn clapped me on the back, laughing his rakish laugh and shaking his head. I felt his hand on my skin without thinking about it; the faint feel of the armchair's backrest was the next thing to a memory. ''I'm going to dig up another drink,'' he chuckled. ''Anything for you?''

The woman asked for a Hellraiser, whatever that was. Phlinn raised his eyebrows at that, but then twinkled his eyes again and glinted his teeth, too, for good measure, and ambled off. ''Phlinn Arol,'' I muttered under my breath. The Adventurer's God—who else could it be? I'd been paying donations to him for years. But why would he mention Max to me unless he knew who I really—

''You like the dress, then?'' said the woman. It was now green and ankle-length with a hoop skirt and bustle.

''Quite becoming,'' I said.

''I've always liked these gatherings,'' she continued, taking a dainty bite out of her goblet. I was sure it had been glass before, but it now seemed to have transmuted itself into a crisp goblet-shaped cracker. ''We have so few opportunities to flaunt our cleverness in public.''

''It is a hard temptation to resist,'' I agreed.

''Yes, but why *should* you resist? I mean, *look* at yourself—you'd think you'd walked in out of the mud. You could at least make an effort to make yourself presentable."

I wondered how many of those Hellraisers she'd already downed. "Some of us are the way we are," I told her, "on our better days, at least." Her remark was reassuring, though. If this entire environment was synthesized, it stood to reason that the appearances people presented here were probably artificial as well. I'd been trying to decide whether you had to go out of your way to construct your semblance for this place as if you were building a wardrobe, say, or whether you got one for free as part of the process; I'd figured the former, but what she'd said just now gave me more confidence I'd guessed right. I hadn't noticed a mirror around, but now I could feel more assured that the transfer hadn't made me look like a snaggle-toothed orangutan to everyone else. On the other hand, that meant I looked like me. I couldn't argue with her. In a crowd of beautiful people, I looked like the guy who brought the supplies in from the cart.

"There's no doubt," Phlinn said. I hadn't realized he'd come back. There he was, though, handing the woman her drink. Arcs of flame like miniature skyrockets were rising out of the fiery red fluid and leaving a small smudge of haze above the rim of the heavy highball glass. "An admirable philosophy."

The woman purred at him and snuggled up, her dress leaving for another quick-change. It was quite boring, really. "We were discussing how amusing these little get-togethers are," I said.

"Right you are!" Phlinn said, loudly enough to make a few nearby heads turn. "Not only these group meetings, the whole damn communication system. One of the best things Byron ever came up with, after the whole genesis thing itself, of course."

"Baby!" the woman said, her purr changing to growl. She looked ready to slap him. "Why bring *him* up, and in a place like this?"

"I'm getting drunk," Phlinn said reasonably. "But whether I'm soused or not, I'll talk about anyone I choose."

"Keep your voice down, then, will you do that much?" She pulled back a step, crossed her arms while carefully balancing her drink, and glared.

"Of course, love, of course." I had to admire his control of his voice; now he'd slid his tone smoothly into sheer raw persuasiveness. Maybe he'd gone to acting school, and maybe his voice effects were augmented for this kind of environment, too. "I'm probably the last one around who'll admit to being a friend of Byron's, you know," he told me, now using a just-you-and-me note of confidence-sharing. "He was the trickiest of us all, that Byron, but not always the most prudent, it's true." He took aim at me again with those eyes of his. I had to admit, he sure did look like a god. "It *is* true, you know."

"What is?" I asked him.

"I was sure you knew. Jardin cast the curse himself, but by then Byron had disappeared, of course, and he'd changed his aural signature, too. I don't know if the curse ever found him or not, but he's almost certainly dead now any way you cut it. He hasn't been heard from in centuries."

I'd heard the rest of what he'd said in a vague sort of way, but my mind had locked around the first word, the first name. Jardin. Where had I heard that name before? "Zhardann?" I said.

"Oh, is that how he's pronouncing it again? He goes through phases, you know, not that there's much difference between them. These old multilingual names, always trying to decide how they should be pronounced. Always some dispute about the consonants. But you came in with him; you must know better than I how he's saying his own name now. Do you think we're up for another of those curses today?"

"We'll have to wait and see," I said. "We'll all have to wait and see."

"Hmm-um, yes, I suppose so."

"Yes, we will," said Soaf Pasook. He was standing on my left. "Arol. I'm surprised you're here, feeling the way you do."

"If you know the way I feel, it shouldn't be a surprise at all. I never like to miss one."

Pasook gave him one of those thin grins that said many things, good humor not among them; the kind of expression these folks all seemed very good at. Maybe they had a particular exercise regimen that included helpful facial muscle calisthenics. "So you've given up your subversive ways? You're willing to join shoulder-to-shoulder with the rest of us in exercising our power?"

"Absolutely," said Phlinn Arol. "Especially when it's aimed against one of our own, for exceeding his franchise and using mortals as his pawns. Among others," he added, flashing Pasook a pleasant smile of his own. "Aren't you pleased to see us all here to help you redress your own grievances?"

"Of course. Glad you could spare the time. If you'll excuse me?"

"Have you done something that needs to be excused?" Phlinn said in mock surprise.

"Hah," Pasook said to Phlinn. Then, to me, "We're almost ready to get started," he went on, laying his hand on my arm and leading me away. He stopped after a short distance, though, just out of earshot. "He's quite the radical these days, Phlinn is. I know you've been away from things and haven't been keeping up, so I thought perhaps I should tell you. A bit of good will between us for you to remember, and all that."

"Really?" I said. My mind felt as abstruse as my remark.

"Perhaps it's not totally his fault," Pasook said thoughtfully. "As the Adventurer's God, he has an outlook that stresses the pitting of man against the forces of man and nature, but not against a totally stacked deck, which is what a world under our thumb often amounts to, to be frank; we all know that. Conflicts with his damnable notion of fair play, I suppose. Steadfast ideals and all that. Or perhaps it comes from a misplaced sense of obligation to his late friend Byron." The name came out in a glob of scorn. I thought he might spit on the cloudtop.

I hadn't asked a direct question of any substance in

days. Maybe I could get away with one here, with Pasook in as abstracted a mood as he appeared to be. Maybe he'd think I'd just been drinking too much. "Byron?"

"Yes, damn him, him and his Abdicationism. If he'd been dealt with properly, no one would ever have heard of the idea again. Just too damn inventive, Byron was. At least it was useful until he turned to politics."

We weren't really alone, but this might be the best chance I'd get to talk with him. "Look, Pasook—"

"May I have your attention, please. Attention, please." The voice was the voice of Zhardann, or Jardin, but it boomed along the cloud as though he had acquired a giant speaking trumpet, squashing all other conversation flat beneath it. I looked around. The cloud had slowed and beached itself against the mountain peak I had observed when the four of us had entered the scene, and Zhardann was perched ten feet up on a clean-swept crag. No speaking amplifier was in sight. He had called the gathering, though, so this was probably his chosen meeting-ground as well; he must know the rules here at least as completely as anyone. Maybe he'd even designed and decorated the place, although that seemed a bit less likely to me. If you could create your own appearance for one of these simulated environments, it stood to reason that you could create your own environment, too. Whether anyone else would be willing to set foot in it was another matter. These gods were a mutually suspicious lot, for good and valid reasons, so I couldn't see them putting themselves into someone else's custom habitat without a very good reason and a whole lot of preparation behind them. No, it stood to reason that this place was a community neutral ground. They might not have many rules, but I was willing to bet that one of them concerned violations of the public meeting-hall.

"Thank you all for coming," Zhardann continued, after the remaining conversations had quickly died out. "The subject of this assembly is Sapriel. Is he in attendance?"

Several seconds of silence passed. No one answered.

"Sapriel has been informed of this assembly and has elected not to attend. His presence is not required at this stage. However, I will now contact Sapriel and ask again, in the sight of this assembly. Sapriel! Sapriel! Sapriel!"

An area of air at Zhardann's altitude but out in front of him, over the front of the beached cloud, spun together in a ball, imparting a crystalline shine and a refractive warp to the clear sky behind it. Then the color of the sky in the ball darkened, becoming cobalt, and the ball began to vibrate. I began to hear echoes of Zhardann's voice, still saying "saprielsparielsapriel," the sound growing and overlapping as the ball's shimmering increased, until all the syllables and component phonemes of the name were ringing together as a clear pure tone.

Suddenly the ball was black. A deep voice spoke from it, a deep voice with an aggravated tone. "Go away," it said. "Don't bother me, I'm busy."

"Is the notification witnessed?" asked Zhardann.

"I witness," said four or five voices scattered around the cloud, stepping on each other.

Zhardann raised his hand. The name-sound of the ball stopped and the shimmering faded almost to nothing, and the color of the ball lightened to the violet-blue of approaching dusk, but the ball itself remained hovering in place. It was clear some ritualized formula was being followed, at least in outline. I wondered how much of this Max knew about. I was sure he'd be interested; after all, he was curious about everything having to do with the gods. It was ironic, really, that *I* was the one who'd been getting to know the gods from the inside. Of course, it was apparent that there was more than one angle to "inside." I was pretty sure my current perspective would have helped to round out Max's, or if not I was being dragged through a lot of trouble for nothing, but unfortunately there was no immediate way to tell him about it.

For that matter, I'd gotten the impression that Max had his own inside sources; he knew too much already to have been relying purely on guesswork. Was one of his sources Phlinn Arol? I glanced around me and spotted Arol off to the right. Not entirely to my surprise, he was watching me. He held my eye long enough to make the point explicit. I gave him a small ambiguous nod and turned back to Zhardann.

"Your attendance is appreciated," Zhardann was saying. "It should be gratifying to us all to see the level of concern such a group is demonstrating for the well-being and reputation of our community. Indeed—"

"Get to the point," someone grumbled in an under-the-breath tone that was clearly intended to carry.

"I acknowledge your indulgence," said Zhardann, using a harder voice of his own for a moment. "This is a serious matter; whatever our differences, we will all agree on that. None among us undertakes it lightly. Does anyone here present question the legitimacy of this forum?"

"Let us move forward," Pasook murmured. I followed him toward the front of the cloud, steering around the clumps of listeners who were standing or reclining on cloud-tufts along the way. A fellow whose form showed not human features or the details of clothing but rather a vista of fields, lush with gently blowing prairie grass under a pleasant sky, as though he was a man-shaped lens punched through the local reality to focus on another world, had raised a question concerning the appropriate makeup of a quorum, and some brief discussion had ensued. To me, it had the sound of an argument that people had been over often enough to get sick of, without anyone having come up with anything new to add in a long time.

"We are a club without by-laws," Pasook said to himself, or perhaps he was really saying it to me. "The only mandatory requirement is self-interest."

The consensus, in line with someone else's quoted precedent, was that the will to act provided the legitimacy. "We will proceed," stated Zhardann. "To present the circumstance, I call Soaf Pasook."

Pasook mounted the cliff-face. Actually, he did as much floating as outright climbing. The snow at his feet remained largely undisturbed, although a few artistically placed footprints did appear in his wake. Facing the crowd, he unreeled roughly the same story I'd heard before. This time, though, he was playing down the involvement of the ring, leading away from it as much as he could. He mentioned "this ring I had" but didn't even allude to the dealings through which he had acquired it or to his connection with me, and certainly didn't bring the name of Pod Dall into the story at all. Instead, he concentrated on his peaceful conduct of business, his responsible and limited revelation of himself to mortals, his attention to the local standards of conduct, and his commitment to the status quo, setting the stage for his sad tale of how this had all been shot to pieces by the unprovoked blunderbuss attack of Sapriel.

It was a reasonable performance, but I could tell that the crowd was only suffering through the exposition so they could get to the meat. I could understand their impatience. After all, stabbing each other in the back was their preferred sport. What would they care if one of their number pulled off a good fast move against somebody else? Pasook by his own admission had left himself exposed by failing to line up with a larger faction and the deterrent value it could provide. When he got to the details of Sapriel's use of the banks, the way Sapriel had disrupted the Oolsmouth business community and the local politics, and especially his interaction with Dooglas, the crowd perked up.

Frankly, I didn't think Sapriel had been all that blatant about his activities, with the glaring exception of his promises to Dooglas. I was willing to grant Pasook additional knowledge I didn't have since he had been the one directly involved, and I'd thrown in a certain poetic license for hyperbole to boot, and of course there was his story of torture, which argued for an unmannerly lack of restraint on Sapriel's part. By Pasook's earlier account to us, Sapriel's desire to get hold of the ring was the reason for the torture. Further, Pasook had told us he'd been about to start shopping the ring around when Sapriel had pounced. I didn't think Pasook's story made quite as much sense with the ring edited down to an incidental role as it had done when he'd told it to us. I'd made that point to the three of them when we'd met before coming here but I'd been out-voted. Zhardann in particular had thought that a full airing of the ring's nature might make folks lose sight of Sapriel in the process since they'd realize that the ring was really the more important issue, and they might even start running out on the gathering to look for it. I didn't think he was wrong, but I was concerned that his tribunal could get equally out of control if someone else brought the ring into the picture and started asking the right questions. Of course, if someone else did bring up the ring, that might be useful information in itself. Zhardann would have been even happier not to mention the ring's existence at all. When Sapriel came in, though, he'd probably refer to it himself, and if the foundation had not been properly set down the ensuing discussion could drop our credibility through the floor. All of this worrying might actually have been moot. By the feel of the crowd, they were taking Pasook's story more-or-less at face value, or even if they weren't, there was enough in what he was saying to make them think something worth considering had been going on.

"Thank you, Soaf Pasook," said Zhardann, when Pasook had capped off his explication by showing the onlookers his recent stigmata. Pasook left his shirt up while Zhardann continued. "Yet this is not the story of Soaf Pasook alone. I have made my own investigation, and I attest to the truth of Soaf Pasook's telling." Not the *whole* truth, I noted, but then I already knew Zhardann was a tricky customer. "Who else will attest?"

"I attest," said Jill-tang. "I also have investigated, and have met with this Dooglas creature. He is clearly enraptured. He believes that Sapriel will elevate him to our own level as his reward."

A hum of conversation rose; that had hit them, all right, as had been intended. Zhardann had thought I should attest, too. With my (or Gash's) reputation for subterfuge, though, who would believe me? I couldn't very well swear by the gods, now, could I? To my surprise, Jill had jumped in to make those points even before I could get my own mouth open. After kicking it back and forth for a bit, Zhardann had reluctantly accepted the problem and backed down. Of course, I could have confounded them all and got up to make a public statement anyway, but I was trying to keep a tighter grip on myself than I'd managed of late. The middle of a ballroom full of gods was not where I wanted to blow my luck with an obvious flub.

"I will want to hear from Sapriel his version of these facts," the floating sphere-creature said, somewhat metallically, as the generalized reaction began to quiet down. "Yet I am troubled. Is there one who will speak for Sapriel?" The interlocking spheres whirred as they tracked around, examining the audience, but when no one piped up, it went on. "I am troubled. We maintain a world of harmony, of equilibrium, working our will with care and prudence. One who is engaged in business with those who inhabit the world has certain responsibilities, for continuity, respectability, predictability. If we are thought of as arbitrary, as flighty, that climate for dealing will worsen."

"Yeah," said a person-sized palm tree whose roots were lost somewhere below the surface of the cloud; its voice was surprisingly conventional, if a bit raspy, although it did seem to emanate from the vicinity of its thick trunk. "They get pushed too far, people may get more inclined to figure out ways of living their lives that don't include us. They may not have power, but they're not dumb. The last thing we want is to start losing our power base or, gods forbid, our legitimacy with the ground-huggers."

The palm's use of that particular imprecation brought a smattering of chuckles from around the area, but it was the sort of nervous snickering that meant a nerve had been touched. "Why should we fear *them?*" said a woman I couldn't spot. "We rule, they serve. They'd better just accept that."

"I don't know you," the palm said, idly bouncing a small coconut up and down on the outstretched end of its longest frond. "Didn't anybody ever tell you about the social contract theory? They stay within certain bounds if they know what's good for themselves, but so do we. Neither side escalates without a lot of careful thought."

"But power—"

"You haven't heard about the threat of power being greater than its exercise, either, have you?" The palm rustled its leaves disapprovingly. A different coconut fell off its trunk and vanished into the cloud. "Will somebody please tutor this girl? Does anybody else question what we're doing here? That it's important to keep any single idiot from spoiling the happy hunting grounds for everybody else? Sounds to me like Sapriel's gone seriously out of line."

"Let's not jump to conclusions yet, shall we?" said the ocelot. "I agree that purely on the evidence we've already presented, of a bank raid that has caused a political struggle and the flaunting or breakdown of the rule of the law in Oolsmouth, an unwise activity is in process. I frown on those who call too much attention to themselves, especially while engaged in plotting and scheming. It goes without argument that much of our mystique emanates merely from being mysterious, unknowable. The more mortals get to see us in action, the more knowable we become. It's difficult to be known and not be tarnished to some degree, since let's face it, we often operate much like excessively endowed people ourselves. If the mortals really understood this, the aura of godliness would melt and people would think that the only thing that differentiated them from gods was their level of power."

Listening to him, it occurred to me that, in fact, this was the attitude I'd gotten used to from Max et al. Excessive familiarity with the ways of the gods had bred in them, if not contempt, at least a realism of appraisal.

There was more back-and-forthing in this vein, and then they got onto the subject of fraternization. It wasn't uncommon for gods to grant personal favors to mortals or to interact with them in one way or another. There was general agreement that adopting a protege or a human pawn, though, should be done carefully. A grouper the size of a cow which had been circulating without apparent concern in the air, breathing freely without an aquarium in sight, stated, as though it was a maxim, that the wrong human could drag the best god into the worst mess. Someone else agreed with the fish, adding that along with the hauled god, of course, came his or hers (or its) commitments, alliances, and entanglements, and before you knew what was happening there went the whole neighborhood.

It wasn't a one-way street, either: not only could gods drag people into their affairs, people could get gods wrapped up in their messes as well. As a god, if you weren't careful who you made promises or binding covenants to, you might find yourself embroiled in an entirely different situation than the one you thought was going on. "Once in, it can be difficult for even one of us to pull out," said an eight-foot guy with a another couple of feet of flowing white hair on top and a few of matching beard dangling down his middle; he had an edge to his voice that smacked of personal familiarity with the problem.

"Even if you do manage to pull out," a woman said, "you do that at the risk of losing your personal credibility or your power, at the least."

Obviously, being a god wasn't the straightforward enterprise I'd always vaguely assumed. I shouldn't have been surprised; after all, I did have a personal (if limited) experience with Gashanatantra, and there were the shenanigans of the last few days to boot.

That wasn't the first thought I'd had of Gashanatantra lately, either. I'd been wondering if he was around. The only one present who looked like Gash was Zhardann, but that was old news and in any case it meant nothing. I had to assume everyone I saw was in disguise. I thought I still might recognize Gash if I saw him, but on the other hand how much did I know, really? The honest answer was "Not very much." With that in mind, there was an equal chance that I'd been shaking Gash's hand and having hor d'oeuvres with him without the slightest idea of who he actually was. Unfortunately, he surely didn't have the same handicap.

With the number of games these guys played, lethal and less so, they clearly made an art of disguise and misdirection. Of course, that meant there had to be an art to piercing disguise, as well. If so—

"Is the view of this assembly, therefore, that Sapriel be summoned and brought before us?" Zhardann said, using his position as chair to move things along. "I declare that this is the assembly's will. I now call for volunteers to assist in performing the summons as an example of our united decree."

He picked five, including the palm, then raised his hands again. "Sapriel!" he called, and as he repeated the name the others joined him. "SAPRIEL! SAPRIEL!" The hanging ball sprang back to life, vibrating, shuddering, shaking beneath the combined ring of the interwoven sounds.

Again, the ball filled with ink. "Go *away!*" said the same deep voice. "I'm right in the middle of—"

"You are summoned!" Zhardann declared. "Come to us now!" His fingers swam through another joint-popping contortion, and the ball began to expand, like the inflation of a balloon. Like a balloon, yes, but if so like one being blown up underwater, against some significant resistance, against a force that was simultaneously trying to crush it. The ball strained outward, power flowing into it from the five volunteers through the modulation of Zhardann, jerking ever larger in a popping series of small wrenches, as a deep-toned howl echoed out of it into the air. A spread-eagled human form took shape inside. The form was full-sized, and the ball had grown large enough to contain it. Then the form was no mere outline, but a dark-bearded man.

Sapriel was thrashing like a freshly-harpooned fish hauled abruptly onto a trawler deck, his hands and feet fixed in stationary globs of what appeared to be shimmering putty but his limbs and body remaining free to lash back and forth in utter futility. I presumed that this was not the flesh-and-blood Sapriel, to speak a tad speculatively about the physiology of a god, since of course I didn't know if they really *were* flesh and blood or something else entirely. Rather, it had to be another simulacrum such as the rest of us were using in this artificial environment. The difference between Sapriel and the rest of us was the element of compulsion, and the fact that Zhardann had undoubtedly done something that equally immobilized Sapriel's physical body wherever it happened to be. Just watching Sapriel writhe made me feel a bit giddy myself, as though someone was dragging me around against my will, too.

"This is a very bad time!" Sapriel snarled. "I am right in the middle of a delicate—"

"Your time is now not your own," said Zhardann. "You have been called to account!"

"To account? For *what?*"

"Step forward," Zhardann called, "Soaf Pasook!"

Sapriel dropped his jaw, then closed it with a small snap. Pasook hadn't actually *stepped* anywhere, since he was still standing on the cliff-side next to Zhardann and a bit below him, but he did raise his own arm to point at Sapriel, and in any case Zhardann's histrionics were good theater. "Hear my charge, O Faithless One!" Pasook began. He rattled off a concise summary of the main points, then wrapped up with a "What say you?"

"I don't have to answer to you or anyone else," Sapriel growled.

"By the force of this assembly," said Zhardann, "you do."

Sapriel looked down and around him at the upturned faces as though the presence of the crowd hadn't entirely registered before. "What is the problem here?" he said. "I had everything under control until you dragged me away. Yes, I heard that Pasook had this ring, and I hoped to acquire it for myself. I used the means that seemed necessary. Pasook persisted in resisting, unwisely, so, yes, I brought him to his knees. He was at my mercy—what's wrong with that? Huh? I see a dozen of you out there who have done worse. Have we all suddenly found religion?"

He looked thoroughly disgusted. "What is the issue here, really? Even when I leaned on him, Pasook never had the grace to admit his defeat, which was ignominious and total." He turned his scowl on Pasook. "You still tried to finesse me, you toad—I thought you were dead!"

"Yet another mistake," Pasook told him. "Your torture was extreme and effective, but again you overestimated."

"The issue here is not one of deicide, attempted or complete," Zhardann said. "Sapriel, you are correct in saying that nothing prohibits you from eradicating whom you choose, except the bounds of good sense and the strength of your enemy's connections; our code of conduct is, if anything, informal. That is not the concern. The true matter is your level of prudence, and your irresponsible and unrestrained conduct with the mortal world."

All of a sudden Sapriel looked scared, he looked *really* scared. "Now wait a second here. Are you running a hearing or a lynch mob? What—"

Sapriel's mouth was still working, but the volume of sound coming through abruptly dropped to a faint whisper. "Despite your protestations," Zhardann continued, "your plots have not succeeded, so you cannot use the defense of justification of means by the desired ends. It may be true that the winner can make the rules; however, you are not the winner." Zhardann raised his voice to address the whole crowd. "I submit the following for your consideration. If one of us cannot behave responsibily with his power, if one cannot restrain himself so as to avoid endangering the common good, one is not fit for one's position. That is the true thesis here.

"You have heard testimony. You have seen Sapriel's response. You understand the serious nature of the issue. Do you wish further discussion? Or is a decision of consensus before us now?"

Sapriel was still immobilized, with the sound-deadening field effectively gagging him as well, but he was flinging himself fruitlessly around his cage and clearly trying to yell at the top of his lungs, his face turning red and sweat running down it. For a projection of his image it was remarkably realistic. Zhardann must have deadened more than his voice, too—there had to be some inhibitor overriding Sapriel's power or he'd have been using every last bit of it to escape. He could sense as well as anyone the expectant taste of blood in the air.

The pause lengthened, as each one present eyed their neighbors and wondered who would be the one to speak up and kick the thing over into action. Finally, a burnoose-wrapped fellow I hadn't noticed before broke the silence. "Mortalization," he said. "I call for mortalization."

The first reaction was a stir that moved like a sudden breeze across the cloud, leaving behind it a murmur like the rustling of leaves, and a turning to and forth like the bending of branches and trunks. The tone was approving. The one who had spoken, though, had wrapped himself again in his burnoose and was holding himself aloof, withdrawn. A thought tickled its way into my mind. If the manifestations of the folks who surrounded me were only that, manifestations, artificial images, why couldn't a single person create more than one of them at the same time? Could someone appear more than once at the same time in the same virtual environment? Could the guy in the burnoose be a ringer?

I made a quick circle through the confusion and approached the fellow from the rear. "Pardon me," I said.

Beyond him in the background, I was able to view both Zhardann and Soaf Pasook. The man stirred as though he was coming awake and turned slowly toward me. "Yes?" he said.

"I don't believe we've met," I told him. "I applaud your resolute statement."

"Thank you," he said, his voice drifting away again. "There is a time for contemplation and a time for action."

Zhardann had been casting his eagle eye across the cloud, waiting for the right moment to plunge back in. At the same time, he was talking to Jill, who had approached him from the crowd and was standing below him on the edge of the cliff. Soaf Pasook was ignoring the group in front of him and spending his own moment in contemplation, his face blank. The man in the burnoose pulled a length of its cloth lower over his face and seemed to go to sleep standing up. At the same moment, Pasook gathered his own attention again and said something to the woman at his side. As he did so, though, his gaze went out across the congregation and happened to meet my own. We spent a moment staring at each other.

Then the voice of Zhardann rolled over us again; I wondered if perhaps he was using a concealed megaphone. "I believe that the sense of this assembly is to mete out upon Sapriel a penalty both punitive and deterrent," he said, "and to remove by this means a dangerous presence from our midst. Is there one who would challenge this?"

The silence had fallen again, the silence of bated breath. No one spoke, no one challenged. I did notice that the crowd seemed a bit smaller than before, as though people had started to slip out during the caucus.

"Is mortalization the decision of this assembly?" said Zhardann.

Again, no one spoke aloud, but an approving murmur rippled across the cloud as the most everyone savored the moment. Most everyone, of course, with the prominent exception of Sapriel.

Zhardann paused once more for effect before proceeding. "Very well. I pronounce in the name of this assembly as its judgment the decree of mortalization upon Sapriel. I further declare that this sentence will be executed immediately. Is there one who would claim the responsibility of leading the infliction? Then I assert my aspect, my office, my power, I, Jardin, Administrator of Curses, Master of Dooms! By my office and my stature, I declare that it is my right, my privilege, my obligation to dispose of this matter speedily and forthwith."

Now I remembered where I'd heard the name Jardin before—Max had mentioned it when we'd been talking about Shaa's problems and the possibility of confronting the Curse Administrator directly. And now it turned out I'd been spending the last week hanging out with him. The way the world works can get to you sometimes. Maybe after this was finished I could bring it up with him, hah hah. Frankly, that would be one of the *last* things on my mind. When we were finished here my first priority was going to be trying to deal with Zhardann and Pasook, and the question of where the ring was and what more did I know that I hadn't been telling them. I could hear a sizzle as the hot water into which I would shortly be dumped was starting to boil.

One thing did make more sense, all of a sudden. Zhardann hadn't hesitated to reveal himself as a solid Conservationist, dedicated to the superiority of gods and the overall status quo. That was exactly what you'd expect from the Curse Administrator, whose power and position stemmed materially from the structure that let gods interfere most directly with the activities of the world.

Zhardann had been building for awhile, but now he'd reached his full scenery-chewing form. "To wander the earth," he declaimed, "the glories of your past lost forever to you, even the memory of your power gone from you like dust, to be one with those who creep across the ground, as one of them to grow old, to grow feeble, and to die—this is your fate, this is your doom, this is your curse. In my full power and vested authority as Administrator of Curses, Master of Dooms, I pronounce upon you now the dread Curse of Namelessness!"

What? I thought. I'd figured Sapriel was going to meet his doom, but I'd had no idea that the shape of that doom was anything other than physical death. Max hadn't said anything to imply that the Spell of Namelessness was used by the gods; he'd only talked about it being turned on people. It was an extremely rare and tricky spell, according to Max, which is why he'd only heard and read about it, never actually seen it in action or had the chance to analyze its full specifications. True, Max *had* implied that a lot of the spells or spell mechanisms used by mortals were also used by the gods; when the gods used them these spells often wound up more powerful, but they weren't necessarily different in operation or even in name. But theory wasn't the biggest thing on my mind just then. The question looming in front of me was major, central in fact, and I hadn't even seen it coming.

Was it possible that what had just been done to Sapriel had, in fact, been done to me, too? Could I have misinterpreted everything? Was I originally a *god?*

Maybe Jill and Zhardann (or Jardin) really weren't mistaking me for someone else—maybe they really *had* known me before the Spell of Namelessness. Before I was mortalized. Maybe they didn't realize I was under that curse. Maybe these trickles of knowledge and expertise I'd been getting every now and then weren't leakage through the metabolic link from Gashanatantra after all—maybe they were leakage from my old self making it through the barrier the Spell of Namelessness had thrown up, across the wasteland of my sundered mind.

Get a grip on yourself, I thought shakily; I was starting to sound as florid as Zhardann. *Calm down.* All this speculation could be nothing more than wishful thinking, wishful that is if you were the kind of person who'd want to be a god in the first place, much less a god tossed out on his ear by his peers. True, from a professional standpoint the Spell of Namelessness sounded more and more like a really useful thing to have around. Sorcerers probably used it on their victims when they wanted an effect from off the usual beaten track, and a magician who knew it could undoubtedly pick up a fair amount of cash by hiring that skill out. For that matter, a spell like that one was most likely part of Jardin the Curse Administrator's normal repertoire. In fact, it sounded like such a handy bit of spellwork that it was a bit surprising you didn't see more of it around. On the other hand, maybe you did. Look how long I'd been walking around without any idea I had no memory of my past, or my identity. The inhibiting field it cast on the people around you, keeping *them* from noticing your lack of name, too, could almost be thought of as the spell's way of hiding its *own* identity.

On the *other* hand, you could understand why maybe the Spell of Namelessness wasn't used that much, after all. Why spend all this time and effort to put somebody on ice when you might as well just kill them outright? Special cases, sure—you might need your victim around for later use, you might want to have a good time watching your former enemy blunder around with their memory gone, you might be using the Nameless one as bait to snare someone else, you might merely lack the power to eradicate your enemy outright, or you might even have some weird moral compunction about murder. Or, as in the current situation of Sapriel, there could be some standard of behavior, or the restraint of politics. But these *were* all special cases, without a doubt.

None of the basic facts of my situation had changed, really, but the scope of possibilities had just gotten wider. I still had to assume that whoever had hit me with the

Spell remained out there somewhere. They might *not* be around, true, but that wouldn't be the smart way to bet. If they weren't, I just wouldn't find them, that's all, but if they were and I didn't, well, like I said, that wouldn't be the brightest way to plan. Before the Sapriel development, though, I'd figured I had to be on the lookout for some human enemy from my past, maybe some sorcerer I'd crossed or a warlord who wanted me out of the way and was willing to pay top ool for the job. Now it looked like I'd been thinking too small. Not only might there be a god with a personal vendetta against me—indeed, possibly one of these very gods I'd been hobnobbing with just now—but I myself might have been one of them. From what I'd seen of the gods so far, that didn't seem like anything to get excited about. Of course, that attitude could have been what might have gotten me in trouble in the first place. . . .

So this was just great. Now I had even *more* stuff to worry about. It just goes to show you—this was the kind of situation people thought I liked.

Zhardann had choked Sapriel off in mid-wail while he set to work. Judging by the pace he was following, he had come prepared with a loaded Namelessness package, he wasn't just whipping the thing up from scratch now as we watched. The face of Sapriel's image was swimming, flowing, *melting*, merging into a blank featureless expanse, the nose flattening and the eye sockets filling. Suddenly I realized that behind that obvious scene, Sapriel's mind, too, was flattening, losing definition and resolution beneath an empty fog. Then I realized, too, that Zhardann wasn't just guiding the Namelessness effect as it continued its lumberjack swath through the forest of Sapriel's memory, he was watching, monitoring, *reading* as the structure evaporated away. I knew what he was looking for, too. He wanted to know where the ring was.

Just watching Zhardann's face I could tell how it was going; that plus my own intuition. He was discovering that Sapriel really didn't have the ring, and in fact he never *did* have it. I didn't know how much time Zhardann had, probably not much, but then the hanging ball fell in on itself and the figure that had been Sapriel, its small spin growing into a whirl. There was a marble-sized black spot in the air, then only a puff of dark smoke.

Zhardann continued looking at the place the ball had just vacated for a moment, the look of puzzlement on his face quickly turning hard. I braced myself for what was going to come next, as soon as the meeting broke up, and he had his chance to come after Pasook and me again. I could still almost feel Zhardann's mind ticking over. Pasook had said that Sapriel had taken the ring. Either he was lying, or for some reason Sapriel's memory had been edited after the fact. That could be possible, too—someone who had stolen the ring from Sapriel could have hidden his tracks by papering over the appropriate memories in Sapriel's mind.

At least those were thoughts I assumed were running past Zhardann's attention. In all these tangled webs, I had to remind myself that none of these folks had ever had the ring in the first place, or at least hadn't had it since Max and I had acquired it in Roosing Oolvaya.

The whole thing had only taken a few seconds—Zhardann's final pronouncement over Sapriel, his unleashing of the Curse of Namelessness and its prompt action in ripping Sapriel's consciousness apart, followed by Zhardann's brief pause in thought. He turned toward Soaf Pasook.

Soaf Pasook was gone.

Then so was my own view of the scene. The gray transport mist was back, shrouding my body, deadening my senses, blocking my vision. I *had* been thinking it was time to go, but had I actually managed to summon the transport field? I didn't think I'd done a thing. The metabolic link had shown itself to be unpredictable, though, and it was worth remembering that I still didn't know how the transport effect had appeared the first time, when we'd arrived at the meeting, so—

The mist lifted. The cataleptic state that I hadn't realized was holding me motionless withdrew. I was still sitting in an armchair, the disguised sword Monoch resting on the floor and leaning up against my knee. The armchair was in a sitting room. The sitting room, though, was different.

I didn't think the room was different because someone had redecorated the place while we'd been out. No, it was a different *room.* It was smaller, and lacked a fireplace, and had a single window on a single wall instead of the two adjoining walls with their multi-pane vista, and although there were indeed artworks on the walls, the style and subjects were entirely different. The main item of furniture in the room was a billiard table.

Jill and Zhardann were nowhere in sight. Across from me, though, was a single chair. Regarding me from it was Soaf Pasook. "That Sapriel," Pasook said. "A simple fellow, at heart."

Pasook was different, too. As I'd known him over the recent hours, he'd behaved as a supplicant, as someone trying to make something better out of an awkward position; as someone who was being acted upon, rather than a prime mover. In manner, he had worn a coat of sheepishness. Now, peering out beyond the sheep was something else entirely.

The idea I'd thought was too loopy to consider when I'd glanced on it earlier had suddenly moved to center stage. Pasook had a jeweled cup at his side. He took a drink, smacked his lips, set it aside. "May I see Monoch, please?" he said.

"You're not Pasook," I said. "You're Gashanatantra."

18
BACKWARD AND FORWARD

"Cast off!" ordered the captain. Zalzyn Shaa, shorn of his own nautical outfit, leaned back against the stern gunwale, keeping his mouth shut. The one-time captain, one-time mate had reassumed his rightful role, although his beard would no doubt take longer to grizzle its way back out to its accustomed station. The captain eyed him now, shifting his attention momentarily from the activities of the crew, probably making sure that Shaa was clear on who was again whom, and what was what. Shaa gave him an approving nod and a small salute. The captain grunted noncommittally and looked away. "Raise sail," he said.

"Raise sail, aye," went the repeated cry.

Shaa turned and looked across at the retreating dock. Haalsen Groot stood on the wharf end with Julio, Julio waiting more impatiently than Groot. Well, Julio would be the one stuck with most of the legwork involved in getting Haalsen Traders rolling again, after all; it was no surprise that he would want to be back at it as soon as he could. Then, too, there was Groot's new controlling interest in the recently disenfranchised Bank of the New Dawn.

The Great Karlini leaned himself on the rail next to Shaa. "When Groot said he was sorry he couldn't accompany us," Shaa said, "did you have the feeling he was entirely sincere?"

Karlini didn't bother to respond. He had more than enough experience with Shaa's straight-faced statements to know which ones were designed for rhetorical effect. "What about that iceberg, then?"

"Still a loose end as far as I'm concerned." Back on the dock, Julio's fidgeting finally took its toll on Groot, and the two of them turned and headed away. "We had too many independent actors running around hatching their own schemes, as usual," Shaa mused, "but everything has somehow managed to come together in the end, at least as far as friend Groot and the greater good of Oolsmouth are concerned. Former Councillor Dooglas, currently languishing in a continued daze under the watchful eye of Groot's erstwhile turnkey, Warder Clang, in the basement of the Hall of the People, probably has a different point of view." The gods, too, having fled the scene, most likely had their own angle on things as well, but they weren't talking. Neither was the Creeping Sword. From the few vague hints he had let slip, he might have been in a position to clarify a good deal, since he had obviously covered a lot of ground since they had last encountered him back in Roosing Oolvaya, but he had been spending his time consumed with his own thoughts. Without even turning to look, Shaa could feel his presence behind them, pacing distractedly on the main deck. He hadn't been out-and-out muttering to himself, but he had clearly been examining scenes that were not those of the ship and river before his eyes.

I couldn't get it out of my mind. All the developments of the past days had come back at me, sure, all the ins and outs and turns and twists, since I hadn't had the leisure to kick back while it was happening to figure out what was really going on, but the one thing running especially through my thoughts was that last bit. "You're not Soaf Pasook," I'd said. "You're Gashanatantra."

"In fact," he'd said easily, "I am both, in a manner of speaking." He held out his hand for the walking stick, and I handed it to him. When I'd first seen him, as Pasook, in the study back at Zhardann's place, Monoch had started to quiver like a puppy returned to the guy who usually took him for a walk; Monoch had recognized him even if I hadn't. Gash muttered the activation word and the sword flamed into life in his hand. As he communed with it, sweeping it through the air, he decided to continue talking to me. "The real Soaf Pasook, I'm afraid, has reached the end of his line. I thought Sapriel was remarkably unconvincing when he told that story about torturing poor Pasook to death, surprisingly so, in fact, since it happened to be true. Of course, Sapriel's sad performance may have had something to do with my presence; I can be quite convincing in a role, I don't mind emphasizing. You haven't done uncreditably yourself."

"Thanks a lot," I said sarcastically, although "Thanks for nothing" would have been closer to the literal truth as far as I was concerned.

"Don't be so negative," Gash said. "This hasn't been a waste of time for you, I'm certain. What you have learned is more than adequate compensation for my continuation of your employment. Nevertheless, I am in a magnanimous mood. Sapriel was a recurring thorn I am pleased to now have out of my path, and without my own personal implication in his departure. This pleases me. My pleasure is your good fortune."

"Oh, really?"

He fixed me with the gaze of a dead fish. "You are a loose end."

Oh. A loose end. By rights, I was something he should be tidying up. Instead, he was going to let me live, or at least I hoped that was what he was implying. "In that case," I told him, "thank you very much." I was hoping he wasn't going to remember the heavy backlash I'd hit him with when I'd siphoned his power through the metabolic link back at the climax of the mess in Roosing Oolvaya; if that *did* occur to him right now his mood might abruptly change. I didn't want to tempt him into getting aggravated at me but I didn't want him to start thinking about nasty stuff like that either, so I figure I'd better try to steer the conversation. I didn't have to hunt for a topic—the assembly we'd just left was preying on my mind. Something wasn't right. Something didn't fit.

Then I had it. "Sapriel *was* lynched," I blurted out. "Unless I'm missing something big, he didn't do enough to justify being demolished like that. When it came right down to it, nobody even bothered to hear his defense."

"Of course he was; of course it was a sham. Haven't you learned anything? Pasook had isolated himself from support but so had Sapriel. Why else do you think he'd have launched so shaky a plot, and relied on *human* support, of all things? He had nowhere else to turn." Gash flashed his carnivore smile again. "Perhaps he had help he didn't realize in reaching that state."

"Perhaps he did," I said. "You mean to say everybody at that meeting had it in for him? No, there'd have been some of them who were there because they'd gotten in position to scavenge some of his holdings, right? And some of them had to be there just for the kicks."

"You see?" Gash said approvingly. "You *have* been paying attention."

"Do you mind if I ask you a question?" I said. "What about Jill? She thought she'd know you anywhere, but she thought I was you and then didn't recognize you when you actually showed up."

"She doesn't know me nearly as well as she thinks she does," Gash said.

"Zhardann, then, what about him? You look different now than the last time—I assume at the moment you look like the real Soaf Pasook—but why did you look before the way Zhardann does now?"

The way he looked at me, past the fiery disk of the unleashed sword Monoch, made me think my moment of grace was just about over, if it hadn't expired already. "This interview is over," he said.

"Are we going to meet again?"

He continued to scowl at me. "Oh, very well," he said, instead of what I'd expected. "Verisimilitude."

"I beg your pardon?" I said.

"Jardin does insurance," Gash said. "I don't. Insurance was one reason I was in Roosing Oolvaya when we met before, if you recall."

"Uh, yeah, I do. But I thought Zhardann was the Curse Administrator."

"How much business do you think there is administering major curses? Insurance gives a much more regular income stream." He let Monoch slow in his twirlings and stretched his left shoulder up, back, around; I heard a squeaking sound like stretching taffy. Gash lifted up his tunic with his left hand and scratched along the side of his ribs. The fresh scars, the stigmata of needles, the flayed skin were like a fading image painted on a fresh canvas; as he eased his hand along his side, the skin rippled and smoothed behind it. He gave a final scratch, tugged his shirt back down, and let Monoch begin to whine again.

"What you said back at Zhardann's place—how if there were gods over you the way your lot is over us, they'd be pretty upset with you all—did you mean that?"

"You of all people should know better than to believe what one of us says," Gash told me severely.

"But if Zhardann could mortalize Sapriel over a case of bad etiquette, wouldn't evidence of outright heresy—"

"After the things I said to them, mortalization would be the least of my concerns," Gash said, in the driest tones I'd heard from him.

"Why did you do it, then, why did you bother? I mean, no one knows it was really *you*, of course, but it was a little off the subject. Why even raise the problem?"

"You're an inquiring fellow," said Gash. "Aren't you interested in politics?" He suddenly paused in his fancy maneuvers with Monoch, and something else seemed to pass between them. Then he swung the sword again and let go. As Monoch cartwheeled up into the air and then came down in a trajectory aimed directly toward my face, Gash said, over the whine of released power, "Here. You hang onto him for now."

I got my hand up, and instead of following my natural instinct to cover my eyes and fall to one side out of the way, an instinct that I knew wouldn't have saved me since I'd seen the kind of fancy footwork the sword could execute when it was seriously going after somebody, I opened my fingers and grabbed. The hilt of the sword smashed into my palm. I slapped my other hand around it for good measure; even so, the sword threw me to the floor, the two of us knocking over the armchair in the process. Monoch was loose and excited and I knew that was a bad combination, but I managed to snarl the shutdown command as we began to tangle ourselves up in the rug. When the sword's whine faded and I pulled the rug off my head, I discovered that Gash was gone.

There was one more obvious thing I could have asked him, if I'd had the chance, but it was just as well I didn't bother; I figured I knew the answer clearly enough and I wanted to keep being alive to appreciate it. Somebody had floated the rumor that had set Sapriel on the warpath, the rumor that Pasook had the ring in the first place. I hadn't been sure who'd been in the position to do that, who had both the knowledge and the inclination, but now I figured there was little doubt it had been Gashanatantra himself. Gash had fed me the same story, too, through the metabolic link, and I'd had enough exposure to the way he worked now to be pretty sure why. A lot of it had actually been true.

Gash and Pasook had indeed teamed up to go after Pod Dall and turn him into a ring. Pasook had double-crossed Gash, perhaps using the late Oskin Yahlei as his pawn, which is where I had come in originally. Gash wasn't the kind of guy to let a double cross go unavenged, though, and he'd seen the chance to take down two enemies with the same plot—Pasook and Sapriel—using me again as his own pawn and surrogate. Gash still didn't have the ring, though. If he'd been keeping close enough tabs on me, he had to know where it was. He could be biding his time before taking it back. He could have decided, too, that it was in a safe enough place for the moment, and that it was succeeding perfectly well in stirring up nastiness without even having to be present. On the other hand, I was sure he'd been out of commission for awhile after I'd hit him with the backlash zap, so maybe the ring's transfer and current location had escaped his scrutiny. If that was true, why hadn't he asked me about it?

You could say that if the first shoe was the stuff he'd pushed me into in Roosing Oolvaya, the other shoe had already dropped with the mess I'd just gone through. I didn't know how big Gash's closet was, though, or even how many scheming feet he had. Things had now gotten more confused than they'd been before, and the field was larger. That's why I couldn't escape the feeling that a veritable hailstorm of hurtling footwear was converging on my head. All I'd felt so far was the first small ones, the little ones that patter down gently just before the torrent hits.

On the other hand, perhaps I was just being optimistic.

It had not gone badly; no, not badly at all. Which wasn't to say that it had gone *right,* or couldn't have gone better. Still, not an operation to be unhappy with, especially when one considered that one was recovering from recently being dead at the same time as the exercise was running its course.

The servant slipped silently back into the dining room through the kitchen door and carefully removed the plate, stacking the used silverware neatly atop it first, also without the vaguest hint of clatter or clink. She didn't want to cross him again, Fradjikan reflected; no one did. If they were smart, that is, and of course if they were still alive to have the second chance. It was good to be alive.

He swirled the wine in his glass, admiring its rich deep red color, its attractive if somewhat forward raspberry-tinged nose. Cabernet with a blend of merlot, surely, but what was that distinctive?—oh, of course, almost as much cabernet franc as sauvignon, that would certainly do it. A bit gutsy behind a youthful streak of tannin, but the tannin along with the acidity gave it a tight backbone, an overall supple texture with a slightly peppery, spicy finish. Ah. Of the many things Fradi had been glad to leave behind in his old body, the gout and the inexorably dulling of his palate, which between them had not only left everything tasting mournfully bland but had provided a next-day residue of extreme joint pain, had been two lumps that had made the greatest dent in his ability to appreciate the worthwhile parts of life. Now, though—ah.

Fradi had realized that Dooglas promised to be the weak link as soon as he'd seen Sapriel rope him in. Still, there was no predicting Dooglas would fall apart to the comprehensive extent he had actually done. The early events had unfolded well: by driving Groot toward insolvency and dishonor, it had become consistent for the river ship to be seized. This would have at the least inconvenienced its passengers. Fradi had hoped things would proceed far enough to strand them in Oolsmouth for awhile, ruin their rendezvous plans in the big city, and most importantly put them in a position where they could easily be observed and monitored. With the collapse of Dooglas and the implosion of the rest of the setup the first two of these had gone away. The third, though, had not been a total loss. And there was The Hand; they should be reporting in soon.

It would have been asking too much to keep a constant line on all the players, and there were certainly significant holes in what he had been able to find out. Since that damned amulet kept anyone from observing Max himself too closely, the major goal of the exercise had been to see what allies of Max could be flushed from the underbrush, as well as to get some feeling for their capabilities and ability for dynamic response.

So now he knew about Shaa, Karlini and his wife and his no-account servants, Haalsen Groot, and that floundering barbarian, in addition to Maximillian himself and the Mont kid. There was also that other fellow who had appeared out of nowhere in time to board the ship out of Oolsmouth, the guy with the cane. Not that he'd looked like anyone of significance, but you never could tell, and it was supporting players Fradi needed to flesh out the cast list anyway. Perhaps the man with the cane was the one who could be turned . . .

So if not much had been accomplished, he *had* set limited objects, and those, at least, had been largely met. The objectives had been limited, but Fradi was still human, or anyway it seemed reasonable to assume that, and so he was still prey to wishful thinking as well. He hadn't wiped anyone from the stage and hadn't even inflicted more than a momentary sting, although if things had fallen a bit differently he very well might have. Now *that* would have made him know he was alive. Intelligence collection and harassment were all fine and good, but when it came right down to it, if you didn't attack, who were you?

In the long run, though, that might have limited the fun. A much larger canvas was ahead, one more suitable for the mounting of a greater extravaganza. And of course for the serious pursuit of his mission; one mustn't forget one's mission in the midst of one's artistry. Fradi knew he'd been going a bit too far when he'd fed Dooglas the torture decree, but he'd decided to allow himself one direct personal touch; a signature piece, as it were. By that time it wasn't going to make much difference anyway, and there were certain standards of style to maintain.

Ego? Fradi thought, holding the glass by one corner of its base and swirling the wine with an adroit movement of thumb and forefinger; the candlelight glinted off the curves of the resulting small whirlpool and accentuated their highlights. Well, yes, ego, but not just that. Fradi was not the only one who considered himself an artist. There was, after all, his patron. It would not do to forget his patron. His patron was another good reason to draw things out. Fradi had not been born yesterday, or even reborn. It would not be a good idea to wrap this up before he knew exactly why his patron was going to all this trouble, why Max and his research made him uncomfortable enough to recruit Fradi from the dead; and until Fradi had a firm enough position from which to ensure his own future well-being. No, it would not do at all.

Any interesting scheme never has a single motivation.

Soon he would leave Oolsmouth, and then the next act would begin. There were so many possibilities in front of him that, like a writer with a blank slate, it was difficult to know where to begin. There was the man with the cane. What about the wife? She might be vulnerable. Wives often were. Fradi's smile widened. They would see. They would all see. In Peridol, the City of the Gadzurian Empire.